MW00681866

OTHER EDGE OF JUSTICE

OTHER EDGE OF JUSTICE

FLETCHER DOUGLAS

Huskion House
PUBLISHING

This is a work of fiction that is a product of the author's imagination, however, many friends of the author have consented to their names being used as fictional characters throughout the novel. Even when settings are referred to by their true names, the incidents portrayed as taking place in those locations are entirely fictitious. The events, characters and businesses described are imaginary and fictitious, and any resemblance to any actual persons, living or dead, business establishments, events or locales is entirely coincidental, save and except as aforesaid. The reader should not infer that the events described ever happened.

OTHER EDGE OF JUSTICE

Hushion House Publishing
www.hushion.com
Published by arrangements with Fletcher Douglas

Contact the author
fdouglas@rogers.com

Cataloging and Publication
Other Edge Of Justice / Fletcher Douglas
ISBN: 0-9733212-5-3

HUSHION HOUSE PUBLISHING LIMITED
36 NORTHLINE ROAD
TORONTO, ONTARIO
CANADA, M4B 3E2

ACKNOWLEDGEMENT

I thank Cathy for her continued support, because without her, I would not have been able to write.

NOVELS BY

FLETCHER DOUGLAS

RIDE A CROOKED ROAD – Spring 2004

Frustrated by a waning law career and the disappearance of Trizzi, the love-of-his-life, Joe McConnell escapes from life's dilemmas, with five other Weekend Warriors, on a motorcycle trip through northeastern United States from Toronto to Alexandria Bay, Boston, Cape Cod, New York, Philadelphia and Atlantic City. One of the bikers secretly steals millions of dollars from a drug plane that crashes in the mountains of Vermont and the gang inadvertently becomes mired in Colombians, cocaine, money and murder. After an associate of the bikers is murdered, Joe risks his life to make a deal with the drug traffickers that could save the lives of his friends. As fate intervenes, money and death draws Joe's world and the dangerous world of his lost love together once again and he has to cross the line for the woman he loves.

OTHER EDGE OF JUSTICE – Spring 2005

For my wonderful boys, Jeff, Chad and Brett,
who have made me a proud father.

"There is no greater gift in life than children
and none of us know what we might be capable of
until one is taken away."

. . . Douglas M. Flett, 1984

OTHER EDGE OF JUSTICE

CHAPTER ONE

On that dull Thursday afternoon during the first week of September, gray clouds filled the dark sky and cast a never-ending shadow over the quiet and still water of Lake Simcoe. The almost square lake, fifteen to twenty miles across in any direction, was in the middle of southern Ontario about fifty miles north of Toronto. The quiescent fall air hung over the mirror-like surface as there was no breeze that day. The red maple leaves on the Canadian Flags were lifeless at the tops of white flagpoles that stood tall in the yards of cottages that meandered along the undulating shoreline. The peacefulness of the overcast afternoon created a very surreal atmosphere that seemed to permeate through the summer community.

As Paul Taylor drove north along the road near the lake, he could tell that the long, hot summer season had come to an end. Most of the beautiful cottages and summer homes scattered along the rocky shore, just south of the Pefferlaw Marina, were empty and alone. It wouldn't be long before the harsh, winter winds and frequent snow-storms blew across the lake from the northwest to keep them company until spring. During the Labour Day holiday weekend that just passed by, most of the cottagers had packed up their summer belongings and their reluctant kids and returned to the city for a new school year. The deserted lake and shoreline showed no signs of life. None of the few permanent residents who lived in the area were out walking that day and there was no boat traffic to mar the calmness of the water. Anyone still around was indoors sitting by their fireplaces taking refuge from a day that screamed fall had arrived.

Paul was behind the wheel of Liz's five year old, dark-green Saab convertible. It had a standard five-speed transmission and a tight suspension that made it perform like an expensive sports car. He remembered, as if it was just yesterday, how happy and excited she had been when he had surprised her with it on her thirtieth birthday.

A couple of years after that happy occasion, Paul's Jaguar had gone off-lease and had been returned to the leasing company because the family no longer required two vehicles. He had been driving Liz's Saab ever since. Every time he drove it, memories of the wonderful life they once had together flooded his memory and his body ached for her. Her perfume still filled his senses whenever he was in the car as if she had purposely left her essence trapped in the fabric of the interior so she wouldn't be forgotten. He missed her with all his heart, with all his being. He thought about her constantly, day and night, but when he was in her car with the scent that was hers alone, it was as if she was right there with him. As if he hadn't lost her. As if she wasn't really gone.

* * *

The Pefferlaw Marina was nestled among the summer homes and cottages on the south side of the lake. Paul drove into the empty parking lot and pulled up to the front of a single-story, gray and white building that was an office and store. It was locked up and appeared to be closed for the day or maybe even the season.

Paul had been in the Saab for over an hour and groaned as he lifted his two hundred pound, six-foot frame out of the driver's seat. He stretched his cramped muscles as he stood beside the car and looked around the deserted yard and docks. There was a Chevy pick-up parked nearby and a number of boats on racks and trailers that were ready to be serviced for winter storage. The smell of burning leaves filled his nostrils as light smoke wafted across the parking lot from a fire in a rusty-red, steel barrel next to a house. As Paul walked toward the building, he noticed a yellow sign taped to the inside of the glass window of the door. It notified potential customers to honk for service if no one was around. He returned to the Saab, hit the center of the steering wheel a couple of times and shattered the silence.

A few minutes later, a short, stocky man dressed in overalls and work boots sauntered across the loose gravel of the parking lot toward the office and the marina's first customer of the day. Paul didn't know the man because he had never been there before. He had only passed by on a number of occasions but knew from the advertising along the highway that the marina had fishing boats for rent. That was what Paul needed that day, a fishing boat.

"Howdy. I'm Fred Hyde, the owner. What can I do for ya' today?"

"Paul Taylor," he said as the men shook hands. "It looks like you're closing up for the season. I was hoping to do some fishing for a few hours this afternoon. Are you still renting fishing boats this time of year?"

"Sure am, but it's kinda late in the day to be goin' out on the lake. There's not a whole lotta daylight left. It can get dark out there pretty quick this time of year."

"I was just planning to go out for two or three hours. I'll be back well before dark. I'm sure that this'll be my last fishing trip," Paul said with a sadness.

"Our usual price is sixty dollars a day and an extra twenty for a full tank of gas. I'll hav'ta charge ya' for half-a-day plus the gas."

"Sounds reasonable."

"I've got a fifteen foot aluminum boat with a small Merc on it tied up down at the gas pumps. It's all ready to go."

"I hope your boats are safe. Do all the boats have life jackets in them?"

"We give everyone who rents a boat a good life jacket and you hav'ta wear it."

"Here's the fifty bucks for the rental and gas. I don't even need a receipt."

"Perfect! We all pay too many damn taxes anyway! Get your gear together and I'll meet you down by the gas pumps," Fred said as he ambled off toward the water.

Paul went back to the Saab and popped the trunk from the automatic opener on his key chain. He reached in and pulled out his fishing rod, a small tackle box, a warm coat and a duffle bag. He piled his gear neatly on the gravel and went to the driver's door, pulled it open and got inside. He needed to bask in the aroma of Liz's perfume one last time. He sat there in a daze, breathing her in, again and again. Tears filled in his eyes and ran down his face as he longed for her. It took a moment to pull himself together. As he got out of the car, he put his car keys into the ignition and a note from his pocket on the passenger seat. He closed the door behind him.

As he walked by the trunk, he put one hand on the lid so the automatic closer would catch. Then he stood there with his hand resting on that place, knowing that Liz's hand had been there before. It was as if he was touching part of her and tears swelled in his eyes again. Paul was about to embark on an odyssey that would take him to places, where years ago, he could never have imagined going. If his nerves and resolve didn't fail him, he would soon open Pandora's Box. If he could gather enough courage to lift the lid and venture into the unknown, there would be no turning back.

He gathered himself together again, wiped his eyes and picked up his fishing gear. He then walked slowly across the parking lot toward the marina docks. A hundred boat slips jutted out from wooden piers throughout the protected harbor and were still half-full of crafts of every make and size. A steel roofing system covered half the slips and the rest were in the open air. A large basin was protected from the wind and waves by a concrete breakwater. As Paul got closer to where Fred Hyde was standing, he could hear the Mercury engine on the back of the small, silver boat. It was purring like a kitten.

"I started the engine to warm it up for you."

"That's great. I'm planning to troll down along the south shore just to see what I can catch. I'm gonna take my time, maybe have a cocktail or two, and enjoy the fall scenery. I just picked up a forty-pounder of Absolut at the liquor store in town," Paul commented to ensure that Fred Hyde knew the direction he was heading.

"Well, be sure you don't drink too much out there. Booze and water don't mix unless they're in a glass on land," Hyde warned. "It's really been a good summer for fishin'. They've been catchin' lots of trout and pickerel and even a few muskies."

It wasn't long before Paul had placed his gear in the small boat and put his life jacket on. He was sitting against the blue, plastic backrest on the rear seat in front of the engine. Hyde untied the bow line and threw it into the boat as Paul did the same at the stern. Paul gave the boat a push away from the dock, and slowly reached back with his left hand, and pulled the gear lever on the motor into the forward position. As the boat moved forward, Paul twisted the end of the steering handle to increase the revs of the engine. The small boat putted away from the wooden gas dock and on toward the marina exit that would take it out of the protected enclosure and into the lake.

"Fred, I'll see you in two or three hours. If I get real lucky, I may even have an extra pickerel to give you for dinner. Even if I have bad luck, at least I'll be able to pour you a shot when I get back."

"Sounds great! Vodka's my drink. Good luck! Be sure to get back here in lots of time. From the look of that sky, it's gonna be a dark and dirty night."

* * *

As the aluminum boat picked up speed, it left a trail of small ripples on the calm water of the marina enclosure. It made its way through the opening in the cement barrier and out into the tranquil open water of the lake. Paul scanned the whole area for signs of life as he moved further away from shore. There was no one to be seen on the land and there were no other boats on the lake. As he looked back in the distance toward the Pefferlaw Marina, he noticed that even Fred Hyde had disappeared and gone back to his chores. He was alone. All alone with the memories of his wife, Liz, and their only son, Ricky. The day seemed to get darker by the minute. As he looked around at the clouds that hung over the lake, he knew that darkness would soon be all over him. The lake was as smooth as glass just like a large mirror and the trees, cottages and boathouses along the shore reflected on the water.

As the boat continued on an angle away from the land, further out into the lake, Paul slowly loosened the ties on his life jacket and wrestled it off his shoulders. He threw it on the floor of the boat well toward the bow and out of the way. He knew that he wouldn't need it that afternoon. Concern for his own life had long left him. The only two reasons for his existence had been taken away from him. He had absolutely no intention of fishing that day. He had more serious matters on his mind.

Paul picked-up the small duffle bag and put it on the seat next to him. He unzipped it and reached deep inside. His hand wrapped around just what he was looking for: the vodka. As the cap came free, he tilted the bottle up to his lips and took a long drink even though he didn't enjoy his martinis that dry. Paul preferred them on crushed ice, with a hint of vermouth. That afternoon, he knew that he would need a few stiff belts not only to keep warm, but to give him the courage to do what he had to do. After a couple of more swigs, he replaced the cap and put the bottle between his feet.

Paul reached back into the duffle bag and carefully pulled out two gold-colored picture frames and set them up on the boat seat in front of him, so he could just look at them again and again. As he stared from one picture to the other, back and forth, again his eyes filled with tears, that soon streamed down his face. He tried to control himself, but couldn't. He started to sob openly and without even realizing it, he reached for the bottle of vodka and took another long drink.

The first frame, on the right side of the seat opposite him, held the likeness of a striking, blonde woman with a beautiful smile. Elizabeth or Liz, as Paul had always called her, had only been thirty-one when the picture had been taken four years earlier.

The picture in the second frame, on the other side of the seat, was two and a half years old. It was of a freckle-faced teenager, a good-looking kid, with hair that was far too long. Paul smiled to himself through his tears as he thought about the number of times that he had playfully pestered his son, Ricky, to get it cut. Richard was their only child and his birth had been somewhat of a miracle because the doctor had almost lost both Liz and their baby. They had been so fortunate.

The boat putted slowly along, further and further out into the lake, and Paul's mind wandered back to happier days. He couldn't take his eyes off the pictures of his family as he sat there, hunched over, sobbing and sipping the warm booze. The three of them had always spent a lot of time together because their son had been an unexpected blessing. Ricky had lots of friends, but always enjoyed hanging out with his parents. It had often been just the three of them planning many wonderful adventures. Paul's wife and child had been his whole life. When he shut his eyes, he could almost hear Liz and Ricky, as they giggled and laughed, right there in the boat with him.

Paul wiped his eyes and nose on his coat sleeve and reached for the bottle of vodka again. The alcohol burned as it went down and the sensation, as the hot liquid seemed to get stuck in his throat, made him shake his head back and forth as if the quick movements would make it taste a whole lot better. He gagged a couple of times and wished that he had brought some ice and vermouth. But under the circumstances, he knew that the Absolut straight out of the bottle would have the desired effect.

As Paul sipped, he turned from the pictures and admired the beautiful summer homes and cottages on the shore. The family had often talked about buying a cottage and a few years back, they had gone on hunting expeditions to see if they could find one to purchase. They had looked in the Muskoka and Haliburton lake areas of the province, both of which were just a couple of hours north of the city. They had wonderful plans for a summer home, but never got around to buying one. He continued to think about his wife and son and all their dreams for the future that would never be fulfilled. He continued to break into sobs. Paul's life had deteriorated to the point where it had become an empty void.

He stared at the two pictures as the boat continued slowly in a westerly direction, about three hundred yards off shore, on its way toward a distant spacing-cut in the tree-line ahead where a deserted concession road made its way through a wooded area down to the water's edge. During the summer months, the area where the road actually met the lake was used as a boat launch ramp and a place to park by weekend boaters. It was virtually abandoned by fall.

Paul concentrated on the pictures of his family as time passed by. He thought about how much he loved them and how much he missed them. As he sat there, hunched over, the terrible blackness of three ruined lives suffocated him. There was an unnatural darkness inside his body; inside his being. It engulfed him internally, and the horrible feeling of despair that had haunted him during the past few years ravaged him once again, as the natural darkness of Mother Nature closed in around him. The night was so black that even if people were standing or walking on the shore, they wouldn't be able to see him out there all alone on the lake. He knew that his fishing trip was over. Time had run out. As he gathered together all of his strength and courage to take the next step, he wondered what Pandora had in store for him.

Paul picked up the bottle of vodka again, took another sip, and carefully reached out over the side of the boat. He slowly dumped the clear liquid into the lake, except for about two inches in the bottom of the bottle. He screwed the cap back on tightly and put it back on the floor between his feet. Then, he took off his coat.

Paul leaned forward and picked up the pictures of what was once his family. They were images of the only two people who had ever meant anything to him during his life, a life completely devastated by tragedy. He pulled the pictures close to his chest and hugged them as tears streamed down his cheeks. He held them close to his face for one last look at the two people he loved so much. He kissed the picture of Liz first and then the picture of his son, Ricky. Through the tears and the darkness, he could barely make out the features of the two people who were once his life. He kissed both images for the last time, one after the other.

A few minutes later, Paul placed the two pictures back on the seat where they had been and made sure that they were facing him. As they stared up at him out of the darkness, he could barely see the likenesses of his beloved family. He thought about when he had first met Liz, the wonderful times they had together and he thought about the day they had married. He remembered the excitement when they learned that Liz was pregnant and the complications on the day that Ricky was born. He questioned why he had to lose them. Life wasn't fair. He continued to think about Liz and Ricky and soon realized that it was time.

As Paul turned off the motor and stood up in the small boat, he mustered together all of the courage in his body; in his being. He put one hand on top of the cowling of the engine and one hand on a corner of the boat and carefully lowered himself over the back transom. He slowly slid into the cold, black water of Lake Simcoe, without making a splash or any other sound, and took one last look toward the pictures of his family. As he sank into the water, Paul let go of the back end of the aluminum boat with a push and it disappeared into the blackness of the night. In an instant, he was lost in the darkness that had become his life.

CHAPTER TWO

At just past three-thirty on a bright, Friday afternoon in late September, a man with dark, slicked-back hair, sideburns and a thick goatee sat patiently behind the wheel of a five year old, dark-blue Taurus, four-door. The car was parallel parked among a number of other vehicles in front of Medford Secondary School. His neatly trimmed beard and sideburns were only four weeks old, but he looked totally different than ever before. He peered intently through his dark sunglasses at each vehicle that passed by or lingered near the students who were all over the busy street at the end of the school day. He was looking for one specific individual.

The man in the Ford was familiar with the neighborhood. It was obvious from the expensive cars and sporty trucks in the student parking lot that the school was located in one of the more affluent areas of the city. As he watched all the teenagers kibitzing, laughing and fooling around as they filed out of the main door to go home for the weekend, the hatred that had been building over the past months surged in his body.

Without even realizing it, he scratched at the uncomfortable mound of hair on his chin as he waited and watched. He thought about the months of planning that he had recently endured and hoped that it would soon pay off. He was getting impatient. He had been near the school on and off for three days, and each day, he had stopped at different locations along the nearby streets at various times. He had been extremely careful not to attract attention to himself by staying in any one spot too long.

On his first day in the area, the man thought that he was going to get lucky, but had been disappointed. He was certain that he had seen the person he was looking for in a black Corvette convertible. The driver had stopped the vehicle three times and talked to various kids. It appeared that he had, very discreetly, passed them small packages in exchange for money. Suddenly and without warning, the black Vette had taken off and disappeared down a side street at the far end of the school. By the time the man reacted, the sports car was gone. The car and driver had not reappeared the next day, but the man was sure that both would return on that afternoon because it was just before the weekend.

Before long, the Corvette pulled into the far end of the student parking lot. The driver of the sports car and the man might finally get to meet. He had waited a long time. The new Corvette, with the top up, was nearly hidden among all the other expensive vehicles that filled the lot. The distinguishing feature of the Vette from the other parked vehicles was a steady stream of students coming and going from it. The man could clearly see that a number of kids, both male and female, would drop by the sports car and get into the passenger seat. They would stay there for a few minutes and then get out and leave. As one student got out of the Vette, another would take his or her place. The man knew that the driver of the sports car had been involved in the same routine a couple of days a week for the past three or four years. That day, he counted sixteen customers. After all, the kids had to stock up on all of their favorite leisure drugs for the weekend.

The Corvette's engine fired up around four-thirty. After an hour of hard work, the dealer pulled it out of the parking lot. He drove down Deevale Road, the main residential street that ran west from Medford, or MSS as it was called, toward Mt. Pleasant Road, one of the main commuter routes that went directly into Toronto's downtown core.

As the sports car went by the parked Taurus, it slowed to let a couple of kids cross the street. The man finally got to see the face of the drug dealer who he hated so much. As soon as the kids passed by, the powerful car roared away. The man pulled the Taurus out onto Deevale and followed at a discreet distance.

The Corvette made a left at the lights and headed south toward downtown. After the two cars passed the Mt. Pleasant Cemetery, south of Davisville, they cruised down into the Rosedale valley, through the densely wooded parklands and on toward the Bloor Street exit in mid-town. The man caught up with the Corvette at the Bloor turn-off where it went west. The Vette turned right on Bellair Street into the heart of an artsy part of the city called Yorkville. At the north end of Bellair, where the street dead ends at Yorkville Avenue, the driver of the Vette drove straight into an outdoor parking lot after making the required pause at the stop sign.

The man pulled the blue Taurus around the corner to the left onto Yorkville and parked among a number of other vehicles on the north side of the street. He waited and watched to see where the drug dealer was going. It wasn't long before he appeared from the lot, jogged across the street through the light traffic, and walked a few buildings to the east of Bellair and Yorkville. The man followed the drug dealer's movements in his rearview mirror and saw him go into a trendy bar and restaurant on the south side called Cowan's Bottom Line.

It was starting to get dark because the fall days were getting shorter but from where he was sitting, he could see the parked Vette in the lot and he could also see Cowan's main door in the rearview mirror. The man settled back in his seat with his eyes glued to the mirror with no idea how long his wait might be. He was excited and anxious and his heart was beating rapidly.

It was close to seven o'clock and quite dark, except for the store business lights and streetlights of Yorkville, when the man caught a glimpse of the drug dealer in his rearview mirror. He came out of Cowan's, all by himself, and immediately crossed the street. The man fired up his engine and waited. A few minutes later, the Corvette passed right by the Taurus and continued west on Yorkville toward Avenue Road. As soon as the dealer's car passed by, the man pulled the Taurus in behind it once again.

Both cars got caught at the traffic lights beside the Four Seasons Hotel on the corner. As soon as the light changed, the drug dealer turned left toward downtown and the man followed. They traveled through the Bloor Street West intersection and on past the Royal Ontario Museum, around Queen's Park, the site of the parliament buildings for the Province of Ontario, and south on University Avenue. The dealer continued for eight blocks until he turned right on Queen Street West. He drove on past all the trendy restaurants and shops and on through the southerly part of Chinatown at Spadina Avenue.

The Vette stayed on Queen until Thomson Avenue where it turned right into an old residential area, with narrow link-houses and a number of large, unique homes that had been converted into small apartment buildings. Three blocks into the neighborhood, the Vette made another right on Ashbury and an immediate left into a narrow, back alley that ran behind the houses on Thomson. It slowed at the third house and drove deep into the backyard beside an old double garage. The Vette pulled up to the rear porch of the house and parked. The man stopped the Taurus at the curb near the entrance to the lane and watched as the drug dealer went into what looked to be an old two-story house.

After a trip around the block to scope things out, the Taurus, with its lights off, pulled into the laneway in the darkness. It stopped directly behind the dilapidated double-garage that was located between the lane and the house on the opposite side of the yard from where the Corvette was parked. The Taurus couldn't be seen from the house. He had rigged the lights of the Taurus so they would turn completely off while the motor still ran. The man thought that the feature might come in handy as he carried out his plans that had been formulated over the past months.

As soon as the man turned off his engine, he reached into his shirt pocket, pulled out a pair of surgical gloves and snapped them on his hands. He got out of his car and carefully looked up and down the alley and into the neighboring backyards as he patted his Glock just to confirm that it was there. All was quiet. As the man looked at the house, he could see the drug dealer pass in front of the two back windows in what seemed to be the kitchen. He walked quietly past the Vette and up onto the wooden porch. He made sure to step only on the outer edge of the steps, near the railing, so they wouldn't creak and announce his arrival. Once on the porch, the man could clearly see the drug dealer seated at a kitchen table at the far end of the room. He was just sitting there quietly, eating something and reading a newspaper. The man on the porch waited and watched for two or three minutes to determine if there was anyone else in the house.

The man took a deep breath as he turned the door handle as quietly as he could. He had dreamed of this moment for a long time and could feel the excitement start to build inside him. He could feel each beat of his pounding heart. He touched the short stubby knife in his jacket pocket with his right hand as the unlocked door opened inward. As he slowly pushed the door open and stepped inside, it made a squeaking sound. The startled drug dealer looked up from the table to see a stranger standing in his kitchen.

"Who the fuck are you?" the drug dealer demanded, as he stood up from the table, not the least bit intimidated by the man's presence because as a drug dealer he had been involved in many deadly encounters and had always come out the winner.

"I wanna buy half-a-dozen dime bags," the man answered with a smile to put the dealer at ease. "I was given your name by one of your regular customers."

By that time, the dealer started to wonder exactly who the intruder might be. Was he a cop or someone who was going to rip him off? The dealer was about six foot two, nearly two hundred pounds, and looked like he could take care of himself. The bearded man standing inside his kitchen door didn't scare him a bit and he walked toward him.

"Any customer of mine that did that is fuckin' dead tomorrow!"

"Your customer who told me all about you used to be a student at Medford Secondary School. The high school where you were doing business until late this afternoon."

"And what the hell is the mouthy asshole's name?" the dealer asked as he moved closer to the man in his kitchen.

"His name is Ricky Taylor!"

"That's bullshit! That little fucker's dead!"

At that exact moment, the dealer threw a right toward the man's chin, but it had been anticipated. The man had seen it coming in the dealer's eyes. He easily blocked it with his left arm and as he put up the block, the man quickly stepped in close. He drilled the dealer with a hard right that landed in the pit of his stomach. The punch nailed him perfectly. At the same time and with lightning speed, the man grabbed the drug dealer by his collar with his left hand and hammered him with two more ferocious rights to his gut. The dealer gasped loudly after each blow and quickly folded over. His knees almost buckled. The man caught him by the shoulders, spun him around and clamped a strong left arm around his neck from behind. At that same moment, the man pulled the small, stubby knife from his right jacket pocket and stuck the point of the blade against the back of the drug dealer's neck. He pressed hard enough to break the skin and draw blood right where his neck meets his skull. The gasping dealer froze immediately as pain flowed all the way down his backbone and into his legs. He realized that he was in serious trouble.

"Fuck, man! That hurts! What the hell do you want? I've got all kinds of money upstairs! You can have it all! Just don't hurt me!"

"Is there anyone else in the house with you?" the man growled.

"No! Christ that hurts! I'm alone! My girlfriend is away for the weekend!"

"She won't be back tonight?"

"No. That fuckin' knife is cutting me! I'll give you all the money I've got!"

"Where's your money and how much do you have?"

"There's gotta be fifty grand in the upstairs bathroom! It's in a bag on a shelf under the sink! That fuckin' knife's hurtin' me! Just take the money and leave!"

"I'm only gonna ask you this once," the man said as he increased the pressure on the small knife in the dealer's neck. "What is the name of your supplier?"

"Jesus Christ! That hurts! I'll tell you, please stop hurting me!" The dealer whined. "He's the fuckin' Italian, Vito Morelli, from Woodbridge!"

"I have a present for you from Ricky Taylor and all the other kids like him who you sold that poison to last year!"

"What the hell are you talking about? I didn't know that shit was bad!"

"I'm Ricky Taylor's father and you're a dead man!"

As Paul finished the sentence, he jammed the short, oyster-shucking knife that was in his right hand into the cervical region of the drug dealer's neck right up to its hilt. The short, wide blade penetrated in between the Axis and Atlas vertebrae just below the cranium, and then he gave it a strong and quick twist, as if he was opening an oyster shell. The loud crunch echoed through the kitchen as the dealer's brain stem separated from his backbone below his skull and the spinal cord was completely severed. The drug dealer died instantly, but all Paul could think of was what the dealer had said to him, *That's bullshit! That little fucker's dead!*

Earlier, Paul had promised himself that he would maintain his composure and self-control as he did all of the terrible things that, in his mind, had to be done. He had planned his revenge for months. He didn't want to do anything stupid that might get him caught before he accomplished his mission, but he snapped after that comment by the drug dealer and kind of lost it for a moment. He jerked the oyster-shucking knife out of the back of the drug dealer's neck as he heavily threw the body to the kitchen floor. The corpse landed face up. Before Paul knew it, he fell to both knees and brought the oyster-shucking knife down with all his might and embedded it deep in the center of the dead man's forehead. As soon as that involuntary reflex happened and was over, Paul seemed to regain control of himself. He immediately got to his feet and took a step back as the reality of what he had just done struck him. He stared down at the dead man.

As Paul's composure returned, he could see the handle of the short, stubby knife protruding from the forehead of the drug dealer who was responsible for his son's death. The man's eyes were wide-open and seemed to be looking right at him, through him almost. He would never forget the blank stare of the first man he killed. It was very difficult for him to avert his eyes away from the face of his victim, but he knew that he had things to do.

Paul was surprised at the small amount of blood that had formed in a pool on the floor near the head of the body. He slowly walked over to the back door and turned off the kitchen lights. He looked out into the yard and alley to see if anyone was around. There was no one in sight. As his eyes adjusted to the darkness and his breathing started to return to normal, he tried to justify in his own mind why this terrible crime had to be committed. He was much more comfortable with it, once it was done, than he had imagined he might be, which he found quite strange.

He made his way down the hall, with the help of a small amount of light from the street lights outside that shone through the window in the front door, and found the stairs to the second level. He took them two at a time. He got to the bathroom quickly and opened the vanity doors wide. There was a small duffle bag hidden on a high shelf in the very back of the cupboard. Unless someone knew it was there, a cursory look into the storage area would not have revealed its location. Paul grabbed the bag and as he pulled it out of the cabinet, a number of other things that were stored in there too spilled out onto the floor. As he exited the bathroom, he grabbed a towel off the shower rack and rushed back downstairs to the kitchen.

Paul checked-out the bag of money on the counter. He also looked out the rear windows to be sure that no one had heard the commotion and that there was no one out in the alley or in the nearby backyards. He then bent down in the dull light and wrapped the large towel around the dead man's head and neck and tucked it together so it would stay in place. He quickly grabbed a small, white garbage bag that he found under the kitchen sink and pulled it over the head of the corpse and tied it tight to keep the towel in place. He then emptied the pockets of the dead man. He soon found a wallet and took whatever money there was in it and threw it into the duffle bag. He pulled out a driver's license and read it in a beam of light, *Steven Shackleton*, and then returned it to the wallet and threw it on the kitchen counter. The drug dealer wouldn't need it where he was going.

In the darkness, Paul picked up the duffle bag, opened the kitchen door to the backyard and slowly walked toward his car as he looked up and down the alley once again. The whole area was deserted. He quietly opened the trunk of the Taurus, which he had previously lined with plastic and a couple of old blankets, put the bag of money to one side and went back to the kitchen. He hoisted the dead man up over his left shoulder and silently carried the body to his car and put it into the trunk. He grabbed the duffle bag of money and closed the trunk quietly. Paul had two more things to do before his evening would come to an end, one planned and one unplanned.

* * *

Paul went south on Spadina Avenue just to stay away from Queen Street which was always busy. As he drove, he thought that it was foolish and dangerous to have moved the body from the house on Thomson, but it was something he had to do. He should have left the drug dealer in his kitchen, but just this one time, he wanted to send a message to the other victims' families and the police. A message that *justice* has been done regarding one of the drug dealers who was responsible for the deaths of teenagers. He then turned on Adelaide Street West, a one-way actually going east, and headed back toward the downtown core. At University, he went north five city blocks and pulled into a circular driveway. He parked in the darkness on the far side, away from the main door of the huge stone building, right where access back on to the busy thoroughfare would be immediate because no one could park in front of him.

Paul, with a ball cap on, his sunglasses in place and Shackleton's small duffle bag in a hand still covered with a surgical glove, slipped out of the car and headed for the main door of the Hospital For Sick Children. As he entered the large lobby, a strong medicinal odor that he would never forget from the many hours that he had spent with his dying wife engulfed him. He wound his way through the crowd of people of many ethnicities who were milling around the reception area waiting for loved ones and drinking coffee. He walked up to a large window in front of an office complex where three women were working at various tasks. A sign on the wall nearby read, *Administration Office*.

"Can I help you, Sir?" An attractive dark-haired gal in a white uniform asked.

"Yes! Christmas is a little early this year! Would you please make sure that this duffle bag is delivered directly to the Administrator. It's a donation to help the children."

After Paul handed the duffle bag through the access window, the woman put it on her desk and looked at it. A moment later, she was shocked as she opened the zipper and saw the contents. Donations to the hospital usually came in the form of a bank draft. When she raised her head to question the pleasant man who had delivered the case, he was gone. There was no one standing outside the windows to her office. Paul had slipped back through the crowd and the confused nurse just caught a glimpse of his back as he went out the door. The nurse rushed through the maze of desks to the hallway, across the lobby and out to the circular driveway, but by the time she got there, the Taurus was lost in a sea of red taillights on a very busy University Avenue.

* * *

Paul continued north once again, around Queen's Park to Bloor Street, east to Mt. Pleasant, north through the Rosedale valley and past the large cemetery. He turned right on Deevale Road toward Medford Secondary.

There were no cars parked in the school lot and very few cars on the street in the neighborhood. The high school was in darkness except for the emergency lights that were always left on inside and the few lights that illuminated the front entrance. Paul had been lucky that it was Friday night because the school often held dances on Saturday nights and then the place would have been crawling with kids.

The north end of the school near the swimming pool and gymnasium was very dark and deserted. As Paul drove toward that area, the only thing he could make out in the darkness was a cement base, about four feet by four feet and two feet off the ground, that held the school's flagpole. It was in the middle of a large lawn near the end of the school building. The red and white Canadian Flag that flies on that pole during the day had been taken down for the night and would be raised first thing in the morning.

CHAPTER THREE

After completing a Bachelor of Arts degree at the University of Toronto, with a major in Political Science, Paul Taylor decided to take a year off school to think about what he wanted to do with the rest of his life. He decided that a decision of such importance could only be made while traveling through Europe. Back in those days, he had very little financial support from his family for his education let alone money for a sabbatical. He realized that he needed to make some quick money to finance his adventure.

After school ended that year, Paul spent the summer months working for a Toronto based construction company on one of its many development sites. He really got lucky because homes were selling faster than they could be built. Interest rates were at an all-time low and the North American economy was booming. The full-time employees had worked all kinds of overtime during the winter months, so most of them wanted to take summer holidays which was unheard of in the construction industry. Paul ended up working as many hours as he wanted to put in. He was passed around from construction site to construction site, from one foreman to another, as he filled in for men on vacation. He worked ten hour days, six days a week, most of that summer and by fall, Paul had saved more than enough money for his planned trip across the Atlantic. He even had enough money put away to go back to school the year he got back.

Late that summer, Paul thought about his future. He wrote his Law School Admittance Test and applied to three Ontario law schools for admittance for the year after his sabbatical. He had always had an interest in a law career, but also needed a reason to come home and settle down after his trip abroad. He thought that he was more likely to get on with something positive when he got back if it was already taken care of before he left. If he changed his mind about a legal education while he was away, nothing would be lost. He simply wouldn't attend law school when he got home.

In October, Paul flew directly from Pearson International, in Toronto, to Heathrow, in London, England. He spent two weeks in London and really enjoyed the uniqueness of the old, historical city. He eventually left for Europe and made his way south through France to Spain where he spent some extended time on the Costa del Sol. He went on to Gibraltar and over to Tangiers, in Morocco. He backtracked north, crossed southern France to Nice and Monte Carlo, and went on to Italy. He spent a number of weeks in Rome walking through the ruins and really enjoyed the history of that ancient city. He got to see the Vatican and St. Peter's Square. Shortly after that visit, he went to Greece and back north through Austria, Switzerland and Germany. He visited the Scandinavian countries and after Copenhagen, Oslo and Stockholm, he returned to London. Before he arranged for his return trip back home to Canada, in time for the new school year, he took a few weeks and traveled through the rest of Great Britain and Ireland.

* * *

Paul's family notified him that he had been accepted at two of the three law schools to which he had applied before he had left for Canada. By the time he got home, he decided that law would not be a bad thing and if he happened to change his direction at a later date, a legal education certainly would not hurt him. He quickly made the decision to go to Queen's University Law School in Kingston, a beautiful town on the north shore of Lake Ontario, about a hundred and sixty kilometers east of Toronto. If Kingston had been good enough for Canada's first Prime Minister, Sir John

A. Macdonald, who had practiced law there before Canada was even a nation, it would be good enough for Paul.

On the Saturday morning before classes were scheduled to begin, Paul took the train, for the two-and-a-half hour trip, to Kingston. He went a couple of days early to find a place to live. The first thing that he did upon his arrival at the law school was check the bulletin board to see if anyone was looking for a roommate. He took two names and addresses off the board and headed to the one closest to the school.

Just two blocks from the law school, Paul found himself in front of an old, red brick four-plex. As he approached the building, he noticed an old Chevy van out in front at the curb. Two girls and a guy were moving boxes and furniture into one of the two upper flats. As Paul reached the walkway to the building, a pile of boxes that had blonde hair blowing all around them came out from behind the van and literally bumped right into him and almost knocked him down. A couple of the boxes nearly fell, but Paul grabbed them from the blonde and saved some dishes. As the boxes were removed, Elizabeth Farwell's messed up hair and beautiful smile came into view. Paul immediately felt an amazing jolt as Cupid's Arrow hit him dead center. As soon as he looked into her pale blue eyes, he knew that she was the girl he would marry. At that moment, his life changed forever.

Elizabeth and her girlfriend, who were in their second year, had taken one of the upstairs apartments, and of course, Paul moved into the one across the hall without a moment's hesitation and with no regard as to who his new roommate might be. He decided that if Elizabeth was there, he was there too. Lady Luck smiled on him that day; the guy who had been helping the two girls move in, dated Elizabeth's girlfriend. After the students completed their chores late that afternoon, they all got together and went out to St. George's Pub for beer and pizza. Paul and Elizabeth, or Liz as he started to call her that evening, became inseparable from that day on. He kidded her that *Liz Taylor* had a nice ring to it. They fell totally and hopelessly in love. They did not want to separate for the summer, so at the end of that school year, Paul and Liz both took summer jobs in the Kingston area just to be near each other. He moved into her apartment after her roommate left town and they lived together in that same place until they finished school two years later.

* * *

Liz graduated with an honors degree in English Literature and decided to teach at the high school level. Paul graduated from law school at the same convocation and they moved to downtown Toronto. They got married that August and soon started their careers. Paul always laughed when he told friends that he was married to Liz Taylor.

Liz became pregnant early that fall and she didn't quite make it through the teaching year when she started to have some health problems. She took a medical leave and put her teaching career on hold for a couple of years. She experienced serious complications during childbirth that put her life and that of their baby at risk. A healthy son was born, but the difficulties had affected Liz's ability to have more children. They named him Richard, Paul's middle name, and also after his father. Rick or Ricky was born just as Paul was called to the bar and began to work for a large firm in downtown Toronto named Gemmill, Farn LLP.

Things went well for the Taylor family during the next ten years or so. Ricky grew into a devoted and wonderful boy who was never in any trouble and was an excellent student. As an only child who was doted on by both parents, it had been a great accomplishment for Ricky to remain so well-rounded. Liz taught English in a high school in the central part of the city and rose quickly to become department head. Paul was liked and respected by his partners, associates and clients and worked his way through the ranks of his law firm to become head of the Estates Section.

Paul was also an only child and his parents had died in an automobile accident while he was in law school. Liz's father had passed away from a heart attack at a youngage just after she and Paul met, and her mother had died of cancer when Ricky was eight years old. Liz and her only sister, Rebecca, had shared a sizeable estate at that time.

Together with the inheritance and a family income generated by a high school department head and a lawyer who was a partner in one of the larger firms in the city, money was never a problem for the Taylor family.

Their beautiful and upscale home in Rosedale, one of Toronto's more fashionable residential districts, was long paid for and their retirement savings and other investments were topped up regularly. They started looking for a cottage in lake country and often took Sunday drives to the Muskokas and the Haliburton Highlands, recreational areas about two hours north of the city, to look for something unique but never found it. They even talked about taking sabbaticals and doing some traveling in the next few years. They were going to take Ricky out of school for a year so he could go along with them. Life was grand.

* * *

It was Liz's thirty-first birthday that Sunday. They stayed in bed later than usual because Ricky had spent the night at a friend's and wasn't expected home until noon. They had gone dancing the night before to a club that played their kind of music. When they got home, they were totally pooped from drinking and wild dancing, so they went right to sleep. At four-thirty in the morning, still half asleep, they made love. The morning was wonderful. They awoke around nine, showered together and got back into bed. They made love again.

After the lovemaking, Liz begged Paul for a massage, one of her favorite things. She loved him to do that for her. He started at her feet and worked his way up her body, as she just relaxed and moaned periodically as he hit those body parts that always feel so good when they are pressed and squeezed. He kissed her in all kinds of sensitive and interesting places as he moved up her body, which released all kinds of uncontrollable giggles and even laughter.

As he reached her shoulders and neck area, he felt something that immediately made him feel sick to his stomach. There was a large, hard lump on the back of her neck, on the right side. Neither one of them had noticed it before that moment. Finding the lump put a real damper on the sensuous morning they had planned. Liz was sure that it had just shown up recently or she would have felt it before. The following day, she went to see their family doctor. To her horror, the doctor found two more, smaller ones, in the armpit area under her right arm during the examination. Another one appeared on her neck before the biopsy of the original one had been returned to the cancer specialist who her family doctor had referred her to. While medical treatment was being planned, a few more lumps appeared on various parts of her body.

After more than a year and a half of chemotherapy, with the usual physical side effects such as hair and weight loss, the family was devastated by more terrible news. At that point, the bad news had to be shared with Ricky. They all cried themselves to sleep almost every night after the prognosis was made known to them.

The cancer had metastasized. It had traveled through the right lung, into the liver, the kidneys and up into the lymph glands. There was nothing that medical science could do for Liz. They were told that it was only a matter of time, so the family prepared for the inevitable. It took the cancer only three months to ravage Liz's body completely and she lost over ten pounds a month. By the time she passed away, she was a shadow of her former self and time had also taken its toll on the family. Paul had a terrible time holding himself together after Liz's death and fourteen year old Ricky was devastated. He and his mother had been extremely close.

* * *

The loss of his mother coupled with the transition into high school was too much for Ricky. Paul tried to comfort his son as best as he could, but he just watched as the kid went into a deep and devastating depression. No matter how hard Paul or the family doctor tried, nothing would pull Ricky out of it. As the months passed by, he seemed to lose control of his life. He had always been a great kid growing up. He had done well at school and had never been in any kind of trouble. Ricky always knew what his parents had expected of him and had always lived up to those expectations.

The loss of his mother changed the young fellow's personality. He became extremely moody, almost a different person. He started to skip classes, not do his homework and often stayed out past his curfew. The kid started to hang out with the wrong crowd and came home smelling like beer and marijuana more than one once. The behaviour was totally out of character for Ricky and he and his dad had serious difficulties dealing with all of those issues.

Paul had problems of his own during that period as he tried to deal with his own grief over the loss of a woman he loved more than life itself. Maybe, just maybe, he hadn't been as understanding as he should have been with Ricky. In retrospect, he couldn't help but blame himself. Paul had wanted to help his son, be there for him, but his own grief consumed him. He became terribly lethargic about life. He lost his ambition. He became a lotus-eater and was barely able to function after Liz's death. He spent a lot of time at the office and buried himself in work, but he wasn't fooling anyone. He didn't accomplish much. He thought that if he worked harder, it would keep his mind off the death of his wife and the problems that he was having with his son. It was simply easier for him just to pretend to keep busy at the office, but that didn't help the situation at home.

Paul and Ricky found it very difficult to deal with each other because each one reminded the other of Liz. No matter how hard they tried to work through their day to day problems, things only seemed to get worse. The father and son never found the bond that had once existed between them when Liz was alive.

Ricky turned to his friends, the wrong friends, for comfort and ended up in all kinds of trouble. He and his buddies experimented with all of the drugs that were available to teenagers from drug pushers who hang around the high schools and target kids his age. One Saturday night, at a school dance, someone laced Ricky's smuggled-in rum and Coke, as well as the drinks of a number of other kids, with Ecstasy that had hit the streets in a dangerous and deadly form because the manufacturing process had been flawed. He and a couple of others at the dance passed out and a number of other kids became terribly sick. They were all rushed off to a local hospital, some in much more serious condition than others.

At midnight that evening, while Paul was watching the news and waiting for Ricky to get home, the doorbell rang. Paul's heart skipped a beat when he looked through one of the windows in the front door of his house. He saw two uniformed police officers, a man and a woman. Concern over what kind of trouble Ricky had gotten himself into that night raced through his mind. After they asked the usual questions, the officers gave him the terrible news. Ricky had somehow taken or had been given a drug overdose and he was gone. He had died. He and one of the other kids had died at the hospital. All of a sudden, Ricky was gone. Paul's only son and only living relative had died of a drug overdose. There was nothing he could do to help his son. It was too late.

* * *

During the following week, the police determined that Ricky and a few of his friends had got their hands on some extra strong dope, part of a bad shipment that hadn't been properly manufactured. A dozen people in different parts of the city had died that same weekend and many more were taken to local hospitals. Ricky and another boy who he hung out with died. One of his friends, who survived the drug dosage, suffered severe brain damage and would likely spend the rest of his life in an extended care facility.

Paul, who had still not recovered from the loss of his wife, was totally devastated by Ricky's death. He had buried Liz months earlier and all of a sudden his only son was gone. Killed by drug pushers. Murdered by drug dealers. Ricky had been the only part of Liz that Paul had left, and with him gone, Liz too was gone forever. At that time, there was nothing left for him in the whole world except a terrible emptiness. He had no living relatives left except a sister-in-law who he had rarely seen since Liz's death. Paul knew that Rebecca had a terrible time with the loss of her only sister. It had been very painful for both her and Paul to get together because the visits brought back all those memories. They both felt that it would be better, easier, not to see each other.

Paul's work also suffered since Liz's death and more so in the months after Ricky passed away. He was unable to concentrate no matter how hard he tried. He realized some time ago that he had to get away from the law firm. He was a total mess.

Thoughts of revenge often filled Paul's mind because the police had made no arrests. He felt that the men responsible for Ricky's death should pay a severe penalty. A plan began to formulate in his head that he started to take seriously. He did some strange things at the office, unlawful things, that were totally out of character for him. He stole passports, birth certificates and drivers licenses from estate files. They belonged to dead clients about his own age who had recently passed away. He made false applications to up-date those passports and documents which gave him a number of aliases. In his own tormented mind, he wanted to make sure that some good would come from his son's death. It was a plan that no one else knew anything about. Even if they had known about it, they would have never believed that Paul Taylor was capable of com-mitting so many illegal acts.

One of the senior partners at the firm, Rod Farn, had spent a lot of time with Paul during the months after Ricky's death hoping to get him back on track. Paul hadn't responded very well and the quality of the legal work that he provided at the firm began to suf-fer noticeably. After a long discussion between Paul and Rod, they mutually agreed that Paul should take two or three months away from the office to sort through his personal problems and once he felt rested and ready, he was to come back to work. Paul knew, deep

down, that it was best for him to get away from the labyrinth that
the practice of law had become.

* * *

All of the free time, with nothing for him to do to keep his mind
occupied, did not have a positive effect on his mental state and
condition. There was no panacea to be found. The plan that had
been going through his mind for months surfaced time and again,
and soon it became all he could think about. Paul thought seriously
about the world and his place in it without his family. He didn't see
where he fit in. He knew deep inside that Liz's death was part of
life's trials and tribulations but Ricky's death was so unnecessary. He
was mad as hell and needed to get even with the scumbags who
killed his son.

Paul turned all of his assets into liquid cash. He immediately put
the family home up for sale in a real estate market where prices had
peaked. He advised Rod Farn that he wouldn't be returning to work
at Gemmill, Farn LLP. Rod and the other partners had reluctantly
made the necessary arrangements to pay him for his partnership
interest in the firm. He cashed in his investments at a time when
the stock market was at an all-time high, so he did extremely well
there too. He also cashed in all of the retirement savings plans that
he and Liz had accumulated because he came to the conclusion that
he had no reason to worry about any kind of a retirement without
his family.

Paul's plan required a secret base of operations so he bought a
small, rustic cottage in the middle of nowhere on a little body of
water called Beer Lake. The property was just outside the Village of
Kinmount, two hours north of the city. He liked the property
because it was on a private lake, about a mile long and a half-mile
wide, and there were only fifteen cottages on it. He cut himself off
from all his friends in the city and told no one about the purchase.
He virtually disappeared. In an effort to be more secretive than
ever before, Paul used an older lawyer from Minden, Ontario, who

didn't know him, to close the cottage purchase and he didn't take title to the property in his own name. He used one of the aliases he had set up when he was practicing law. The purchase was a sweet deal in that the vendor had held a mortgage for most of the price and mortgage payments could be made locally in cash. Paul set it up so he could walk away at any time with no paper trail that would lead to him.

Before he actually disappeared from the city and moved into the cottage, he took a four-day weekend trip to the Cayman Islands, and a week after that, he went to Bermuda for a few days. The following weekend, Nassau. The trips had not been holidays but to arrange secret offshore banking connections. They were a necessary part of his long term plan. The next week was spent making his money disappear through a number of transfers to various banking institutions in Bermuda, The Channel Islands, Switzerland, the Bahamas and Grand Cayman. All of Paul's wealth ended up in an offshore corporate account in the Caymans with no paper trail and the funds could be accessed from anywhere in the world with an international debit card.

His wife and son's memory was constantly on his mind. He was consumed by their images day-in and day-out, especially his son's, because he had died so senselessly and at such a young age. During the months that followed, Paul developed a growing hatred of drugs and the people who dealt them. He especially developed an intense hatred of drug dealers who prey on young children and hang around their schools to try and get them hooked on their deadly and dangerous products. The intense hatred eventually became a force that enslaved his very being. It gnawed at him every waking moment. It became his juggernaut.

During the months in the wilderness at Beer Lake, the hate for those people who were responsible for his son's death grew daily. Paul took an obsessive interest in physical fitness and survival techniques. He worked out with weights for hours each day. He studied martial arts by video and learned how to defend himself. He learned how to survive in the bush for two or three nights at a time without any supplies or equipment. He took up jogging and could run through the forest for fifteen miles without stopping. Physically, he was in the best shape of his life; he hardly recognized himself when he looked in a mirror.

His only social contact during all of those months was at the Kinmount Gun Club that operated out of an unused gravel pit on the northern edge of that small village. He became a member under his new name. He attended the shooting ranges two or three times a week but didn't get close to any of the other gun enthusiasts. He practiced on weekdays when no one else was around the club and rarely met other members. He became a loner. He took a serious interest in his Glock 25 and became more than proficient in the use of that weapon.

* * *

On the Wednesday after the Labor Day Weekend in early September, just as the summer was heading toward fall, Paul left Beer Lake and went to Toronto. He checked into a room at the Royal York Hotel in the heart of the downtown business district. After all the months of training, planning and waiting, there was only one thing he wanted to do before he went north on his last fishing trip. He wanted to have dinner with his old friend and law partner, Rod Farn, who had always been there for him. Paul wanted to see him once more just to let him know that he appreciated his friendship and help over the years.

As Paul thought about having dinner with Rod, memories of his partnership years at Gemmill, Farn flooded into his mind. A mind that was continuously tormented by the loss of his wife and son. He could almost understand Liz's passing from her terrible disease, but Ricky's senseless death was another matter. His hatred of drug dealers continued to consume him.

On Wednesday evening when Rod walked into the lower level of Bymark, one of the city's premier restaurants, on Wellington Street West, he was totally shocked at the change in Paul's appearance. He didn't recognize his old friend and almost walked right by him.

Paul had lost weight, bulked up and seemed to be in perfect physical condition. He was very toned and muscular. He looked like a young athlete.

Dinner was low-keyed and the two friends talked generally about how Paul had been getting along. Rod could immediately tell that the death of his wife and son still affected him terribly. Paul thanked Rod for all of his support over the past years and for being his good friend. Rod read something in Paul's voice and demeanor that suggested that there was still a problem, but he couldn't quite put his finger on it. Paul alluded to the fact that his son's death had not been in vain and that some good was going to come from it. He mentioned something about turning to the *other edge of justice* to ease the pain but Rod had no idea what Paul was talking about or what he meant. Paul also hinted that he had disposed of his assets and Rod was left with the impression that Paul might have given a lot of his money away to charities. Rod was very confused and uncomfortable listening to Paul speak. He really had no idea why Paul had wanted to meet with him or where the conversation was going. Rod even wondered if he shouldn't be trying to help him even more than he had in the past. The tone of the conversation appeared very strange.

When dinner was over, Paul embraced Rod and told him again that things were going to be just fine and thanked him for his friendship. After the men said their goodbyes, Rod walked back to his car shaking his head and wishing that there was something more that he could do to help his friend. It was obvious to Rod that Paul had still not recovered from the loss of his family. He couldn't understand why Paul had called him after so many months had passed by. He also wondered what Paul had meant about turning to the *other edge of justice*.

CHAPTER FOUR

The senior basketball team at Medford Secondary School had a scheduled practice at eight o'clock every Saturday morning. This weekend was no exception. The work-out forced the players to behave themselves on Friday nights because there would be hell to pay from Coach Stu Acton and his assistant, Steve Chisholm, if they were not at the gym on time and were not ready to play ball. The kids started to arrive on schedule.

Brett Jamieson and one of his friends, Terry McCausland, had picked up three of their teammates on their way to the early morning practice. As the carload of players arrived at about quarter to eight, in the early morning darkness, Brett pulled his car onto the blacktop driveway that ran beside the gymnasium to another parking area at the rear of the school. All of a sudden, Brett saw something strange out on the school lawn and slammed on the breaks of the vehicle. As it screeched to a complete stop, the guys in the car bounced forward.

"What the hell's that guy doing by the flagpole?" Brett asked his buddies. "The way his head is hanging, it looks like he's asleep."

"Christ! He's just sitting out there in the darkness and the cold," Terry replied as he pressed the power window button. "Hey, buddy! What the hell are you doing?"

As Terry leaned out of the car window and yelled to the shadowy figure that was sitting motionless on the flagpole base, his breath clouded in the cool morning air. There was no answer or movement from the solitary form that was alone in the darkness, on the square of cement, under the flagpole on that late October morning.

"Run over and see what the hell he's doing," Brett suggested to his friend.

Terry opened the passenger door and jogged over to the place where a man was sitting. It was too dark to get a good look at the guy until he was right up close to him.

"Hey, buddy! What the hell . . . Jesus Christ! Brett, get over here fast!" Terry screamed, with his voice full of urgency and his arms waving frantically.

Brett, and the other three guys in the backseat, jumped out of the car and quickly ran over toward where Terry was standing in front of the seated man.

"What the hell's happening?" Brett asked, as he was the first to arrive next to his friend. "Holy shit! Is the guy dead?"

"It sure looks like it. There's a fuckin' knife stickin' out of the middle of his forehead!"

"Jesus! That's Stevie, the guy who sells drugs around here. I bought some pot from him just last week. I think his last name is Shacklestone or Shackleton or something like that," Brett said, as he kind of backed slowly away from the dead body as if something terrible might happen to him if he stood too close.

Stevie Shackleton was just seated there on the cement base and he had been propped up against the flagpole as if he was resting. Whoever had killed the drug dealer had taken great pains to sit him there in plain view, at a spot where he would be easily found, right in front of Medford Secondary School.

"We'd better call 911!" Terry exclaimed.

"It sure the hell doesn't look like he'll need an ambulance. He looks real dead. My cell's in the car," Brett said as he turned and left the other guys.

By the time the 911 call was made, two more carloads of basketball players had arrived and one of the guys had gone inside to find Stu Acton and Steve Chisholm. They immediately joined the small crowd of onlookers, mostly their basketball players, on the front lawn of the school as it started to get light. Each member of the crowd voiced an opinion and speculated as to what had happened to the drug dealer while they waited for the police and ambulance to arrive. As soon as the cops arrived, the coaches and their players were moved well back from the area where the body was sitting. It was an attempt to preserve any evidence at the crime scene that hadn't already been trampled on by the crowd. The two coaches formally cancelled the basketball practice.

Detective Graham Everdell and his partner, Jack Carpenter, were the first two detectives to arrive on the scene. The patrolmen who had arrived earlier had cordoned off the area around the dead body and most of the school lawn near the flag pole with bright yellow crime scene tape. All the sightseers were well back and out of the way. There was the possibility that the police might find some evidence that related to what definitely appeared to be a murder. That was very unlikely because there had been a whole basketball team walking all over the site for about twenty minutes before the police had arrived. The lawn was covered in footprints and cigarette butts.

"It's pretty obvious that whoever killed this guy set him up on that concrete base as if he was sitting there. He wanted the body to be found," Everdell commented.

Carpenter asked, "What the hell is that thing sticking out of his forehead? Is it a knife or is it some kind of a tool or something?"

"You know what it kinda looks like? One of those small knives or tools that you open oysters with, do you know what I mean?"

"Yeah, could be. I think they call them oyster-shucking knives," Carpenter said as he bent down for a closer look. "There's blood on the back of the guy's neck at the base of his skull. It looks like there might be a second stab wound back there."

Everdell bent down and took a closer look, "It does look like another wound and from the look of both of them, either one would have killed him."

"The kids who found the body told one of the officers that the dead guy is the local drug dealer. His name is Stevie Shacklestone or Shackleton or something similar. They also said that the guy's been around this school off and on almost every week for the past few years," Carpenter went on.

"I'm sure those athletes would only know him from a distance," Everdell laughed. "It's unlikely that any of those jocks ever smoked the odd joint or popped a pill."

"Yeah, right," Carpenter added with a laugh of his own.

Ten police officers and detectives scoured the grounds in the area where the body was found and searched the nearby streets for clues as to exactly what had happened. They were unable to come up with anything other than a probable name of the victim. They knocked on a number of doors nearby but none of the residents had seen or heard a thing. The damp morning grass around the body had hundreds of footprints and dozens of cigarette butts that likely belonged to the school basketball team. The two detectives interviewed Coach Acton, his assistant, Steve Chisholm, Brett Jamieson, Terry McCausland and all of their teammates but didn't learn anything helpful.

It was just after twelve when the ambulance, without the benefit of its siren, rolled out of the high school neighborhood on its way to the city morgue. The body of Stevie Shackleton, with the oyster-shucking knife still protruding from the forehead, was tucked away inside in a black body-bag. The victim's head had been covered with a small, clear plastic bag to preserve any fingerprints that might be on the knife. The technical unit would continue the investigation at the Coroner's office downtown.

* * *

Everdell and Carpenter returned to their unmarked Ford Crown Victoria and called headquarters with all the information they had about the murder victim found at Medford Secondary. All they really had to go on was a name and the fact that he was a drug dealer. They figured that the dead man's name would probably appear in the police computer. It did. Even with that little bit of information, it didn't take long. A couple of minor, prior drug related arrests showed up, together with what they hoped would be a current address for the victim.

"I know where Shackleton lived on Thomson Avenue. It's just west of Queen and Spadina and forty-seven should be two or three blocks north," Carpenter advised.

"We may as well head over there now and check it out before someone else gets there. Let's go through this Krispy Kreme drive-through and grab some coffees and a couple of donuts. I didn't eat anything this morning and I'm starving," Everdell said.

The two detectives were almost finished their breakfast by the time they pulled onto Thomson. As luck would have it, there was a fire hydrant in front of number forty-seven, so they parked next to it. Once they got on the porch, they knocked on the door once and then a second time. There was no answer. They tried the door-knob, but the door was locked. The cops looked up and down the street and decided to walk down to the corner of Ashbury and go around to the back of the houses. They knew that the whole neigh-borhood had back alleys for access to the backyards for parking and garbage collection. It wasn't long before they found themselves walking past the black Corvette convertible at the rear of number forty-seven and up onto the back porch. They knocked loudly one more time.

"This door is partly open," Carpenter said as he gave it a push and it opened wide.

The detectives stepped into the kitchen, stopped inside the door and looked around. They immediately saw some evidence that had to relate to the murder of the drug dealer. They reached into their pockets, pulled out pairs of latex rubber gloves and pulled them on their hands before they touched anything.

"Well, I'd say that this is where Stevie was killed. Look at all those scuff marks and the dried blood over there on the floor," Everdell observed.

"You're probably right! It looks like there was a fight. With a little luck that'll be the deceased's wallet on the counter near the sink," Carpenter answered as he carefully picked it up. "It is Shackleton's and it has been cleaned out. I'd better bag it in case we can get some prints. Why don't you take a look around the house?"

Carpenter put the wallet in a small, plastic bag and looked around the kitchen for any more evidence. Everdell wandered through the main level of the house without seeing anything out of the ordinary so he went upstairs. He inspected all three bedrooms and didn't see or find anything of great importance to the murder investigation except the scene in the bathroom looked a bit strange. He went back down to the kitchen.

"There's no sign of a struggle in the rest of the house and everything seems to be quite normal except for the upstairs bathroom," Everdell advised. "The vanity has been left wide-open. There are a number of plastic bottles of cleaning stuff and other things spilled out onto the floor as if someone was in there looking for something. There might be some prints up there."

"Look at the dishes, food and newspaper on the kitchen table. It looks like Shackleton was having dinner when his buddy arrived," Carpenter said and added with a laugh. "He should've offered the guy somethin' to eat!"

"We'd better get the Crime Scene Search Unit over here before the place is crawling with people. We'll also need a couple of uniforms to put at the doors to keep everyone outta here until the Forensic guys are done."

"What about upstairs? Does it look like anyone else lives here?"

"The master bedroom has some woman's clothes in the closet and in the chest of drawers so Stevie may have a wife or girlfriend."

"I wonder where the hell she is," Carpenter mused.

"Maybe the neighbors can give us some information. They may have seen or heard something last night. Jack, why don't you call it in to Forensics and I'll go out and knock on a few doors."

It was just after three o'clock when Everdell and Carpenter left two patrolmen and the Forensic Identification Services Team at Shackleton's house and went back to the Homicide Squad headquarters on College Street. There was very little evidence in the house and the neighbors who Everdell spoke to were no help. None of them really knew Shackleton or his girlfriend, as she turned out to be, because they had always kept to themselves. They hadn't heard or seen anything the night before. The detectives hoped that the patrolmen who were still knocking on doors and the Forensic Team, who were hard at work, might turn up something.

* * *

At headquarters, Everdell and Carpenter sat at their abutting desks on one side of a large squad room. There were a number of other desks and filing cabinets scattered throughout. They were going through their notes in an attempt to piece together the meagre evidence that they had found at the high school and the house. Carpenter called the morgue and got a preliminary report from the pathologist who was on duty that afternoon to see if he could add anything that might help them.

"The only thing out of place at the house was the way that the vanity in the upper bathroom had been ransacked by someone. The guy was a drug dealer. Maybe that's where he stashed his drugs or cash. It looked like he had built a shelf high up in the back of the cabinet," Everdell said, thinking aloud.

"The pathologist says that it was the oyster-shucking knife entry in the back of the neck that killed Shackleton. He died instantly. The brain stem was completely severed at the base of the skull at the top of the cervical region. It was done in the same kind of a motion as if the killer was actually opening an oyster."

"Does that mean the killer pulled the knife out of Stevie's neck after he killed him and then buried it in his forehead?" Everdell questioned. "Why would he stab him in the face after he was dead? He had to know the first wound killed Stevie immediately."

"Christ, who the hell knows? Maybe the lunatic just didn't like the guy!" Carpenter said with a smile.

"Well, the only thing that the evidence tells us at this point," Everdell said with a laugh, "is that we're looking for a killer who loves oysters!"

The two men continued to sift through the evidence that they had put together and bantered their thoughts back and forth hoping to come up with something. Everdell was shuffling through the stacks of papers on his desk and Carpenter had just got coffees when the Chief of Detectives, William Speer, stuck his head into the room.

"Graham, take line four! It might be a call about your dead drug dealer."

"Thanks, Billy," Everdell answered as he punched the flashing button, picked up his hot coffee with his other hand and leaned back in his old, wooden chair.

Carpenter, who was across from him, looked at his partner in quiet anticipation.

"Detective Graham Everdell. Can I help you?" There was a slight delay as he listened. "Yeah, that name is certainly familiar. My partner and I are investigating the death of a Steven Shackleton and this whole thing may have something to do with it."

Carpenter looked at the expression on his partner's face and kind of opened his arms, as if he were asking, *What the hell is the person on the other end of the line telling you?* He was anxious to find out who the caller was and what new information about the case was being provided. The fact that they had so little evidence to go on really bothered him.

"Thanks very much for calling. My partner and I are on our way. We'll be there in about fifteen or twenty minutes."

"What the hell's all that about?"

"It's the Administrator at the Hospital For Sick Children. Someone dropped off a duffle bag of money containing over fifty grand last night. When the guy left it with the gal who was working, he told her that, *Christmas is here a little early this year!*"

"What's that got to do with us and this case?"

"There's a name written in ink inside of the bag! It belongs to someone named *Steven Shackleton* who lives on *Thomson*. There's a pretty good chance that the bag of money they have at Sick Kid's came from the vanity in Stevie's upstairs bathroom."

CHAPTER FIVE

Darkness slowly engulfed the Pefferlaw Marina while Fred Hyde had dinner. He was about to settle in and watch some television when he suddenly remembered that his only boat rental customer that day had not returned. He had almost forgotten about Paul Taylor. Fred remembered that he was a very friendly guy who had promised to bring him a fish or if he didn't catch one, he had said that he was at least going to pour him a drink of vodka when he returned.

Fred decided that the television would have to wait until later. He went into his mudroom and pulled on his work boots and a warm jacket before he headed outside to see if his customer had returned to the marina. He turned on the yard lights and picked up a flashlight as he went out the door. As soon as he walked off the porch, he noticed that Paul Taylor's Saab convertible was still parked where it had been left earlier in the afternoon.

The night was as black as Fred had ever remembered and there was no sign of his boat or his customer. He walked down to the gas docks and looked out over the marina basin to see if he could locate the boat but it wasn't there. He stood at the end of the dock and waved the beam of his flashlight out over the lake and yelled his customer's name a couple of times. Paul Taylor did not respond to the light or the hailing.

Fred wasn't sure what he should do about the situation because it was already quite late. He decided to call the Ontario Provincial Police detachment at Beaverton, a small town about ten miles away. Forty-five minutes later, a black and white OPP cruiser pulled into the marina parking lot and stopped right next to the Saab with its lights on. Fred walked over toward the two cars as the policeman got out of his vehicle.

"Howdy, I'm Fred Hyde. I made the call to the police station."

"Good evening. I'm Constable Michael Murphy. What seems to be the problem?"

"I rented a fishing boat to a Paul Taylor at three o'clock this afternoon. That's his Saab. He said he was going fishing for a couple of hours but hasn't come back yet."

"Well, the lake hasn't been rough. Maybe he had some engine trouble and pulled in somewhere," the officer said as he walked to the driver's side of the Saab.

"I think if that happened, he would have called me by now just to let me know that he was all right. The marina phone number is on the inside of the boat so he couldn't miss it," Fred explained.

By that time, the policeman was seated in the driver's seat of the Saab with the glove compartment open and said, "The keys are in the ignition. Let's find out exactly who this guy is and where he came from." The cop opened a small, plastic folder with the ownership in one side and the insurance particulars in the other and laughed, "The vehicle is in the name of an *Elizabeth Taylor* at a Toronto address. You don't think that it belongs to the movie actress do you?"

"If this guy was married to the actress, he wouldn't be out here in the middle of Lake Simcoe in one of my small rental boats. He'd be on a yacht in the Caribbean or the Mediterranean," Fred replied smiling.

"There's a note on the passenger seat," the policeman noticed.

"What's it say?" Fred asked.

"It says that the proceeds of the sale of this Saab should be given to the Hospital For Sick Children in Toronto."

"Christ! It sounds like a suicide note!" Fred commented.

"I'll see if I can get a phone number on my cell and call his wife. Do you know if he took a cell phone out there on the lake with him?" Constable Murphy asked.

"I didn't notice if he had one or not!"

"The number for a *Paul Taylor* at the address on the ownership is no longer in service and there's no forwarding number. I don't know what the hell that's all about."

"What do you think we should do?" Fred wondered.

"Do you have access to a decent sized boat around here that has a spotlight? We should take a look out on the lake just in case he's in trouble and is sitting out there in the darkness," Murphy decided, "but I sure as hell don't like the sound of this note."

"I've got the keys to a twenty-seven Regal that's here on consignment. We can use it and there is a rotating spotlight on the bow," Fred advised.

"That's great! Get the boat ready and I'll call the detachment to let them know what your call was about and what we're going to do," Murphy answered.

"I've got one of those really bright spotlights that will plug into the cigarette lighter. I'll go and get it and the keys to the Regal," Fred said as he walked off.

Constable Murphy called his detachment and informed them about the situation at the marina. He advised that he and the marina owner were going on a search and rescue mission to see if they could find the lost fisherman. He also told them that he wouldn't be in his cruiser for the next couple of hours and could only be reached on his cell. As soon as he made his report, he joined Fred and they walked toward the docks.

"This Regal has lots of fuel. I put some in the other day to show it to some people who were interested in buying it. Do you mind giving me a hand with the mooring cover? It weighs a bloody ton," Fred explained.

"Not at all. This is a fair sized boat." Murphy answered.

The men rolled up the heavy canvas cover and left it on the dock. Fred got into the boat first and turned the blower on for a minute or two to get rid of any gas fumes in the bilge. He turned the keys and the twin, three hundred and fifty cubic inch v-eights came to life. Fred untied the front and rear lines and threw them on the dock. The policeman jumped in as Fred slipped the two engines into gear and the boat slowly began to move out of the slip.

"Which direction do you think the guy went when he left?" The policeman asked.

"He was going to troll down the south shore. We should probably head that way and if he's out there, he will be able to see our lights."

Fred plugged the portable light into the lighter and handed it to the cop.

"Christ! This is bright! He should be able to see this from anywhere on the lake."

"It is a great light. It's got the same power as those lights they put on airplanes for landing at night," Fred explained.

The Regal cruised slowly down the shore and as the spotlights searched the dark water, they yelled for Paul Taylor. They traveled for about an hour without any luck. The boat made a large, arcing turn further out into the lake and went back the way it had come. The men used the same searching techniques on the way back. They moved the two searchlights all over the calm water of the lake, along the shoreline and yelled periodically to attract the attention of the lost fisherman. They had absolutely no luck finding Paul Taylor, or the boat, and arrived back at the marina after two and a half hours of searching. The men put the Regal back into its slip, covered it with the mooring cover and found themselves back in the parking lot near the cars.

"We really can't do much more tonight," Constable Murphy decided as he opened the door of the cruiser. "Maybe Taylor will show up in the morning. You're right though, if he is in trouble and pulled in somewhere, he would have called to let you know, but I really don't like that note."

"Well, he seemed like a real nice guy and he was acting normal. I can't imagine that he wouldn't call if the motor quit or if he stopped somewhere. Something's fishy. He'd have to realize that someone would be out looking for him if he didn't come back before dark."

"I'm off my shift at midnight, but I'll have another officer who comes on duty in the morning come around and see you first thing. If Taylor hasn't shown up by then, or called in, another search will have to be done in the daylight. I hope you hear from him soon," the constable said, "and if you do, let us know. Thanks for calling."

Constable Murphy left the marina and headed straight back to Beaverton to file his missing person report. Other than the missing fisherman, it had been a quiet night. After the report was filed, he went back out for an hour or so. At the end of his shift, he left a memo about the missing fisherman for Constable Tom Meredith, who would arrive for the day shift at eight in the morning. He asked him to immediately contact Fred Hyde and do a follow up at the Pefferlaw Marina.

* * *

By ten o'clock the following morning, there were four Ontario Provincial Police Officers, including Constable Meredith, standing around the gas dock at the marina. They were chatting with Fred Hyde about the missing fisherman and what kind of search was done the night before. A police boat was already in the water and another search and rescue mission was about to get underway. The missing fisherman had not called the marina or come back. They all started to think about the significance of the note that had been found on the seat of the Saab and began to realize that it was most likely a suicide note.

It was another of those overcast days and a slight wind had come up overnight. The lake was a bit choppy with one-foot waves hitting the cement breakwater one after the other. Fred accompanied Constable Meredith and a female officer in the OPP boat as they cruised down the south shore. It was twelve-thirty when Fred spotted his fishing boat. It had washed up on a rocky shore, out in front of a beautiful year round residence, six or seven miles west of the marina. It looked like the small boat had been bouncing against the rocks next to the cement and wooden dock for some time. Fred could see that the rocks had dented the boat and the lower unit of the motor was damaged. The officers tied up the poliee boat to the private dock.

"That's my boat all right," Fred acknowledged. "The way it's hitting those rocks means that the engine is probably screwed."

"There's no sign of your fisherman and the life jacket you gave the guy is still in the boat," Meredith commented. "There's a lot of other stuff on the floor too."

"I'll get into the water and move the boat off the rocks so no more damage will be done to it. Will one of you guys stay on the dock and I'll push it over there so we can tie it up?" Fred asked.

On the calm side of the private dock, Constable Tom Meredith listed the items found in the boat in his memo pad. There was a fishing rod with the line still rolled up on the reel even though there was a Rapala on the end of it. It looked like it had never been used. There was also a life jacket, a coat, an almost empty bottle of Absolut Vodka, an empty duffle bag and two framed pictures. One picture was of an attractive woman in her thirties and the other was of a teenage boy.

"Damn it! Look at the family pictures and the booze! I'm afraid that this doesn't look very good," Meredith commented.

"That bottle of vodka was full when Taylor left the marina. He showed it to me and said that we'd have a drink when he got back," Fred added.

"I'm afraid this looks like a classic suicide," Meredith stated.

"He had the life jacket on when he left my marina," Fred observed.

Two more police boats arrived during the next couple of hours together with six more police officers. Four of them were divers and they had all of their gear with them. The divers spent most of the afternoon in the fifteen to twenty-five feet of cold water along the shoreline. The speculation at the end of the day was that bodies usually sink when they first go into the water. All the police officers agreed that Paul Taylor's body would probably surface at some time during the next few weeks. As bodies deteriorate and decompose, the various gases that form inside the chest cavity usually bring them to the surface.

The body was never found.

* * *

Rod Farn picked up the Saturday Star and read all about Paul's fishing trip and his drowning death in Lake Simcoe. He wasn't totally surprised at the contents of the story. There had been something very odd about Paul during the dinner meeting. He had been acting quite strange. At the time the newspaper had gone to press, the authorities were still looking for Paul's body. The article went on to speculate as to what had happened to the missing man, *Paul Richard Taylor*. The evidence strongly suggested a suicide. The police had found pictures of the missing man's wife and son in the boat, both of whom had died in recent years. There was also an almost empty bottle of vodka and an unused lifejacket. There was a fishing rod in the boat with a line that had never seen the water. The story went on to report that the missing man's vehicle was found at a nearby marina with a note on the front seat but it didn't elaborate. After he read the article, Rod decided that the evening dinner date had been Paul's way of saying goodbye.

CHAPTER SIX

etectives Graham Everdell and Jack Carpenter parked their unmarked police car in the circular driveway on University Avenue near the main entrance to the Hospital For Sick Children and went inside. They crossed a large foyer filled with people who were coming and going or seated in comfortable chairs reading and waiting. They walked past a small crowd near a coffee counter and went directly to the internal windows where the Administration Office was located. As he was requested to do during the earlier call to the Homicide Squad offices, Everdell asked the friendly woman in the office for Peter Strybosch, the Hospital Administrator.

Strybosch had not been working the night before. He and his wife had slipped away to Niagara Falls, an hour and a half west of Toronto, for a romantic weekend in a city famous for honeymoons. More recently, gambling was in the spotlight with the construction of two Vegas-style casinos right near the falls. They had planned to do some gambling at the border city casino so aptly named Casino Niagara.

Joan Markey, the gal on the nightshift the evening before, tried to contact her boss as soon as the man dropped off the duffle bag of cash, but he didn't answer his cell. She wondered what to do with the money for the night and decided to lock it up in a cabinet in her boss' office until the next morning. The hospital staff finally caught up with Strybosch around noon Saturday when he checked his messages. It wasn't long before his romantic getaway in the honeymoon capital of North America was ruined. In all of the years that he had been a hospital administrator, nothing as strange as this had ever happened before. He returned to the hospital to deal with the cash that had been left there under such extraordinary circumstances.

* * *

"Gentlemen, please come right in," Strybosch said as he shook hands with the detectives. "I want you to know that whoever dropped off this money screwed up a romantic weekend in Niagara Falls with my wife, Heather. My first weekend off in a month."

"Well, we have to work the odd Saturday too and our wives are not the least bit thrilled about the number of hours we have to put in on the job either," Carpenter replied.

"That won't make Heather feel any better because I cancelled the last get-a-way that we had planned. When we left Toronto for wine country, she even commented that our planned weekend escape was too good to be true!"

"That's really too bad, but other than that, how are you?" Everdell asked.

"I'm fantastic," Strybosch answered with a belly-laugh. "We all know that a whole weekend alone with your own wife is far too long anyway."

"Tell us about the large unexpected donation the hospital received Friday night," Carpenter asked as he sat down in one of the leather chairs in front of the oak desk.

"Well, we often get large donations, but never in cash."

"I'm sure that it was a pleasant surprise for the hospital," Everdell answered.

"It was and here it is! This is how it arrived, in this duffle bag," Strybosch explained. "It was dropped off last evening around eight o'clock. It's mostly small bills. My assistant and I counted it earlier today and there seems to be just over fifty thousand dollars. The name printed on the inside edge of the bag indicates it belongs to a *Steven Shackleton* who lives on Thomson."

"Mr. Shackleton was murdered early last night and we're right in the middle of a homicide investigation." Everdell went on, "We think that he was killed at his home on Thomson, near Queen and Spadina, and some time shortly after the murder took place, this money was dropped off at the hospital. We think it was taken from Shackleton's house, probably by the killer, at the same time the murder was committed and then the killer came directly here."

"Which employee was on duty when the money was dropped off?" Carpenter asked.

"One of our administrators, Joan Markey, told me that a man walked in around eight o'clock last night and handed her that bag through the Administration Office window. He just said, *It's a donation to help the children.*"

"We'll have to ask her a few questions. Did she happen to give you a description of the person who dropped off the bag?" Everdell asked.

"Joan said that the man was white, about six feet tall and weighed a couple of hundred pounds. He had slicked-back, dark hair and some kind of a beard, a goatee, she thought, and long sideburns," Strybosch explained. "She also said that he was wearing dark glasses, probably sunglasses and a baseball cap of some kind."

"All the guy said to her was that the money was a donation?" Carpenter asked.

"That's it and he made some reference to Christmas coming early this year. By the time Joan realized what was in the bag and looked up, the guy was on his way back through the reception area and almost out the door."

Everdell asked, "Did anyone happen to see his car or get the license number?"

"No. By the time Joan got out of the office, across the lobby and through the front door, the guy had disappeared."

"Joan Markey can't be working today if she worked last night?" Carpenter asked.

"No, she has the day off, but she doesn't live far from here if you want to talk to her. She has a condo over on McCaul, two or three blocks west of here. My assistant will give you her address and phone number."

"I'm afraid that we'll have to take the money with us because it is evidence in a homicide. It is tied directly to the murder we're investigating and it's quite obvious that it belonged to the victim," Everdell explained.

"What happens to the money after the case is solved?" Strybosch asked. "Will the hospital eventually get it back?"

"The deceased was a drug dealer, so the money may eventually be classified as *Proceeds of Crime* and if so, certain rules, regulations and procedures will have to be followed. It might even go to the estate of the deceased. If there's any way that we can arrange for the hospital to get some or all of it, we will," Carpenter advised.

"Thanks very much for your co-operation," Everdell said as he and Carpenter got up to leave. "We'll get the information on Joan Markey from your assistant on the way out and let you get back to enjoying your weekend."

"It's too late to carry on with my romantic weekend in Niagara Falls so I think I'll just take my wife out for dinner tonight."

"I had an anniversary dinner at Mediterra, a seafood restaurant at York and Richmond, about two weeks ago and the food was excellent," Carpenter commented.

"That sounds perfect, maybe I'll try it."

"Have a nice time tonight," Everdell commented on the way out of the office.

* * *

The detectives left the hospital and their first stop was Joan Markey's condo on McCaul. They called her from their car and made an appointment. As the only eye witness, she confirmed everything that Strybosch had told them earlier. She didn't provide any new evidence, but more clearly described the man who had dropped off the money. On the way back to the police station, both detectives mulled over the facts of the case.

"We can pretty well rule out robbery as a motive for this killing. The guy wouldn't have killed Shackleton for his money if he was just going to give it away to the hospital. There's a lot more to it than that," Carpenter said.

"You're right. That means that the murder was likely premeditated and planned, and in all likelihood, committed by someone who knew him."

"I wonder how Medford Secondary School fits into all of this?" Carpenter said, thinking out loud.

The two detectives drove the rest of the way to headquarters in silence. They were both trying to decide what their next course of action should be.

CHAPTER SEVEN

As the small aluminum boat disappeared into the darkness that enveloped him, Paul Taylor began to slowly and methodically breaststroke his way toward shore. The water of Lake Simcoe was extremely cold on his hands and face, but it didn't take long for his body to get used to it because he was prepared. It only took a few minutes for the cold water that had seeped into the wetsuit that was under his clothing to reach his body temperature and once that happened, Paul was almost warm. He continued to stroke at a regular pace, noiselessly cutting through the water, toward that part of the shore where the road allowance came down to the lake.

Twenty minutes later he reached the sand and gravel shoreline of the road that sloped gently into the shallow water. It was graded as a ramp for use during the summer season. As he hit the bottom and quietly rose out of the water, his eyes searched the blackness of the shoreline to be sure that no one was in the vicinity. It was imperative to his plan that no one saw him walk out of the lake that night. He continued to be vigilant as he dripped and sloshed, as quietly as possible, the three hundred feet to the road that ran along behind the cottages in that area. He also kept a lookout for any cars that might be traveling on the country road. If one came along, he would have to slip into the thick brush and trees that lined the roadside to avoid being seen.

At the corner, where the cottagers' road crossed the road allowance, Paul turned to the right and walked behind the lakefront cottages to the fourth cottage. He stopped at a garage that sat just off the road and looked around once again. He quietly opened the garage doors and quickly slipped inside. As he got into the dark blue Taurus, he was careful to sit on the old blanket that had been spread over plastic on the driver's seat because his clothes were sopping wet. He didn't want to take the time to change into dry clothes. He started the engine and backed out of the garage into the blackness with his lights off. After he closed the garage doors, he got back into the car and drove slowly toward the concession road. As he turned right and headed away from the lake, he pulled the light switch and lit up the roadway. A mile down the road, he turned left at Woodbine Avenue and continued to drive north-easterly in the direction of Beer Lake.

* * *

Two nights before, Paul had driven his Taurus to a friend's cottage on Lake Simcoe. It was owned by one of his associates at Gemmill, Farn LLP. He knew that his friend had packed up his family the weekend before and had taken them back to their home in the city to get the kids ready for the new school year. He also knew they would only use their cottage on weekends, and probably wouldn't even be back to the lake until Thanksgiving weekend. The empty garage was always left unlocked. After he left the Taurus in the garage that night, he walked the mile or so to Woodbine and then a few hundred yards south to a Shell gas station. He used his cell to call a Beaverton cab to pick him up. He explained to the driver that his car had broken down and that he had to get to Fenelon Falls, a small town about forty miles to the east. From there he took a local taxi to Kinmount, ten miles further down the road, and walked the last mile or so into his cottage on the lake.

* * *

As Paul, soaking wet, turned the Taurus north on Highway 48 on his way back to his cottage, he congratulated himself on how well the plan for his demise had been executed. It had gone off without a hitch. He knew that it wouldn't be long before Fred Hyde at the Pefferlaw Marina would be wondering what had happened and would be out looking for him and the small fishing boat. He thought that it was very unlikely that the boat would be found that night.

The idea to take the law into his own hands had started to fester as his hatred of drugs and drug dealers took over his whole being. He knew that the legal system would never punish the man responsible for the death of his son. He would make him pay for what he did. He was going to kill him. When that mission was completed, he was going to kill a few more drug dealers and traffickers who hung around the other high schools where teenagers had died or been maimed on the same night that Ricky had died.

After Ricky's death, he had read all of the newspaper articles about the students at the five high schools in the metropolitan area who had been sold Ecstasy from the same bad shipment. Seven teenagers died and a number were hospitalized with terrible injuries as a result of bad drugs on that same weekend. Paul decided to find the drug dealers who had ruined so many lives and avenge those unfortunate deaths too.

The more Paul thought about his loss, and the losses that other families had endured along with him, revenge was foremost on his mind. Those thoughts were all he had left and they kept him going day after day. As the idea of revenge and justice continued to haunt him, he wondered how he could get to the guilty men. He soon moved to the planning stage. He thought that if he were dead, there would be no chance that he could be a suspect or get caught. His plan started to take shape.

* * *

Paul, as head of the Estates Section at Gemmill, Farn LLP, had full access to the personal records, including birth certificates and driver's licenses, of a number of men his own age who had recently passed away from various causes. He chose the identities of two of his clients, Gordon William Thoburn and Clive Edward Lyons. Over the past few months, he had fraudulently applied for and received two Canadian Passports, each in the name of those men, with a different picture of him in each one. He had grown a mustache and sideburns for the first one and added a goatee for the second. His hair was longer than usual for both. He knew that it would take the government years to cross-reference passports with deceased Canadian citizens.

In his capacity as a lawyer, Paul had the authority to certify the identity of those people who applied for passports through the Department of Foreign Affairs and International Trade. Once his signature was on an application and a picture of the applicant, the only further check that civil servants ever carried out was a telephone call to his office to verify that he had signed the paperwork and did in fact know the party described in the submitted documentation. When Paul got the calls, he merely certified, verbally, that he was the lawyer involved and that he knew the applicant. The passports had been issued without a hitch. It had also been just as easy to have the licenses replaced by the Ministry of Transportation in the names of the dead men with Paul's picture on each one.

The third identity or alias was an afterthought when one of Paul's good friends passed away after a long illness. Paul became concerned that his new aliases could be tied to Gemmill, Farn LLP, so he decided it would be prudent to take some extra care with his third and final identity that he applied for during those months. Jack Melville Randall, a long-time family friend who was Paul's age, had passed away with cancer and his wife, Georgia, asked Paul to drop by her home to give her advice in relation to the finalization of Jack's estate. Over the years, Jack had taken all of Paul's advice to heart so when he died, all of his assets had transferred immediately to Georgia by right of survivorship. There was virtually no estate. Things were so simple there was no reason to open a file at the firm. Paul dropped by to answer estate questions for Georgia on three occasions and after the second visit, Jack's birth certificate and his driver's license were *misplaced*. Paul assured the widow that they would never be needed for anything.

By the time Paul picked up the *Jack Melville Randall* passport from the ministry and got a new driver's license, he was ready for any emergency that might develop. He was in a position that would allow him to travel internationally, incognito, if the need ever arose. He decided that the Randall identity would be saved for last and at some point, he might just have to actually become his old friend. The other two identities would be used to facilitate his plans for revenge.

* * *

The trip back to the solitude of the little cottage on Beer Lake that night was uneventful. As soon as he got back, he peeled off his wet clothes and took a long, hot shower. As the warm water soothed his cool, clammy skin, the reality of what he had done finally hit him. He thought, *I no longer exist! As far as all of my friends and business associates are concerned . . . as far as the world is concerned, I'm dead!* Each member of the Taylor family had died so tragically, one after the other.

Later that night, as he was sitting in his favorite chair and relaxing by the fire with a J & B on ice with a little water in his hand, his eyes focused on a wooden box of oyster-shucking knives that sat in a far corner of the room. He thought to himself, *Why the hell did I buy those things at that garage sale so many years ago? I wonder why I've kept them all this time?*

Paul's mind turned to more deadly matters. He thought about how he was going to kill the sleazy drug dealer who had killed his only son. The street dealer from Medford would be his top priority in the days to follow. He decided that not only was he going to kill the bastard, he was going to be sure his victim knew why he was going to die. The killing would send a message to every drug dealer who had ever preyed on high school students across the city. The street dealers who had caused havoc at five high schools on the weekend that Ricky died would not escape. He was also going to kill the street dealers' drug suppliers higher up the drug chain. They were responsible too.

Paul decided to lay low for a couple of weeks to let the news of his drowning death be forgotten. The down time would give him an opportunity to carefully plan his next move because he was going into uncharted waters. He was quite relaxed for a man who had just taken his own life.

Pandora's Box had been opened wide and for Paul . . . there was no turning back.

CHAPTER EIGHT

After the body of Steven Shackleton was found leaning against the flagpole at Medford Secondary School on that Saturday morning, Detectives Everdell and Carpenter continued their investigation. All of the evidence that they had in their file had been found during their initial enquiries.

The experienced detectives went through their memo pads and reports with a fine-toothed comb. They discussed the murder backwards and forwards in an attempt to come up with something they had missed. They really thought something would break if they kept digging. They read the Coroner's Report, time and again, and even interviewed the pathologist personally. The cause of death was confirmed to be the stab wound in the back of Shackleton's neck. The way that the short, wide blade of the oyster-shucking knife had been pushed and twisted in the cervical region of the neck had the immediate effect of severing the brain stem near the Atlas Vertebra. The victim had died instantly. The killer would have realized that at the exact moment of death because the victim's body would have gone totally limp in his grasp. The detectives were unable to figure out why the killer had pulled the knife out of the back of the dead man's neck and buried it in the middle of his forehead. That act made no sense because the guy was already dead. The body yielded no other information or evidence.

On the Monday following the murder, the two detectives spent two hours with Steven Shackleton's girlfriend, Alison Flaherty. She had lived with him for six months prior to his death, but was unable to add much to the investigation. She did confirm that her boyfriend was a drug dealer and that he did hide his money on the specially built shelf in the vanity in the upstairs bathroom. She was very upset by the fact that she could have actually been there when the murder took place and could have been killed too. She immediately moved back to her parent's home.

Carpenter and Everdell also revisited Medford on the Tuesday, to see if any of the students would be able to shed more light on the murder. They arranged for the principal of the high school to make an announcement over the personal address system. It requested that any students who had seen Shackleton in the area of the school during the past week should drop down to the Guidance Office to chat with the detectives who were investigating his murder. The turnout wasn't great. Most kids who knew Shackleton didn't want it to be publicized just in case their parents found out. The two brave students who did show had little to add to what the detectives already knew, except that the drug dealer had been hanging around the school on at least two different days the week he was killed. On the Wednesday, and again, on the Friday.

The detectives walked the crime scene again that afternoon. The whole area was still cordoned off with yellow crime scene tape and designated as off limits for the students. They wandered around the area for about an hour and tried to make some sense out of the evidence they had put together but didn't have much luck. The scene was much the same as it had been on the Saturday morning. The only difference was that the body had been removed. They were unable to find anything helpful to their investigation.

The following morning, Everdell and Carpenter went back to Shackleton's residence with the hopes that they might have overlooked something. On their way to the back door, they took time to look around the yard where the Corvette was still parked. The gravel and some uncut grass had all kinds of tire tracks and wheel marks that belonged to a couple of police cruisers. The area had been compromised because the uniforms had been too lazy to park on the street and walk down the lane to the house. Nothing else jumped out at them.

The detectives spent another hour going through the different rooms of the house looking for anything that might help. Things looked pretty much the same as they had on the previous Saturday.

They also went up to the second floor and concentrated on the bathroom where the contents of the cupboard under the sink had been scattered on the floor. Everdell and Carpenter got down on their hands and knees to take a good look inside the vanity. It was obvious that a secret shelf had been specially built by Shackleton well out of the line of view of anyone who might take a cursory look inside. The Forensic Team found some fingerprints in the bathroom, but they belonged to the dead man and his girlfriend.

They went back downstairs to the kitchen and sat at the table where the deceased had been sitting when he was interrupted by the killer. They discussed all of the evidence but still couldn't make it fit together. They needed a break in the case.

On Thursday, Everdell and Carpenter made prior arrangements to meet Peter Strybosch, the Administrator at the hospital, together with the three women who had worked on the evening shift when the duffle bag of money was dropped off. One small piece of new evidence that surfaced was that a woman who had been on duty that night at the coffee counter in the lobby had remembered seeing a man come into the hospital around eight o'clock in the evening carrying a small, dark bag. He had been walking so quickly through the crowd that he had caught her attention. A few moments later, she just happened to look up and had seen him once again, without the bag, walking at a fast pace toward the front door. She merely confirmed Joan Markey's description of the man. Other than that, she supplied nothing new.

In the few weeks that followed the Shackleton murder, Everdell and Carpenter seemed to be at a dead end with no new leads. Forensics had found no extra prints in the kitchen or bathroom. They decided to work late that day because contacts on other files could only be made in the evening. They were going through the seven different cases that they had on their plate. The last one they reviewed was the Shackleton murder file.

"I know that this thing seems to be at a dead end, but why don't we go through the file one more time before we put it away? I sometimes think that we're just missing something that's right there in front of us," Everdell suggested.

"Let's do it. There are a lot of things that just don't make sense. Let's go through them again and I'll write all the facts on the black-board," Carpenter agreed as he stood up and wiped off some of the unnecessary chalk notes. "Let's start right at the beginning."

"Right. The one kid at Medford said he had seen Stevie around the school on the Wednesday afternoon, two days before he died. The other one said that when he went home on the Friday at about four-thirty, he had seen the dealer's Corvette convertible parked in the school parking lot among the other cars with Stevie behind the wheel," Everdell recalled. "Stevie was probably there doing his weekend business. Neither of the witnesses could pin-point the time the black Vette left the school parking lot."

"Sometime after four-thirty, Shackleton must have finished his business transactions. Then he left the school area and made his way downtown to his house on Thomson," Carpenter went on.

"It appears, from what we think is the time frame, that Stevie was in his kitchen having something to eat and reading the news-paper somewhere around seven o'clock. About two hours had passed from when he left the school. We don't know if he went straight home or not, but he was home around seven."

"Presumably, Shackleton's dinner was interrupted by someone who came to the back door while he was sitting there at the table eating. The killer was either invited into the house or just burst in," Carpenter added.

"The food on the table had been partially eaten, so when who-ever arrived came into the kitchen, Stevie must have got up out of his chair to confront him in some manner in the middle of the room. The killer is probably a male."

"It's quite obvious that some kind of a fight took place because there were a number of black shoe marks in the middle of the kitchen floor where the blood was found."

Everdell continued, "That's probably when Stevie got the oyster-shucking knife stuck into the back of his neck. The coroner said that it took a forceful stabbing motion and a lot of brute strength to insert the knife and twist the blade enough to sever the top of the spinal column from the brain. The killer has to be fairly strong."

"Look at Shackleton! He was well over six feet and at least two hundred pounds, maybe more, and he looked to be in good shape. He could probably take care of himself, so the killer has to be a fair size as well as tough and strong."

"So the guy grabs Stevie, sticks the knife in his neck and gives it a hard twist. Is Stevie on his feet at that moment or is he lying face down? The killer is either holding the body up and drops it or the body's already on the floor. When does he pull the knife out of the back of Stevie's neck? Either the knife is pulled from the body as it falls to the floor face up or he was stabbed lying face down. If it's face down, the killer has to kneel down and roll the limp body over. Either way, he pulls the oyster-shucking knife out of the neck and plunges it into the middle of the dead man's forehead. What the hell was that all about?"

Carpenter went on, "The pathologist said the stab wound in the back of Shackleton's neck killed him instantly and that the killer would have known that because the body would have gone limp immediately. Who the hell kills someone as if they're opening an oyster? The killer must have planned to kill Shackleton that way. He knew he would die instantaneously."

"Why the hell did he pull the oyster-shucking knife out of the back of Stevie's neck, if he knew Stevie was already dead, and then bury it up to its hilt in the middle of his forehead?"

"That is really strange. The second wound, could have been done in a fit of rage. Maybe for some reason or another, the killer hated his victim," Carpenter surmised.

"If that's the scenario, then the killer must have previously known Stevie."

"Now, we've got Shackleton dead on the kitchen floor. Then the killer goes upstairs and finds the duffle bag of money that's been stashed on a hidden shelf in the back of the bathroom vanity. How the hell did he know it was there? You couldn't see it by just looking into the cabinet."

"There are two ways that he would have known where the money was hidden," Everdell went on. "One, he was a friend or someone who Stevie knew and trusted, or two, Stevie told him where the money was hidden."

"I'm sure you're right! A friend or partner might know where Shackleton kept his drugs and money. If the killer was a stranger and Shackleton was overpowered and thought that he was about to die, he might have begged for his life and offered the money to save himself."

"Jack, both of those scenarios make sense. Either way, the guy killed him and took the duffle bag of money from the bathroom."

"OK, so he pulls the bag out of the cabinet and knocks all that stuff onto the floor," Carpenter added. "It didn't look like the killer ransacked the other rooms so he had to know exactly where the money was hidden."

"To make matters even more confusing, on the way to Medford, the killer dropped into the main lobby of the Hospital For Sick Children, a place that's crawling with people, and drops off Stevie's duffle bag of money containing over fifty grand. He tells the woman in the office that it's a donation to help the children. What the hell is the perp's motive? He obviously didn't kill him for the money!"

"That's right, now the hard part of this whole thing! Why did the killer move the body to Medford Secondary School and set it up in front of the school for everyone to see? After he does the murder in the privacy of Shackleton's house and it's over and done with, why does he risk moving the body? Someone could have seen him at the house, the hospital or the high school."

"The body wasn't just moved, it was moved to a very public place where it could be easily found. The fact that the killer took Stevie's body to Medford must have been important to him because he really did risk being seen."

"It appears to be just a murder, not a robbery, a premeditated and planned murder with a personal twist," Carpenter concluded.

"You're right and three things bother me about the scenario. First, the way the small knife was jammed into Stevie's forehead after he was dead, second, the money being dropped off at the hospital as a charitable gesture and, third, the body being moved to a specific location all the way across town. Why Medford?"

"Well, I think that we've hit a brick wall on this one, so why don't we put it away and wait and see if something breaks for us in the next couple of days," Carpenter suggested.

"You're right. Let's get back to that rooming house fire where the old guy died last week. We still have a number of people to talk to while we're waiting for the Fire Marshall's Report."

CHAPTER NINE

P aul Taylor was totally shocked at how easy it had been to kill someone he hated so much. The Shackleton murder didn't bother him at all. He often thought of Ricky and the other teenagers across the city who had died that night and the students who had ended up in the hospital. He thought about the kids with neurological damage who would spend the rest of their lives in an extended care facility and he sympathized with the families whose lives had been ruined. He thought about the major suppliers, the bosses, the men who put the drugs on the street. They too would have to pay.

Even though Paul had planned to kill the drug dealer for months, he was never really sure if he could actually do it. Once it was over however, he actually felt ecstatic. A drug dealer who had preyed on high school kids in Toronto was off the street. The one who had killed Ricky. Paul knew that there were more of those vultures out there. He considered them the scum of the earth. He made an oath to himself that the drug dealers who frequented the other four high schools where students had died that weekend would all meet the same fate. He knew in his heart that the murder of Steven Shackleton was just the beginning.

It was important to Paul to move Shackleton's body to Medford Secondary School where he had done his dirty work. He wanted the police, students, parents, teachers and other drug dealers to know that justice had been served. He wanted to show them that someone had finally had enough of the inaction of the local police to get these guys off the streets and hold them responsible for their actions. They would all soon find out that there was much more to come in the future. If the cops couldn't do it before more lives of innocent teenagers and their families were ruined, then Paul would do it for them.

After he left Shackleton's body in the schoolyard, Paul drove north to Highway 401 and headed east out of the city. During the two-hour drive back to Beer Lake, he was very careful to stay within the speed limits. Even though his driver's license and Taurus were in the name of *Gordon William Thoburn*, he didn't wanted to risk being stopped for a speeding ticket. Now that he was dead to the rest of the world, he wanted to be sure he stayed that way, at least until after all his work was done.

He thought about the events of the past months as he drove north. His mind raced through all the planning, all the training and all the waiting and finally, the actual *execution* of his plan. As he thought about how he had carried out his plan and about the word *execution*, he smiled to himself at the pun. He was feeling quite proud and took great pleasure in the fact that everything had gone so smoothly. Steven Shackleton, the Medford high school drug dealer, was out of business.

Paul arrived back at his cottage at eleven-fifteen that night and the first thing that he did was fill a glass with ice cubes, three ounces of J&B and top it off with a little water. He took a couple of long sips and set it on the table beside his favorite black, leather chair. He threw some wood and paper into the fireplace and watched the colored flames from the paper ignite the logs. As the smell of a new fire filled the room, he sat quietly and watched the flames devour everything they touched. He felt warm, relaxed and comfortable as he thought about the day's events. In his state of mind, he knew that he had done something good.

At one o'clock in the morning, Paul finished the last of his strong drinks and decided that it was time to hit the hay. Tiredness began to engulf him as all of the day's excitement slowly drained from his body. He was somewhat surprised that he felt so good, but deep down, he had always known that he would have a good night's sleep. He closed the fireplace screen, turned out all of the lights and went to bed.

* * *

Paul slept in later than usual. He was up and getting organized by ten-thirty. He had a change of heart as he started to shave off the goatee and left the thick, bristled mustache in place. It had been a long time since he had a mustache and sideburns and he felt that he looked totally different. As he showered and washed his hair, his thoughts went back to Medford. He was sure that the body would have attracted a crowd by then. He pictured a crowd of people milling around to get a closer glimpse of the corpse and the police trying to keep them back. He wondered if the sightseers and the police would get the message he had left for them. Would they realize that they were looking at the body of the drug dealer who had sold the bad dope that had killed the two teenagers and maimed another at that high school so many months before? If they didn't realize that fact that morning, he thought that the police would eventually figure it out.

Paul dressed in his work clothes and went outside onto the cedar deck that he had built at the front of the cottage. Beer Lake was like glass. The maple, oak and fir trees in the surrounding forest all along the shoreline reflected on the mirrored surface. Paul was able to wipe the events of the previous day out of his mind as he did the various chores that had to be done around the property before the winter set in. He winched his dock up onto the shore so the ice break-up in the spring wouldn't tear it apart. He finished cutting a number of logs for firewood that he had started and left the week before. At about five o'clock, he fired up the barbeque and cooked a thick Porterhouse to perfection and had it for dinner, along with a baked potato and a mixed vegetable salad that he threw together from the things in his crisper. He sat down to eat in his favorite chair and flipped on the television so he could catch the six o'clock news on Global, one of the local Toronto stations.

After some local political news, Beverly Thomson got right into the story about a body that had been found at one of the high schools in the central part of the city. "At about eight o'clock this morning, the body of a man who had been stabbed to death was discovered in the schoolyard of Medford Secondary School by some members of the school basketball team who were at an early morning practice. The police said that the body had been left on the cement base of the school flagpole, in an actual sitting position, propped up against the pole. The police have not yet released the name of the victim pending notification of next-of- kin, but they did indicate that the Homicide Squad is in charge and a murder investigation is underway. Further information will be reported as it becomes available."

The news had been short and sweet. Paul really hadn't expected much more. He decided that he would drive into Kinmount the following morning and pick up a copy of the Sunday newspaper just to see what further information had been made available to the public. He had another very quiet evening as he sat by the fire and watched television. He went to bed early and enjoyed another good night's sleep.

After a light breakfast, he got into the Taurus and drove the five minutes into Kinmount. While his gas tank was being filled at the local garage, he went inside to pick up the Sunday Star. Back in his leather chair by the fire, Paul glanced over pages one and two and found what he was looking for on page three. There was a picture of the dead man and two small columns of print. He started to read: *"Steven Shackleton, 30, of Thomson Avenue, was murdered early Friday evening in the kitchen of his home in the downtown area. His body was found at Medford Secondary School, in the schoolyard, propped up against the flagpole. The police have advised that the deceased was a drug dealer who frequented the school area. Shackleton died of a stab wound to the back of the neck, but was found with an oyster-shucking knife stuck right in the middle of his forehead. The police don't know why the body was moved from his residence to the high school, but said that the person who committed the murder, may have dropped off a duffle bag containing over fifty-thousand dollars at the Hospital For Sick Children while the body was being transported from the residence to the school. The bag of money apparently belonged to the victim. The police are looking for a white male, thirty-five to forty years of age, with a goatee, sideburns and slicked-back, dark hair for questioning. If anyone has information about seeing that man on Friday evening on Thomson Avenue, at the Hospital For Sick Children or near Medford Secondary School, they are asked to contact Detective Graham Everdell or Detective Jack Carpenter who are handling the investigation at Metro Homicide at 1-416-999-INFO."*

Paul was confident that the police had very little evidence to go on from both the house and the school. He wasn't the least bit concerned because he felt that he had done his homework and had executed his plan perfectly. He was sure that he hadn't made any mistakes. The trip to the Hospital For Sick Children hadn't been part of the original plan, but turned out to be an added bonus. Maybe some good could be done with the drug dealer's money. Someone who worked at the hospital had quite obviously provided the police with the very general description that had been made public in the media.

For the next ten days, Paul stayed close to home and enjoyed the beautiful fall weather at the lake. He rarely ventured out to the village and quit going to his local gun club. He didn't want to be seen in public anymore. It was almost time to formulate some new plans. He kept thinking about the other four high schools where drug dealers preyed on teenagers. He spent a lot of time on the internet, reading back issues of the Toronto Star from around the time of Ricky's death. He read all about the other kids who had died or would be in extended care facilities for the rest of their lives. Paul knew that he would soon visit their neighborhoods too, because their deaths and the destruction of their families were so closely tied to Ricky's death.

* * *

After taking it easy for a week and a half, Paul got itchy. He got up early on a Wednesday morning and as he showered and shaved around his mustache and sideburns, he decided that it was time to continue on with his crusade. His mustache had become quite bushy and his sideburns rivaled Elvis'. Paul then packed a small overnight bag with enough personal belongings to last for three days, just in case he needed that much time, but he didn't take his tools with him. He wouldn't need the Glock 25, the surgical gloves or an oyster-shucking knife. He was only going on a reconnaissance mission.

After he got dressed and ready to leave, he slipped on his dark sunglasses and stood in front of the large mirror in the main room and looked at his image. He thought to himself, *Who is that person in the mirror?* He knew it wasn't Paul Taylor. He had drowned in Lake Simcoe a number of weeks ago.

The drive to the city took the usual amount of time because the traffic moved very well until he got close to Pearson International Airport in the west end. He took Highway 401 to the Highway 427 exit and went south from near the airport to Lakeshore Boulevard on the shores of Lake Ontario. He knew there was a strip of small, cheap hotels and motels right on the water where he could get a room for a day or two.

Paul used his new identity as *Gordon William Thoburn* to check into the Sea Horse Motel for two nights. He chuckled to himself as he walked into his room because the motel's theme was for romantic getaways. All of the spacious rooms had been decorated for lovers with waterbeds, heart-shaped bathtubs in the middle of the room, mirrored ceilings and an assortment of adult movies. The time period of sexual freedom and debauchery that are synonymous with the Roman era had inspired the names for each room in the complex. Paul had been fortunate enough to have booked into one named after the Roman Emperor, Caligula, whose reign was one of the most adulterous and bloodthirsty in ancient Roman times. As he got settled, the romantic décor brought memories of Liz flooding back into his mind.

It had been a long, long time since Paul had felt any interest for the opposite sex. A part of him had died with Liz. After her death, he couldn't think about other women, but he always felt that the lack of interest in sex would pass with time. Then there were the troubles that he and Ricky had coping without her. His days and nights had been full of frustrations and disappointments. When Ricky died, another part of Paul died too. There were absolutely no feelings left.

Two of the high schools that lost students on the weekend that Ricky had died were in the west end. Trudeau Collegiate Institute was just off Kipling near Dundas Street West, about fifteen minutes from where Paul was staying. He arrived at the school before noon and cruised through the streets nearby just to get a feel for the area. He ended up in the parking lot of a small strip plaza across from the school in the afternoon and stayed until close to five o'clock but there was nothing out of the ordinary to be seen.

The next morning, just before noon, Paul found himself back in the strip plaza parking lot near the school again. He realized that the weekend was approaching and many foolish kids would need their stash. If he kept a lookout, he should be able to pick out the local drug dealer at lunchtime or after school without much difficulty. They were usually young guys who drove fancy cars.

No suspicious vehicles showed up at the school during the lunchtime break so Paul left the school area at about two o'clock and drove around while he waited for school to get out. He went into a drive-thru at a local Burger King and picked up a couple of burgers and a shake. Shortly after three o'clock, he was back in the plaza parking lot waiting and watching. About ten to four, a white Mustang coupe, with a single male inside, stopped beside four separate groups of teenagers along the street. Yet, as far as Paul could tell from his distance, there wasn't any business done during those visits. By the end of the day, that was the only suspicious car that Paul had seen. He gave up the ghost at around five o'clock, as most of the high school kids had disappeared, and drove back to his romantic room at the Sea Horse.

On Friday, the start of the weekend, Paul thought that there might be a little more action out in front of Trudeau. His booking at the motel was over, so he loaded his things into the Taurus before he left for the high school. He parked in a different part of the plaza parking lot and waited. Nothing happened during the lunch break. The white Mustang didn't reappear and there were no other suspicious vehicles in the vicinity. At three-fifteen, the Mustang showed up again. As it drove past the school, the driver stopped and talked to half a dozen groups of students, but once again, it didn't look like any exchanges had taken place.

At the far side of the school, the white Mustang did a u-turn and drove back toward the plaza and pulled into the parking lot where Paul was parked. The car stopped in a parking space facing the road and away from the stores in the same line of cars where Paul waited. The Mustang was only four cars away from him. He could see the driver through the windows of the other vehicles that were parked between them. He was nice looking, about thirty, with dark hair and a mustache. Paul could only see the guy's head and shoulders from his car, but he would never forget his face.

Paul just sat there and watched. Then it started. The students who the driver had talked to near the school made their way to the plaza parking lot and started to visit the Mustang. They got in and out of the car one after the other. It was obvious to Paul that he had found the guy he was searching for during the past three days. He was looking forward to eventually meeting the street dealer up close and personal.

Forty-five minutes later, the drug dealer fired up the engine of the Mustang with a roar and left. As the dealer peeled out of the plaza onto Kipling Avenue, the tires burned rubber with a squeal. Paul pulled out behind him, far less conspicuously, and followed the white Mustang to Dundas where it turned left and went west for three kilometers. Suddenly, it pulled into the parking lot of a strip joint called Sweethearts which boasted all kinds of exotic women dancers. The Taurus followed the car into the lot, and eventually, Paul followed the man into the Etobicoke establishment.

The large room of the club was dark, but the stage and runway where a pretty, large-breasted redhead in a G-string was dancing, were brightly lit. The light from the stage flooded out over the seats that were close by and left the rest of the room in a state of semi-darkness. It took a few minutes for Paul's eyes to adjust to the lighting but he didn't lose sight of the man he was following.

The drug dealer walked over to a table where a few scantily clad girls were seated and joined them. The dancers were smoking while they waited for their turn on stage. As Paul headed for a nearby table, he heard one of the girls call him *Eddie*, so he knew that he was a regular customer. Paul sat in a dark area of the room on the opposite side of the runway. He ordered a Molson Canadian from the waitress who came by his table as soon as he hit the chair. As he sat there and watched Eddie, his eyes often wandered to the nude girls who were dancing, many of whom were quite attractive. Memories of Liz flooded back into his mind as he thought about how long it had been since he had made love with her; made love with anyone. He had never been with anyone else since the day they had met. He hadn't had the urge or desire during the past few terrible years, but he found himself unable to resist looking at the great bodies.

Paul was in the middle of his second beer when the drug dealer got up from his table and went toward the men's room with another guy following him. He waited for about three minutes and headed there himself. As Paul walked through the door, the two men were standing by the sinks talking and money appeared to be changing hands. It was obvious that the dealer was making another sale. As Paul ignored them and walked on by to the urinals on the left wall. Eddie looked right at him, but turned away and finished the trans-action. The two men were gone by the time Paul finished. He went back to his table and continued to pretend that he was watching the girls on stage. Actually, his thoughts were drawn to them regularly, but he kept an eye on Eddie too.

The drug dealer left the club an hour later. Paul followed him out into the darkness of the evening, but not too closely. Eddie pulled the Mustang back onto Dundas and continued west, past the city limits, to Highway 10 in Mississauga, and turned north. Three blocks later he turned into a parking lot next to a high-rise condominium building and stopped. Paul pulled in too and watched him go through the front door of the building into the reception area. He used his own key to get inside, so Paul assumed that Eddie lived there.

It had been a good day. Paul had not only found the drug dealer who frequented the high school where a teenager had died from the bad drugs, but he knew the make of his car, where he lived and what appeared to be his favorite hangout. Paul decided he had all of the information he needed about *Eddie* for the moment, so he drove north toward the airport and Highway 401, crossed the city, and headed back to Beer Lake. He knew that he and Eddie would become better acquainted very soon.

He had accomplished everything that he had wanted to during his trip. He had found the pusher who had sold the bad drugs to the students of Trudeau Collegiate Institute that had caused so much anguish for so many families. As Paul drove north, he decided that he would go back into the city the following week to find another one of the drug dealers on his list. He spent some quality time at the cottage for the next four days and just took it easy as he continued to get the place ready for the change in seasons. While he worked, he never stopped thinking about finding his next victim.

* * *

The following Wednesday morning, Paul was fully packed for his visit to *The Big Smoke*. This time he was going to take his tools with him. He decided that he wanted to be ready just in case he got the urge or an opportunity to take care of some business. He had his loaded Glock 25 tucked in a holster under his left arm, two pairs of surgical gloves and a couple of oyster-shucking knives, that he had never touched with his bare hands, wrapped in cloth in his glove compartment. He wasn't sure whether or not he would need those things that day, but he wanted to be ready, just in case.

Paul planned the trip to arrive at Cedarview Secondary School by the lunch break. The high school was located in the east end, on his way into the city, just off Kingston Road, near St. Clair Avenue East. It only took him about an hour and a half to get there because he didn't have to drive across the city through the traffic. He did what had become part of his usual routine on these trips. He hung around the high school waiting and watching. He knew that the local drug dealer would show up sometime during the next couple of days.

The first day, Paul picked out a sharp looking, blue BMW, two-door coupe, early in the afternoon. It cruised through the streets near the high school and the driver stopped and talked to a number of students. The *Beemer* eventually disappeared and never came back that day. About five o'clock, Paul drove back to Kingston Road, picked out a small motel from the dozens that lined the street and checked in for a couple of nights. He spent most of Thursday afternoon around the school but didn't see the BMW again or any other suspicious cars until Friday. He soon began to realize that most of a drug dealer's business was done just before the weekends.

Paul watched from a distance as the dealer completed a number of transactions. It had just started to get dark by the time the guy pulled onto Kingston Road and went east toward Highway 401. Paul tailed him, a couple of hundred yards back. They continued east for five minutes until the Beemer took Centennial Road into the West Hill area of the city. The drug dealer turned into a small subdivision that was full of those old, story-and-a-half, wartime houses that all looked the same. The BMW pulled into the driveway of one that was in complete darkness and disappeared along the side of the house. Paul could tell that there was no one else in the house. As he drove by slowly, he saw the back end of the car slip into a detached garage in the backyard. The driver must have used a remote to open the garage door because Paul could tell from the lights of the BMW that the door was already on its way back down.

Paul continued up the street to the next corner, stopped in a dark area between two streetlights and got his gear together. He put on a pair of surgical gloves, double-checked to see that the Glock under his left arm was ready to go, took one oyster-shucking knife out of the glove compartment and put it in his right jacket pocket. As he drove back down the street, he noticed that the house had no outside lights on at all, either in the front or at the back. He could see a light and what appeared to be a television in the living room, faintly shining through the sheer curtains of the front window. Paul turned the lights of the Taurus off as he got close to the driveway and slowly coasted into the darkness beside the house. He quietly got out of his car, without closing the car door tightly, and looked around. Things appeared to be quiet and normal.

Paul walked carefully to the back corner of the house and looked through the windows near the back porch. The rear room was in total darkness. He then walked slowly and silently toward the front of the house with his eyes peeled for any neighbors who might be out and about. After he made sure there was no one in the street, he climbed the five cement steps of the front porch in the darkness. Paul opened the screen door with his left hand and gave one of those cute, *shave and a haircut, two bits*, knocks that sound so friendly. His Glock was cocked in his right hand.

The door opened to the darkness and the occupant didn't even bother to turn on the outside porch light. Suddenly, the drug dealer was standing right in front of him. To Paul's surprise, the guy was Asian, but he wasn't sure of his nationality. He was about five foot nine and about a hundred and sixty pounds. He appeared to be in his late twenties with spiked, dark hair with the tips bleached blonde.

"What can I do for you?" the dealer asked, with a slight accent, as he looked at Paul whose image had been lit up by the light shining out from the living room.

"We have to talk," Paul said as he pointed his gun at the drug dealer's chest.

The Asian immediately raised his hands in the air and moved

slowly away from the door. As he backed into the living room, Paul quickly and quietly stepped inside and noiselessly closed the door behind him.

"Who the fuck are you and what do you want?" the startled dealer asked again.

"I'll ask the questions," Paul said as he lifted his handgun higher and pointed it right at the drug dealer's head. "Is there anyone else in the house?"

"No, I live alone! What do you want? I don't have much money here if you're here to rip me off!"

Paul made the drug dealer lie down on his stomach on the living room carpet between the television and the coffee table. With the Glock pushed against the back of the guy's head, he tried to find out if the dealer had a stash of money in the house so it could also be donated to a good cause. The terrified guy convinced Paul that all his cash was in a safety deposit box in a nearby bank, so it could not be given to charity. Paul took a few minutes to explain why he was there. He made the guy remember the episode of the bad drugs and the kids who had died or whose lives had been ruined. He made him remember the students who had attended Cedarview Secondary School.

"What's your name?" Paul asked as he put the Glock back in its holster and pressed the oyster-shucking knife against the back of the Asian's neck.

"Jesus Christ! That hurts like hell! My name is Liang Chung. What do you want?"

"I want to know the name of your supplier," Paul asked as he put more pressure on the small knife, "and I want to know his name right now!"

"Fuck! Stop please! I'll tell you! His name is Ruffus Allan from Scarborough"

"Where does the son-of-a bitch hang out?"

"Willie's pool hall . . . at Eglinton and Victoria Park . . . the one that's upstairs!"

The drug dealer's pleading that he hadn't known that the drugs were bad fell on deaf ears. The crunch echoed through the small house as the Atlas and Axis Vertebrae separated under pressure. Paul turned off the lights and the television so that the house was in complete darkness. The drug dealer was left laying on the carpet, in the middle of the living room, with an oyster-shucking knife sticking out of the back of his neck just below the base of his skull. Once again, with Ricky and the other teenagers on his mind, it had been very easy for Paul to kill the scumbag. About fifteen minutes after he arrived, Paul had finished his job and quietly slipped back out the front door to his car in the darkness beside the house.

* * *

It was still early on Friday evening as Paul drove toward the freeway. He had one more oyster-shucking knife in his glove compartment and was feeling a real rush of adrenaline, so he decided not go back home just yet. Instead, he took Highway 401 west through to the airport and continued west to Highway 10 south. About forty minutes from West Hill, Paul pulled into the parking lot of the high-rise condo building just north of Dundas where Eddie lived. He drove slowly among the rows of cars, but didn't see the white Mustang. He thought that he would try to find him at Sweethearts, and if Eddie wasn't there either, he would call it a day and head back to Beer Lake.

It wasn't long before he pulled into the busy parking lot at the strip joint. Eddie's car stood out because it was parked right up front, beside the main door, where the best customers got priority parking spots. Paul figured that Eddie was at his favorite haunt, probably celebrating a number of lucrative Friday afternoon drug sales to the students at Trudeau Collegiate and other nearby schools.

Once inside, Paul wandered through the darkness and the throngs of other men until he saw Eddie. He and another man were sitting at what appeared to be Eddie's usual table. A voluptuous, nude, blonde girl was going through a number of gyrations on a stool between them. He couldn't help but notice the wicked body on the gal who was doing the lap-dance. His feelings of virility hadn't returned to him until he had begun to exact his revenge on drug dealers. As he looked at the naked woman at Eddie's table, his groin began to stir, but the feelings ended quickly as Liz's memory flooded into his mind.

At an empty table, Paul was very careful not to touch anything with his hands. He pulled the chair out with his foot and sat down. He also drank his beer with a tissue that he had taken from his pocket placed around the bottle. He wouldn't be leaving any fingerprints anywhere in the establishment, just in case. His table was located between where Eddie was sitting and the men's washroom. Paul knew that Eddie would have to take a piss at some point and that he would have to walk right past him to get to the can. He was still pumped and full of confidence. His adrenaline had been high since he left West Hill. He was foolishly beginning to think that he was invincible.

Twenty minutes later, the evening's feature presentation was introduced and appeared on stage. Cindy was one of those gals who starred in porno flicks and when she wasn't making movies, appeared in strip clubs throughout North America. She had all the necessary cosmetic surgery required to make her a big star, *big* being the operative word. She had billed herself as having *Triple H Breasts*. Each breast was the size of a man's head. When Paul saw her come out onto the stage and saw how big her boobs were, he assumed that her act would be to just try to remain standing without falling over. He was quite surprised when it turned out that the entertainer actually had an act and was much more talented than the local gals. She really did put on a show.

The eyes of every man in the room were glued to her. They cheered and hooted as she swung and bounced those beauties across the stage and up and down the runway. Most of the men in the crowd got up from their tables and squeezed toward the stage to get a better look. It wasn't long before most of the room was standing and had moved forward with their backs toward Paul. Cindy was scheduled to do six numbers in her first set so she would keep the audience busy for quite awhile. As Paul kept Eddie in his sights, he also stood and stretched his neck to see what was happening on stage. The dancer's breasts were so large that they seemed to move back and forth and up and down in slow motion as if they were on film. As the first song ended, the second started to play immediately, so the large breasts never did stop moving. The audience was enthralled and the clapping and cheering was almost deafening. All the eyes in the place were on Cindy.

Paul was standing with the rest of the crowd in the darkness, but well behind them at his own table. He caught a glimpse of Eddie heading toward him and the can. Paul put his beer down quickly and went to the washroom before Eddie got there. The room full of men, none of whom were in the washroom, continued to cheer the star of the Special Feature. Paul slipped directly into the fourth stall, the one in the right corner opposite the urinals, well away from the door. He pushed it open with his wrist and quickly pulled on the surgical gloves as the door swung shut. He could feel Eddie's presence nearby and heard him step up to a urinal in front of where he was hidden. As soon as the gloves were on, he put his hands in his jacket pockets and stepped out of the stall. As Eddie continued to urinate, he looked directly at Paul who walked on past him, toward the bathroom door, as if he was leaving. He was merely double-checking to be sure that no one else was coming their way. A quick look confirmed that the whole crowd was fixated on Cindy. No one was walking toward the men's washroom.

Paul turned quickly and walked back toward the stalls and the urinals. Eddie had just finished taking a leak when he stepped up close behind him. Paul wrapped his left arm around the front of Eddie's neck and stuck the sharp blade of the short oyster-shucking knife into the back of Eddie's neck. As the tip of the knife penetrated the skin and into the spinal cord, severe pain shot down his back and into both of his legs. Eddie knew that he was in trouble and froze in agony without a word.

"Move! Now!" Paul growled in Eddie's ear as he turned him around and led him toward the open corner stall.

Eddie did exactly what he was told because the pain in his neck, back and legs was unbearable. He could feel blood run down the back of his shirt as he tried to walk with what felt like electricity running through his body. The dealer fully cooperated without any quick movements until the two men were right inside the stall and the door had closed behind them.

"Do you remember the students from Trudeau who died from the bad drugs they were sold about a year and a half ago?" Paul snarled in his ear.

"Yeah, I remember that bad shipment!" Eddie said as he grimaced in pain. "That wasn't my fault! I didn't know that shit was dangerous!"

"Who was your fuckin' supplier? Who sold that poison to you?"

"Rousinsky! Vladmir Rousinsky from Hamilton!"

"Today, drug dealers who kill teenagers at the high schools in this city are going to die!" Paul whispered in his ear.

At that precise moment, Paul pushed the oyster-shucking knife hard into Eddie's neck right at the base of his skull and as he gave that quick twist, he heard the cracking sound in the cervical region as the vertebrae were pried apart and the spinal cord was disconnected from his brain. Eddie's body immediately went limp in Paul's grasp without making another sound. Paul quickly sat him on the toilet and leaned him into the corner against the wall. He then stepped out of the stall and shut the swinging door tight so it would remain closed.

Paul, slowly and nonchalantly, walked out of the washroom and back into the crowded main room with his hands in his jacket pockets. The featured act, Cindy and her Triple H's, still had the audience of half-looped, cheering men enthralled and infatuated. Not one man in the crowd took his eyes off the stage and runway or even turned around. Paul left the washroom unnoticed, turned and walked toward the front door of the strip joint. He quietly slipped out into the night.

* * *

As Paul calmly drove back to Beer Lake, he was pleased at how well his day had gone and about how efficient he was getting at his new career. He did, however, seriously start to think about the chance that he had taken by killing Eddie in a public place that was full of people. He thought that he had been very foolish. He would have to smarten up and be more careful the next time. He would have to develop a proper plan that wouldn't put him at risk of being seen or caught. He had been feeling too cocky because killing the Asian had been so easy. He needed to get his adrenaline under control. He couldn't believe it. He had killed two of those bastards on the same day and both of them had coughed up the names of their suppliers. He had three names in the drug hierarchy, Vito Morelli, Ruffus Allan and Vladmir Rousinksy.

His head was spinning as he pulled off Highway 401, well east of Toronto, and went north on Highway 35/115 to his quiet cottage on Beer Lake. He was thinking about how much he was enjoying the excitement and danger of his mission. He liked ridding the world of drug dealers who poison, maim and kill the teenagers of Toronto. The risk that he had taken in the strip joint continued to bother him. He would have to be more careful. He thought, *It would be a shame to get caught just as my work is getting started!*

CHAPTER TEN

At just after seven o'clock on a Friday night, Dectectives Everdell and Carpenter decided that they had beaten the Shackleton murder into the ground. They had gone through the file, frontwards, backwards and sideways and had discussed all aspects of the evidence over and over again. They had come up with nothing positive to continue their investigation so they decided to close the file for a few days. They had a number of other files in their case load that needed attention.

The detectives decided to work the late shift on another case that had involved a fire in a downtown rooming house a number of days earlier where one of the residents had died. They had not been able to reach witnesses during the day. The fire had started in an old rooming house, in a seedy part of the inner city, near Queen Street East and Parliament. The fire had gutted one room and damaged the floors above and below. There was evidence of arson, which would turn it into a murder case, but the Fire Marshall's Report had not been finalized. While the detectives were waiting for the report, they had interviewed a number of witnesses who lived in the rooming house and had known the old man who died in the fire.

After their initial investigation, Everdell and Carpenter determined that the victim had often picked up local street-prostitutes and took them back to his room. There had been a history of booze-fueled arguments and fights over money and the police had been called on more than one occasion. The detectives thought that the fire might have been the result of the non-payment of the required fee to the hooker-of-the-day and in a drunken fight, the whore may have deliberately torched the room. The policemen had a lead on where to find a close friend of the dead man who might possibly know the names of the old guy's regulars, so they headed downtown to pursue that investigation. They hated the late shift but had to do their time along with the rest of the detectives.

At eight-thirty, as they were driving south on Sherbourne toward the area where the fire had taken place, Everdell and Carpenter got a call on their cell from Bill Speer. The Chief of Detectives rarely called them directly so they knew that the call was important. As Carpenter picked up the phone, Everdell glanced in his direction.

"Jack Carpenter. What's happening?"

"I just got a call from two uniforms who are at a strip joint called Sweethearts which is located way out on Dundas Street West in Etobicoke and they may have some news for you about the Shackleton murder case."

While Everdell continued to drive, Carpenter answered the Chief. "We've worked that case for a month and are nowhere. What've you got for us?"

"About half an hour ago, one of the patrons at the strip joint found a male body in a stall in the men's washroom. The victim has been stabbed to death."

"What's that got to do with the Shackleton case?"

"The patrolman said that the knife is still in the body and it's sticking out of the back of the victim's neck. He says it looks kind of strange. He thinks it's one of those oyster-shucking knives that he read about in the paper in the Shackleton murder case."

"Another killing with an oyster-shucking knife! How far out is the strip club?"

"It's just west of Highway 427 on Dundas. I told them to keep everyone away from the scene until you two get there, so move it!"

"We'll get back to you. Graham, Sweethearts…on Dundas just west of 427!"

Everdell commented, "Don't tell me that we might finally get a break in Stevie's murder. The lack of evidence and leads has been driving me crazy."

"I keep thinking that we're missing something," Carpenter answered and explained the telephone call to his partner. "I think we should just go south to the Gardiner Expressway and head west. That'll be the fastest route."

Everdell put the flashing red light in the center of the dashboard of the car and turned it on. It wasn't long before it was doing its thing and the heavy Friday night traffic started to move out of their way. It would take them at least half an hour to get to the west end of the city. They were both really pumped because they thought that this might be the break they needed.

* * *

By the time the detectives got to Sweethearts, there were four patrol cars and an ambulance already there in the parking lot near the main door. There were also a lot of people, probably patrons, milling around outside. Everdell and Carpenter parked their car next to the cruisers and worked their way through the crowd. They were immediately directed to the men's washroom where three patrolmen were chatting and blocking the door so no one could go inside. No one was interfering with the crime scene.

"I'm Detective Graham Everdell from College Street and this is my partner, Jack Carpenter. It sounds like this might be just like the one that happened downtown. Who called it in?"

"I did. I'm Derek Baker. I remembered that strange knife thing from the newspapers or the news about that other murder. We've kept everyone out of the washroom since we got here, but we don't know what went on before that," the young, good-looking patrolman advised.

"Great! That's a good bit of police work, Derek, to remember the Shackleton murder from a month or so ago," Carpenter answered. "I guess we'd better take a look."

Everdell and Carpenter walked into the large men's washroom, with Baker right behind them, and began to look around. There were four sinks and mirrors to the right and two towel dispensers and a couple of condom machines on the wall to the left. Further along on the left, behind a divider, there were five urinals on the wall and right opposite those, on the right, there were four toilet stalls. The detectives found what they were looking for in the last stall. A body of a thirty-something male was sitting on the toilet and leaning against the walls where they met in the corner of the small cubicle.

"Derek, were you able to find out who this guy is? Is he a regular at the club?" Carpenter asked.

"The manager said that he's in here nearly every day. He was a good customer who never caused any trouble," the policeman advised.

"Jack, take a good look at the back of his neck. It sure looks like an oyster-shucking knife just like the one that was in Stevie's forehead!"

"Yeah, I think it's identical."

Everdell turned to Baker, "Does anyone know much about the dead guy, his name, where he lives, what he does for a living?"

"A couple of the dancers said that his name is Eddie Firestone and he lives a few miles west of here in a condo. The manager said that he makes his living as a drug dealer in the area, but also said that he had a deal with Eddie not to do any business on the premises because the company didn't want to jeopardize the liquor license."

"Well, Graham, old buddy," Carpenter said to his partner, "there's the second tie-in with Shackleton. They were both killed in the exact same way, stabbed in the back of the neck with an oyster-shucking knife, and they were both drug dealers."

"Let's hope that the Forensic Team can come up with something here. The killer left nothing at Stevie's house or at the high school."

"One of the guys said that a Forensic Identification Services Team has just arrived in an official van of some kind. Do you want them to come in here right now?" Baker asked.

"Sure, send them in. We've seen enough," Carpenter answered.

"Jack, we'd better see if we can find some witnesses to talk to before they all disappear through the cracks."

"Here's a list of the people who I spoke to when I first got here. I asked them to stay around because you guys would want to talk to them. It sounded like they would," Baker explained.

"You've done a fine job here today, Derek," Everdell said to the patrolman, "let me know where you're stationed and I'll send a letter to your Unit Commander."

As the three men vacated the washroom, two forensic experts, in white rubber gloves and carrying all their paraphernalia, went inside and had the place to themselves. Everdell and Carpenter decided to interview some of the people who were in the club at the approximate time that the murder took place so they went looking for whoever was in charge. They found the bar manager talking to a few scantily clothed dancers.

"How long will it take to remove Eddie's body from the bathroom so we can get back to work?" The manager asked. "After all, it's Friday, one of our busiest nights. We also have Cindy here tonight, our Special Feature, who gets paid a fuckin' fortune."

"The show must go on! I'll tell you what I can do for you. If you've got an office that we can use to talk to a few witnesses, we should be able to let you get things back to normal fairly quickly," Carpenter said.

"Sure, there's a room off the main foyer that you can use if it'll get the girls back dancin'. Just give me a couple of minutes to clean it up."

"Once things get rockin' and rollin' again, you're gonna have to work out a way for everyone to use the women's washroom for the rest of the night because the forensic guys are gonna be busy in there for hours. The men's washroom will be off limits tonight for sure and likely tomorrow. I think you should put someone at the women's washroom door so there's no trouble," Everdell explained.

Carpenter turned to Constable Baker, "Will you find the witnesses who you talked to earlier and see if they'll come to the front office and see us in a few minutes?"

As the patrolman started to leave, Everdell spoke to him, "Derek, would you mind asking anyone outside who was in here before they found the body to come back in now? We may as well find out if there are any other witnesses who can help us."

"No problem, I'm on it!.."

The impatient crowd that gathered outside, moved indoors quickly and took their seats near the runway and stage. As soon as Everdell got up on the runway to say a few words and came into everyone's view, a guy called to him from the crowd.

"Take it all off!"

Another man near the door, who had way too much to drink, yelled, "Show us your tits!"

"I know I'm a good-lookin' guy, but I'm sure that none of you would want to see me with my clothes off," Everdell answered. "Could I please have your attention just for a couple of minutes then we'll let the show start again? My partner and I have a job that we have to do. It looks like one of Sweethearts' good customers, Eddie Firestone, was murdered in the men's room about an hour and a half ago. It's our job to find out who did it. The murder likely took place while many of you were watching the show. I want you all to think back over the past couple of hours and try to remember if you saw Eddie and who he was with and what he was doing. Also, think about the fact that he must have walked to the washroom during the show. Did anyone see him do that? Did anyone notice if someone followed him in there? Did he go in there with another person? If you all promise me that you'll think about these things, I'll let the music and dancing get started." There were a number of hoots and cheers from the crowd. "I would like anyone who can remember anything about Eddie tonight or any other time that might help us, to please come to the office out in the front lobby and talk to us. We promise that we won't keep you away from the entertainment for long, but anything that you think might be helpful, probably will be. Don't worry about how trivial or unimportant you think the information might be. If it's about Eddie, please talk to us. Thanks for your help."

* * *

Everdell jumped down off the runway. As he and Carpenter walked toward the front door and the manager's office where they would continue their investigation, the music started to play again and the lights were turned down low. The office was ready for them and as they went in and sat down, they noticed that Derek Baker had three of the witnesses who he had previously spoken to ready to be interviewed. He brought two of them in together.

"Well, who have we got here?" Carpenter asked as he tried to keep his eyes on the faces of the two girls, with great bodies, who were busting out of their small outfits.

"I'm Candy and this is Honey. We'd been sitting with Eddie at a table close to the runway for a couple of hours before he went to the washroom and never came back."

"Yeah," Honey added. "We were all watching the Feature Act, Cindy, the girl with the huge tits. I think they're triple H's or something, and while she was performing, Eddie got up to go for a pee."

"How long was he away before you missed him?" Everdell asked.

"We were both just watching the show and didn't really notice. The gal with the big boobs was really good and very funny, so I'm not sure how long it was before we noticed that Eddie wasn't around," Candy said.

"I noticed that he didn't come back," Honey added, "but I just assumed that he was making his rounds and was in another part of the club talking to someone."

"Do you know what time the Feature Act started?" Carpenter asked.

"Yeah," Honey answered. "It's always scheduled for seven o'clock, but most of the time it starts fifteen minutes late so the crowd will drink more booze."

"So you could say that Eddie left your table around seven-thirty?" Everdell asked.

"Yeah, that's right," Candy said. "I think the dancer with the big tits was doing her second or third number when he said he had to take a piss."

"While you two were watching the Special Feature, did you notice if anyone followed Eddie to the men's room or if anyone went in there with him?" Carpenter asked.

"Nah, we didn't see nothin'," Honey replied and Candy agreed with a nod.

"OK. If you two gals think of anything else that may be of help to us, please give us a call," Everdell said as he gave each of them one of his cards.

The next girl who came in to be questioned was quite tall and attractive, but she wasn't a dancer. She had on a short T-shirt that hung well above the top of her tight blue jeans, flat stomach and belly button ring. The two detectives noticed that her eyes were very red and bloodshot as if she had been crying. It turned out that she was the bartender. The detectives introduced themselves and began the interview.

"My name's Danielle Campbell, but everyone calls me Dani, and I've been bartending here for about a year. I've known Eddie since I started and we dated for quite a few months, but we broke up about six weeks ago. Lately, I've only seen him when he came in here, but he dropped by almost everyday."

"You look a bit upset. Even though you weren't dating anymore, did you still have a thing for Eddie?" Everdell asked.

"Yeah, I still really did like him a lot. We always had a lot of fun together, but he couldn't keep his hands off the other girls who dance in this place."

"So if you still liked him, you probably kept an eye on him to see what he was up to when he was here," Everdell suggested.

"Yeah, I guess so, he was always talking to some bitch with no clothes on."

"Did you happen to notice what time Eddie got here today?" Carpenter asked.

"He got here shortly after five and spent most of his time sitting with those dancers who just left here, Honey and Candy. He spent a lot of time with those lesbos lately and he was always sitting with them when he was here."

"Did you happen to notice him at the time he left their table and headed for the washroom just after the Feature Act started?" Everdell asked.

"Eddie got up and joined people at other tables all the time, but he always went back and sat with those two sluts. I think he had a thing going with both of them and they kinda like each other a lot too, if you know what I mean."

"Where were you actually standing in the place when the Feature Act started?" Carpenter asked.

"I was behind the bar, where I was supposed to be, pouring drinks and keeping an eye on what's happenin' in the crowd. The gal with the great big boobs really put on a good show. She's a bit of a comedienne."

"Dani, you must have been keeping an eye on Eddie too! Did you see him get up and go to the washroom during the show?" Everdell asked.

"Yeah, I saw him get up from the girls' table and head toward the washroom about five or ten minutes into the performance."

"Did you happen to notice if he went to the washroom alone? Was he with someone or did anyone follow him?" Carpenter asked.

"The only thing that I seem to remember is that some other guy from one of the back tables, over near the washroom, got up at about the same time and headed in that direction too. I think that Eddie followed him into the washroom."

"Can you describe the guy who was ahead of him?" Carpenter asked again.

"No, it's always too dark in here to see very well. They really turn the lights down low when the features are performing."

"Is there anything else at all that you can think of that might help us find out who killed Eddie and why?" Everdell went on. "Did he have any enemies?"

"No. Everyone liked him. That's about all I know."

Everdell asked more questions, "He was a drug dealer! You must have known that? I assume that you only hung out with him when he wasn't working and had no involvement in his business. Did he mention any disputes with anyone over money, drugs, territory or anything like that?"

"No, not that I can remember. During the months we dated, he seemed to get along with everyone who he did business with and there were never any problems."

Carpenter added as he handed her his card, "Thanks Dani. Here's our phone number. If you happen to think of anything else that might help, please give us a call."

The bartender left the room. The detectives were alone so they took a few minutes to chat and consider the information that they had learned from their initial enquiries.

"What do you think?" Everdell asked his partner.

"Well, it sounds like Eddie followed another guy into the washroom while the feature was on, but it seems that everyone else had their eyes on the stage and on the girl with the big boobs. What did they say her name was? Cindy?"

"Let's see if anyone else remembers a guy going into the washroom ahead of Eddie. Derek, please send in the next witness."

Carpenter and Everdell interviewed five more dancers. They had serious trouble asking questions because they couldn't concentrate with the nearly naked women in front of them. A couple of girls came to the office bare breasted on purpose just to bug the cops. They even talked to Cindy to see if she saw anything from the stage during her performance but had no luck. They had serious trouble looking her in the face while they chatted, as her breasts were quite amazing.

In the end, they really didn't get much more positive information because everyone had been watching the special act. They were both starting to get tired when Constable Derek Baker announced that there was a guy and a girl left who wanted to talk to them.

"Howdy, I'm Jack Spratt and I don't want to hear no fuckin' jokes about my name. I've heard 'em all."

"No problem, Jack," Carpenter answered. "Did you know Eddie or did you see anything that might help us find out what the hell happened here tonight and why?"

"Eddie was an asshole. He thought he was a fuckin' big wheel, but he didn't deserve to get killed. The only thing I saw that might be helpful is that during the Special Feature, I just happened to turn around and saw Eddie heading toward the can. I also noticed another guy, who had been sitting all alone in the dark area near the washroom, get up and go in there ahead of him. Eddie went in after he did. I really didn't think anything about it at the time, just a couple of guys goin' for a piss."

"Did you happen to see the other guy come back out into the main room?"

"Yeah, I don't know why, but he did catch my eye when he came out. He was about six feet and a couple of hundred pounds. He looked like he was in pretty good shape, like he worked out or somethin'. It was hard to see in here but I think he had dark hair, long sideburns just like Elvis used to have, and a big bushy mustache."

"Only one other person saw the guy go to the washroom too, but she can't describe him. Would you recognize him if you ever saw him again?" Everdell asked.

"I'm not sure I would because the lights were turned down so low, but I guess I could try if you happen to pick someone up," Jack said as he stood up.

"Here's our card," Carpenter said. "If you think of anything else that might help, give us a call. Thanks for talking to us."

As Jack Spratt left the office, Carpenter turned to his partner and said with a laugh, "Do you really think that Jack eats no fat?"

"You had better not let him hear you talk like that or he'll give you a swat!" Everdell answered and added, "Derek, please send in the last witness."

"Hi, I'm Lori-Ann Murphy. I served that guy who sat near the men's washroom. He drank Molson Canadian."

"Lori, thanks for coming to see us," Everdell said and continued. "Do you go by Lori or Lori-Ann?"

"I answer to both of them."

"Did you happen to get a good look at the guy? Can you describe him for us?" Everdell went on.

"The lighting isn't turned down so low before the feature starts, so I got a pretty good look at him. I noticed right off that he was a nice looking guy, really well-built, with long sideburns and a bushy mustache. He was wearing some kind of a baseball cap."

"Did you have a conversation with him?" Carpenter asked.

"No, he didn't say much at all. He was kind of a quiet guy."

"Did you see him go to the washroom?" Carpenter asked.

"No, I didn't see him go to the washroom or leave, but I did clear off his table while the gal with the big boobs was doing her show. All of a sudden the guy was gone."

"Do you think you would recognize him if you saw him again?" Everdell asked.

"I think I could," Lori-Ann answered.

"That's great. Here's our phone number, so if you think of anything else that might help us with our investigation, please give us a call," Everdell said as Lori-Ann got up and went back to work.

"You know, Graham, this whole fuckin' thing is starting to look just like the Shackleton murder. All we've got so far is another vague description of a guy who could be the killer. There's probably no real evidence here at the scene. My guess is that Forensics aren't gonna come up with anything here either."

"The victims were both drug dealers. It's also pretty obvious that they were killed by the same person, in the same way. I don't remember anyone ever being killed with an oyster-shucking knife before, do you?" Everdell asked.

"No, I can't recall any murders like that either. Think about the description of the guy who came out of the washroom that our buddy Jack Spratt gave us. Lori just told the same story. The man that dropped the money off at the Hospital For Sick Children was described basically the same, but he had a goatee. It's been awhile since we found Shackleton, so the guy could have gotten rid of his beard and kept the mustache and sideburns."

"That might make sense," Everdell answered and went on. "I wonder how many of those bloody oyster-shucking knives the guy has tucked away?"

CHAPTER ELEVEN

Paul got back to Beer Lake shortly after ten o'clock that Friday night and was so pumped up after his rampage in the city that he grabbed the bottle of J&B as soon as he walked through the door of the cottage. He poured himself a stiff drink, started a fire and sat down in his favorite chair to think about his accomplishments of the day.

He thought about the Asian, Liang Chung. He had dealt drugs in the east end of the city and had spent the last few years poisoning the students at a number of schools, including Cedarview. The fact that he was lying there dead, in the middle of his living room in that war-time house in West Hill, didn't bother Paul at all. He remembered that the house had been left in total darkness and the drug dealer had hidden his own car in the garage in the backyard. Paul had a gut feeling that the body might not be found immediately.

However, Paul thought that the body of Eddie Firestone had probably been found already. It would not have taken very long for one of the customers to stumble across the dead man in the men's washroom at Sweethearts. Paul guessed that the police were already at the strip club combing the washroom for clues. They were likely interviewing potential witnesses as he sat by the fire and sucked back his favorite drink. He was feeling so good, he poured himself another one.

Paul was confident that the murder of Liang Chung, in West Hill, had gone off without a hitch. He was positive that he hadn't left any evidence in the house or out in the driveway. He was also fairly sure that no one had noticed his Taurus in the driveway because he had pulled it into the total darkness along the side of the house where it was not visible from the street. The terrified, little Asian had remembered the bad shipment of Ecstasy that had killed all the teenagers. He had been more than willing to provide the name of his supplier, on the chance that by cooperating, the intruder would spare his life. Paul had stored away that information in the back of his mind for another time because he knew, deep down, that he and Ruffus Allan would be meeting in the near future.

Paul was concerned about the way that he had handled the murder of Eddie Firestone because it just seemed to happen without much care or planning. He hadn't really intended to kill Eddie in a public place because of the risks involved, but his adrenaline had been flowing. He had been so excited about how easy it was to kill the Asian that he felt that he was on a roll. He felt that nothing could stop him that day. There was Eddie, enjoying himself at his favorite hang-out, and it just seemed to be the right time to take care of him if an opportunity presented itself. There had been a special show on stage that evening holding the attention of the other patrons. Paul had decided to do it very quickly, without really thinking about it, which was dangerous because he could have made a mistake. One thing that Eddie managed to spit out quickly, before he died, was the name of the drug trafficker who supplied the drugs for distribution in the west end. Eddie's supplier was a Russian named Vladmir Rousinsky who lived in Hamilton, a small city about forty-five minutes west of Toronto. Paul also put his name on a mental list of things to do and began to look forward to meeting him too.

* * *

The next morning, Paul got up early and did some chores around the cottage. At ten o'clock, he decided to drive to Minden, about twenty miles north, to do some grocery shopping and pick up some other things that were needed around the house. He also bought a copy of the Toronto Star because he was interested to see if there was any information in the paper about his previous day's activities.

By the time he finished shopping, it was almost noon, so he dropped into the Rockcliffe Hotel for a couple of beers and a burger before he went home. He rarely went out in public for a drink and he enjoyed the change of pace. There were people around and he felt that he fit right in with them. He actually did with the long hair, Elvis sideburns and bushy mustache.

Back at the cottage, in his leather chair, Paul opened the front section of the paper. He found the story about the murder that had taken place the night before in the west end of the city on page three. The story was short and sweet and to the point. It provided very little information to the public: *"At seven-thirty last evening, the body of a man was found in the men's washroom at Sweethearts, a strip club, on Dundas Street West. The victim had been stabbed to death and left in one of the stalls. The name of the deceased has not yet been released pending notification of next-of-kin. There have been no arrests at this time, but police are investigating the death as a murder and will release further information as the investigation continues. Anyone with any information is asked to call Detectives Everdell or Carpenter at 1-416-999-INFO."*

Paul noted that the kind of knife that had been used to kill the victim and the fact that he was a drug dealer weren't mentioned. Maybe the police were reluctant to tie it to the murder that had taken place at Medford. He looked through the rest of the Saturday paper, which was about three inches thick, and didn't find any mention of a murder in West Hill. It was quite obvious that Liang Chung had not been found yet. Paul was sure that it wouldn't be long before someone discovered the body. He thought that family or friends were likely wondering where he was right at that moment.

It turned out to be a wonderful autumn weekend and Paul got lots of things done. The cottage was just about ready for winter. Paul watched the news report on Saturday evening and it basically reiterated the information that had been in the morning paper. There were no additional facts released by the police. On Sunday, there was absolutely nothing more about the murder at Sweethearts and nothing about finding a body in West Hill. Finally, on the

Monday, Beverly Thomson on the Global evening news gave a full report on the body that had been found at the strip joint: "The body found on Friday evening at the Dundas Street West strip bar called Sweethearts has been identified as Edward Firestone, thirty-one, of Mississauga. The police have advised that the murder victim was well known to them as he had been arrested a number of times on drug related charges. The police have asked anyone that may have information about the deceased and his activities during his final few days, or why he was at the strip club on Friday evening, or any other information that might help with the investigation, to immediately contact Detectives Graham Everdell or Jack Carpenter at 1-416-999-INFO."

Paul found it hard to believe that the body of the Asian lying on his living room floor had not been found. Three full days had passed and there had been no mention of the second body. Paul thought, *Surely someone should be looking for the guy by now! He knew that it would just be a matter of time.*

Paul relaxed and enjoyed the fall weather around the cottage for the next couple of days. There was always something that needed to be done around the place. As he puttered, he spent time thinking about his next move. There were still two more drug dealers out there who had to be dealt with. He wouldn't be able to rest until they were taken care of once and for all.

On the six o'clock news on the Wednesday evening, Beverly Thomson finally provided him with the additional information that he had been waiting for: "Global has just learned that the body of another drug dealer has been found in West Hill. The body of Liang Chung, twenty-eight, was found in the living room of his home early today by friends who had not seen him for a number of days. The police have informed us that the victim died of a knife wound to the back of the neck and they have put the time of death at sometime late Friday or early Saturday. This is the third recent murder of local drug dealers and the authorities have not been forthcoming with information to the media. It has been confirmed that all of the deaths are related, in that each victim was stabbed to death with what appears to have been an oyster-shucking knife. Anyone knowing the deceased or his movements late last week are asked to immediately call the investigators, Detectives Graham Everdell or Jack Carpenter at 1-416-999-INFO."

Paul continued to take it easy for the next six days and thought a lot about the two drug dealers who he still had to visit. One of the high schools where one teenage student had died was in the Beach area in the east end of the downtown part of Toronto. One young girl had died under circumstances very similar to his son Ricky's and another boy had ended up in the hospital for a long and indefinite stay with serious brain damage. The fifth and last high school was located in the northwest end of the city in the Jane and Sheppard area. Two teenage Jamaican students had died from drug overdoses on that weekend and a couple more kids had been taken to the hospital but had eventually been released. They had been the lucky ones.

* * *

Almost two weeks passed by before Paul went back into the city to see if he could find one of the other two men on his original list. Even though it was only going to be a scouting trip, at the last minute, Paul decided that he would throw his tools into the car, just in case. He also decided that he was going to stay away from public places when the time came to kill his victims. The strip club had been way too public and he wasn't going to risk being seen or caught in the act again. He decided that he would take care of any future business in more secluded surroundings. Paul also decided not to kill two drug dealers on the same day as that had been asking for trouble. He had been stupid. He decided that he would take his time and be much more careful.

On a Wednesday, Paul found himself at Pinehurst Secondary School in the Jane and Sheppard area in the northwest end of the city, a few kilometers north of Highway 401. After the usual cursory surveillance of the school neighborhood, he found himself in a parking place that would give him a good view of the abutting street and the school parking lot. It wasn't long before Paul found the man who was to be his next victim. The guy was blatantly selling drugs to students right out in the open. He was a black guy, in his mid-twenties, and was driving a fancy, red sports car. From a distance, Paul thought that it was a Porsche. As it started to get dark and all of the business died down, the dealer left the school and drove south on Jane Street. Paul followed the guy, at a respectable distance, to a parking lot behind a restaurant just south of Jane and Wilson. The dealer parked and went inside for almost two hours. Paul waited in the darkness near his car and introduced himself to him as he was about to leave.

Clarence Jones was left lying on the pavement behind his red Porsche 911 with an oyster-shucking knife in the back of his neck just below his skull. Just before the crunch that had become music to Paul's ears, the drug dealer had remembered the bad drugs that he had sold and gave up the name of his main supplier. Vito Morelli from Woodbridge. It was a bit disappointing because that name was already on Paul's hit list.

As Paul drove back to Beer Lake, he couldn't believe that it had all happened so quickly again. He had expected to be in the city for two or three days, not just one afternoon and evening. One of the remaining two drug dealers was dead on the pavement behind his fancy car. He started to think about the possibility that he could deal with the final drug dealer who had sold the bad drugs to the students at The Bluffs Collegiate Institute before the weekend. He thought that it would be great to finish off the last scumbag in the next few days, so he could take some time off from his endeavors and relax. He knew that he had to rest up and plan some real strategy before he went after the big guys. They would be harder to get to know. By the time he got home, he had decided that he would get up bright and early in the morning, get all packed again and go back to the city to find the last street dealer on his list. One more dead drug dealer who hung around The Bluffs high school would complete the list that he had somehow, in his mind or subconscious, committed to Ricky.

* * *

After his usual drive through the school area at noon Thursday, Paul found an inconspicuous place to park and hung around most of the afternoon. The only suspicious car that he saw moving slowly through the neighborhood, was a brand new white Cadillac CTS with very dark, tinted windows. The driver had stopped and talked to a couple of groups of students, but the car quickly disappeared. Paul spent the night in one of the seedy motels on Kingston Road that was filled with refugees, gypsies and other transients. There were noisy children everywhere.

He was back at The Bluffs by noon Friday waiting, but the white Caddy didn't show up until school was out. It was immediately met by a number of students who transacted some weekend business with the driver. At close to five o'clock, the car headed west on Queen Street East and right into the commercial section of the Beach. The car was moving so slowly along Queen, Paul figured that the driver was looking for a parking spot. He knew it would be tough to find one at that time of night. Eventually, the CTS turned left at the McDonald's at Lee Avenue. It made another immediate left into a public parking lot off the main street behind the buildings. As the Taurus followed the Caddy around the rows of parked cars, the white car took the last open spot at the rear of the parking lot near the back fence. A black man got out of the car as Paul passed by and drove back toward the street. He found a parking spot next to the entrance. Soon, a man who had that Rastifarian look about him, probably Jamaican, sauntered past the rear of Paul's car and disappeared around the corner on his way back to Queen Street.

Hours later, Paul left the drug dealer seated behind the wheel of his car parked in the last row of the parking lot. His eyes were wide-open and looking straight ahead, but Paul had left his calling card. The noise of the crunch, as Paul had twisted the oyster-shucking knife in the back of his neck, had filled the interior of the car. It was a wonderful sound to Paul. The guy was the last drug dealer on his list. Before the dealer died that night, Paul made sure that he knew why he was going to die. The guy had remembered the bad Ecstasy but denied that it was his fault. Before Paul killed Darvel Rastone, he convinced him to tell him the name of his supplier. Ruffus Allan who lived in Scarborough was already on the new hit list thanks to Liang Chung.

* * *

Paul got back to the cottage late that night and was totally relieved that the first part of his mission was over. The drug dealers who had sold the bad drugs were dead. He had never been sure that he could kill all five of them as he had planned. He had thought of his son Ricky each time he plunged the oyster-shucking knives into the necks of the dealers and twisted them with all his might. He believed that some kind of good had actually been done because those drug dealers were off the streets once and for all.

Paul was thrilled with his ability to make his plans for revenge and carry them out successfully. The only evidence that he knew he had left for the police was that they had all been killed by the same person, in the same way, with an oyster-shucking knife in the back of the neck. He had left them a clue that the murders were related to the deaths of the teenagers, nearly two years earlier, when he moved the body of Steven Shackleton back to the scene of his crime, Medford Secondary School.

* * *

Paul decided that the first phase of his mission was over and he was going to take some time off. There would be no more killing . . . for the moment. His hit list for the street hustlers had been depleted and a new list had been put together with only three names on it, an Italian, a Russian and a Jamaican. They would have to pay too. They were the major suppliers who distributed drugs to the street dealers in the city, the big guys, the upper echelon who bring the drugs into the country and put them on the streets. They were probably more to blame for the deaths and maiming of the students than the local drug dealers. As Paul sat in his favorite chair, with a J & B and water in his hand, he thought to himself, *I won't be totally happy until I get to know the three big guys a whole lot better, but that will have to wait for now.*

CHAPTER TWELVE

After the body of Edward Firestone was found in the men's washroom at Sweethearts and the investigation was well underway, Detectives Everdell and Carpenter immediately went back to their file on the Shackleton murder. They were reluctant to release any information about the similarities between the murders to the media. All the city needed was a report that a serial killer or a mission killer was on the loose. They felt that the media and public should only know the basic information for the time being. However, investigative reporters have their own sources to find out information. It wasn't long before the media had dubbed the killings The Oyster-Shucking Murders.

Earlier in the week, the two detectives had interviewed four more people who had been at the strip club on the night of the murder. None of them had anything to add to the information obtained at the scene. There was little evidence. It was the Shackleton murder all over again. The detectives were totally frustrated by mid-week, when out of the blue, they got a call. Another male body had been found in the living room of a small house in West Hill in the east end. An oyster-shucking knife was sticking out of the back of the victim's neck.

As soon as Everdell and Carpenter walked into the wartime house, they knew that the victim had been dead for some time. The pungent, putrid odor of death seemed to attach itself to their taste buds. The detectives immediately placed handkerchiefs over their noses and mouths as they reluctantly made their way into the small front room. Everdell was the first to speak.

"Christ! Let's get the hell in and out of here quickly so Forensics can take over."

"I'm with you! I'm gonna be sick to my stomach."

"Jack, if those guys outside are right and this guy was killed about five days ago, that could be Friday, the same day that Eddie Firestone was found at Sweethearts."

"Christ, Graham! If this victim is a drug dealer, that means the guy might have killed two dealers on the same bloody day!"

"This is starting to become an epidemic! I'll bet anything you want to bet that this guy, Liang Chung, is a local street dealer too!"

"Do you think there might be more than one person involved in these murders?" Carpenter asked. "Two the same day, in different parts of the city!"

"More than one person could be involved. If it turns out that this guy is a dealer too, it could be some sort of turf war."

"The Asians and Jamaicans are always trying to steal business from the bikers."

"The only problem with that theory," Everdell went on, "is the Shackleton murder. If this whole thing was gang related, fifty grand in cash wouldn't have been dropped off at the Hospital For Sick Children as a donation for the kids."

"That's true," Carpenter agreed.

"Well, let's get the hell outta here and let the Forensic Team get to work. I've gotta get some fresh air. We may as well knock on a few of the neighbors' doors while we're out here," Everdell suggested.

"What really pisses me off is that there probably won't be any witnesses and there likely won't be any real evidence, just like the other murders."

Everdell and Carpenter spent the rest of the day in West Hill. Between them, they talked to at least a dozen neighbors and kept in close contact with the forensic crew as they completed their work in and around the house. The detectives, again, came up with nothing concrete that would help them in their investigation of what appeared to be the third murder in a series. They were becoming concerned that they had a mission killer on their hands rather than a gang war. Mission killers kill certain types of individuals to cleanse society. During the week that followed, they interviewed family members and friends of Liang Chung. They confirmed that he was in fact a drug dealer who had been operating in Scarborough for the past three or four years. The deceased had never been arrested before, so there was no information in the police computer about him.

The progress in the investigations of the two new murders was tedious and time consuming. It was almost painful for the detectives since there were no leads. After the partners did everything that they could do regarding the West Hill investigation, they decided to concentrate on the Firestone murder again and go back over the evidence. They returned to Sweethearts and interviewed a number of the witnesses again. They talked to the strippers and much to their disappointment, the girls were almost naked. They did find a couple of new people to talk to who had been there the night of the murder, but they added nothing. The detectives thought that they were missing something, some angle that they hadn't considered.

After talking to the two homicide investigators about all three murders, Chief Bill Speer agreed that there was a real possibility that a mission killer was on the move. He decided to give Everdell and Carpenter their own private room at headquarters so they could concentrate on all three murders at the same time away from all of the other detectives.

"We have to find out how and why all of these murders are related. As of this moment, you two are off the usual shift rotation and you are to concentrate on this string of murders," Speer decided. "You decide what shifts you work so your time fits into whatever leads you are following at the time. We've got to catch this guy before there are more killings. Spend a minimum of time on your other cases."

"What do we do about all the overtime?" Everdell asked. "Is there a budget?"

"There's never a budget. Don't worry about the extra hours. I'll make sure to find the money and you can have some extended time off at Christmas."

"We're on it and we'll keep you up-to-date regularly," Carpenter answered.

The Shackleton, Firestone and Chung files were spread out on two long tables joined together side to side with half a dozen chairs placed around them. The ten by twelve room had no windows. Their work area was about six feet from a wall that held a huge blackboard covered with names, dates, arrows and other chalk marks. The detectives had tried, over and over again, to come up with similarities in the files. The only facts were that all three dead men had been drug dealers who had been murdered in the same way. They just couldn't put their fingers on anything else. They had to find a lead.

* * *

The following Wednesday, Everdell and Carpenter worked in their small office until nearly seven o'clock. They were both dead tired from the pressure that Speer was putting on them and from beating their heads against the wall trying to turn up some new evidence in any one of The Oyster-Shucking Murder cases. The media was having a field day and the cops were having no fun at all. Everdell was at home, around nine o'clock, watching a Toronto Maple Leafs game on television when he got a call from headquarters that another male body had been found in a parking lot in the Jane and Wilson area of the city. The victim had been found lying on the ground behind an expensive car with a funny looking knife sticking out of the back of his neck.

Everdell had not been able to find Carpenter at home, but eventually located him on his cell as he was walking through Sherway Mall with his wife. She always shuddered when she heard his cell phone ring when they were out together and he was off-duty. Usually, it meant that Jack had to go back to work for one reason or another.

Both detectives knew that they had to get to the scene of the fourth murder quickly. The new crime scene might yield them the clue they needed to break the murder investigations wide open. When they got to the parking lot, there were two patrol cars and an ambulance already parked near a bright red, sports car. One of the patrolmen filled them in on what they had found when they had arrived about an hour earlier.

"We know the dead guy behind the Porsche. His name is Clarence Jones and we've arrested his ass twice in the last few years for selling drugs in this part of town."

"All these drug dealers sure drive expensive cars," Carpenter commented as he and Everdell walked past the Porsche. "I think this car is worth well over a hundred grand."

"There's no fuckin' doubt that we're in the wrong line of work," Everdell said as he bent down over the body with a flashlight in his hand and aimed the beam of light at the back of the dead man's neck and head and then looked toward his partner. "Jack, take a look at this, the same kind of oyster-shucking knife that was used on the others."

"I don't want to think about how this investigation will play out. There'll probably be no witnesses and no other evidence."

Unfortunately, Carpenter was right. The murder scene gave up absolutely nothing that would help the detectives in their investigation and there were no real witnesses. No one had seen or heard anything. There was not even a partial description of the killer or of a strange car in the vicinity. The detectives spent the rest of the evening and part of the next day talking to people at the nearby restaurants and businesses without any luck at all. By Friday, they had gathered as much information as they were likely going to get. By that time, they had also received the Coroner's Report on the death. Again, the victim had died instantly. The similarities to the previous three murders were all they had. The deceased was a known drug dealer, with a record, who frequented the streets of Downsview. He had been murdered in the same manner as the other three victims.

* * *

Saturday morning, at about ten to eight, just after they arrived at the office to start their shift, Everdell and Carpenter were sitting in their private room. The evidence relating to the four murders was scattered all over the large table. They were drinking coffee and looking at their scribbled notes on the blackboard. All of sudden the door sprung open and Chief Speer burst into the small room in an agitated state.

"You guys aren't gonna fuckin' believe this! They just found the body of Darvel Rastone, a Jamaican, out in the Beach. Guess what? Darvel just happens to be a known drug dealer in that part of the city. Wanna know how he was killed?"

Everdell answered, "He probably has an oyster-shucking knife sticking out of the back of his fuckin' neck."

"You sure are quick this morning," the Chief said, as he threw them his report.

"Jesus Christ! That's number five! If this shit isn't gang related, and it doesn't appear to be, we've got a mission killer on our hands," Carpenter said. "The only good thing about all of this is that he's not a serial killer out there killing innocent members of the public. He's just doing our job for us and getting rid of the drug dealers!"

"OK, Chief. We're outta here! The guy's still a bloody killer even if he is helping us do our job. Jack, at least this time they didn't find the victim on our night off."

The detectives soon arrived in the Lee Avenue public parking lot right behind a McDonald's, just off of Queen Street East, in the Beach area of the city. They found exactly what had been described to them in the report from Speer. A fairly large Jamaican was sitting behind the wheel of a brand new Cadillac. He looked like he was sitting there resting. The wooden handle of the same kind of knife that the others had been killed with was clearly visible at the back of the victim's neck. It appeared to everyone at the scene that the drug dealer had been killed the night before. The blood on the back of the victim's neck had dried to a hard crust and the skin color was much darker than normal. The vehicle also exuded the gut-wrenching smell of human decay.

The reason the body hadn't been found until morning was because the black tinted windows of the car made it impossible to see into the vehicle unless someone was right up close to a window. A husband and wife, on their way to an early morning breakfast at Karas, had parked beside the Caddy. When the husband had stepped out of his car, he noticed the outline of a man seated, motionless, behind the wheel of the car next to him. The man inside didn't move and appeared to be staring blankly out through the windshield. There was no response to knocks on the window so the guy had opened the unlocked door. As soon as the odor hit his nostrils, he cancelled breakfast and called the police.

* * *

The Saturday investigation took the same form as the others and, as usual, nothing very helpful was found in the car or in the area around it. Later that afternoon, the detectives were back in their room on College Street waiting for the Forensic Report and the Coroner's Report. They knew what the contents of both reports would reveal. They would be similar to the other ones that they had recently read.

"There has to be something that ties all of these murders together and we're just missing it. I think we should erase the blackboard and start over. Let's write down all the information that we have about each of the five murders. We'll list everything side by side for comparison and see if we can come up with something common to all of them. It's probably right there in front of us," Everdell suggested.

"I'm with you," Carpenter agreed, "but I have a gut feeling that we're only going to rehash all those things that we already know."

"Think about this! The killer made public appearances when he killed Stevie Shackleton and Eddie Firestone. We even got a couple of half-assed descriptions of him in both of those instances. They weren't identical, but at least they were descriptions with some seri- ous similarities. The last three murders were done much more carefully, almost in private, away from members of the public."

"You're right, Graham. I don't know why, but I keep getting the feeling that the guy who committed these murders is trying to tell us something or give us a message of some kind. We haven't been able to figure it out."

"Jack, the only fuckin' message I'm getting is that the killer really doesn't like drug dealers! We have to find out why!"

"If you think about all five murders, the only one that was different was the first one. For some reason, Shackleton's body was moved from his house downtown, all the way up north to Medford Secondary School. He was also stabbed twice! Maybe we should concentrate on that case. There must be a reason why the killer went to all that trouble. The first murder has to be the key; there's some reason why Shackleton was treated differently!"

As Everdell started to erase the blackboard and Carpenter began to sort out the contents of the five murder files in sequence across the long table, the door of the room opened. Chief Speer came in and shut the door behind him. He sat down in one of the empty chairs at the end of the table.

"I've had a number of calls from the Mayor recently. He told me that he's being hounded by his pals in the media because of the lack of information being released by our department about *The Oyster- Shucking Murders*," the Chief stated and continued. "He's insisting that the department hold a news conference and let the media know what the hell's going on."

"Billy, if we make all of the information public, at least one good thing will happen here in the city," Everdell answered.

"And what's that?" Chief Speer asked.

"All of the fuckin' drug dealers will head for cover and go into hiding until we find the guy responsible for these murders."

"That wouldn't be a bad thing," Carpenter suggested.

Speer went on, "I'm going to schedule a news conference for Monday afternoon at two o'clock. I'll introduce you, since they are all your cases, and one of you can describe to the public what we've learned to date. The way things seem to be going, it might not be a bad idea to ask for some help too."

"We were just about to start over and go through everything that we've got on all of the murders from day one. We'll draft a statement for the press and put a copy on your desk for Monday morning," Everdell commented. "If any changes are required, we can make them before two o'clock."

The detectives got through all of the evidence before they went home, but didn't learn anything new. They both felt that the key to the whole thing was the Shackleton murder and the reason why the body was moved from his home to Medford high school, but they couldn't put their fingers on it. They decided that they would return to Medford the following week and speak to the principal about all the drug problems at the school. Some kind of helpful information might come out of the visit because they knew deep down that Medford was the key. Before leaving, the men prepared a draft of the public statement for the news conference and left it on Speer's desk.

* * *

The Chief approved the contents of the public statement and no changes were required. The news conference was scheduled at City Hall early enough in the afternoon that the newspapers would have time to write their stories for the late editions and the radio and television news departments could put together their detailed broadcasts for the evening news. The news conference would be televised live. The Mayor could show big business and the community just what kind of clout he had in dealing with the police department. He tried his best to turn it into a political event that would put a few feathers in his cap for the next election.

The Mayor called on the Chief of Police to introduce the Chief of Detectives from Homicide, who introduced the two seasoned detectives in charge of the investigations of The Oyster-Shucking

Murders. Each member of the hierarchy had a few choice words to say while they were in the limelight.

Detective Graham Everdell spoke on behalf of the department: "As the police department has already reported to you on five different occasions during the last few weeks, five Toronto area drug dealers have been murdered in different parts of the city. The murders started with the death of Steven Shackleton, who was killed at his home in the downtown area. Fifty thousand dollars was taken from the victim's home and while the killer was moving the dead body to Medford Secondary School, he dropped the money off at the Hospital For Sick Children. Two weeks later, Edward Firestone was killed in the men's washroom at Sweethearts, a strip club in the west end of the city. A few days later, the body of Liang Chung was found in his home in West Hill. That murder may have taken place on the same day as the Firestone murder. Ten or twelve days later, two more drug dealers were found murdered. The body of Clarence Jones was discovered in a parking lot behind a restaurant in Downsview and Darvel Rastone's body was found in his car in the Beach area of the city. All of these men appear to have been killed by the same person or persons and in the same manner. Each victim was stabbed with an oyster-shucking knife in the cervical region of their neck, at the base of their skull, where the spinal cord attaches to the brain. They all died instantly. We have been unable to come up with a motive as to why these men were targeted other than that all of the victims were known drug dealers. The murders do not appear to be gang related. The suspect is described to be a muscular, white male, thirty-five to forty years of age, with long dark hair, sideburns, a large bushy mustache and sometimes a goatee. If anyone out there has any knowledge or information about this man, the victims or their murders that might help us with our investigations, please call us as soon as possible. Please ask for either Detective Graham Everdell or Detective Jack Carpenter at 1-416-999-INFO. We will not be answering any questions at this press conference. Thank you all very much."

CHAPTER THIRTEEN

Paul got up bright and early Saturday and showered and shaved. He got rid of his long sideburns and trimmed his mustache back to something much smaller and neater than it had been during the past few weeks. As soon as he was dressed and cleaned up, he headed ten kilometers down the road to Fenelon Falls to do some grocery shopping. As he drove, he felt a real sense of accomplishment as his original mission had been completed. He had killed the five guilty drug dealers, after they acknowledged their part in that terrible weekend. The need for revenge that had gnawed at Paul in the past had subsided.

Back in his cottage at the end of the day, he looked in the large mirror on the wall and barely recognized the old Paul Taylor. He was totally different. It was the hair, the mustache and the exceptional physical shape of his body. Since he hardly knew himself, he was sure that past friends and acquaintances would never recognize him. Along with those changes, he always wore his dark glasses and a ball cap, something that he had never done in the past.

Paul listened to the Sunday evening news. He learned that the Toronto Police Department had scheduled a news conference for Monday afternoon to bring the public up-to-date on the investigations into the murders of the five drug dealers. Monday, as Paul worked around the cottage, the time for the two o'clock special news report finally arrived. As soon as the City-TV newscast started, the camera immediately broke to the City Hall and panned over a number of people until it zoomed in on the Mayor. There were four men standing behind him and after a few words, he introduced the Chief of Police. The Chief, without any fanfare, introduced William Speer, the Chief of Detectives of the Homicide Squad. Speer outlined the reasons for the news conference and introduced the two senior detectives in charge of the murder investigations. He then asked Detective Graham Everdell to speak to the public and media on behalf of the department.

Paul sat quietly and listened to the full news report. He couldn't believe what he heard Everdell say: *We have been unable to come up with a motive as to why these men were targeted other than that all of the victims were known drug dealers. Paul thought, The cops still haven't figured it out! They just don't get it!* Paul thought that his message had been loud and clear as to why Shackleton was chosen as a target. He had even moved the body from his house to the high school where he had committed his crimes to leave a clue for the police. The body had been moved at some risk, and to top it off, the bag of cash had been delivered to the Hospital For Sick Children. *Surely those two things must have meant something to their brilliant investigative minds!* he thought. The cops had been unable to draw a connection between the dealers in the different areas of the city and the deaths of so many teenagers at all those high schools almost two years earlier. *Why haven't they been able to figure out that the dead men had all been responsible for the deaths of all those innocent kids?* he wondered.

He thought that they should have been able to figure out the connection between the murders and those areas of the city where the students had died from the bad drugs. *What the hell was the matter with them?* He thought. *Do I have to spell it out for them?*

As those questions went through his mind, he decided that he would have to give them a push in the right direction. He wanted the police and the public to know that there was a specific reason for each killing and that the names had not been just pulled out of a hat. Those five men had to die because they had ruined the lives of so many families.

What Paul didn't know was that the deaths of the kids had originally been in the jurisdiction of Narcotics and the Homicide

Squad did not investigate them. Also, the detectives had investigated dozens of other murders since then.

* * *

On Tuesday morning, Paul was up early and got ready for a trip to Toronto. He couldn't make a phone call to the police from his cell or from one of the small towns nearby because he realized that the police had ways of finding out where specific calls had originated. After he showered, he had a good clean shave for a change, except for the trim new mustache. He had really hated the long sideburns and the goatee and was glad they were gone. He wasn't going to break anymore laws for awhile, so he decided that he could relax and try to be more like himself. He did realize that he had to continue to dress differently than he had in the past. He always wore his dark glasses because Paul Taylor was actually dead to the whole world. He didn't want to just happen to bump into someone who might recognize him from his other life.

Now that his list had been depleted, he was going to take some time off from handing out his form of justice and just relax. However, since he had decided to go into the city to make a phone call anyway, he thought that he might just slip into Woodbridge in the north end of the city and look around on his way home. The name Vito Morelli kept lingering in his mind.

Paul was in no hurry so he decided to travel the country back roads. As he drove through the Town of Markham, he saw a sign that reminded him that he really needed a haircut. HairWays Salon and Spa, located right on the side of the highway, jumped right out at him. Paul knew that he would never meet anyone he knew there so he stopped and got about half of his long hair cut off. Chris, the owner, a very friendly and personable guy, cut his hair and tried to talk him into all kinds of fancy things like a perm or some blonde tips. Paul just got a haircut, but it was a great haircut.

Just before eleven, Paul pulled into the huge parking lot at Bayview Village on the northeast corner of Bayview and Sheppard, three minutes north of Highway 401. He wandered through the mall for about fifteen minutes, window-shopping, until he found the escalator to the lower level where there were fewer shoppers. As soon as he arrived, he found exactly what he needed. There were two pay phones in a private alcove not being used. Paul picked up one of the telephones with a handkerchief in his hand so no fingerprints would attach to the receiver. He pushed the dial buttons with the rubber end of a pencil, 416-999-INFO, the number from the media.

"May I speak to Detective Graham Everdell, please?"

"One moment, sir, he'll be right with you," the polite operator answered.

"Detective Graham Everdell. What can I do for you?"

"I watched your news conference yesterday. You guys sure haven't got very far trying to figure out what the hell's going on with the murders of all those drug dealers! You just don't get it, do you?"

Everdell's senses perked up almost immediately and for some strange reason, a chill ran through his body.

He concentrated and asked, "Are you a witness to one of the murders that we're working on? Do you have some information that might help us with our investigations?"

"Actually, I'm a witness to all of the murders! I stabbed each guy, personally!"

"What the hell are you saying?" Everdell asked somewhat shocked.

"I'm only gonna say this once! I moved Shackleton to Medford to give you guys a clue! The five drug dealers that finally got justice were responsible for selling that bad shipment of Ecstasy that killed all those high school kids a couple of years ago!"

"What are you saying? You killed all five of them?"

"Detective, it was really nice talking to you!"

Paul smiled to himself as he carefully hung up the phone and slowly walked back toward the escalator. He returned to the main level of the mall and window-shopped as he headed toward the exit where his car was parked. Ten minutes later, he was cruising along the entrance ramp onto Highway 401 heading west. It wasn't long before he was driving north on Highway 400 toward Woodbridge.

* * *

As Paul entered the Woodbridge area, he spotted a Denny's and pulled into the restaurant parking lot. It was nearly noon and he was hungry. Besides, he wanted to find a local phone book and look up the name Vito Morelli. He didn't really expect to find a listing but he would take a look. If Paul could just find out where the guy lived during this trip, the useful information would be stored away for a later date.

After some toast, corn beef hash with a couple of poached eggs on top and a large glass of milk, Paul was shocked when he found exactly what he was looking for in the phone book at the payphone just outside of the men's washroom. The Vito Morelli who Paul was looking for may live at 14 Deercreek Court, but he had no idea where the street was located in the small community. As Paul walked toward his parked car, a uniformed Purolator driver was on his way into the restaurant for lunch.

"Do you happen to know where Deercreek Court is?"

"Sure do," the driver answered. "Go to the far end of town on Highway 7 and you'll see a small plaza on the right called Deercreek Plaza and Deercreek Court is the next left, just at the east end of the plaza. You can't miss it."

"Thanks a lot," Paul said as he got into his car and followed the driver's directions.

Paul turned left onto Deercreek Court. It was an impressive street. All the homes were in the five thousand square foot range and they all had three-car garages. It was a dead-end, with only about thirty homes on it, and number fourteen was about halfway down. As Paul drove by, he noticed that there was a gray, 700 Series BMW in the driveway, and parked right beside it, was another very expensive, white, V12 Mercedes convertible. They were both worth well over a hundred thousand dollars. After he saw the property and the vehicles, he was sure that he had found the right house.

Paul drove to the end of the cul-de-sac and turned around in the turning circle. On the way back past the Morelli house, he jotted down the car makes and models, as well as the license numbers, on a pad on the front seat of his car. The information would come in handy for when he went back to work on his mission of revenge against the men in the higher echelons of the drug world hierarchy.

* * *

The trip back to the north-country was long and tedious because Paul went further north to Newmarket and then east through farm country. He eventually ended up driving north on Highway 48 past the Pefferlaw Marina. As he looked in at the yard that was full of boats, he wondered what had happened to Liz's Saab. He hoped that it had been sold and the money had gone to charity. He continued cross-country to Fenelon Falls, then on to Kinmount and Beer Lake. He arrived just after four in the afternoon.

As usual, he poured himself a J&B and water on ice and sat down in his favorite chair, without the television on and without starting the fire, and just looked out over the lake and thought about life. He thought about his conversation with Detective Everdell and wondered how shocked the cop had been when he realized that he was talking to the actual killer of the five drug dealers. Paul knew that it would take Everdell and his partner some time to dig back through their files and the old newspapers to get the whole story about the bad shipment of Ecstasy. It would take even longer to put together the names of the devastated families around the city that had suffered on that same weekend when Ricky had died. The detectives would soon link the names of the dead and maimed children to the schools they had attended and tie the dead drug dealers to those high schools and neighborhoods. They would eventually be reminded of the losses that so many innocent families had suffered.

In Paul's state of mind during those days, he was almost proud of what he had accomplished. He knew that he had broken the law, but rationalized that once the detectives knew how much pain had been caused by the dead drug dealers, they might even thank him. The police would soon figure out that the killers of the high school students in the various parts of the city, all those months ago, had never paid for their crimes until now. The authorities had failed to make any arrests. *They might even be grateful*, he thought.

Paul was beginning to look forward to going after the big guys, the real drug traffickers, who import the drugs into the country and supply the street dealers. The wealthy fat-cats further up the food chain. The five men who Paul had killed were almost justified when they had begged for their lives saying that the bad shipment had not been their fault, but the fault of the real drug traffickers who had supplied them. He had understood what they were trying to tell him, but in his mind, they had been just as responsible as the men in the upper echelons. They hadn't brought the drugs into the city, but they had put the bad drugs into the hands of the teenagers who had died. Paul would make sure that the big guys paid for their crimes right along with them.

CHAPTER FOURTEEN

Detective Graham Everdell couldn't believe what had just happened. As soon as the phone line went dead, he slowly hung up the receiver. All of the blood in his face had drained away leaving him very pale as he stared at his partner in disbelief and looked for words. He sat up straight and shook his head back and forth.

"I can't fuckin' believe it!"

"What's the matter?" Carpenter asked. "You look like you've seen a ghost!"

"I didn't see a ghost, but I think I just spoke to one!" Everdell answered as he leaned forward, put his elbows on his desk and rested his head in his hands.

"What the hell are you talking about?"

"I think I just talked to the oyster-shucking killer! The guy said he killed all five of the drug dealers! He just called the hot-line and asked for me!"

"What did he say? You look like you're in shock!"

"He didn't say very much at all or stay on the line very long. He basically suggested that *we just don't get it!* He said that *we haven't been able to figure out what's going on!*"

"He's sure as hell right about that!"

"He said something like, *I'm only gonna tell you this once,* and continued on and said, *the five drug dealers who were murdered sold the bad shipment of Ecstasy that killed a bunch of high school students about two years ago!* I remember something like that happening. Do you remember anything about it?"

Carpenter thought back to the past and answered, "There was a bad shipment of drugs that hit the city nearly two years ago and I think about a dozen people died and a lot of others were hospitalized. A number of the victims were high school kids. The bad shipment of drugs came out of a home-lab somewhere down south and I think that a number of people died south of the border too. We weren't involved in any of those investigations though because Narcotics claimed that they were all in their jurisdiction."

"I'll bet any amount of money that Medford was one of the schools. That has to be the reason why Stevie's body was moved there. The killer wanted us to find him there," Everdell guessed. "I think he thought that we would have pieced it all together once we found Shackleton at Medford."

"The other drug dealers were killed all over the city. So if you're right, we will probably find out that the other high schools where students died will be somewhere near where the dealers operated or where their bodies were found."

"I'd better try to locate the call just in case he used a pay phone, but this guy hasn't left us any evidence yet," Everdell decided.

He picked up his telephone and called the official Bell Canada number that the department had for such emergencies. He provided the special operator with his name, rank, code and return number and explained that he needed the information as quickly as possible. He then dialed Chief Bill Speer to tell him about the break in the case.

"I remember that fiasco two years ago. Narcotics investigated a number of deaths all over the city and I think they found out that the bad shipment of Ecstasy came from the southern United States, California, I think. I'll arrange for Narcotics to transfer all of their files on those deaths to our department immediately," Speer said. "I should have them for you within a couple of hours."

"Great! I'm doing a locate on the call just in case the guy used a pay phone and we'll hit the Internet to pull up all of the newspaper articles about those Ecstasy deaths. Get those files to us as soon as you can," Everdell said as he hung up.

"I've already found some back issues of the Toronto Star from that time period and I'll print every article I can find. We should also take a look at the Globe and Mail, the Financial Post and the Sun," Carpenter said.

"Billy is getting us all the files that Narcotics has on those drug deaths. We'll have them in a couple of hours."

As Everdell finished the sentence, his telephone rang. It was the special Bell Canada operator with the telephone information.

"That was quick! Tell me that the call was made from a pay phone!" Everdell said to the Bell operator.

"It was made from a pay phone on the lower level of Bayview Village on the corner of Bayview and Sheppard Avenue East. The phone should be located in the east end of the lower level and its serial number, which you'll find on the front of the telephone at the bottom, is TO-19483."

"Thanks very much, Operator," Everdell answered as he finished making notes and then hung up and immediately dialed an internal office number. "Forensics? . . . Is Bill Konkle there? . . . Bill, its Graham Everdell. Can you drop everything you're doing and come with me? We've gotta go to Bayview Village to lift some prints off a pay phone. We have to do it right now!"

"Christ! I just had a sandwich delivered. I was gonna have an early lunch because I already missed breakfast. I guess I can take it with me," Konkle answered. "You're driving! I'll get my stuff together and meet you out back in a few minutes."

"I'll see you in the garage," Everdell said as he hung up his phone and handed his partner the Bell Canada information that he had written down. "Jack, call a *Black and White* and get it over to Bayview Village right now and find this pay phone on the lower level of the mall. Have them make sure that no one touches it until Bill Konkle and I get there."

"Right. While you're gone, I'll fight my way through the newspapers and copy anything I think we'll need. By the time you get back downtown, we should have all the old files from the Chief and we can try to put all this shit together."

"I'll be back as soon as I can. Maybe then we'll be able to figure out exactly what this guy is trying to tell us."

"Good luck with the prints."

"I'm not optimistic. This guy hasn't left us anything yet, but we have to at least go through the motions," Everdell said as he disappeared out into the main part of the Homicide Squad offices.

* * *

Everdell drove the unmarked police car north, through the fairly light traffic, while Konkle ate his triple-decker clubhouse sandwich. It took them about half an hour to get to Bayview Village and park. The men snaked their way through the shoppers and got to the lower level as quickly as they could. As they got off the escalator, they caught a glimpse of police officers guarding two pay phones that were almost hidden in a small alcove.

"We got here as soon as we got the call and there has been no one near the two phones since we arrived," Constable Tom Poupore advised the detectives.

"Great! Let's give Bill Konkle some room so he can do his thing. We might just get lucky and get some prints that might help us with our murder investigations," Everdell said as he and the two policemen stepped back out of the expert's way.

"Now that you're here, we'll hit the streets," Constable Poupore commented.

"No problem, we can handle things now. Thanks for your help," Everdell answered as the two cops turned and left the area.

"Graham, it looks like there are lots of prints on both phones."

"I thought there would be. Bill, can you smell the coffee? There's a Starbucks just down the hall. Do you want anything? "

"Yeah, just a black coffee."

It took the forensics expert almost an hour and a half to complete his analysis. Everdell stood by and studied all of the different procedures with interest. He had often watched the guys from the Forensic Identification Services at work on many occasions and always found it fascinating. As Konkle finished, he spoke to the detective as he packed his brushes, powders and spray cans back into his large case.

"There are a few finger prints that I was able to lift, but I have to tell you that there are a number of clean spots or smudge marks on the hand piece. That indicates to me that someone probably used it fairly recently with gloves on or a handkerchief in their hand. I also did the other phone, who knows, he may have touched it."

"I kind of expected you to say something like that because the guy we're dealing with is extremely careful. He's left us nothing at the murder scenes. I didn't really expect to find his prints on the phone, but we had to try."

"Who knows? Maybe he made a mistake. I'll be able to process what I've got by noon tomorrow and I'll make sure that a full report lands on your desk as soon as it's done," Konkle advised.

On the drive back to College Street, the men chatted about the investigations that Everdell and Carpenter were working on. Everdell provided Konkle with intimate details about the cases that he would not have known about. He thought that if he bounced all the information off of a third party, it might lead to some startling new way to look at things. Nothing positive came out of the discussion.

* * *

As Everdell walked through the station toward the private domain that he and Carpenter called home, he bumped into Chief Bill Speer. He had an armful of brown legal-size files all stamped in red with the word, *NARCOTICS*. There were sixteen in all. The files were handed over to Everdell right there in the hallway.

"How'd you make out? Any chance you might get some prints off the telephone?"

"Konkle was able to lift some prints off both phones in the alcove," Everdell replied, "but I'm not getting too excited. He seems to think that someone had used the phone with gloves on or with a handkerchief or something."

"Let me know what you learn from the files as soon as you get through them," Chief Speer ordered as he turned and headed back toward his own office, "and make sure that I get a copy of the Forensic Report on the telephones."

Everdell joined his partner in the room and put the pile of files on one end of the table. He told Carpenter what had taken place at the mall and that they would have a full Forensic Report by noon the next day. Carpenter showed him a pile of copied newspaper articles about the bad shipment of Ecstasy and the damage it had caused. The terrible news had been splashed over all of the major newspapers about two years earlier. He had printed double copies, a pile for each of them, and was ready to start reading.

"I'll get us both a coffee and then we can go through these newspaper articles together. As soon as that's done, we can compare our findings to what's in the files that the Chief rounded up for us and then go back to our own files," Carpenter suggested.

"I'll clear one end of the blackboard because I'm sure that we'll need the space if we're dealing with five different drug dealers, five different schools, five different parts of the city and a dozen or more dead or injured high school students and their families."

It was close to five o'clock when the two detectives finally got through all of the material. They both leaned back in their hard, plastic chairs to stretch and as they did so, concentrated on all the information on the blackboard.

"You know, I do remember that bad shipment of drugs and all those deaths now, but the fact that Shackleton's body was moved to Medford didn't ring a bell." Carpenter pondered. "I don't know why one of us didn't twig!"

"Christ! It was nearly two years ago and we didn't investigate them. Look at how all the information on the board fits together. It looks so simple now, doesn't it?" Everdell added. "Each one of the drug dealers who have been killed may have been the main supplier at each of the schools where students died."

"So what the hell do we have on our hands? A distraught father, brother or other relative of one of the teenagers who died or some kind of a vigilante or mission killer who is taking the law into his own hands?"

"Who the hell knows? If we had just paid a little more attention to the Stevie Shackleton murder we might have figured it out. His murder was not only the very first one, but if you look at it closely, it gives us most of the answers to the questions that we have been asking ourselves all these weeks," Everdell lamented.

"You're right! Medford had two students die and one ended up in the hospital indefinitely with brain damage. One article said that the kid would probably be there for the rest of his life. It has been confirmed that Shackleton was the main drug supplier for that school and had been for a few years. The killer took the trouble to move his body from his home to the school, for what appears to be no other reason than to give us some kind of a message, so we could figure out why Shackleton had been targeted. The bag of money that was delivered to the Hospital For Sick Children was a clear indication that the murder was not drug or gang related. The guy didn't want money, he wanted revenge. It was all right there and we probably would have got the connection if Narcotics had let us get involved in those investigations," Carpenter surmised.

"I guess that's why the caller said that, *we just don't get it*, when he spoke to me. In his mind, he left us all the answers to all of the questions. All we had to do was look a little closer at the Stevie Shackleton murder."

"So the killer may have some kind of a relationship with one of the teenagers who died. Maybe one of the victims from Medford because it was his first choice. On the other hand, there may be no relationship at all and the killer is just a crazy vigilante who wants to make sure that justice is done."

"I think that we've put enough time in on this shift, Jack. Let's sleep on all the information and wait until tomorrow and see if there are any prints from the mall phone. Let's get the hell outta here. I've had enough for one day."

CHAPTER FIFTEEN

Paul Taylor went back to Beer Lake and decided to take it easy for the balance of the week. It was time for a rest. Steven Shackleton and the other drug dealers who had caused the deaths of the students were dead. It wasn't that he didn't care about the adults in the city who had died from the same bad drugs, but there was something about the animals who target young people. Kids are so often easily swayed into experimenting with the various kinds of drugs that are rampant in the streets.

As Paul tracked down the street dealers and killed them, he always made sure they knew why they were about to die. Each of them had made the very same statement, *It wasn't my fault, I didn't know that the drugs were bad!* Paul decided they were probably right and the distributors and traffickers in the higher echelons of the business were really to blame. As time went on, Paul decided to expand his list of targets to include that group.

During the few days off, Paul thought about the three men whose names he had been given by his victims. He would formulate plans to visit each of them in the near future. There was Vito Morelli in Woodbridge, Ruffus Allan in Scarborough and Vladmir Rousinsky in Hamilton. In time, they would all pay the same price as the street dealers at the bottom of their distribution system.

Liz and Ricky never left Paul's mind as he worked around the cottage. Liz especially, because he felt guilty. He still missed her so much it hurt, but after almost three years of celibacy, he found himself thinking about other women. He noticed them when he was out in public and missed the tenderness that he had once shared with her. It had been a long time since he had been able to think of anyone but her, however, things were changing. Paul hoped that she would understand.

Even though he kept busy during the day, visions of his lost family floated into his mind and would not leave. He remembered how much he loved them. It was a good thing for him to remember them but he still missed them terribly. Paul felt absolutely no remorse for the five drug dealers he had killed even though he knew they too had families and loved ones of their own.

Paul thought about the higher level men whose names he had been given by his victims. Men like them never had second thoughts about the havoc that their bad drugs wreaked on so many young lives and families. Other people's losses were always on Paul's mind because of his own tragedy. He wondered if they were enjoying their life. He wondered if they had families of their own. Families that would miss them after they were gone. He hoped that they were happy because their happiness was about to come to an abrupt end.

The longer Paul spent at the lake, the more his hatred grew for those men hiding in those fancy homes. He thought about each of them in their privileged lifestyles. He envisioned killing them, one by one, the same way that he had killed the lowly street dealers. Before they actually died, Paul would make sure that they knew why they were about to die. He knew they had long forgotten, not only all the high school students, but all of the others, whose lives had ended in a grave or in a hospital bed that weekend so long ago. He was anxious to meet them all.

Finally, Paul completed the fall work needed to prepare his place for the winter. He hadn't ventured very far from home for quite awhile. He went to Kinmount a couple of times to get newspapers and to Haliburton for an afternoon to get groceries, beer and scotch. He even stopped at the Rockcliffe for a couple of draught beers. He did some fishing, and actually caught a good-sized Bass, which he grilled for dinner one night. He continued his strenuous exercise regimen, daily work-outs and hiked for miles in the bush.

In the evenings, he watched television. He needed to get a few good nights' sleep and be well rested. He did a lot of thinking about the three men he would be visiting soon. He knew that it wouldn't be long before he was very busy again.

On Sunday, the last day of his short vacation, Paul thought about how he would deal with his next victims. He knew where Morelli lived, so he decided to locate the other two men on his list. When he knew where they all lived, what they did day-to-day and where they hung out, he would formulate some plans to make them pay for their crimes. He realized that he would have to be more careful because they would always have others around them. He decided to find the Russian and the Jamaican and when that was accomplished, he would get to know them all, one at a time. He would learn their likes, dislikes and habits. He was looking forward to it.

CHAPTER SIXTEEN

Graham Everdell and Jack Carpenter both had sleepless nights thinking about the killer's phone call. The guy had actually made a personal call to headquarters on the hotline, asked for Detective Everdell and spoke to him about the murders. If the call was legitimate, and the two detectives thought that it was, the killer had provided Everdell and Carpenter with the missing link. He had shared just enough information to connect all the killings together and that was why they felt that the guy who had called was for real. The new information indicated that the recent deaths of drug dealers were directly related to a number of drug deaths that Narcotics had investigated nearly two years earlier. The detectives finally had some leads.

"Do you think it was the killer on the telephone or just some crank caller being an asshole?" Carpenter asked the next day.

"I honestly think it was the killer. He really didn't say very much at all, just got right to the point. He wanted us to know that all five murders weren't just random killings. Each drug dealer was killed for a specific reason. They had supplied that bad shipment of Ecstasy to those high schools where a number of young people had died or were injured."

"Your gut feelings have been right on before."

"I also feel that he's not a stranger," Everdell said and went on. "He may have a relationship with one of the victims. I think we have to review all the information that we've put together one more time and find the connection."

"Well, let's get started," Carpenter answered.

"Seven students died at five schools across the city. Two are still in extended care facilities with severe brain damage and are not expected to recover. If the killer has a relationship with anyone, it has to be with one of those nine kids."

"Is there any significance to the sequence of events?" Carpenter asked. "The killings started with Shackleton at Medford. Trudeau was next with Firestone's death at the strip joint in the west end and then Cedarview, Pinehurst and The Bluffs."

"Medford is the most important. Stevie Shackleton's murder was different from the others. The killer has a connection to one of those kids. I just know it. We didn't get the message because we were kept out of the loop by Narcotics!"

"I guess if you think about it, if someone was pissed off enough to start killing drug dealers because they killed a bunch of young people, wouldn't he target the drug dealer who had killed or maimed his loved one first?" Carpenter added.

"Makes sense to me. Let's take another look at the families of the two kids who died and the one who was permanently disabled from Medford. We might just get lucky."

The detectives sorted through the paperwork they had on the three victims from Medford Secondary School with enthusiasm. They were pumped. They spoke to each other as they made notes of information that was compiled from the various files.

"Kenneth Wilson and Richard Taylor are the two boys who died of the drug overdoses that day and Andrew McKenzie is in extended care. We should start by making an appointment with the principal of Medford to obtain some preliminary information about the boys and their families," Carpenter decided.

"Why don't you call the school and set that up? While you're doing that, I'll keep putting together the information that we've got on the other victims."

* * *

At Medford, a secretary led the detectives into the principal's office.

The principal was an attractive and extremely well-dressed woman of about forty, with a very friendly way about her.

"Hi! I'm Linda O'Leary. I've been the principal here at Medford for the past five years and I'll be happy to share any information that I have. I understand that you want to talk to me about the students who died from the drug overdoses a couple of years ago."

"That's right. I'm Detective Graham Everdell and this is my partner, Jack Carpenter. We're investigating a number of murders that may be related to the deaths of those kids here at your school and across the city on that terrible weekend."

"I had my secretary pull the files on our students who were involved. Two boys died and one is permanently disabled."

"We're looking for information on the families of the victims. Did you have any contact with the parents of the boys before or after the incidents ?" Carpenter asked.

"Yes, I try to get to know the parents of all our students. Kenny Wilson was a great kid. He was a good student who excelled in all the sports here at Medford. He has two sisters who still attend this school. His parents, Charles, a Chartered Accountant, and his wife, Betty, live just a few blocks from here. I'll give you their address before you leave. I actually had a chat with them on Parent's Night, a few weeks ago."

"How have they seemed since the death of their son? Do you think that they were able to cope with the tragedy and eventually get on with their lives?" Everdell asked.

"They were totally devastated when it first happened, especially Charles, because Kenny was his only son. Their daughters are sweethearts and I'm sure that they helped their parents get through those terrible days."

"Has Mr. Wilson shown any signs of not coping with the loss of his son during the months since Kenny's death?" Carpenter went on.

"No, Charles and Betty appear to have been able to put Kenny's death behind them and get on with their lives. They are both quite religious and I'm sure that their faith and their involvement in their church have helped them a lot."

"Do you know the parents of Richard Taylor and have you seen them since the death of their son?" Everdell asked.

"That's another terrible tragedy! Ricky's mother passed away with cancer about a year or so before he died. The young fellow was totally devastated and heart broken. His father, Paul Taylor, a lawyer with a large firm downtown, had a terrible time dealing with the loss of his wife. When Ricky, his only child, passed away, he was a wreck. It was awful. I feel sick to my stomach just thinking about that poor family."

"So Mr. Taylor has had some difficulty coping with his loss?" Carpenter asked.

"Oh, he coped with it all eventually, . . . he drowned in Lake Simcoe in September. He had gone fishing and all of the evidence indicated that he committed suicide. It was in all the newspapers."

"That is terrible," Everdell commented, "the whole family gone. Do you know if Mr. Taylor and Ricky had any other relatives that live here in the city or anywhere else who we might be able to talk to?"

"No, as I recall from Ricky's funeral, there weren't very many relatives there. Just his father, Paul, and I think maybe an aunt. She may have been a sister of Ricky's mother or something like that but I'm not sure. I do remember that the grandparents on both sides had passed away sometime earlier."

"It almost sounds like the aunt who attended the funeral is the only living relative now?"

"I'm sure that's right. I remember seeing her at the mother's funeral too."

"Do you remember the name of the funeral home?" Carpenter asked.

"Yes, both Ricky's and his mother's funerals were at Stoddarts Funeral Home on Bayview Avenue, just south of Eglinton."

"What can you tell us about the McKenzie family? Were they able to deal with Andrew's injuries and the fact that he'll likely spend the rest of his life in a hospital?" Everdell went on, probing for more information.

"Andrew's father had been killed in an automobile accident, years before, and June McKenzie has raised her kids on her own. Andy has two sisters and a brother. They are a family that had dealt with tragedy in the past and they seem to be coping with their terrible situation with Andrew. They take turns making daily visits to the hospital to feed Andy his dinner."

"Thank you. That's about it," Carpenter said. "If you would be kind enough to give us the Wilson's and McKenzie's addresses, you can get back to work. We'll find out the name of Ricky Taylor's aunt from the funeral home."

Linda O'Leary quickly jotted down the required information on a sheet of paper and as she handed it to Detective Everdell, she commented, "I'll give you the work numbers for Mr. Wilson and Mrs. McKenzie so you should have no trouble contacting them. Sometimes people are hard to catch at home."

Carpenter spoke as the two men stood up to leave the office, "Thanks so much for your cooperation. If we have any further questions, we'll give you a call."

"If you are investigating the deaths of the drug dealers who caused those terrible things to happen to my students, I'd rather not be of anymore help to you if I can avoid it. The city should give the person who's killing those men a medal or something."

* * *

As the detectives left the school, they silently looked toward the flagpole where Shackleton's body had been. Neither one said anything as they thought about their conversation with the principal and her comments that praised the work of the killer. Carpenter spoke first as the unmarked car turned south on Mt. Pleasant toward downtown.

"It's very clear that Linda O'Leary is certainly not on our side in this investigation."

"I'm sure that there are a great number of other people like her in the city too."

"It's a shame that we have to contact all these people and rehash the pain that they're trying to forget, but there's not much we can do about it. As soon as we get back to headquarters, we'll call the Wilsons and the McKenzies for an appointment. We'll also have to call Stoddarts Funeral Home and get the information on Ricky Taylor's aunt."

Everdell answered, "It doesn't sound very promising after hearing about the families of the Medford victims, but we have to do the interviews anyway."

Back at the office, Everdell went across the street to the deli to get them both a drink and a sandwich. Carpenter stayed behind and called to make appointments to meet with the three sets of family relatives. Stoddarts did have Ricky Taylor's aunt's address and phone number on file. He had no problem contacting all of the people on his list. The meetings were set for times that were convenient for all parties. The detectives would have to do some night work again.

* * *

The meeting with Charles and Betty Wilson was first on the agenda that evening and it turned out to be quite pleasant. They were very down to earth and appeared to be able to get through whatever life had dealt them by leaning on their faith. They were religious, in a friendly sort of way, and not the least bit overbearing. The detectives enjoyed the meeting and felt that Mr. Wilson, and the rest of the family, had dealt with their loss. Their girls were great comfort. Everything appeared quite normal.

It was much the same story with the McKenzie family. They all seemed to rally together and were able to pitch in and help with the terrible situation that had developed. June McKenzie was very hard working and the other three kids pulled their weight around the house and someone visited Andrew in the hospital everyday. The family appeared to be coping as well as they could with the burden of having a young family member in an extended care facility.

Ricky Taylor's aunt, Rebecca Farwell, was also very cooperative and easily conversed with the two detectives during their meeting. She was a friendly woman who had never married and when she spoke of the Taylor family, a deep sadness came over her.

She explained to the detectives that she had cared a great deal for her sister, Elizabeth, and was elated for her in her life with Paul Taylor, the man of her sister's dreams. She had also been extremely happy for Liz when Ricky had arrived. She shared that Liz had some serious problems with the birth of her child and believed that her nephew had been a gift from God. Rebecca described a very loving couple who doted on their only child.

"It really does sound like your sister and her husband were very much in love and had a very happy family life together," Carpenter commented.

"They were the ideal family until Elizabeth got sick," Rebecca explained. "Paul loved Liz more than life; she was his world. She loved him just as deeply. When Ricky was born, they showered him with that kind of love and they became the perfect family. As the cancer ravaged Liz's body, Paul slowly deteriorated physically and mentally. After she was gone, he just fell apart. If Ricky had not been there with him, I'm sure that he would have taken his own life sooner than he did. There was nothing for him but Ricky who was the only part of Liz that he had left. When Ricky died, I always knew that it would be the end for Paul. He had nothing more to live for. It didn't surprise me in the least when I heard that he had actually committed suicide. It was as if I always knew that he would someday."

"Are there any family members who were close to the Taylors, either in Toronto or anywhere else?" Everdell asked.

"No, I'm the last of our family. My parents are long gone and Elizabeth was my only sister. Paul's parents died a number of years ago and he was an only child."

"We're sorry that you had to revisit all of these tragic events. That's all of the questions we have at this time. Thanks for your help," Carpenter added.

"I think it's shameful that you're wasting taxpayers' money trying to find the killer of the drug dealers who killed my nephew and so many other children in our city. Those criminals all deserved to die for what they did."

* * *

The next afternoon, Everdell and Carpenter were in their room at headquarters discussing the interviews that had taken place.

"I think that we can pretty well forget the relatives of the victims from Medford. The Wilsons and the McKenzies look like they have a handle on life's problems. Rebecca Farwell, Ricky Taylor's only surviving relative, doesn't look like a killer or like someone who would hire one," Everdell commented.

"You're right. I think we've hit a dead end at Medford even though it was the logical tie-in because the facts of that murder are so different from the others. Let's take a look at the families of the victims from Trudeau Collegiate since the Firestone murder was second. Then, I guess it'll be on to Cedarview, Pinehurst and The Bluffs, in that order."

"Jack, why don't I take Trudeau and Pinehurst? They're both in the west end of the city. I'll make the calls, go to the schools and do the interviews. You take Cedarview and the Bluffs, they're in the east end, and do the same. At some point in the next couple of days, we can sit down and put all the information together."

"Yeah. That'll save us some time and with a little luck, we'll get a lead or two."

The detectives agreed to finish the interviews as soon as possible. They were hopeful that some new information would surface that would help them in their investigations.

CHAPTER SEVENTEEN

Paul Taylor stopped for gas and a coffee at the only station in Kinmount, a Shell, shortly after eight o'clock Monday morning. A short goatee was back in place, his hair, covered by his Raiders cap, was not nearly as long as it had been and he wore his dark glasses. He planned to cut directly across the top of the city, north of the airport, and go west to Hamilton, an industrial city of five hundred thousand people, about fifty minutes west of Toronto.

His plan was to locate Eddie Firestone's supplier, Vladmir Rousinsky, the Russian. Paul wanted to find out where he lived, what car he drove and where his favorite bars and restaurants were located. The trip was only intended to be a fact finding mission. He had decided that he wouldn't get carried away if he happened to find Rousinsky. Paul knew that he would have to be more cautious dealing with the distributors because they would be much better organized than the street pushers. They might even have bodyguards. He realized that he could easily get himself into trouble if he didn't have a game plan for the last three men on his list. He had to be more precise than he had in the past. The level in the drug organizations that he was about to deal with could mean his own sudden death if he made any mistakes. He was in no hurry. He would take his time and plan carefully.

* * *

The busy industrial city had an odor all its own. Dark smoke lingered in the air above the steel mills on the shores of Hamilton

Harbour. He looked at his watch and noted that it had been two and half hours since he left Beer Lake.

Paul stopped at a Seven-Eleven in a small strip plaza as soon as he got off the expressway. He bought two local newspapers, the Hamilton Spectator and Hamilton This Week. He left his car parked near the variety store and walked to the last store in the row, a greasy-spoon that advertised an All Day Breakfast. As he entered the foyer, he stopped at a payphone and looked up the name Rousinsky in the phonebook. He had a gut feeling that he would not be as lucky as he had been with Morelli in Woodbridge. He was right. There was no such name listed. He would have to do some digging.

During breakfast, Paul scanned the newspapers looking for some sort of Russian connection. He looked for restaurants, bars and strip joints. Two ads jumped right out of the Spectator at him. The first, advertised Lovely Natasha's, a strip joint that touted the most beautiful strippers in the city direct from Moscow. The second, The Russia House, which appeared from the ad to be an upscale steakhouse. Paul felt that they would both be worth checking out. He knew that if Rousinsky was around town, he would be involved with, connected to, or hang out at Russian businesses.

As Paul ate his breakfast and looked through the newspapers, he decided that he would likely have to stay in Hamilton for a couple of days. As soon as he finished eating, he drove around the downtown core of *The Steel City* to get a feel for where things were located. During his search for the Russian, he would likely have to do some driving but would take cabs whenever possible, especially if he was going to have a few beers. He found the strip club first because it was right on one of the main streets. He had a lot more trouble locating the fancy restaurant. In the end, he had to get some directions from a cab driver. As soon as he knew where both businesses were located, he found a small downtown hotel, a Days Inn, checked in for one night and parked his car in the underground parking garage. By the time he got settled in his room and was ready to hit the streets, it was close to one o'clock in the afternoon.

* * *

The white and green United Cab dropped him at the front door of Lovely Natasha's and he wandered into the darkened room. As his eyes adjusted, he noticed that the room was quite large. It had a lit-up stage along one side, opposite the main door, with a runway that came right out into the middle of a room full of tables and chairs. The runway and stage also had seats running along the edges so patrons could sit close to all the action. It looked like every other strip joint that Paul had been in over the years on those special occasions that had required that kind of entertainment.

Paul walked to the bar in the center of the room, opposite the stage and runway, and ordered a Molson Canadian. He decided to stand at the bar until his eyes got totally adjusted so he could get his bearings and have a good look around. It was still fairly early and it was only Monday, but there were about sixty or seventy bodies scattered around the large room watching a tall, thin blonde doing her routine. She was quite attractive and appeared Russian, or at least, eastern European. To the right of the stage, there was a VIP lounge that was enclosed in dark, tinted glass. Persons sitting inside can see out, but the other patrons cannot see inside. It held about a dozen guys and about half a dozen dancers for private shows away from the crowd.

Paul finished his beer at the bar and walked over toward the VIP lounge and an empty table near the runway. He sat within earshot of the bartender who was on duty. Four guys were seated at the next table with a nude table dancer, on a stool, doing a private dance in their midst. Paul couldn't help but look at her thin, smooth body and recognized her as the girl who had been on the stage a few minutes before. He ordered another beer from the waitress, who was fully clothed, but well built and pretty enough to have been a dancer. In time, the guys beside Paul started to get bombed and the one seated closest, spoke to him periodically. During the breaks between dancers on stage, Paul and his new buddy chatted.

"Are all the girls who dance here really Russians?"

"I've been coming here for about three years. The place used to be called *Dominos* or something. I heard that it was taken over by Russians about two years ago and that's when the name changed. Most of the girls who have danced for me have some kind of an accent, but who the hell knows if it's Russian," the guy answered.

"What's that glassed in area for over there?"

"The Russian guys who own the place and their friends watch in private and they often get the dancers to go in there for private shows if you know what I mean."

"When do the owners use the private area? Do they hang around very much?"

"I'm here a couple of afternoons a week and they're often here. They usually drop by in the early evening and stay for a few hours. Then they all usually bugger off."

The loud music started once more and one of the most beautiful women in the world sashayed out into the center of the stage. Paul and his new buddy stopped talking and concentrated on the show. During the next couple of hours, the place got much busier and most of the tables had men sitting at them. Paul continued to talk to his new friend every so often, but he was just putting in time to see if the VIP's were going to show up. He had a gut feeling that if Vladmir Rousinsky was not one of the owners, he would be one of their friends. If he hung around, he would learn something about his target.

At four-thirty, four burly foreigners sauntered into the club with an important air about them. They went directly to the stand-up bar where Paul had been earlier. Paul couldn't hear everything they talked about because of the loud music. They spoke some Russian that was mixed in with English, but the words that he did hear convinced him that they were the guys who he had been waiting for all afternoon.

The man who appeared to have some air of authority spoke to the bartender behind the bar, "Have Sasha bring two bottles of Cristal to the lounge."

"How many glasses will you need?

As the song ended and the dancer on stage finished her dance, the main man in the group answered the bartender, "I'd better have six glasses. Vlad is supposed to be here in about half an hour with a friend, so make sure that you send them right to the lounge. We'll be hanging around here until about seven-thirty or eight and then we're going to the Russia House for dinner."

"That sounds great, Ivan. I'll send them right over as soon as they arrive."

"Be sure that Sasha takes good care of us because I want to impress these guys."

"No problem. I'll talk to her right now and make sure she's onside."

Paul could hear a lot more when the music wasn't blaring so the break between dancers was perfectly timed. He was within earshot of most of the discussion and he could almost feel the excitement build in his body when he heard the name Vlad. Paul knew deep down that they were talking about Rousinsky.

Just before six o'clock, two dapper Russian-types came in and walked directly to the bar. One spoke to the bartender and reached across the bar and did some sort of handshake as Paul watched and listened.

"Vlad, it's great to see you again," the bartender said and went on. "Ivan is in the lounge and asked me to send you directly there as soon as you got here."

"OK, Comrade, see you later," Vlad answered as he turned and walked toward the smoked glass private enclosure with his friend right behind him.

The two men passed within three feet of Paul as he sat at his table. He got a good look at his target and would be able to recognize him anywhere. He was slightly taller than Paul, but had a slighter build, maybe ten or fifteen pounds lighter. He had very short hair that mostly stuck straight up into the air which gave him a real European look. Paul sat there for another half an hour deciding on his next move. The first group of Russians indicated that they had made plans for dinner at the Russia House for around eight o'clock that evening. He assumed that they would all likely stay hidden in the darkened lounge until close to that time. Paul decided that he couldn't accomplish anything further sitting in the strip bar, other than drink too much, so he left. He went outside, hailed a cab, and went back to his hotel.

As soon as Paul got back to his room, he went through the newspaper once again, picked up the phone and dialed the number for the restaurant.

"Is this the Russia House? . . . I would like to make a dinner reservation for one for seven-thirty this evening . . . Thoburn . . . That's great, I'll be there."

Paul wanted to be sure that he got there before the Russians arrived. He would be seated at his table with a drink in his hand and maybe even eating. Then there would be no possibility that anyone would think that he had followed them there, if by chance, he had been noticed earlier. He ordered a carafe of coffee from room service because he'd had a few beers during the afternoon and he wanted to drive his car to the restaurant. He thought that he might have to follow the Russian later that evening to find out where he lived.

Paul jumped into the shower and got cleaned up. He put on a pair of dress pants, a coordinated sport shirt and a jacket. He knew where the restaurant was located and left in plenty of time to make his reservation. He parked his car at the far side of the parking lot, well away from the main door, so he would be well back from all of the people who would be coming and going over the course of the evening.

* * *

The restaurant was modern in design. The reception area had a large cloakroom just inside the main door. The hall to the main eating area opened up into a huge room with four different levels. There were customers seated on each level even though it was not busy. The various seating areas could be seen, each one from the other, over the railings of the balconies that separated them. There were many private, and even romantic, dining areas in different alcoves. The opulent décor was very dark with oak paneling and deep brown carpeting. At one end of the expanse, tucked into an intimate corner, was a piano bar that exuded quiet music into the eating area. Paul thought that the restaurant was as upscale as any of the places that he and his cohorts used to frequent in downtown Toronto.

As Paul was led into the eating area, the Maitre d' asked him if there was a particular part of the restaurant where he would prefer to sit. In a rear corner of the main level, he noticed a *Reserved* sign on a table for eight or ten in what looked like a special area. It was an exclusive, private seating area. Paul took a chance that was the table that had been reserved for the Russians, so he chose to sit on one of the upper balconies nearby. He was introduced to a waiter and followed him up the rear stairs to a table for two located against a rail overlooking the private corner. From his perch, Paul could still see the main entrance behind him. He would be able to sit there in relative obscurity and listen to the diners below. A waiter arrived shortly after and provided him with a thick wine list and a menu for consideration.

He ordered a dry, vodka martini to start and indicated that he would take a few more minutes to order dinner and wine. He took his time perusing the wine list because he knew that he would probably be there for awhile. As the martini arrived, Paul settled in for a relaxed and enjoyable dinner.

Fifteen minutes later, Paul heard some commotion in the reception area and glanced in that direction from his perch above the main level. Eight men, six of whom Paul recognized from the strip joint, talked and laughed as they headed toward the rear of the establishment. They were well known to the staff and were treated like royalty. They were either the owners or good customers who tipped well. Paul soon realized that his instincts were right as the group was led to that special table just below him. The Maitre d' did not leave for the longest time and two waiters hovered over the group of special guests.

Paul was on a balcony about ten feet above the group. He was close enough to hear them talking and laughing, but was hidden behind a wooden railing. He could lean slightly forward or backward and look through the rungs and see the men very clearly without looking suspicious. He was just another evening diner in the restaurant.

Paul could tell that the Russians intended to have a leisurely dinner so he decided to take his time and just sip his drinks and order his courses one at a time. He started with dill pickles, black olives, cottage cheese and garlic bread that were put on every table right after diners sat down and ordered their first drink. When the martini was nearly gone, Paul ordered a bottle of Chateauneuf-du-Pape, one of his favorite reds, and let it sit on the table and breathe awhile. He rarely got out for dinner anymore so he decided to treat himself. He started with cream of potato soup, then moved on to a small Caesar salad, an appetizer of grilled calamari, and for the main, King Crab legs. He took his time eating and tried to learn whatever he could from the conversations going on at the table on the lower level.

Dinner turned out to be absolutely fabulous. Paul finished up with a black coffee and a double Grand Marnier, straight up. He had listened to the conversations below him all evening. They spoke mostly in English, with some Russian mixed in, and the conversation covered many subjects. Paul found out that three of the men at the table, including Vlad, had an interest in Lovely Natasha's and the Russia House, and they all laughed about how well the two businesses were doing. There was absolutely no talk of drugs or the drug business. The men talked about going on a ski trip or holiday to Vail, Colorado some time early in the new year, but no specific date was mentioned. At ten-thirty, the whole gang sounded like they were going to have one last after-dinner drink before leaving the establishment.

Paul took that conversation as a hint to make the necessary arrangements to pay his tab which he did using cash. He left his table before the men below him left theirs. He didn't even look in their direction as he left because he didn't want to have eye contact with anyone. He wound his way back to the main entrance through the opposite side of the restaurant so he didn't have to go near them. He decided that he would wait in his car until Vlad left and then follow him. All he still needed to do on this trip was find out where he lived. He would get to meet him soon enough.

* * *

It wasn't long before two of the men appeared outside the main door and stopped in the lighted reception area. One was Vlad and the other was the man from the strip joint who had been called Ivan by the bartender. They stood and talked for a few minutes, when all of sudden, they hugged each other and Ivan went back into the restaurant. Vladmir Rousinsky walked toward a large, gray Mercedes, got in and started it. Paul jotted down the license plate number while he had a chance. It pulled out onto the busy street and Paul followed at a safe distance. He kept another vehicle or two between them.

As the Mercedes approached a traffic light at Dunvegan Street, on the edge of an upscale residential area on Hamilton Mountain, the light turned yellow and Vlad scooted through and made a left turn. Paul was stranded behind another car in the intersection. He was a fair distance back and there was nothing he could do about it. After the light finally changed, Paul drove slowly up Dunvegan, past all of the beautiful homes, but the gray Mercedes was nowhere to be seen. He drove to the very end of the street and then in both directions for about four blocks and turned around and went all the way back to the traffic lights without any luck. He wasn't able to locate the Mercedes anywhere in the darkness. He had lost the Russian at the lights, but at least Paul had some idea where he lived. He decided that he would look around Vlad's neighborhood early in the morning to see if the car could be located. Paul knew two of his haunts and could likely find him anytime he wanted to in the near future.

* * *

After a good night's sleep on a full stomach, Paul was up and out of the hotel by seven o'clock. Within half an hour, he was driving along Dunvegan looking for the gray Mercedes. Finally, he spotted it at the far side of a circular driveway in front of a two-story, stone mansion. Paul could only make out three or four of the license plate numbers on the rear of the car, but they matched the ones that he had written down the night before so he was certain that Vladmir Rousinsky lived there.

All in all, Paul was more than satisfied with the results of his investigative techniques into the whereabouts of the Russian drug distributor. He now knew where Morelli and Rousinsky lived and hung out, so he would be able to find them when their number came up on his list. All Paul had left to do was find the Jamaican, Ruffus Allan.

CHAPTER EIGHTEEN

Dectective Graham Everdell called the principals at Trudeau Collegiate Institute and Pinehurst Secondary School and made appointments to see them the next morning at nine-thirty and at eleven-thirty respectively. He decided to visit Trudeau Collegiate first because the traffic from the downtown area out into the suburbs, to the Kipling and Dundas area of Etobicoke, would be relatively light. Most of the commuters would be heading into the city. After that appointment, he could easily swing north to Highway 401 East to Jane Street and then go north to Pinehurst Secondary School.

The detective got to Trudeau five minutes late and was immediately led into Olivia Percival's office. She had been waiting for his arrival. The meeting with the principal went very well and the dead student's file was handed to the detective. He slowly leafed through the dozen or so pages.

"That whole situation was terrible!" Ms. Percival recalled. "Colleen Thomas, the little girl who died, had just celebrated her fifteenth birthday. I was told by the other students that she was really a good girl who had never tried drugs before and had only done so that night at the urging of a few of her friends."

"That always seems to be the way with kids."

"The friends who Colleen was hanging out with that night will have to live with the tragedy for the rest of their lives."

"Any other night," Everdell commented, "she would have likely survived the experiment. As I'm sure you remember, a bad batch of Ecstasy took its toll across the city and in some parts of the United

States that weekend. A dozen or so people in Toronto died and many ended up in the hospital. Seven young students in a number of high schools scattered across the city died and a few other kids suffered brain damage."

"Here are the address and phone numbers for Mr. and Mrs. Thomas. As I recall, Colleen had a younger brother and sister. I think she was the oldest child."

"I assume you went to the funeral and had some contact with the family at the time of the tragedy. Do you happen to remember how the family members took the death of their daughter? Did they appear to be coping with the tragedy?"

"They were totally devastated at the loss, as anyone would be, because Colleen had always been such a wonderful girl. She had never done anything foolish before that night. I happened to bump into Harold and Margaret Thomas a few weeks ago at a nearby mall and she was expecting another child. It appeared to me that they were moving on with their lives," Ms. Percival explained.

"Do you recall what Mr. Thomas does for a living? Does Mrs. Thomas work outside the home or is she a homemaker?"

"As far as I can remember, Mrs. Thomas is at home and Mr. Thomas has his own rig or truck of some kind. I think he travels to the United States a lot so he's away three or four nights a week."

"That's all of the information I need for now. I want to thank you for your help."

"You mentioned that you are investigating the deaths of the five drug dealers who have been murdered around the city. You should spend lunch hour in our staff room and listen to the opinions about those murders. The teachers at Trudeau would like to personally thank the man who is ridding the streets of those drug pushers."

"They're not the only ones who have expressed that opinion."

* * *

Detective Everdell took Dundas to Highway 427, drove north and caught Highway 401 East to Jane Street. He made it to Pinehurst about ten minutes early, but the principal, Richard McCarthy, was waiting for him when he arrived. They actually bumped into each other in the hall. Mr. McCarthy led him through the main office directly into his own office and closed the door.

"David Packard was really a bright kid with a lot of potential. What happened that night was terrible, not just here at our school, but across the city. As I recall, a number of people in the city died from that same bad drug shipment."

"It certainly was terrible. I need some information about the Packard family and how they took the death of their son. Can you give me some background on the family?"

"I understand that you're wasting taxpayers' money investigating the recent murders of all those drug dealers. The guy should carry on until they're all gone. Most people feel that drugs are far too rampant on our streets and more should be done to stop young people from having access to them."

"Believe me, I've heard that sentiment everywhere I go. However, you and everyone else know that's not the way our system works. Vigilantes can't take the law into their own hands. If they could, a lot of innocent people would likely die too."

"I hear ya'. I didn't know Ed and Karen Packard very well until the tragedy. They took the death of their son pretty much like any other family would under the circumstances. They were devastated and angry at the world," Mr. McCarthy advised.

"Have you had any contact with the family since the funeral?"

"Not really. I called their home two months after it happened to see if there was anything that I could do, or the school could do, and I spoke to Mr. Packard. He declined any help, but he was quite pleasant and thanked me for my call. That was about it."

"So Mr. Packard seemed quite normal at that time?"

"Yes he did. He sounded like the family was trying to put their loss behind them."

"Do you recall what he does for a living?"

"He's an engineer and I think he works for a plastics company north of the city."

"If you would be kind enough to give me whatever information you have, such as their full names, address, phone numbers, place of work, if you have it, etcetera, I'll get out of your hair and let you get back to work."

* * *

After Pinehurst, Everdell headed back to headquarters to sort out his notes while the conversations were fresh in his mind. He would make arrangements to meet with the parents of the two dead teenagers as soon as possible. He also had a few calls to make on other cases that had been ignored recently.

It turned out that Everdell was able to see Ed and Karen Packard early that evening. They spent about an hour discussing the death of their son and the other victims of that terrible weekend. He arranged to meet with Harold and Margaret Thomas the following evening. The interviews brought a lot of pain back into the lives of both families, which really bothered the detective, but he had a job to do. Neither of the interviews made him the least bit suspicious about the fathers and there were no extremely upset brothers or uncles. The two families appeared to be coping with their tragedies as best they could and seemed to be carrying on with their lives.

* * *

Detective Carpenter had spent the last few days going through a similer process dealing with the deaths of the students from Cedarview Secondary School and The Bluffs Collegiate Institute. The principals had been more than cooperative, but came across with the same sentiments about the deaths of the drug dealers that Everdell had heard during his interviews. The people Carpenter spoke to also thought that it was a waste of public money to be chasing a killer who deserved a citation.

The parents and families of the deceased kids seemed to be quite normal in the way in which they had dealt with their tragedies.

There was no indication that any of the parents, relatives or friends had the potential to take the law into their own hands. Carpenter also came up with nothing to help the investigation.

* * *

Three days later, Everdell and Carpenter sat in their office at head-quarters and compared notes and discussed the information they had obtained during their interviews.

"I didn't find anything out of the ordinary in my discussions with the principals or the parents I met," Everdell stated. "Did you have any better luck?"

"No, everyone I spoke to appeared to be quite normal and fairly well adjusted. They seemed to have put their lives back in order and I had no indication of any extreme hatred of drug dealers or anyone else. The deaths were a tragic part of their lives that they wanted to put behind them."

"Everyone I talked to thought the oyster-shucking killer was doing the community a service and should keep up the good work. I couldn't believe it," Everdell added.

"I found the same sentiments too. Where do we go from here?"

"I guess we keep digging. I still have a real gut feeling that the Stevie Shackleton murder has more to do with this than any of the rest of them. I think that we are going to find the key to all of the murders at Medford."

CHAPTER NINETEEN

After Paul had located Rousinsky's Mercedes parked in front of one of the most beautiful homes on Dunvegan Street, he left Hamilton. He had a busy day planned in the east end of Toronto which was an hour and a half away during the morning rush hour. Paul knew that the Jamaican drug distributor, Ruffus Allan, lived in Scarborough. He decided to find him as he passed through the city on his way home. The drug dealer's pool hall hangout was just off Highway 401.

The trip into the city was a disaster and it took forever just to get to Oakville, which was only about a third of the way there. The traffic was bumper to bumper. The traffic report on CHFI, by Mad Dog and Billie, advised that there was a three car pile up around Highway 10 and cars were backed up for about ten kilometers. Paul decided to head north on Highway 403 which connected with Highway 401 near the airport, but the traffic was just as bad. He crawled across the north end of the city and finally got to his exit at ten-thirty. His destination was ten minutes south on Victoria Park Avenue to Eglinton.

Just before the oyster-shucking knife had crunched into his cervical vertebrae, Liang Chung had told Paul that Ruffus Allan was his major supplier. He also told him that he hung out at Willie's Billiard Hall on the second floor of the Golden Mile Plaza. Paul knew exactly where the pool hall was located. He recalled that when he was a kid, one of the great American Billiard Champions, Willie Mosconi, had put on an exhibition there and that it had been named after him.

It was too early in the day to start shooting pool, so Paul pulled into the mall parking lot and found a restaurant. He took his time and read the morning paper while he had brunch. At twelve-thirty, he headed for the pool hall.

* * *

Willie's Billiard Hall was a huge room with forty tables of varying sizes. Most were four by eights, all with different colors of felt. Many tables had numbered balls and were ready for Spots and Stripes or Nine Ball games to begin. Some were set up for Snooker with fifteen red and six colored balls. About a third of the tables were busy.

Paul's eyes went directly to the far corner opposite the main entrance. Two black men were shooting pool and four brothers were watching. They were dressed *cool* in bright colors and four of the six wore those pull-on knitted hats that covered all their hair. It was easy to pick out the guy in charge. As soon as Paul saw him, he thought, *Dat gotta be da man!* He sat on a stool at the bar and ordered a bottle of Canadian. As he sucked it back, right out of the bottle, a guy sitting near him spoke.

"How about a couple of games of Spots and Stripes?"

"Sure, why not. I'm Gord." Paul extended his hand. "What are we playing for?"

"Ben," the guy said as they locked hands. "How about five bucks a game?"

"Great! You call it for the break," Paul said as he tossed a *Looney* into the air.

"Heads! . . . my break!" Ben answered as they walked towards the nearest table.

Ben made two balls right off the break, one spot and one stripe, so he had his choice of which ball to shoot next. He chose solids and sank two more before he missed and turned the table over to Gord. Paul sank one easy shot and missed the next one on purpose. He had played a lot of pool over the years and rarely lost.

"Ben, do you play here a lot?"

"Yeah, I live in the neighborhood and I'm in here most afternoons when I work the four to twelve shift down at General Electric on Warden."

"This seems to be a busy place. What's with the group of black guys down there in back corner? Are they regulars?"

"Everyone who plays here knows them. Stay away from those guys. They do business out of here all the time, if ya' know what I mean. I've heard that they're major dealers. Also, they're not good losers if you happen to beat them shooting pool."

"I heard one of them call one of the others Ruffus. What kind of a name is that?"

"They're all members of a Jamaican gang of some kind and the one they call Ruffus is the leader. I think his last name is Alin or Allan or something."

"Which guy is called Ruffus?" Paul asked to make sure.

"Don't be starin' at them because it doesn't take much to piss them off and they don't mind startin' trouble. He's the one in the purple shirt with the matching hat."

"Thanks for your advice. I'll stay the hell away from them," Paul said as he sank two more balls and missed the next shot. "Do they hang around here much?"

"This is their main place. I've been in here lots of afternoons and evenings and they've been here almost every time. Somebody said that they have some money in the place, but I don't know if there's any truth to that story."

Paul missed the next shot and set Ben up for the win. He sank the remaining solids without any trouble. Ben won the next game too.

"They were good games, but I've got to hit the road. Here's the ten I owe you and maybe you'll let me get it back the next time I drop in here."

"Be glad to anytime. It was nice meetin' ya'."

Paul paid for his beer and for the table since he had lost the games. He waved to Ben and left the pool hall.

Paul decided that he didn't have to hang around to find out where Ruffus actually lived because Ben had said that he was at the pool hall everyday, so he hit the road. In no time, Paul was back on Highway 401 on his way to Beer Lake. He had gathered all of the information that he needed about the last two men on his list. He needed to get home to make some serious plans to dispose of those pieces of garbage as soon as possible.

* * *

The fall weather was phenomenal. Beer Lake was quiet and the surface was like glass because the other cottagers had closed their places for the winter. The calm water reflected the surrounding tree-lines and hills and different bird and animal sounds resonated through the surrounding woods. The weather was crisp and cool with the sun high in a light blue sky. For the next couple of days, Paul kept busy around the property and continued his work-outs. He also thought about what his next move would be in his personal fight against the drug traffickers.

He decided to make a plan and stick to it, so he wouldn't do something stupid and get into trouble. His plan put Vito Morelli at the top of the list because he had supplied Steven Shackleton. He decided to go back to Woodbridge and get better acquainted with him. Paul knew where he lived and could find out fairly quickly what haunts he frequented. It would be easier to track Morelli on weekdays, so early Friday morning, he got into his car and headed to that small community north of the city.

Just after eight o'clock, Paul drove slowly to the end of Deercreek Court, turned around at the turning circle, and went back toward the main thoroughfare, Highway 7. As he passed Morelli's house, he noticed that both the BMW and the Mercedes were parked in the driveway. Paul pulled into the small strip plaza across the highway from the Deercreek exit and parked so he could see the intersection. He slipped into a nearby Starbucks, grabbed a coffee and returned to his car. He waited for the Morelli cars to leave Deercreek and hoped that Vito Morelli would be driving one of them.

At eight-thirty, the Beamer stopped at the highway, and turned toward Paul. He was about to follow it, but quickly realized that the driver was a woman. She was alone in the BMW. Paul sat back and continued to sip his coffee. Half an hour later, the white Mercedes, V12 Convertible stopped at the highway and turned in the opposite direction. He could tell there was a man behind the wheel and assumed that it was Morelli. He pulled out onto Highway 7 and followed at a discreet distance.

The sports car went into a Petro Canada station a few minutes later, so Paul drove on by and stopped on the roadside among some parked cars. It wasn't long before Morelli headed back the way he had come toward the downtown business area of the community. Paul carefully made a U-turn and followed.

Morelli parked the Mercedes in front of an Italian restaurant called Papa Mario's so Paul stopped short and parked on the same side of the street. He watched as a short, stocky, broad shouldered Italian, with dark hair, got out of his car and walked toward a sign advertising, *The Best Breakfast In Woodbridge*. The man bounded up the front steps of the restaurant, two at a time, and disappeared inside. After a good five minutes, Paul walked nonchalantly toward the establishment. As he entered, he glanced toward the last booth on the right and saw the back of Morelli's head. He was seated and talking to three other swarthy-complexioned men. Paul passed by a number of stools in front of the bar to the left and chose one near the booth where the men were seated. He sat down with his back to them, but he could hear their conversation.

As Paul sat down, a waitress took the breakfast order from the men behind him. A waiter behind the counter approached Paul for his order.

"Coffee?"

"Black, please, with three eggs, over-easy, Canadian bacon and brown toast."

"Coming right up," the guy said as he placed a mug of coffee on the counter.

Paul settled in and tried to look as nonchalant as he possibly could. He reached for the Toronto Sun that was lying on the counter nearby and began to scan it. He automatically turned to the daily Sunshine Girl. Women had been on Paul's mind much more lately. As he perused the paper, he focused on what the guys in the booth were talking about. They changed from English to Italian with ease.

"*Paesanos, we gotta set a date for the Lauderdale week or we're not gonna get down there,*" the man opposite Morelli commented. "*Vito, when can you get away?*"

"*The week after next and Luigi said his place is available. I think that's American Thanksgiving so there'll be all kinds of pussy around that week,*" Morelli answered.

"*Vito, that week's good for me,*" a third man answered.

"*Me too,*" said the fourth.

"*Then it's settled. The trip to Fort Lauderdale is U.S. Thanksgiving Week,*" the first man who spoke confirmed. "*We'll all leave a week from Saturday.*"

"*I'll call Luigi later today and tell him we'll take his condo on the Galt Ocean Mile for that week. It is fairly central and big enough for all of us,*" Morelli said.

"*Vito, be sure to do it today so he doesn't give it away to someone else. You said you have to talk to him anyway,*" the guy beside him added.

"*I'm lookin' forward to hangin' out around Shooters. Remember how many broads were there last year, especially for those bikini contests that they hold in that bar next door,*" Morelli reminded them. "*I think it's called Bootleggers.*"

Paul ate his breakfast and pretended to read the Sun while the men talked, periodically in Italian and then in English, about their holiday the year before. They only talked about fun things and did not discuss any illegal businesses in a public place. They chatted about all of their plans for American Thanksgiving that fell on the Thursday, two weeks away. Paul got no information to indicate that Morelli's friends or business associates were in the drug trafficking business as well.

As Paul finished breakfast, he thought about Florida and the fact that he hadn't visited Fort Lauderdale in years. He had been there many times and knew all the places that the men talked about. Past clients had owned condos on the Galt Ocean Mile at the north end of Lauderdale beach. Paul knew Shooters well. The more he thought about Morelli's trip to Florida, he thought that might be where they should meet.

The men were still eating breakfast when Paul left. He felt very comfortable with the thoughts that were going through his mind since he had listened to the men's plans. As he pulled out into the traffic and headed east toward Beer Lake, he formulated a plan of his own. Paul knew that the police were working hard to solve the five recent murders of drug dealers in Toronto. It was time for a change of venue. There was no reason why he couldn't be in Fort Lauderdale for the week of American Thanksgiving too.

CHAPTER TWENTY

Everdell and Carpenter spent a lot of time in their room at headquarters where all the evidence on The Oyster-Shucking Murders was kept under lock and key. The room was a mess. The tables that had been pulled together to make one large area were scattered with files, reports and papers. The blackboard had so many chalk marks, underlines and arrows overlapping and going in all directions, it could hardly be read. Dirty coffee cups were scattered around and some of the papers were stained with spillage. The frustrated detectives had shuffled and reshuffled through all the evidence they had collected over the past several weeks. They were going nowhere fast and felt like they had hit another dead end.

"Damn it! Here we are again. We've talked to everyone we can think of about these murders and haven't come up with a damn thing," Everdell snarled.

"You're right, Graham. We've done about as much as we can and have absolutely nothing to go on. The only thing I can suggest is that we clean up this dump and make sure that all of the pieces of evidence are in the right files. Then let's put them in sequence and go through them again piece by piece."

"All right, Jack, but let's get rid of most of this shit on the blackboard. We'll keep the key stuff and just rearrange it, then maybe, as we go through the files again, something might jump out at us. We'll list each murder in sequence and jot down all the evidence and try to piece it all together one more time."

"If we're going to basically start all over and take the time to go through the evidence again, let's get Speer in here and make him sit through it with us. Maybe a new set of eyes will pick up something that we've been overlooking."

"Good idea. I'll go and talk to Billy," Everdell said as he headed for the door.

Forty minutes later, the small room where the detectives had been spending all of their time looked totally different. There were five neat piles of folders and papers on the tables that each related to a different murder. They were in a time sequence, from left to right, starting with Steven Shackleton, then down the table with Edward Firestone, Liang Chung, Clarence Jones and Darvel Rastone. The blackboard was divided into equal areas with a name, date, time and place with space underneath for the evidence relating to each murder to be clearly listed in a proper sequence.

As Everdell put the finishing touches on the five areas of the board, Bill Speer walked into the room carrying a coffee.

"I've told everyone out in front not to bother us until I surface," Speer said and sat down. "Let's take a look at each murder and see what the hell you guys have got."

"We've been through all this stuff ten times and have come up with very little. We've interviewed all the witnesses and family members of each victim and can't come up with any evidence to point us in any direction," Carpenter explained.

"Billy, I really think that we've hit another dead end," Everdell confirmed.

"Well," Speer answered, "you've got two hours of my undivided attention so lay it on me and let's see if I can be of some help."

"The thing that keeps coming back at us is that first murder. Steven Shackleton was killed downtown, moved to Medford and the bag of money was dropped off at the Sick Kid's. It was different from the rest," Carpenter commented.

"That was explained by the killer when he phoned me. He basically said that he had moved the body of the drug dealer to the school where Shackleton had caused the deaths of two students and hospitalized another as a message to us. He thought that we would figure out why that specific drug dealer had been targeted."

"If those assholes in Narcotics would share more information about the homicides they investigate, you guys would have put it all together long ago," Speer added.

"Even with that explanation," Carpenter commented, "there must be a more significant reason why Shackleton and Medford were first on the hit parade."

"Carry on. Maybe I'll see something you guys have missed," Speer said.

CHAPTER TWENTY-ONE

Five days after Paul's first up-close-and-personal encounter with Vito Morelli and his buddies at Papa Mario's Restaurant, he returned to Woodbridge for another two day visit. He wanted to confirm that the trip to Lauderdale was on schedule. Paul had to stay overnight because he had been unable to locate Morelli the first day. He went by the drug kingpin's house in the morning and the Mercedes wasn't in the driveway. He drove around the small community, starting at Papa Mario's, to see if he could spot the car somewhere, but that didn't happen. He spent most of the day hanging around the town, but Morelli never did show up. He stayed at a small, dump of a motel on Highway 7, at the east end of town, that even offered hourly rates.

The next morning, Paul was more successful. The Mercedes was in the driveway on Deercreek Court, and after a short wait in the plaza, the sports car came out of the cul-de-sac and turned down the highway toward the business section and Papa Mario's. Paul followed Morelli to his favorite restaurant and sat on a stool nearby. He ate breakfast while Morelli and his cronies finalized their plans for their boys' week away in Fort Lauderdale. They confirmed, partly in English and partly in Italian, that they would all be flying out of Pearson International Airport on the Saturday afternoon, via West Jet, a charter airline that flew to Florida a couple of times a day.

* * *

Later that Thursday afternoon back at Beer Lake, Paul considered alternative ways to get to Florida to minimize the risk. He had three options. He could cross the border by car at Gananoque, east of Lake Ontario, and drive south on Highway 81, The American Legion Highway, through the eastern states. That would take close to thirty hours each way in his old car, so he decided that it would be better to fly.

He had two choices to hit the friendly skies. He could catch an Air Canada flight from Toronto direct to Lauderdale, or alternatively, he could cross the border at Niagara Falls or Fort Erie and fly out of Buffalo. Southwest and Jet Blue had regular flights. The more he thought about it, he felt that the Buffalo route would be safer for two reasons. One, he could bump into someone he knew from his past life in Toronto and that wouldn't likely happen in Buffalo. Two, he wouldn't have to go through customs and immigration line-ups and answer a lot of stringent questions in Buffalo.

Paul packed for a week in the sun and shaved off his goatee. He left his mustache in place because he would be traveling as Gordon William Thoburn. The birth certificate had no picture but the passport and driver's license had a picture of Paul with a full mustache so he wanted to look the same as his documentation at the border crossing.

As he gathered all of his things together, Paul looked at the box of oyster-shucking knives in the corner of his living room. He briefly thought about taking one with him, but soon realized that would be a stupid thing to do. He could buy one in Florida. He was actually looking forward to spending a few days in Fort Lauderdale because it was always a fun place. There were lots of people, many bars and restaurants, and usually great weather. After all, Florida is *The Sunshine State*.

* * *

The following day, Paul drove across the top of the city once more. It would have been faster for him to take Highway 407, a toll road, but he didn't want his license plate photographed and recorded. He caught Highway 403 west of Pearson International, and went south to the Queen Elizabeth Way, which looped around the west end of Lake Ontario and on into the Wine Region of southern Ontario in the Niagara Peninsula. He eventually pulled into the long-term parking at Casino Niagara in downtown Niagara Falls. He planned to leave his car there for a week or so.

He carried his suitcase to the main foyer of the casino and used a pay phone to call the *Airport Express*, a local company that specialized in pick-ups and deliveries at the airports in Toronto, Hamilton and Buffalo. Their vans cross the border at Queenston, Niagara Falls and Fort Erie several times a day with travelers from both Canada and the United States who use the various airports for connections. There were usually half a dozen passengers with luggage and the immigration officers were used to them coming and going, so they only asked for identification, where the travelers were going and how long they were going to stay. The crossings were usually informal and straightforward.

The large van, with Paul and four other passengers, was waved through after the usual cursory inspections. It took half-an-hour to get to the Buffalo Niagara International Airport and the driver's first stop on arrival was right beside the kiosk for Jet Blue. It only took Paul a few minutes to pay for his ticket, check his bags, and clear security. He had a couple of scotches in a nearby lounge while he waited for his flight to leave and chatted with an attractive redhead on her way to Chicago. Even though he still missed Liz terribly, he had been noticing other women more regularly.

* * *

The temperature in Fort Lauderdale was in the high seventies, without a cloud to be seen. Paul rented a white Lincoln Town Car and drove directly to the Marriott Hotel on S.E. 17th Street, in the south part of the city. He checked in for three nights with an option that, if the weather was good, he might stay for the whole week. He paid extra for a poolside room on the main level, so he would be near all the action on the patio. The upscale complex was his favorite place in Fort Lauderdale. It was right on the inland waterway, had a great secluded marina that held boats up to about seventy feet long and an absolutely beautiful pool area with a gazebo bar with a grass roof, hot tub and palm trees. The dozens of comfortable chaise lounges were often used by beautiful women in bikinis. The hotel had an excellent restaurant and a nightclub that was one of the local hot spots.

Paul spent the rest of Friday afternoon around the pool bar and enjoyed a quiet dinner in the Witches Watch, the restaurant in the hotel. He had only one drink in the club and ended up going to bed at a reasonable time so he would be well rested the next day. First thing in the morning, Paul drove to the downtown business area of Lauderdale, inland and away from the tourist section on the ocean, and found a huge hardware store. He found exactly what he was looking for; an oyster-shucking knife just like the ones he had back home. After shopping, he went back to his hotel, lounged by the pool, sipped cocktails and took in the sun. As he sat at the Gazebo Bar and socialized, he wondered if Vito Morelli and his buddies from Canada had arrived in the sunny south yet.

Back in Woodbridge, Paul had heard Morelli and the others mention Shooters as being one of their favorite hang-outs. He knew that the whole group would show up there for a full shift on Sunday afternoon because the weekend bikini contests were second to none.

Paul woke up early Sunday morning and ordered fruit, bacon and eggs and whole wheat toast from room service. He relaxed as he ate and watched the sports channel. At noon, he headed out to the pool area and found a lounge chair close to the bar. He had a short swim to cool off and then wandered over to the hut and ordered a strawberry Daiquiri to take back to his lounge. He spent the rest of the time looking at the eye-candy around the pool. Just after two o'clock, he went back to his room.

Paul had never had any urges for the opposite sex since Liz had passed away, but just recently there had been a resurgence of his interest in women and the guilt that he had experienced in the past was no longer there. He found himself thinking that perhaps it was time to move on.

After a quick shower, he dressed in a sports shirt, shorts, sneakers and a Forty Niners peaked cap. He put his dark sunglasses on his sunburned face and stood in front of the mirror as he got ready to head for north Lauderdale. He thought he would fit right in with all the other tourists. Even if by chance, he bumped into someone he knew from Toronto, he would never be recognized. In the classy reception area of the hotel, he had the doorman hail him a cab. He knew he would be having a few cocktails and didn't want to drive the Lincoln. The bikini contest usually didn't start until around four and he knew that Morelli and his friends would be there for the show.

* * *

The cab went north on N. Atlantic Blvd. through the tourist and beach area of Fort Lauderdale which was a two mile stretch of sand and bars that attracted young people. It was party central for the thousands of guys and gals in bathing suits. There were advertisements all along the strip, touting bikini contests and cheap drinks.

About a mile north of the strip, the cabby turned left off the ocean highway and drove three blocks toward the inland waterway. Shooters was a huge complex and a very busy meeting place for booze and good food. It was located on the east side of the inland waterway and was rumored to be owned by Canadians. The huge complex was twice the size it had been originally because the owners had purchased Bootleggers, a similar spot right next door, with it's own poolside entertainment. There were hundreds of feet of boat dockage, three or four eating areas and four or five bars.

Paul got dropped off at the front door on the valet parking ramp and walked directly inside and back toward the water. The first level had a round bar to the left and an eating area that sat about a hundred people, which was pretty well full. He went down about six steps to the ground level where the main bar, patio and more casual eating sections were located along the water. The docking area was full of boats that were rafted off each other, four or five deep. The music was booming and the place was really rocking. He could tell that the pool area next door was starting to fill up in anticipation of the bikini contest. The place was packed.

The stand-up bar in the middle of the restaurant, on the edge of the patio, was the best place for him to be until he got his bearings, so Paul stopped on the water side of it and ordered a Sea Breeze. He enjoyed the vodka, cranberry and grapefruit juice, with lots of ice. He decided earlier that he wouldn't drink much that afternoon because he had to keep his wits about him. From where he stood, he could observe most of the restaurant and the docking area. There were about three hundred people in his sights, but he didn't see the group from Toronto. As he finished his first cocktail, he ordered a double in a tall plastic cup to take with him to the pool area at Bootleggers, next door, because recent announcements by the Master of Ceremonies had suggested that the bikini contest was about to begin. As he squeezed his way through the crowd, he kept his eyes open for his Woodbridge friends.

There were a hundred and fifty people crowded in, shoulder to shoulder, and a third of them were women. The first arrivals had taken the best seats around the pool on the relatively small patio. Paul inched his way through the bodies and up onto the small, raised wooden deck of the poolside patio bar. He was squeezed in against the wooden railing and had a perfect view of the walkway over the middle of the pool where all of the action would take place. He scanned the pool area and crowd of partiers and spotted the Morelli group seated at a front table on the far side of the pool. They must have arrived at the complex early to have one of the tables right up front.

All of the women in the contest were quite spectacular; young, tanned and well-built. The bathing suits they wore were almost non-existent. Eight of them lined up next to the Master of Ceremonies, a local disc jockey, whose sexist remarks made the whole crowd hoot and holler. Paul had a feeling that the owners of the bar had paid a number of the gals to enter the contest because they were all absolutely gorgeous. There was also prize money for the one the audience chose as the winner.

The announcer sent the first gal on her way. She walked all around the pool once, with a bounce in her step, so that everything moved at the same time. She squeezed by close to all of the guys in the front row. She crossed the bridge from one side of the pool to the other and stopped in the middle to do a little routine. The crowd cheered as she moved back and forth across the bridge with a spring in her step that made the bare cheeks of her ass move perfectly and her large breasts bounce up and down. After a final turn in the middle, as onlookers whistled and screamed, she walked back to the Master of Ceremonies.

As the performances continued, Paul couldn't help but notice the girls. He also kept an eye on his friends from Canada. They were right in the middle of all of the excitement. The girls had to brush by them. Vito Morelli and his three friends were seated together enjoying the show. They were dripping with gold neck-chains and bracelets and each of them wore a couple of diamond rings that sparkled in the sunshine. They were dressed in summer shirts and shorts and fit right in with everyone. Their table was covered with glasses of drinks and they seemed to be enjoying themselves.

As the contest progressed, the cheering crowd continued to drink and the noise got louder and louder. When all the contestants had completed their walks, the announcer had them line up on the bridge. He then walked along and put his hand above each contestant's head and asked the audience to cheer for their favorite. The loudness of the cheers would decide the winner. As usual, two of the most well-built girls tied, so all the other contestants had to leave the bridge and stand back on the side of the pool.

Each finalist had to do another walk around the pool, as sensually as she could, to see if they could make the audience scream and yell loud enough to make her the winner. Paul thought that they were both Playmate material. As the announcer pointed at the blonde, the audience clapped, hooted and screamed so loud that Paul was sure she had won. When the announcer pointed at the brunette, she put her arms in the air and jumped up and down, like a boxer who had just won a fight, and her silicone twins popped out of the top of her bikini and bounced around in all directions. The noise from the crowd was almost deafening. That afternoon, blondes did not have more fun. The dark haired beauty won the big bucks.

As soon as the contest ended, Paul exited the pool bar from the back side, well away from the Canadians. He made his way back to the stand-up bar in the main part of Shooters. Everyone usually moved over there when the bikini contest was over. He wanted to be there before his buddies from Woodbridge, so he would just be another partier and blend right in with the crowd.

A few minutes later, Morelli and his friends stepped right up to the end of the long bar, six feet from Paul, and ordered a round of drinks. Paul's adrenalin started pumping when he saw them coming toward him and for some unknown reason, Paul quickly introduced himself to two girls from New York as *Jack Randall* and started a conversation so he would look nonchalant. His nerves slowly settled down. Even though he was talking to his new friends, he was paying close attention to the men at the end of the bar and listening to their every word. He finished his drink, so he ordered another Sea Breeze and included his new friends in the round.

"What do you do up north?" Paul asked the gorgeous, well built redhead, who had introduced herself as Laurie Crawford.

"I'm a stockbroker with a firm in downtown Manhattan and I live in Greenwich Village fairly close to where I work."

Paul turned his attention to the attractive blonde who had also introduced herself, "And how about you, Cress? What a great name!"

"I had a great time at Octobers last night," Morelli was saying. "That nurse I met wants me to meet her at eleven tonight at her place after she gets off work."

"Thanks. I'm a lawyer with one of the top labor firms in the state and live and work in the city near Laurie," Cress answered. "What about you?"

"I thought that you were gonna have dinner with us at Yesterdays tonight?" A friend of Morelli's asked.

"I was an estate lawyer but I gave it up to pursue other interests," Paul said.

"I'm still going with you. After dinner, I'm gonna leave you guys and I'm gonna get laid," Morelli answered. "I won't leave you guys until close to eleven o'clock."

"So Jack, where are you staying and when are you going back to Canada," Laurie asked with the kind of smile that Paul thought showed some interest in him.

"I'm staying at the Marriott in south Lauderdale, over on S.E. 17th Street, and I'm planning to stay until next weekend if the weather's good."

"Don't get hooked up with a broad so early in the week," one of Morelli's friends offered. "There're lots of them around that look like those broads in the bikini contest."

"What part of Lauderdale are you gals staying in," Paul asked glancing at both of them.

"We arrived yesterday and we're here for twelve days. We're just at the Ramada on Galt Ocean Mile," Laurie answered. "It has a beautiful beach on the ocean that's just great if it isn't too windy."

"That's just north of here, where all of the condos have been built right on the ocean," Paul commented, remembering that Morelli's gang was staying there too.

"Don't worry," Morelli went on, "I'm not gonna fall in love. I'm just gonna go to Boca Raton, bang her and tomorrow she's history. I'll be right back out there on the prowl with you guys."

"Yeah. The Ramada is about halfway along the strip," Laurie answered and then asked. "Jack, why don't you join us for dinner tonight? Cress and I don't know where we're going yet, but you're welcome to join us."

"Damn it! I would really like to join you two for the evening," Paul said glancing at Laurie, "but I've been invited out for dinner by a friend. He and his wife are going back to Canada in the morning. Why don't we get together for drinks tomorrow at the Ramada or at the Marriott? My hotel has a beautiful pool area and patio bar that would be a great place to hang out and I'll even buy lunch if you're interested."

"Let's have one more drink and then we'll go back to the condo and get ready for dinner,"Morelli said to his cronies."I can almost taste the food at Yesterdays. Those twenty ounce New York strips are fantastic."

"That sounds all right with us, Jack," Laurie answered looking at Cress. "We'll come over to the Marriott around noon and we can just have a relaxing afternoon around the pool."

"I'll be on a lounge chair right by the gazebo bar at the pool, so come right out there when you arrive. If you have to change, you can use my room because it opens onto the patio. It looks like we're ready to get outta here," Paul said as he noticed that the bar was starting to clear out and the numbers were dwindling.

Paul left enough money on the bar to cover the tab and walked out with the gals, right past Morelli and his group, and they didn't even look his way. He followed Laurie and Cress to the main entrance of Shooters where they said their goodbyes, hailed a cab and disappeared. Paul went back inside and stood at the rear bar just inside the door and ordered a beer. He could see the guys from Woodbridge from where he was and would know exactly when they decided to leave Shooters.

* * *

Fifteen minutes later, the men left the main bar area and wandered toward the front door. Paul finished his beer and paid as they walked by the smaller bar where he was standing. He reached the main entrance just in time to see Morelli and his friends get into a Cadillac on the valet ramp. As the Caddy pulled away, the doorman waved for a waiting cab and Paul slipped into the backseat and gave the driver directions.

"Head north to the Galt Ocean Mile. I'm looking for some friends who are staying there and if I drive by, I might recognize the building where they stayed last year."

As Paul's cab pulled out onto N. Atlantic Blvd. and turned left, he caught a glimpse of Morelli's Caddy ahead. It had turned right onto Galt Ocean Mile. As it continued along the row of exclusive, high-rise condominiums right on the ocean, Paul's cab driver unknowingly followed the Canadians.

"Slow down a bit. I can't seem to remember what building I was in last year."

As Paul's cab slowed, he saw Morelli's car turn into one of the nicer buildings called the *Galt Ocean Club* and stop at the front door. Paul now knew where they were staying. He had his cab continue north past the Ramada where Laurie and Cress were staying. At the Howard Johnson's at E. Atlantic Blvd., the driver turned south on the ocean highway and traveled along the strip where all the young people were partying. The cab then took Seabreeze Blvd. west to S.E. 17th Street and the Marriott. Paul was very happy because he not only knew where Morelli and his friends were staying, he also knew where they were dining that evening.

It was close to six o'clock when Paul walked into his room at the Marriott. As he thought about the afternoon events, he was excited about the prospect of Morelli going off on his own to meet a nurse later that evening. He was going to leave his buddies behind. It was a stroke of luck. Paul hadn't imagined that an opportunity to meet Morelli, one-on-one, would present itself so early in the week. He had figured that getting him alone, away from his entourage of tough guys, would have taken a lot more planning. He decided that his best opportunity to do what he had come to Florida to do might be that evening. He would exact his revenge on Morelli that night if the opportunity presented itself. The more Paul thought about the evening and Morelli's plans, he knew that he had to be ready. He was glad that he had controlled his drinking during the afternoon.

As soon as Paul got to his room, he thought about dinner because he hadn't eaten much all day. He thought to himself, *If those fuckin' drug traffickers can go out for a nice dinner at one of my favorite restaurants, so can I!* He had a feeling that the Italians wouldn't go for dinner until around eight and that they would likely take their time eating and drinking. He called Yesterdays from his room and made a dinner reservation for seven-thirty in the name he had been traveling under, *Gord Thoburn*. The more Paul thought about his previous visits to the excellent restaurant, the hungrier he got.

Paul regretted that he had introduced himself to the girls from New York as *Jack Randall* because that was the name that he was saving to use after he retired from killing drug traffickers. The comment had been made in haste, in a very nervous and excited state, as Morelli and his three friends had approached the bar. He had quickly wanted to blend in with the two women in the crowd. It was another wake-up call. He had to think more clearly and be more careful. As he thought about it, the New Yorkers could call him *Jack*. No harm done.

As he showered and got dressed for the evening, his thoughts changed from food to something much more exciting. Laurie kept coming into his mind. The two of them had clicked and she had shown some interest in him while they talked. Paul was looking forward to spending the next day with her.

* * *

Yesterdays, one of Paul's favorite eating places in Lauderdale, was a huge three story building that looked like an old mansion located on the west side of the inland waterway just off Oakland Park Blvd. It too had docking facilities for large yachts. There were two floors of dining, with a couple of small bars where dinner guests waited for their tables, and on the third floor, there was another bar and night club. The upper bar had a huge buffet of free finger foods during happy hour. Another room had a dancing area that featured middle of the road music supplied by a disc jockey.

Shortly after seven-thirty, Paul had the valet park the Lincoln and he stepped inside the main door. He was led to a table for two on the lower level of the restaurant along the north side of the building. From there, he could see the main entrance and anyone coming and going. He ordered one glass of California Merlot, a garden salad with blue cheese dressing and a twelve ounce Texas Longhorn filet. He had finished his salad and his steak was just being set on his table when he spotted the Morelli group being led to a table at the far back of the large restaurant. They had arrived at the expected time.

Paul took his time eating and enjoyed the excellent steak. The place was full and the usual dinner buzz filled the room. He only had one glass of wine with dinner because he would be driving and he wanted to keep his wits about him. Paul finished eating shortly after nine o'clock and decided to go to the upper level bar because he knew that Morelli wouldn't be leaving his buddies until at least ten thirty or so. He had some time to waste. The stairway to the upper level went right through the lower dining areas so most of the tables could be seen from one place or another. It didn't take long for Paul to spot the foursome seated by the windows overlooking the waterway. They were in the middle of their dinner and seemed to be enjoying their food and having a good time. Paul continued up to the third level bar and ordered a sparkling water on ice.

* * *

Forty-five minutes later, Paul was sitting quietly behind the wheel of the Lincoln, in a parking area on the street across from the restaurant, while he waited for Morelli to show. He soon came out of the main door and the valet hailed a cab for him. Paul decided to follow him to wherever he was going and see what developed. It might be the only opportunity to get him away from his friends. With a little luck, they would have a chance to meet. The Lincoln followed the cab inland to Federal 1, one of the main Florida highways that runs parallel to the coast, and then twenty minutes north to Boca Raton. The cab, with the Lincoln a respectable distance behind, turned left on N.E. Mizner Blvd. and into the large parking lot of a town house development called Palmetto Estates. While the passenger paid the cab driver for the ride, Paul parked near the first building and turned off the lights and engine.

The townhouse development had been built like a *U* with two rows of about twenty houses each facing the other about two hundred feet apart with another dozen at the far end. The center of the development was a park filled with a mix of trees and shrubbery which offered some privacy because the wooded areas partially blocked the view from one side of the complex to the other.

Morelli walked down the sidewalk in front of the townhouses on the west side and Paul quietly paralleled him on the east side. As the two men walked, Paul kept an eye on his target through the breaks in the trees and bushes. Morelli stopped and knocked on the door of what turned out to be the thirteenth townhouse and was let inside. Paul thought, *Bad Luck!* He found a very secluded spot in the trees and bushes, halfway between the nurse's home and the parking lot. He knew that Morelli would come back the same way after his one-night-stand. Paul was invisible as he waited in the shadows and darkness of the shrubbery.

At four-thirty in the morning, the nurse called a cab to pick her friend up in the parking lot of the townhouse development. The Cabbie arrived and after twenty minutes, he got tired of waiting for his fare and pulled his empty cab out onto N.E. Mizner Blvd. and disappeared into the night.

Morelli didn't make it through the park.

CHAPTER TWENTY-TWO

Everdell and Carpenter spent more than the two hours allotted with Bill Speer. They went through all the evidence that had been collected in relation to the five murders and painfully sorted through all the official reports and other documentation. Everything they knew about the victims was listed on the blackboard. They noted dates, times, locations and the names of witnesses. The men tried to find one small piece of evidence that had been overlooked, something that was missing, or a new clue that would spur on their investigation. They came up with absolutely nothing. Bill Speer felt that the two detectives had done everything by the book and that the evidence was just not there.

The following week, the detectives continued to work on other files in their caseload, but every day or so, they met in their private room where all the evidence was kept for what everyone, including the public, now called *The Oyster-Shucking Murders*. They sat there and chatted, shuffled through the papers and looked at the notes on the blackboard. They bounced ideas and theories off of each other. They were looking for something, anything, that might catch their attention and give them a break in the case.

"I'm still really convinced that the Stevie Shackleton murder and Medford are the keys to this whole bloody mess," Everdell said, thinking out loud.

"We've been through all this before," Carpenter said almost tired of the scenario.

"The murder took place in his own home, and then for some reason, the body was moved to Medford. Was it just to give us a clue as to why Stevie was a target for murder? The killer thought that we would remember the previous drug related deaths at that school and figure out why Stevie was killed. To top it off, the killer dropped off fifty grand at the Hospital For Sick Children as a donation for the kids. Nothing as strange as those two events happened in any of the other murders."

"You're right!" Carpenter agreed. "But there's another distinguishing feature . . . the oyster-shucking knife was pulled out of Shackleton's neck and plunged into the middle of his forehead! What the hell was that all about?"

"I don't know, but Stevie's murder is definitely more personal."

"What are you thinking?"

"Jack, I have no fuckin' idea what I'm thinking. Stevie was stabbed a second time in the forehead, maybe in a fit of anger, and the killer risked moving his body to another location. He was not afraid to be seen when he dropped the money off at the hospital. There has to be a connection between one of the victims from Medford and the killer."

"That makes sense but we have nothing to go on. Why don't we take another look and see if we can come up with something new."

The men opened the thick Shackleton File and spread out all of the evidence in front of them. They both went through the stack of information, probably for the tenth time, and made new notes on the blackboard. Everything was listed and tied together by arrows. The list of witnesses was expanded to include some people who knew the families of the victims but had never been interviewed.

"We talked to Stevie's girlfriend who lived with him, but she was away at the time of the murder. Her story about being at her parents checked out," Everdell said.

"She couldn't, or wouldn't, tell us very much."

"We talked to June McKenzie, Andrew's mother. He is the kid who is expected to be in extended care for the rest of his life."

"That family seemed to be coping with the tragedy but maybe we should take another look. There might be a boyfriend, uncle or someone else who wants revenge. What if something like that happened to one of your kids?" Carpenter asked.

"You're right, Jack, and I have a fuckin' gun! I guess we should take another look at Mrs. McKenzie's relatives and friends."

"That story about the Taylor kid and his family is terrible. His mother died of cancer a few years before the kid's death and his father committed suicide a year or so later. Did he have any other relatives or close friends that we may have overlooked?"

"We talked to the dead mother's sister, Rebecca Farwell. She was the only living relative on both sides of the family. She had never married," Everdell recalled.

"Yeah, you're right. The father who killed himself a few months ago had no relatives at all."

"Maybe we should take a look at the sister again, but didn't she say that she wasn't as close to Ricky Taylor and his father after her sister died? She didn't seem to have the tenacity to hire someone to revenge the loss of her nephew. Another look will probably lead nowhere," Everdell said as he started to show his frustration.

"Maybe we should talk to some of the father's friends and associates. He was a lawyer at one of the larger law firms downtown," Carpenter suggested as he made notes.

Everdell continued, "The other kid who died at that time was Kenneth Wilson and we met with his folks, Charles and Betty. He was an accountant. They had two other daughters and were a very religious family."

"The principal at the school seemed to think that they had been able to get on with their lives after the death of their only son."

"We had better take a look at the male relatives and we should also make arrangements to speak to Mr. Wilson again and his accounting associates."

"The killer appears to be a man in his mid to late thirties, who is in extremely good shape based on the vague descriptions we got at the hospital and Sweethearts. He has to be a tough bastard too, because he had no trouble handling all of the victims."

"There is the possibility that even though the killer is a man, he could have been hired by a woman!" Everdell thought out loud.

"That could be, Graham. Let's start with the family of the kid in the extended care ward, McKenzies, and then move to the Wilsons. After that we'll go back to Ricky Taylor's aunt. Then we'll find out if Ricky's father had any close friends or law partners who might have spun out and committed these murders."

* * *

Everdell and Carpenter seemed to get new life and renewed enthusiasm as they started to look at the Shackleton murder with a new perspective. They started with the McKenzie family. The police spoke to relatives and neighbors who all felt that the family had coped with the tragedy. Two of Mrs. McKenzie's brothers and a brother-in-law were also interviewed without anything suspicious coming to light. Her work associates passed the tests too.

The detectives turned their attention to the parents of Kenneth Wilson. The couple was quite religious and leaned on their church for support. They interviewed the boy's two uncles, brothers of both the father and the mother, and did some background checks and everything seemed normal. They also did their homework in relation to two of the husband's best friends and accountant partners and didn't come up with anything or anyone suspicious. The only thing that kept surfacing over and over during the interviews was the disgust people expressed when they found out that the police were wasting taxpayers money investigating the murders of the drug dealers.

The detectives interviewed Ricky's aunt once more and another couple who were her best friends. Her friends had been adamant that although she had been devastated, she had put the tragedies behind her. Further background checks revealed no red flags from her past that suggested she would be capable of hiring someone to commit murder. Her mental state had always been normal and she seemed to live an ordinary life.

Everdell and Carpenter made an appointment with the managing partner at Gemmill, Farn. David Gemmill was happy to provide them with a list of the lawyers in the firm who Paul Taylor had associated with when he was alive. He remembered Paul fondly, as a wonderful guy who worked hard and kept to himself. David's relationship with Paul had been mainly business. The other lawyers told the detectives that Paul hadn't socialized much because he was a real family man who doted on his wife and child. They all confirmed that he had been devastated when his wife died of cancer, but thought that he had overcome the months of depression. It was their opinion that the death of his son put him over the edge. Before the detectives left the law firm, they were directed to another of the senior partners, Rod Farn, who was closest to Paul.

"I knew Paul as well as anyone at Gemmill, Farn and I knew his family. Paul and I were not what you would call best friends, but I did socialize with him and Liz a few times a year. I got to know Ricky as he grew up. Paul was a hard-working family man. He truly loved his wife and he always thought of Ricky as a special gift. At the time they married, Liz had been told that she likely wouldn't be able to have children. In fact, Paul almost lost both of them during Ricky's birth, so they were extra special to him."

"We're really trying to find out if Paul had a best buddy, someone who might have been totally devastated when he killed himself. Someone who might want to take the law into his own hands and get even for the loss of his friend," Carpenter said.

"No, Paul was never that close with anyone in the firm or in his personal life. Like I said, he spent a lot of time with Liz and Ricky and did a lot of family oriented things."

"He didn't have a best friend outside the office?" Everdell asked.

"That's right. He was friends with a few of his partners here at the firm, but did little socializing with them. If he wasn't at work, he was at home with Liz and Ricky."

"Thanks for your time, Mr. Farn," Everdell said as he and his partner stood up to leave the well-decorated, spacious office. "If you happen to think of anything that might relate to the Taylors and the murders that we're investigating, please give us a call, no matter how insignificant you think it might be. Our direct line is on the card."

* * *

The policemen had exhausted the list of their additional witnesses and came up with nothing new that would break the case open for them or point them in a new direction. Their investigation of The Oyster-Shucking Murders was at a standstill, so they went back to their other cases. They worked hard on their other investigations, but often found themselves sitting back in their room full of evidence, sorting through papers, looking at the blackboard and bouncing thoughts off of each other.

Things remained at a dead end until mid-week when Bill Speer burst into their room and interrupted their morning coffees. They had been sitting there studying all of the information written on the blackboard. He threw a folded copy of The Toronto Star into the middle of the table. It was folded over to page nine and there was an article that had been circled in black marker. Carpenter could tell from the small headlines that it was about a Canadian who had been killed in Florida.

"I think that you guys might find the news in today's paper kind of interesting! Read that story that I've marked for you!"

"What's it all about?" Carpenter asked as he picked up the paper.

"Just read the bloody thing!"

Carpenter took a few moments as he read the first few paragraphs of the circled story and then started to get excited.

"Jesus Christ! Graham, look at this!" Carpenter exclaimed as he handed the paper to his partner.

Everdell grabbed the paper, turned it around and read the circled article as Carpenter and Speer waited for his response.

"I can't believe it! Vito Morelli! Murdered in Boca Raton, Florida! He's that trafficker from north of the city, Woodbridge, I think. We've been trying to nail his ass for years," Everdell said and was even more surprised as he read on. "They found him dead in the gardens of a townhouse development a couple of days ago. Jesus Christ! A fuckin' oyster-shucking knife!"

CHAPTER TWENTY-THREE

The dawn of another beautiful day filled the eastern sky as Paul pulled into the parking garage at the Marriott. As soon as he got to his room, he poured himself a large scotch on ice, with a little water, and gulped about half of it down. He was feeling great. He excelled in his new vocation and the fact that he had killed one of the major distributors made him feel even better. Paul closed the curtains on the patio door to stop the morning light from entering the room. He adjusted the pillows on his bed and turned on CNN just to calm down a little before he tried to get some sleep.

Paul was relieved that the work part of his trip was over so early in the week. He had thought that it would have been much harder to get Morelli away from his buddies because guys on vacation usually spend a lot of time partying together. He knew that the world was well rid of him. As the events of the evening raced through his mind, he laughed to himself, *I did that piece of shit a favor because I could have killed him before he screwed that nurse!*

It was only Monday and he had completed his mission. He would stay the rest of the week and relax. It had been a long time since he had been in Florida. He looked at his watch and realized that it was six and remembered that Laurie and Cress were coming over around noon. He was looking forward to seeing Laurie. Paul set the alarm for eleven-thirty and turned off the lights and television. He slept like a log.

* * *

Just before noon, Paul left his room through the patio door and left the door unlocked since he would be in and out all afternoon. He ended up in a lounge chair close to the gazebo bar. As he sat there, he felt quite tired and groggy so he dove into the pool and did a couple of laps and then laid back and dried in the heat of another gorgeous day. An attractive waitress came by a couple of times to see if he wanted a cocktail of some kind, but he declined to wait for his friends to arrive.

As he was resting in the sun, he thought about Liz and how much he still missed her. Although he went through a long period when he didn't even notice women, that seemed to be changing. He found himself staring at the attractive women around the pool and admiring their bodies. Maybe it was time for him to start thinking about getting back into the mainstream. At that moment, Laurie and Cress walked across the deck toward him and when he looked at Laurie, a warm feeling passed through his groin. There was something about her that excited him. He liked her.

"Good morning, Jack, or is it afternoon?" Laurie said as the girls approached.

"I think it's just afternoon. You two found the hotel all right?"

"We took a cab," Cress answered. "The guy drove us right down the ocean strip in all the traffic. It took us about forty minutes to get here."

"That's too bad, but you're here now. How about a Strawberry Daiquiri or a Pina Colada to start the day?" Paul asked.

Both of the girls ordered daiquiris, so Paul went to get three of them. They already had their bathing suits on, or what there was of them, underneath their tops. They undressed while Paul was at the gazebo bar. As he waited, he looked back toward them and noticed that they were both in great shape and had fantastic figures. As he watched Laurie strip down to her bikini, he had that feeling again. They both had great tans even though they had only been in Florida for a few days.

They sunned and drank all afternoon and took a dip in the pool each time the heat got too much for them. They had burgers about two o'clock and continued to cocktail the afternoon away. About four or so Cress found herself at the gazebo bar talking to two guys who were in the party mode, so Paul and Laurie were able to spend some time together. They both could tell that there was something special between them. They ended up in the pool, not really hugging, but close together and touching each other a lot.

"I think that I should take you two out for dinner and dancing tonight," Paul said to Laurie who was starting to feel her cocktails.

"That sounds great and we might even get lucky and Cress will get invited out by one of the guys she's talking to over at the bar," Laurie smiled and pulled him closer.

"I think that would be a good thing too."

"Jack, let's both keep our fingers crossed then," she laughed and pulled him close.

They kissed a couple of small kisses while they talked. Paul had to wait a few minutes before he could get out of the pool without being embarrassed, but the party continued. Cress spent a lot of time at the patio bar with her new friends. Periodically, there were bursts of laughter from where they were standing and they all seemed to be having a good time. Paul and Laurie were delighted to be alone. They had fun together just talking, lying in the sun and swimming. Laurie told Paul about her life in New York. She had been divorced for two years and wasn't dating anyone seriously. Paul didn't share a lot of details about his personal life, but did mention that his wife had lost a battle with cancer a few years ago and he hadn't felt like dating since. Laurie thought that it was time he started. It was after four o'clock when Cress came back to them.

"Those guys at the bar are from Atlanta. The one guy has a date tonight and the other guy has invited me out for dinner with them," Cress explained. "They're gonna go to a hotspot called the Bimini Boatyard for dinner and dancing. It's in this end of town, just on the other side of the inland waterway. Why don't you guys join us."

"That sounds all right with me," Paul answered. "What do you think, Laurie?"

"Sure, it sounds like fun."

"I'll go and tell them you guys are going to come too and make arrangements to meet at about seven. That should work for us shouldn't it?"

"Yeah, that's great. Why don't I give you guys a ride back to your hotel? I'll just slip over to my room and get out of this wet suit and grab my car keys while you're talking to them," Paul decided.

"I'll go with you," Laurie said, "I want to use your bathroom."

"Cress, we'll see you in a few minutes."

As Paul and Laurie crossed the patio around the pool, they noticed that many of the sunbathers had disappeared. The busiest spot was the gazebo bar where people had gathered for one last afternoon cocktail. As soon as the two of them went into Paul's room, Laurie noticed that the drapes were closed and the television was on. She spoke first.

"Jack, you don't mind me coming to your room with you, do you?" She smiled and gave him a quick kiss on the lips as she went toward the washroom.

"Not at all, let me get a towel so I can get out of this suit while you're in the bathroom," Paul answered as he grabbed a large bath towel off the rack inside the door.

Paul dropped his wet bathing suit, dried himself off and slipped on some jockey shorts. Just as he pulled them up, Laurie came out of the washroom, walked over to him, and pushed him onto the bed. She then gently lay down on top of him and smiled.

"Jack, I've wanted a real kiss all day! When we were in the pool earlier in the afternoon, I almost dragged you off to your room," she said as she moved against him.

"As I mentioned, it has been a long time," Paul said as he felt himself begin to bulge in his underwear. "I don't know if I remember how, but you're the first person I've wanted to kiss in a long, long time."

She kissed him gently, two or three times on the lips, so they could get a feel for each other and then they kissed deeply. Paul slowly put his arms around her. She felt so good. He realized at that moment just how much he had missed the warm touch of a woman. Laurie continued to kiss him and her pelvic area rubbed his groin. Back and forth. Back and forth. It felt good for both of them. She kept rubbing. He kissed her again and again. He had a serious hard-on. He couldn't help it.

"God!.. That feels so good!.. Oooh, Christ!.. Oooh!.. Oooh! I'm so sorry, I didn't mean to do that! It has been so long since I've even kissed a woman, let alone done anything else," Paul said totally embarrassed. "For some reason, when I'm with you, all of the guilt that I've had about seeing another woman since my wife died seems to be gone."

"Jack, you don't have to feel bad about anything, I understand. You do feel good and you definitely didn't forget how to kiss."

"You really have no idea how long it's been since I've been in this situation with a woman."

"Don't feel bad, just enjoy it. I'm glad I have that effect on you," Laurie said.

"If I'm going to drive you and Cress back to your hotel, you had better get off me and let me change my underwear. This is really embarrassing."

"Don't worry about it, Jack, I think it's great. I'm glad that I make you feel that good," Laurie said as she got up off the bed. "Later, we can spend some more time together and I'll show you what you've really been missing."

A news broadcast just began as Paul came out of the bathroom. As he pulled on his shorts and slipped on his shoes, he took a moment to listen.

"Let's take a minute and see what the weather is going be like tomorrow," Paul suggested.

The newscaster soon got to the part that Paul was interested in listening to: "The body of a Canadian tourist was found in the gardens of a townhouse development in Boca Raton at about nine o'clock this morning. The police are investigating the incident as a murder, but no further details are available pending the notification of next-of-kin."

"A Canadian came all the way to Florida to die. What a shame!" Laurie said.

"That sort of thing happens all the time," Paul said as he finished dressing.

Before they left the room, he pulled Laurie close to him and kissed her again and rubbed himself against her and said, "If we don't get the hell out of here, Cress will have to find her own way back to the Ramada."

As the two of them walked across the patio toward the bar, Paul's body slowly returned to normal. Liz was on his mind and he felt guilty. The closest thing to sex that he had experienced since Liz had died were a few wet dreams. He had always wondered how he would feel if and when he interacted with another woman. He felt good, except for the premature ejaculation. He still loved Liz, but now realized how much he missed a woman's warmth. He needed to make love. He was looking forward to the rest of the evening because he knew that this was going to be his lucky day.

Laurie and Cress' room at the Ramada was like most hotel rooms with two double beds, a sitting area, a balcony overlooking the ocean and a bathroom. Laurie took a cold beer out of the small fridge, opened it and handed it to Paul.

"Those guys from Atlanta are going to pick me up here just before seven, so we will meet you two at the restaurant," Cress decided.

"Why don't I just get ready for the evening now," Laurie said, "and I'll go back to the Marriott with Jack while he gets ready. We'll meet the rest of you there."

"That's great," Cress said. "I'm having a Cran and Vodka. Do you want one?"

"Sure, pour me one," Laurie said. "I'm gonna jump into the shower."

It was after six by the time Laurie was ready to go out for the evening and as she came out of the bathroom, Paul's heart skipped a beat. She was dressed in a low-cut, slinky dress that clung to her gorgeous body and as far as he could tell, she had absolutely nothing on underneath it. She was definitely not wearing a bra and there were no panty or even thong lines. She looked terrific and the moment Paul saw her, he felt movement in his groin. He crossed his legs so no one would notice and tried to make it stop.

"We'll catch up to you guys," Laurie said to Cress as she and Paul left the room.

The drive back to the Marriott was fairly quick because Paul went inland and took Federal 1 rather than the ocean highway down along the strip in all the traffic. Laurie held Paul's hand in hers on her lap all the way there and he enjoyed her touch. Things were stirring in his body that he had forgotten even existed. He was feeling good and alive. He was anxious to get back to his place just to kiss her again.

"I haven't been out for dinner and dancing for so long I can't even remember the last time," Paul commented.

"I'm looking forward to bringing you back to the real world," Laurie smiled.

* * *

As Paul and Laurie crossed the patio, he picked up two Sea Breezes at the bar. The anticipation of sex later in the evening was all Paul needed. He couldn't believe it! He had a chubby by the time he got to the room. He flipped on the television to the music channel as soon as they got there and headed for the bathroom.

"Make yourself at home, I'm gonna have a quick shave and shower and I'll be ready to go," Paul said. "Are you hungry?"

"Not really," Laurie answered as she took a sip of her drink, "I'll want to eat sometime tonight, but I'm not in any rush."

Paul came out of the bathroom covered in shaving foam, "I don't have a bar in the room, just scotch. I wasn't expecting to have company this week."

"You don't need booze because the patio bar is so close," she answered as she slipped her shoes off and fixed the pillows on the bed so she could lean back and relax.

As soon as he finished shaving, Paul jumped into the shower and was back out drying in two or three minutes. He combed his damp hair straight back and wrapped one of the large towels around himself and stepped out of the bathroom to go to the closet. He looked toward Laurie and was pleasantly surprised. She was nude between the sheets. The television and the light had been turned off and the radio was playing quietly.

"I think you should come over here and practice that kissing a bit more," she smiled and noticed from the bulge in the towel that the thought excited him.

"That's a great idea," Paul said as the towel fell to the floor and he joined her.

They cuddled and kissed for a few minutes and it became quite obvious that Paul was more than ready to take that next step.

"I had no intention of meeting someone while I was down here, so I'm not really prepared for this," Paul said.

"Well, I'm an emancipated divorcee from New York City and it's better to be safe than sorry. There are a couple of condoms on the night table whenever you're ready."

"You drive me crazy! I think I've been ready for this for a long time and just didn't meet the right person. I want to apologize right now because it has been a long, long time since I've even thought about doing this and I think it could be over before it begins, but I promise that the second time will be a lot better."

Paul and Laurie didn't make it to dinner that evening. They stayed in bed and made love. Paul was like an animal, he couldn't get enough. They did everything and they did it for hours. They fell asleep around midnight and woke up together about four in the morning and started all over again. By six thirty, they were down on the Fort Lauderdale strip walking along the beach and looking for a place for breakfast.

The rest of the week turned out to be a lot of fun for Paul. Cress had latched onto one of the guys from Atlanta and spent her free time with him. Laurie had basically moved most of her things to the Marriott and she and Paul really had fun together. They had so much fun, Paul extended his stay until the following Wednesday when the New Yorkers were scheduled to go home.

Paul took Laurie to meet Cress and her new boyfriend for lunch at Shooters on Friday afternoon and something strange happened that was totally unknown to Paul. As he and his friends finished their lunch around two o'clock, two official looking men walked into the main part of Shooters from Bootleggers and stood at the end of the bar and drank some sort of non-alcoholic beverages. One was in a business suit and the other was a Deputy Sheriff. As Paul and his friends left the restaurant, unbeknownst to both parties, Paul actually rubbed shoulders with Detective Graham Everdell. He was in Florida meeting with the local authorities to gather evidence about the murder of Vito Morelli. He was in the process of following the dead man's itinerary in Fort Lauderdale prior to his death. Even though it was a very warm day, as Paul's arm brushed Everdell's arm as he left the restaurant, both Paul and Detective Everdell felt a chill run through their bodies that neither one quite understood.

* * *

Paul took all of the information that he needed to get in touch with Laurie again in New York, but made some excuse about moving his residence back in Canada so he couldn't give her a contact number. He told her that he would be in touch with her by phone and e-mail when he got settled. He really did want to see her again.

The flight back to Buffalo was uneventful. He was picked up at the airport by the airport service that he had used to get there and was taken back to his car at the Casino Niagara parking lot in Niagara Falls, Ontario. The return trip to Beer Lake went well and by the time he got there, he was ready for some sleep. The last few days in Florida had taken their toll. It had been years since he had that much of that kind of exercise.

CHAPTER TWENTY-FOUR

Everdell and Carpenter had flipped a coin to see which one of them would get to go to Florida. Everdell had won, or lost, depending on how one looked at it. It was scheduled to be a very quick trip, very hectic and not much fun, just to see how the evidence in Fort Lauderdale compared with the murders in Toronto. It would be for one night, maybe two, and then right back home. Everdell was disappointed that he had won the toss because his wife was already mad at him for working so many hours.

* * *

Everdell flew out of Toronto on Thursday evening via Air Canada and was picked up at the Fort Lauderdale Airport by a deputy named Richard Krysiak from the Boca Raton Sheriff's Department. Krysiak was a cordial guy in his early thirties and had been working on the murder of the Canadian because the body had been found just as he came on shift. He took Everdell to a Super 8 Motel near the station and dropped him off for the night. They arranged to meet first thing Friday morning to go through all of the Florida evidence that had been accumulated. The Toronto detective took the opportunity to get a good night's sleep, so right after the eleven o'clock news, he turned out his lights and crashed. Everdell didn't so much as move all night until the alarm rang at seven. He actually felt well rested and refreshed in the morning.

The police station was a white brick, two-story building, that was five or six years old. It was on N. Ocean Blvd. in central Boca Raton, not far from Mizner's Mall. Everdell had read about the upscale shopping center in one of the magazines in his motel room and wondered what it would be like to have valet parking when you went shopping. He wouldn't find out on this trip. He didn't have time.

Krysiak and he sat together in a small interrogation room with a white file folder on the table between them. The Florida cop pushed it toward him and picked up a mug of coffee and took a sip before he spoke.

"This is everything we've got on the murder," Krysiak advised and then asked, "Who the hell was this guy anyway, to bring you all the way down here from Toronto?"

"Believe it or not, I don't give a rat's ass about the death of Morelli. He was one of those major drug traffickers who we just couldn't seem to get our mitts on. He won't be missed up north," Everdell answered.

"What brings you down here then?"

"A couple of years ago, a bad dose of Ecstasy hit the streets of Toronto and a dozen or so people died, including a number of high school students. During the last couple of months, five local drug dealers have been murdered who dealt drugs at the schools where the kids died, and now, Morelli, may be number six. We think he was more than likely the main supplier to one or two of the dealers who were killed so our killer may now be going after the big guys."

"So you really think that Morelli's murder might have been committed by the same guy who killed the drug dealers in Toronto," Krysiak commented. "Do you have any evidence that suggests the killings are related?"

"As I mentioned, all five of the drug dealers in Toronto were killed in exactly the same manner. Each of them had an oyster-shucking knife stuck into the back of their neck right at the base of the skull and then twisted, just like the guy was opening an oyster. They all died instantly."

"So you think that your man may have come all the way to Florida just to kill this guy? Why wouldn't he just do it in Toronto? There's no death penalty there."

"I have no fuckin' idea why he would come all the way down here. Probably, just to screw up our investigation. This oyster-shucking knife that you have in the bag here is not exactly the same knife that he used up north, but it's very similar."

"If it is the same guy, he would be smarter than to try to bring one of his own oyster-shucking knives down here on an airplane since 9-11."

"I'm sure you're right. It looks like Morelli and his associates got here Saturday and you seem to have notes on their itinerary from the time they got here," Everdell said reading from the file. "Was the nurse he spent the night with helpful?"

"She didn't really add much we didn't already know. She had met Morelli the night before at Octobers in Lauderdale, and that night, he got to her place around eleven. She called him a cab at four in the morning. He left her house, but it seems he never made it to the parking lot or the cab."

"What about the cab driver? Were you able to locate him?"

"Yeah, we talked to him too. He arrived at the address at four forty and waited for his fare for about twenty minutes and when he didn't show, he left," Krysiak answered.

"It looks like you guys have covered everything. There was no physical evidence where the murder took place? Did any of the neighbors hear anything during the night?"

"There was nothing at the scene. Whatever happened, happened very quickly and quietly. We talked to all the neighbors and no one heard a thing."

"Can you arrange for me to get copies of everything in your file? The only other thing I'd like to do before I head back to Canada is see the murder scene and maybe follow in Morelli's footsteps for the couple of days he was here before he died."

"No problem. They can copy the file while we're gone. I know all the places that Morelli visited so I can take you by them. We'll do the murder scene first."

"Then let's go by the place where he was staying. Are his buddies still here?"

"No, they all went back home as soon as we were finished with them, so the condo is empty. Some guy from Toronto apparently owns it."

After they left the murder scene, the trip to the Galt Ocean Mile condo took about half an hour. Everdell had seen enough after he walked through the six rooms for about five minutes. Anything that had belonged to the Italians was gone and all of Morelli's personal belongings were at the police station. The police officers then went south on N. Atlantic Blvd., turned right at Oakland, over the inland waterway, and immediately drove into the lavish front entrance to Yesterdays.

The sign indicated that it wasn't open for business until eleven, but one of the doors was ajar so they walked into the lobby. After the men introduced themselves, a waiter showed Everdell the reservation list for the previous Sunday evening. It indicated that Morelli's group had arrived for dinner around eight o'clock. He asked the waiter for a photocopy of the Sunday page in the book. They also dropped by Octobers, the late night dance club where the men had spent Saturday evening, but it was locked up tight and no one was around.

It was two o'clock when Everdell and Krysiak walked through Bootleggers and over to the main bar and restaurant at Shooters. They stopped at the bar for a cold drink of soda. Neither one of them drank alcohol on-the-job. As they stood at the end of the bar sipping on their drinks, Krysiak spoke.

"That's basically where Morelli and his gang went from the time they arrived in Lauderdale to the time of the murder."

"Well, it seems like they were just on a holiday because they had booked the condo for a full week. I've never heard of those guys doing business down here."

"Is there anything else you need to do before you head back?" Krysiak asked.

"No, you've done a great job. I've seen everything I want to see so the only thing left is to go back to the station and pick up the file that you had copied for me. I might take a look through Morelli's belongings once more before I leave," Everdell said, making sure to praise the work of the local cop.

"We can head back now and get that stuff done. What time are the flights if you want to fly back to Toronto today?"

"I've got a tentative return flight at five-thirty this afternoon."

"Let's head back and then I'll drive you to the airport."

As the two policemen were chatting at Shooter's bar, four people from a nearby table got up to leave the restaurant after their lunch; two nice looking gals with New York drawls, and two men, one with a mustache. Everdell glanced at the attractive girls and didn't even notice the men, but as the man with the mustache brushed by him, a shiver ran through his body. Everdell thought that it was very unusual and couldn't figure out what had caused that very strange sensation. After all, the temperature was in the eighties.

Back at the Sheriff's Office in Boca Raton, Everdell went through Morelli's personal effects and found nothing that would add anything to the investigation. A duplicate copy of the file was given to him, including copies of all the reports, pictures and any other evidence that had been collected. Everdell put the copy of Yesterday's reservation book page for the day of the murder in the file with the other information. He and Krysiak then headed to the airport for his flight back to Canada.

The local police had turned over all of the stones that Everdell would have looked under had he been the investigator so his trip turned out to be shorter than it could have been. The Sheriff's Office had done a great job. As he sat in his window seat on the plane, he opened his file on Morelli's death and pulled the copy of the reservation book page from Yesterdays out of it and stared at the names on it. He returned it to his file, leaned back and shut his eyes. He was glad to be going home.

* * *

First thing Monday morning, Everdell, Carpenter and Speer sat at the tables in their small room at headquarters with copies of all of

the evidence and information that Everdell had brought back from
Florida. Carpenter and Speer got a first hand report on what had
happened in Boca Raton. Everdell briefed them on the evidence
that he had seen and explained the information in the file, piece by
piece. The murder could just as easily have happened right on their
own doorstep because it was the same modus operandi. As far as
Everdell was concerned, Morelli was the sixth victim in The Oyster-
Shucking Murders case.

"Graham, what do you think? Is it our guy?"

"Hell, it has to be! Everything's the same. If we dig a little deeper,
we're going to find that Morelli was the supplier for one of the
street hustlers killed here in Toronto. I get the terrible feeling that
this guy has decided to go into the upper echelons of the drug business to make the big guys who contributed to those teenage deaths
pay too."

"If you're right," Carpenter added, "he's not done yet. The five
street dealers who were murdered across metro didn't all deal with
Morelli."

"That's for sure. There have to be a few more major traffickers
here in the city who supplied some of the other victims."

"That makes sense," Speer said as he got up to leave the room,
"you guys better try and find out who might be next on his list."

CHAPTER TWENTY-FIVE

Paul's first night back at Beer Lake was restless, not because he had committed another murder, but because both Liz and Laurie were on his mind. He felt guilty about having been with another woman, even though deep down, he knew he had to get on with his life. His first dream was about Liz and she was right there with him. She wasn't upset, she knew that he still loved her and she also knew that he needed to move on. When the dream ended, Paul woke up and looked around the room. It had not been a bad dream. His problem was that after three years, he still really missed her.

His next one was about Laurie, a woman he didn't know very well. A liberated and divorced New York girl whose company he enjoyed. When he woke up, he had what could be called a serious *woody*, but still felt pangs of guilt as he thought about Liz.

In his next dream, both women were there on the deck of the cottage at Beer Lake, sitting on summer chairs, enjoying a beautiful day. They chatted together and everything was fine. In the morning, when Paul woke up, he seemed to know that Liz had no problem with him moving on with his life and finding someone else to love too.

Paul put the coffee on as soon as he got out of bed. He then wandered back out to the fireplace, threw in some paper, kindling and a couple of logs and lit the paper in four or five places and sat down in his leather chair. The smell of the burning wood and brewing coffee relaxed him. He felt tired as he carried his mug back to his chair and as he sat there quietly near the warm fire, thoughts about his past and present lives went through his mind.

Paul had enjoyed meeting Laurie and spending time with her, but she was really his first date in close to three years so he wasn't sure if she meant anything special to him. He definitely knew that she was one great piece of ass and the two of them had actually had a lot of fun together. He decided that he would like to see her again, but he wasn't quite sure when that could be arranged.

Paul still had a couple of things to take care of before he could think about taking some time off for a little rest and relaxation. He hadn't given a lot of thought about what he was going to do once his work was finished. He had no serious plans about continuing his crusade because, deep down, he really didn't enjoy what he was doing. He didn't like killing people. His mission was to avenge the deaths of his son and the other young victims. He felt that would be accomplished when his list was completed. Paul had provided the detectives with enough information over the telephone that they would be able to figure out why the men who died were killed. Surely the words *justice* and *revenge* would soon come to the minds of the detectives.

Of the two things to be done remaining on Paul's list, one was a Russian and the other was a Jamaican. As he sat in front of the fire, he wondered, *Which one of those lucky bastards is going to be the next one to meet me up close and personal?* Christmas was less than three weeks away, so if he made the decision to kill one more trafficker, he had to do it before the holiday season got underway. He thought, almost out loud, *I'd hate to screw up somebody's Christmas!* and laughed to himself.

Paul thought about the close encounters that he had previously had with Vladmir Rousinsky, in Hamilton, and Ruffus Allan, in Scarborough. He recalled that as he sat in The Russia House during dinner and listened to Rousinsky and his friends talk, they discussed going on a skiing holiday to Colorado in the New Year. As he contemplated his next victim, he marveled at the success of the Florida trip. He had even enjoyed himself. Maybe he would leave the lucky Russian until after Christmas because he hadn't been on a skiing holiday for years. Paul would join Vlad and his buddies on the trip to Colorado. Besides, Ruffus Allan was just down the road. He would be easy to locate and fairly easy to take care of, if Paul could just find a way to separate him from his posse. It wasn't difficult to decide his next move. The Jamaican would miss Christmas.

Paul spent the next few days just relaxing around the cottage. He went to Minden to do some grocery shopping to stock up on food that he could store in his freezer because the holiday season was approaching. He was intending to hang around home. Laurie kept coming back into his mind and he wondered what plans she had for Christmas. He was sure that Paul Taylor wasn't going to get invited anywhere for the holidays because he was dead. After shopping, he dropped in at the Rockcliffe Hotel for a beer and ended up shooting a few games of pool with one of the locals. He realized that if he was going to visit the pool hall in Scarborough, he needed to practice. The weekend came and went and all of a sudden it was mid-week. Paul watched the news on television regularly and read the daily newspapers. All was quiet. There was absolutely no news about how the investigations into The Oyster-Shucking Murders were going.

On Wednesday night, Paul gathered all his gear together and got ready for the trip to Toronto that was planned for the morning. He slept well and was up bright and early. He wasn't in any great rush because the regulars at the pool hall wouldn't show up until noon, so he cooked himself a full breakfast and watched the morning news. While he ate, he wondered what he could do to impress the Jamaican at the pool hall and he decided that the only thing that would really turn his crank was money and lots of it. He went to the old pair of rubber boots in the corner of the living room and pulled out a large stack of bills. He counted off five thousand dollars in hundreds and put the small roll in his jacket pocket. He thought that should be enough to get Ruffus' attention. He stood in front of the full length mirror and even started to recognize himself. The sideburns were gone but the goatee was starting to grow back although is wasn't nearly as thick or full as it had once been. He put on a Toronto Blue Jays cap for a change and decided that he was almost ready. Paul puttered around until about ten-thirty when he gathered up his things and headed out to the car.

* * *

Just after twelve, Paul pulled off Highway 401 and took the 404 north about half-a-mile to Sheppard and exited on the cloverleaf. At the lights, he drove straight through to the Ramada Inn parking lot. Paul booked in, went directly to his room and got himself organized for at least a one night's stay, maybe two. It wasn't long before he was back in the lobby and hailed a cab to take him to the pool hall at the Golden Mile Plaza.

It was just after one o'clock when Paul wandered into Willie's Billiard Hall on the second level of the plaza on the northeast corner of one of the busiest crossroads in Scarborough. He went directly to the bar, sat at one of the stools and ordered a Molson Canadian. As he took a swig of the beer, he glanced around the room. About a third of the tables had guys playing various games of spherical arts, but the pool table in the back corner was not being used. The gang of Jamaicans was nowhere to be seen. Even though Paul had eaten a decent breakfast, he felt a twinge of hunger so he ordered a banquet burger as he waited. He knew that Ruffus and his posse would eventually show up.

After he finished eating, Paul thought that he may as well shoot some pool so he arranged for a table with the bartender. He chose the third table from the back corner and took another beer with him as he wandered down along the windows toward the far end of the room. As he walked by one of the tables, a familiar looking man who was playing pool with another guy spoke to him.

"Gord, I see that you have decided to come back for some more punishment."

"Ben, I really just dropped in to get my money back from ya'."

"Maybe we'll have a couple of games a little later."

"Sounds great, I'll just be down here practicing. You better not let me play for too long or you might be in serious trouble today."

"I'll catch up to you in awhile," Ben said.

As Paul continued on toward his table, he heard Ben brag to his buddy that he had taken some money off the guy that had just walked by, a few weeks ago. Paul recalled that he had let him win the games because Ben had been providing him with information about the pool hall and the Jamaican drug dealers who hung out there. Paul didn't really care if Ben showed up over confident. He thought that he might just make the braggart pay for a few beers that day.

Paul played two games of snooker by himself and by halfway through the second, he found his eye. He was playing extremely well and knew that he would be hard to beat unless he laid off, which he might have to do. As he recalled, Ben worked shift work at one of the local plants and he wasn't a bad guy. Paul decided that he wouldn't beat him up too badly because he wanted to spread some money around in public.

Just as Paul sank the last red ball in his second game and was about to start shooting the colored balls, he noticed five Jamaicans come into the pool hall. He recognized three of them as guys who had been at the corner table the first time that he had visited Willie's. He immediately picked out Ruffus Allan. He was the mouthy guy giving orders to his boys. They walked past Paul and took their usual spot in the corner, two tables away. Paul was close enough to hear everything they said. His only concern was whether he could decipher the Jamaican patois. Just as Paul sank the black ball and ended his game, he noticed Ben walking toward him with a beer in his hand.

"Gord, do you want to keep practicing for awhile or are you ready for a lesson?" Ben asked as he walked toward Paul's table.

"You sound pretty cocky. You must have just won at that other table, but I gotta warn you, I'm really on today."

"I did win sixty bucks from that guy I was playin' with, but he wasn't that good, I'm sure you'll kick my ass!"

"Well, I'm glad that we're playing for the other guy's money so I won't feel too bad when I take it from you," Paul laughed.

"Rack'em. Let's get at it. What do you want to play for, ten or twenty bucks?"

"Ten is fine with me. I don't wanna take all your money in the first couple of games. Do you have to go into work later today?"

"Naw, I got the day off so I hope you brought lots of money with you. Let's play for twenty a game if you don't really care. I feel kinda hot today."

Paul didn't care what amount Ben wanted to play for because he intended to lose a lot of money to him if the Jamaicans were watching. He wanted to show them his bankroll and spend some time near their corner table, so he could listen and find out what they were all about. He hoped to learn enough about Ruffus to find a way to get him alone, away from his gang, at some point during the next two or three days.

Paul played pool with Ben all afternoon, two tables over from the Jamaicans, and the games continued into the early evening. Just before seven, Ben had to leave so it was time for Paul to pay up. Paul peeled four hundreds off his large bankroll and threw the money on the table. He made a big deal about the loss. The Jamaicans noticed. Ruffus watched the exchange and got a good look at the handful of cash that Paul was carrying. As Ben left, with a big grin on his face, the Jamaican leader spoke to Paul.

"Hey, mon, my name is Ruffus. You wanna play a few games fer some real money instead of dat chicken shit you were playing fer over dere?"

"Why not," Paul answered as he walked toward the five men who were hanging around their corner table. "I'm Gord," he said as they watched him fold his large wad of money and put it back into his pocket. "What do you want to play for?"

"Can ya' 'andle a 'undred a game?" Ruffus asked.

"No problem, that'll be fine. You call it for the break," Paul answered as he tossed a two dollar coin into the air and it landed on the table.

The Jamaicans were playing Solids and Stripes and not Snooker. The first game went to a black ball game. Ruffus won. Paul wasn't sure who was conning who because they both missed shots they should have made. As the second game continued, Paul had a stroke of luck as his balls had all been set up right over the pockets and he couldn't do anything but win the game. During the third game, Paul decided that the best way to get to know his partner was to lose some money to him and make him feel good. As time went on, he made sure that Ruffus was always up a few hundred dollars.

"Do ya' live or work 'round 'ere, mon?" Ruffus asked as he watched Paul line up a shot.

"I live in Agincourt and work at the Pickering Nuclear Plant," Paul answered and thought that it wasn't a total lie in since his hotel was in that part of the city.

"Ya' must 'ave a good job to be carryin' all dat money wit ya'."

"Yeah, I got a decent job. I also have a cash business with a lot of the guys at work that keeps me in the green stuff," Paul explained without saying too much more.

He wanted Ruffus to think that maybe he was a drug dealer on the side and that's why he had the bankroll. That kind of scenario would fit right into Ruffus' plans because drug dealers like to rip each other off. The two men played about twenty games as Ruffus' buddies watched their leader in action. By about nine-thirty, Paul was feeling no pain because he had been drinking beer since he got there and as Ruffus sank the black ball and won the game, he decided to call it a night.

"I owe you five hundred bucks," Paul said as he peeled five one hundred dollar bills off his roll of cash and threw them on the table, "and that's enough for me tonight. I've had too much beer today, I'm pissed. I can't put the balls in the pockets anymore."

"Well, I sure don' mine takin' all yer money, but we'll play agin another time."

"Nice meetin' you guys. Maybe I'll see you tomorrow," Paul said as he shook Ruffus' hand and turned and headed toward the bar.

Paul paid for both tables before he left because he had lost games to both Ben and Ruffus and also sent a round of drinks to everyone at the corner table. Paul knew that he had made an impression with the size of his bank roll. He had lost a total of nine hundred dollars and even bought them drinks when it was all said and done. He knew that the next time he bumped into Ruffus and his friends, they would remember him.

As Paul went through the door and down the stairs to the outside, Ruffus sent one of his posse to see what Paul was driving. The wad of money had impressed him and he wanted to get the rest of it from his new friend. Paul got into a waiting cab and went north on Victoria Park. His mode of transportation was reported back to Ruffus who had hoped that his new friend, with all the money, drove a big fancy car so they could watch for it to return to the parking area near the pool hall. He wanted to see Paul again.

* * *

The next day, Paul was hoping to be able to finish the job that he had come to the city to do. He actually slept in until ten. After he got showered and dressed, he checked out his equipment. He put his Glock 25 in a holster under his left arm, put a pair of surgical gloves in one jacket pocket and the oyster-shucking knife in the other. He was going to go back to Willie's Billiards and see what developed.

Just before two, Paul was at the bar having a burger, fries and a beer when Ruffus Allan and his entourage came in and passed by the bar on their way to their regular table.

"Eh, mon, yer back 'ere fer more punishment," Ruffus said when he saw him.

"If I can shake this hangover, I want to get my money back."

"As soon as yer ready, come o'er to ma' table and we'll go at it."

Paul finished his lunch and read the newspaper. He wasn't going to rush down to the back corner because the Jamaicans would be there all day. About an hour later, with a beer in his hand, Paul walked slowly back toward the corner table and his new friends. He and Ruffus played pool all afternoon and the winners of the games went back and forth, but Paul made sure that his Jamaican buddy was always up a few hundred dollars. Paul had a couple more beers, but took it easy on the pretense that he had a headache and a hangover from the day before. By eight o'clock, three brothers who had been watching the games left the pool hall indicating that they would all meet later that night. As a guy named Artie watched, Paul and Ruffus played about ten more games over the next hour and as the Jamaican won another one, he spoke to Paul.

"That's six 'undred. I don think yer gonna get yer money back today, mon. Why don' we all git the 'ell outta here and go to a club down on the Danforth?"

"I'm for doing something else. This fuckin' game has already cost me enough money," Paul answered as he pulled out his roll of money, peeled off six hundreds and tossed them on the pool table.

* * *

Ruffus drove a white Mercedes, with darkened windows, and as Paul got into the back seat behind the driver, he opened and closed the door with his jacket sleeve in his hand so he wouldn't leave any fingerprints on the door. He didn't know what was going to happen as the night progressed, but he wanted to be ready. Ruffus had an unbelievable sound system and purple lights that flashed under the front end. The bass from the music gave Paul an immediate headache as they drove down Victoria Park toward the Danforth. He got a feeling that things weren't quite right as Ruffus turned into Shoppers World on the southwest corner and drove toward the darkness at the rear of the mall. He had a premonition that something was about to happen so he got ready for trouble. In the darkness, he slipped his handgun out of its holster, quietly cocked it as the music blared and put it on the seat beside him. Then he gently pulled on his rubber gloves. He had been very careful not to touch anything in the car.

"Where the hell is the club we're supposed to be going to? I don't remember seeing one in this plaza."

Ruffus answered, "It's jus' down on da Danforth at Pape. We jus' gotta meet someone out back o' here fer 'bout five minutes."

As the Mercedes went around to the back of the complex, Paul could see a huge, almost empty, parking lot that went west behind a couple of dead end residential streets that accessed the Danforth, well away from the stores and shoppers. It was almost black in that far western corner of the lot and there was no one around as the car came to a stop. Ruffus turned off the ignition.

"Who the hell do you guys have to meet back here?" Paul asked as his right hand found the gun that was on the seat beside him.

At that moment, Artie turned half around in his seat and pointed a handgun directly at Paul and said, "We jus havta see that roll o' money ya' got in yer pocket!"

"Are you guys gonna rob me, for fuck sake? I thought that we were friends!"

"Don't fuckin' kill 'im in the car, it'll mess thin's up. Gord, give Artie the money and get the 'ell outta here, now!" Ruffus yelled.

"OK, OK, I'm gonna give him the money and get out. You guys don't have to shoot me for Christ Sake, it's only money."

"An' ya won' be a witness no more!" Ruffus said.

Paul couldn't believe that the two assholes in the front seat were going to kill him and leave him in that parking lot for a few thousand dollars. He knew that he had to act fast or he would be dead.

"Here's the money and I'm gonna get out of the car, but you gotta let me go. I won't tell anyone about who robbed me, I promise I won't call the police."

Instead of a handful of money, Paul's empty hand went toward Artie's gun and pushed it to his left, but as his hand hit it, it discharged with a deafening explosion and bright flash in the interior of the car. He got creased in the upper left arm on the side of the muscle. At the same moment, Paul brought his Glock up off the backseat and shot Artie in the face. The bullet went into his right eye, through his head, and lodged in the post between the side door and front window. The glass didn't shatter, but blood and pink brain matter splattered all over the front seat. In the same motion, Paul sat forward and placed his gun right against Ruffus' right temple and he froze in a total state of shock.

"Put both of your hands on the fuckin' steering wheel and if you move even a little bit, I'll blow your head off just like I did to your buddy over there!"

"Who the fuck are ya, mon. I wasn't gonna kill ya, just rob ya!"

"You are so full of shit, *mon*. You would have killed me for a few grand and never thought a thing about it."

"Don't hurt me, mon. I can get you some money, lots of money!"

"I want you to tell me about your drug distribution business. Who buys your shit from you and where do they sell it?" Paul ordered.

He leaned forward against the back of the driver's seat, put his left arm around the Jamaican's neck and pushed his Glock against his head a number of times so he would know that it was there. Paul then lowered it and put it back onto the backseat. In the same motion, he slowly pulled his oyster-shucking knife from his jacket pocket and stuck it in the back of Ruffus' neck so he could feel it. He then tightened his arm around the trafficker's neck and pushed the small knife deeper into his favorite spot, enough to make it really hurt and draw some blood, just to let him know that he was deadly serious.

"Fuck, mon, that hurts! What the 'ell are ya doin'?"

"Answer the fuckin' questions that I asked and do it now!" Paul said as he put a little more pressure on the blade.

"Fuck, mon, I sell ta 'bout twenty street hustlers and they sell all over Scarborough. I'm jus' a middle man. The drugs jus' pass trough me 'ands."

"Where do they sell their drugs?"

"Dey sell 'em all over the place, bars, clubs, high schools, places like dat."

"Do you remember that incident a couple of years ago when some bad Ecstasy hit the streets and a number of high school kids across the city died?"

"Yah, mon. I remember all dat shit."

"My son was one of the kids who died that weekend and all of you fuckers who put that shit on the streets are going to die too!"

As Paul finished the sentence, he jammed the oyster-shucking knife into Ruffus Allan's neck and gave it a hard twist and left it there. The sound of the crunch, as the bones separated, was louder than usual because it filled the interior of the car. He let go of the body as it went limp and fell against the steering wheel. Paul quickly looked at his shoulder that was stinging and realized that the wound wasn't very serious. He could make out the form of his handgun where he had placed it on the seat and immediately picked it up and put it back in its holster. Then he took his gloved hand and rubbed it all over the right side of the back seat and soon found what he wanted before he left the scene. He picked up the shell casing from his bullet and put it into his pocket.

He got out of the car in the darkness, looked around and slowly headed for the nearest residential street where he walked north to the Danforth. Paul continued west past all kinds of nightclubs and restaurants and there were lots of people on both sides of the street. He fit right in with them. Five or six blocks away from the side street, he slipped into the back of a cab that was parked right in front of an English pub called Brass Taps.

"Highway 404 and Sheppard."

"No problem," the cabby said as he pulled out into the traffic. "There certainly looked to be lots of broads going into that spot tonight, was it busy inside?"

"It sure was, but unfortunately, I have to leave."

* * *

The cabby didn't need to know where Paul was staying so he got dropped off at the Fish House, a great seafood restaurant, right on Sheppard Avenue East near his hotel. Paul didn't go inside, but walked through the back parking lot and out onto the street where the Ramada was located. As he walked toward the hotel, he could really feel his shoulder burning.

Back in his room, he took off his jacket and shirt and was glad to see that the bullet had just creased his arm and it had nearly stopped bleeding. His jacket and shirt were ruined and a small amount of blood had seeped through the arm of his coat and left a dark, wet spot that just looked like a stain of some kind. Paul got a small bottle of vodka out of the mini-bar to treat the wound and ripped his shirt up for a bandage. By the time he finished, he felt fine and flipped on the television to the eleven o'clock news. There was no mention of the guys who Paul had left in the car in Scarborough. He thought that they might not be found until morning.

Paul got up at seven thirty, had a shave and a shower, and changed the bandage on his arm with another piece of his shirt and another application of vodka. It stung like hell but the wound looked fine. He would put some proper disinfectant on it when he got back home. He packed up all his things, including the gloves, jacket and remnants of his shirt and was ready to leave about eight-thirty. He could see the busy 401 from his window so he decided to take advantage of the complimentary continental breakfast nook off the main lobby. He went down, got something to eat and took it back to his room. Paul was back at Beer Lake by noon and as soon as he sat down in his favorite chair, with the fire going and a scotch in his hand, he thought to himself, *I'm now officially on my Christmas Holidays!*

CHAPTER TWENTY-SIX

After Everdell returned from Florida and showed Carpenter and Speer all the evidence provided by the Florida police, the consensus among them was that Morelli had been killed in Fort Lauderdale by the same man who committed the five murders in Toronto. It had all the same earmarks and Morelli was a drug trafficker. The killer had been just as careful down south as he had been up north and there was very little evidence left at the scene where the Boca Raton police had found Morelli's body. The two detectives were back in the same place they were in before the Florida trip, as far as lack of evidence was concerned, but they knew that the Morelli killing was the sixth in what they now also called The Oyster-Shucking Murders.

"We have to keep looking at the Shackleton murder. I know I keep saying it over and over, but it's gotta be the key to solving this case," Carpenter commented.

"You're right, but I think we should contact the few airlines that fly directly to Fort Lauderdale from both Toronto and Buffalo and get a copy of their passenger lists on the flights for the week before the Morelli murder," Everdell decided. "Who knows, maybe a name we recognize will pop up."

"Let's do that right now. You put a list of airlines together and I'll go across the street and get a couple of sandwiches. It's a little early, but I'm starving."

Just as Everdell finished making a list of all of the airlines with flights into Fort Lauderdale from Toronto and Buffalo, Carpenter returned with food and drinks. They split the airlines up and made the calls and then turned to their sandwiches. As they sat there eating and talking about the Shackleton murder, the door to the room sprung open and Bill Speer burst in quite unexpectedly.

"We just got a call about two dead bodies in a car in a parking lot behind Shopper's World, on the southwest corner of Danforth and Victoria Park," Speer blurted out excitedly. "It's a call that you guys will want to take."

"What the hell are you saying Billy, we're at number seven and eight?" Carpenter said almost shocked at what he had just heard.

"It sounds like it. There are two dead, one was shot, apparently in the head, and the other has an oyster-shucking knife sticking out of the back of his neck," Speer explained. "You two had better get out there right now."

"We're on our way," Everdell said as he stood up with a half a sandwich in one hand. "We'll have a report on your desk as soon as we get back."

The detectives quickly put their coats on, grabbed their food and drinks and left the room. It wasn't very long before they were heading north toward Bloor Street and would soon be traveling east along the Danforth into Scarborough. Even with their red light flashing, it would take them at least half an hour to get to the scene of the murder.

* * *

Everdell and Carpenter pulled off the Danforth and into the large parking lot in front of Shopper's World which was half-full of cars. They drove through the lot, past the large retail buildings and out into the rear parking and delivery areas. There was an expanse of black pavement that went from Victoria Park to the west, behind three residential streets, and stopped at a tall wire fence. The two hundred yards of rear parking area was almost deserted except for a few delivery trucks at the back of the stores. The detectives immediately saw two black and whites, with their lights flashing, parked about two-thirds of the way to the fence, beside a white car. The unmarked police car with its red bubble-light flashing turned and headed in that direction.

"It looks like a Mercedes," Carpenter commented as they came to a stop.

"Who was first on the scene?" Everdell asked as he pulled on latex gloves.

"I'm Constable Hawley Day. My partner and I saw the car sitting in the middle of the lot about an hour ago and it looked suspicious. It was all alone and parked sideways across the parking spaces so we checked it out. What you see is what we found."

"Has anyone touched anything since you got here?" Everdell continued.

"Not really, all we did was open the doors to see what was inside and we touched the bodies to see if there was any sign of life. There wasn't. They must have been in the car for awhile because that smell of death was fairly strong when the door opened."

"What does it look like to you, Hawley?" Carpenter asked.

"You guys will know better than me, but it looks like the shooter was in the backseat of the car. He obviously shot the passenger in the head and I have no idea why the driver was stabbed to death instead of shot like the other guy."

"Well, Jack, let's take a look and see what we've got," Everdell said.

The two detectives opened all four doors of the car and peered in each one from different angles to get a feel for the crime scene. They both looked closely at the two dead bodies to determine the causes of death.

"The driver died the same way the other six died and it's exactly the same kind of oyster-shucking knife that the killer has used all along," Everdell commented. "What about the passenger?"

"Look at the spray on the front and side windows. This guy was certainly shot from the backseat, but he must have been looking back there when he got it," Carpenter surmised. "The gun was fired by someone sitting behind the driver and the bullet went into the victim's right eye, through his head and his brains splattered all over the place here in the front seat."

"Where the hell did the bullet end up? None of the windows are shattered."

"There is a hole in the plastic covering on the door jam beside the front window. It looks like the bullet may be lodged in there," Carpenter answered as he stuck his finger in the small opening and felt nothing but steel.

Everdell moved to the back passenger door on the driver's side, "Look at this window and door. Someone who was bleeding leaned against it."

"This Colt on the floor of the front seat must belong to the passenger," Carpenter answered as he held it up with a pencil through the trigger hole and smelled the barrel. "It has been fired. If he was looking back when he got shot, there may be a bullet back there."

"There's a small hole in the leather, at the top of the seat, right near the door."

"That's likely where it went and if there's some blood smudged on the door, there's a chance that the killer got hit."

"If he did, this'll be the first bit of evidence that he ever left at one of the murder scenes," Everdell commented. "We should be so lucky that he's starting to get sloppy! There might be something else here too."

"The dead guys look like a couple of street punks. I'll bet any amount they're traffickers," Carpenter said as he pulled a wallet out of one passenger's back pocket.

"I won't be taking that bet. Our guy is off street dealers and is targeting the actual traffickers or suppliers," Everdell answered as he went through the pockets of the driver.

"The passenger's name is Arthur Jacobi and he lives at 55 Tumpane Street."

"His buddy here is Ruffus Allan and he lives at the same address."

"Let's call and see what's keeping the Forensic Team and leave it all for them. We might just get lucky for a change. Let's see if these guys have a sheet."

"Forensics should have been here by now," Everdell commented.

Everdell and Carpenter were not surprised to learn that both men had a long history of drug related charges. The detectives, and the four other police officers there, walked the scene of the murders in a large circle around the Mercedes looking for anything that might relate to what had happened. Nothing turned up. The detectives walked around the car again and looked in each of the doors, from different directions, to try and piece together what had happened at the time of the murders. They both agreed on the facts but would wait for the full Forensic Report. Finally, the forensic crew arrived on the scene.

"It's about time you got here, Bill," Everdell said as a greeting to the Forensic Team and Bill Konkle, who had helped him with the public telephone at Bayview Village a few weeks back. "I think we have it all figured out for you."

"We need all the help we can get. What the hell happened here?" Konkle asked.

"The shooter was in the backseat and he shot the passenger first, in the head, and splattered his brains all over the windows. Then, rather than shoot the driver too, he took the trouble to kill him with an oyster-shucking knife," Carpenter explained.

"Well, we'd better get to work before the coroner gets here to pick up the bodies. We'll probably have to take the car downtown for further investigation so we won't have a full report for you until the beginning of next week."

"No problem, Bill," Everdell said, "but would you mind calling me when you guys are done here and just give us a verbal as to what you think happened?"

"I'll do that later this afternoon. Talk to you then."

Everdell and Carpenter went back to their car as the Forensic Team started to do their job. They took pictures of the whole scene including the inside of the Mercedes. It was obvious to everyone what had gone down inside the vehicle, but the detectives couldn't understand why their killer had changed his pattern.

"Graham, this certainly adds a new twist. Our guy has never used a gun before."

"I think that he was always ready to use a gun if it ever became necessary, but he was always able to kill his victims in the way that he had planned."

"This whole scene is sure different from the others," Carpenter added. "Do you think that some kind of a copycat killer is trying to blame this on our guy?"

"I have a gut feeling this is our guy and something went wrong, but let's wait until we hear from Konkle. I think we'll find that the oyster-shucking knife is identical to the other ones."

"There's not much more we can do here," Carpenter said. "Let's take a look at the victims' residence. Maybe we'll find something there that'll piece all of this together."

The unmarked police car slipped back out onto the Danforth and turned north at Victoria Park. It only took them fifteen minutes to find Tumpane Street which was tucked into a quiet, exclusive enclave in the center of Scarborough. The five bedroom brick home, with a three-car garage, was built on a ravine and looked like it was out in the coutry with trees all over the street. The home was shared by the two victims and a couple of other members of Ruffus' posse, one of whom, let the policemen into the house for a cursory look around since they were investigating the death of their leader. There was a swimming pool in a beautifully landscaped backyard and the master bedroom, which belonged to Ruffus Allan, looked like it belonged in a bordello.

* * *

Later that afternoon, Everdell and Carpenter were sitting in their private room at headquarters drinking coffee, shuffling papers and discussing the new murders. They had just finished a short report for Chief Speer when the phone rang. Everdell was closest, so he answered it. It was Bill Konkle with his verbal report that he had promised.

"Thanks for calling. Jack is here with me, so let me put you on the speaker."

"You guys had pretty much figured it out. The murders took place sometime last night, probably before midnight, and the killer was definitely sitting in the back seat behind the driver. It looks like the passenger fired at the guy in the backseat first, or he wouldn't have got the shot off. He died instantly. The shooter in the back shot him directly in the right eye. The bullet went through his head and into the post between the door and the front window. We found the bullet in the post, but it's in such bad shape it won't tell us anything. We had absolutely no luck finding a shell casing from the backseat shooter's gun. It wasn't on the floor or in or under the backseat."

"Will you be able to tell what caliber it is?" Carpenter asked.

"Not likely, but we'll do our best. The bullet that was shot from the front seat is intact in the backseat upholstery and it's obvious that it came from the passenger's Colt. It looks like the guy in the backseat got hit, but of course there's no way of telling how badly he's hurt. His injury is probably not too serious for two reasons. First, he killed the driver with the oyster-shucking knife after he was shot and second, the backseat only had a small amount of blood smudged on the door and window as if he had leaned against them. He likely had an arm wound and leaned against the door as he killed the driver."

"Do you think that the car will give up anymore evidence?" Everdell asked.

"We're still working on it. There are all kinds of prints, but who knows if the killer touched anything. He didn't leave prints at any of the other crime scenes. What are there now, six counting Florida? These two guys make eight."

"You don't have to remind us," Everdell complained. "I'm sure that Speer will be in here any minute to make sure we don't forget."

"I'll have a full written report for you late Monday and I'll do my best with the crushed bullet and the blood on the back window. Talk to you then," Konkle said.

"The only chance we have is that these murders are totally different from the rest of them, almost as if they hadn't been planned properly. The killer may have been forced into doing something that he wasn't really ready to do and he might have been sloppy for the first time," Carpenter commented as his partner hit the buttons on the phone and hung up.

"I think it's time for us to go home and sleep on all this new information. Maybe at the first of the week, Konkle will have some good news."

CHAPTER TWENTY-SEVEN

While Paul sat quietly in his chair by the fire and sipped on his scotch, he threw the remnants of his bloody shirt and his ruined jacket into the fire and watched them turn into flames and smoke. As soon as his first scotch of the day was gone, he went into the bathroom and took the makeshift bandage off his shoulder and looked at his wound. He was thankful that the wound was just a crease because if he had needed medical treatment for a gunshot wound, he would have been in serious trouble. He winced as he washed the cut with a warm washcloth and once it was patted dry with a soft towel, it actually looked clean. He thought that it would heal fine, but it would likely leave a one and a half inch scar where the bullet had creased the side of his upper arm. He cleaned the wound with some rubbing alcohol and then smeared it with Polysporin, the only disinfectant he had around the place. He wrapped it properly in gauze and taped it so the bandage would stay in place while the healing process started.

Paul just relaxed for the rest of the day and read by the fire until it was time for the six o'clock news broadcast on Global. He wanted to hear the report about the two Jamaican drug traffickers who were killed in Scarborough.

Beverly Thomson started with the local news: "Early this morning, metro police found two bodies in a car in the Victoria Park and Danforth area. The men appear to be two more victims in what has been commonly called The Oyster-Shucking Murders. The total number of deaths attributed to the same killer is now seven. One of the victims had been shot in the head and the other had been stabbed to death with an oyster-shucking knife. The police have advised that the two dead men have long record sheets and are members of a well known Jamaican gang of drug traffickers who operate in the east end of the city. The police are concerned about the more violent and out of control nature of these murders and ask anyone who has any information about the victims or the killer or killers to contact Detectives Graham Everdell or Jack Carpenter at 416-999-INFO. The police are still probing the recent murders and will provide further details as the investigation continues."

As the newscast ended, Paul was a little ticked off about the tone of the comments supposedly made by the police that the murders had become *more violent* because one of the victims had his brains splattered all over the front seat of the car. They had no idea what had happened that night and they were blaming him for being violent. The Jamaicans were going to kill him for a few grand. *Perhaps it's time to have another chat with Detective Everdell and straighten him out again*, Paul thought.

Paul wondered about the total number of murders to date being reported as only seven and had a feeling that the police and the media hadn't picked up on the death of Vito Morelli in Boca Raton, Florida. If the police knew about Morelli's death, they had not shared that information with members of the public or the media. As Paul sat back and relaxed, he thought to himself, *Only one more to go!*

Paul took it easy for the rest of the night and read until the nine o'clock movie started. At the end of the movie, he watched the news but there was no more information about the killings, so he went to bed. He slept well, but had dreams about Liz, Ricky and Laurie. The dreams were not bad dreams, they were about missing people he loved and cared about. He was developing a strong urge to spend some more time with Laurie and the Christmas season was fast approaching. Holidays were always a very lonely time for Paul. Still in bed, he decided that he would call Laurie and see what her plans were for the Christmas season. It had been a long time since he had been to New York.

Paul eventually got up and soon found himself in the bathroom shaving. The sideburns that tend to lengthen all on their own came off. The goatee disappeared too. He left the mustache in place because he was actually starting to like it. As he was in the shower, Paul noticed that the water was hesitating so he made a mental note to check out the water pump. Once out of the shower, Paul changed the wet bandages on his shoulder and dressed the wound again. It was almost at the stage where it wouldn't need to be covered, so he thought that the next day, he would leave the bandage off and let the air heal it.

* * *

After a good breakfast of coffee, toast, bacon and eggs, Paul grabbed his tool box and went out to the back porch to inspect the water pump to find out what was causing the water flow problems. He quickly saw that there was water all over the place and that one of the joints had sprung a leak. He turned the pump off and found that the washers needed to be replaced. He didn't have any so he decided to drive to Oshawa. As he drove the sixty-five miles to the automotive town near Toronto, he decided that he would make two phone calls; one to Laurie and one to Detective Everdell.

After Paul picked up the materials that he needed to fix his water pump at a hardware store in the Oshawa Centre, he found a bank of telephones on the lower level of the mall in an area with not many shoppers around. He held the receiver with a gloved hand and used a pencil to dial the toll free number that had been given in the newscast; the same one that he had used before.

"Is Detective Graham Everdell there, please?"

"One moment, sir."

"Detective Everdell. Can I help you?"

"I watched the news report last night about the dead Jamaicans in Scarborough and I'm a little concerned that you seem to think that these killings are becoming *more violent and out of control.*"

"Who's calling please?" Everdell asked as a chill ran through his whole body when he realized that he was speaking to the killer for the second time.

"You know who's calling. I want to clear up a few things."

"What kind of things?" Everdell asked, and quickly motioned to Carpenter and Speer that the killer was on the line and to quickly get someone to try to trace the call if he could keep him on the line long enough, just in case he wasn't using a pay phone.

The two men got up quickly and rushed toward the outer offices to do what had to be done.

"I just want you to know that those two Jamaicans were going to rob me of only a few grand and then kill me! The passenger in the front seat pulled his gun first. That's why all that shit went down in the car. I only intended to kill Ruffus Allan, the leader of that gang of drug traffickers."

"Can I ask you a question?" Everdell asked as he tried to keep him talking.

"Sure, but do it quickly, it's almost time to hang up."

"Did you kill Vito Morelli in Fort Lauderdale?"

"All I can say is that I have a nice tan. That piece of shit deserved to die too," Paul answered and went on. "I have some good news for you!"

"And what's that?"

"There's only one more victim. Then it will all be over!" Paul said as he hung up.

* * *

As Paul drove back to Highway 401 and took the east ramp, he got up enough nerve to call Laurie on his disposable cell phone. He had a great time in Fort Lauderdale and really enjoyed making love with her, but for some reason, this shy complex came over him as he wondered if she might already have a date for the holiday season. *What the hell!* he thought. He dialed her New York work number and crossed his fingers.

"Smeenk Securities!"

"I'd like to speak to Laurie Crawford, please."

The call was put through to a pleasant woman who almost acted like she knew him when she found out who was on the phone.

"Ms. Crawford's assistant, Nancy, can I help you?"

"Hi! Jack Randall calling. Is Laurie Crawford available?"

"Mr. Randall!" She sounded excited. "Ms. Crawford is with clients, but I'm sure that she will want to take your call. Please hang on while I interrupt her."

There was about a two minute pause on the phone and Paul got the feeling, from listening to her assistant, that Laurie might have mentioned the new guy who she had met on her trip to Florida and that he might call her sometime. Paul was glad of the response.

"Hello, Laurie Crawford."

"Hi, I just called to see if you have any plans for dinner?"

"No, I don't. Why, are you in New York?"

"No, but I really wish that I was. I thought that if you had plans for dinner then you would have already met a new guy and I'd be outta luck."

"Jack, you stupid ass! Why are you getting me all excited? I thought that you were here and you were really going to take me out for dinner tonight!"

"I would love to but I'm in Canada. I'm calling because I've been thinking about you and I want to see you. What have you got planned for the Christmas holidays?"

"Christmas is on Wednesday so I'm taking the following week off and going home to Boston to see my folks, but I don't have to stay there right through to New Year's Eve! What are your plans for the holidays?"

"I don't have any commitments, that's why I'm calling you."

"If I spend Christmas with my folks, I can be back in New York on the Friday. Why don't you come here on the Friday or Saturday and stay through New Year's Eve? We'll go to Times Square or something."

"That sounds great! New York on New Year's Eve! I'm sure that we'll find something fun to do. I'll plan on being in New York on

Saturday by noon, depending on the flights. I'll call you and let you know my schedule and don't worry about picking me up, I'll just take a cab to your place from the airport. I can't wait to see you."

"I'm really looking forward to seeing you too. I'm sure we'll have lots of fun, but Jack, bring a sports jacket and slacks, because my boss, Frank Smeenk and his wife, Jan, are having a cocktail party that we'll be invited to during the holidays."

"Ya know, I was a little reluctant to call you because I thought that you'd be busy, but I'm really glad I did. I am looking forward to seeing you again."

"Me too, Merry Christmas and I'll see you on the Saturday."

Paul was excited because of Laurie's response to his call. It appeared that she hadn't found someone new and had been hoping that he would call. He was glad that he decided to contact her. He had no plans for the Christmas season and definitely no plans for New Year's Eve, mainly because he was *dead*, but he could be *alive* in New York City. He loved that city even though he hadn't been there for about five years. He remembered that he could almost feel the city vibrate as soon as he got off the plane. He and Laurie had enjoyed each other so much that he was sure that the vibrations would continue during his visit.

* * *

The drive back to Beer Lake was pretty ordinary and Paul felt so good about the pending trip to New York that he didn't even notice how long it took to get there. Driving the speed limit always made the drive longer. Christmas would pass by easily and quickly now. He would have all of the excitement of New York City to look forward to for New Years and the arms of a gal who he hadn't been sure about when he left Florida. He assumed that she would go home to a number of boyfriends and never think about him again, but he had been wrong. He knew from the tone of her secretary's voice that Laurie had mentioned him to her.

Paul was glad that he had called Detective Everdell too and

straightened him out. He thought that the police would be happy to hear that the killings were coming to an end soon. He kept repeating to himself, *Just one more!*

At the time, Paul didn't realize the effect that his relationship with Laurie was having on his mission for revenge. He would be finished killing people soon, because deep inside he didn't like doing it anyway. The memory of Ricky and all the other victims spurred him on to finish his list of those people who were responsible for ruining the lives of so many families.

Paul decided to put the fact that he had one more drug trafficker to kill out of his mind until after the holiday season was over. The only thing he was going to think about was Christmas all alone at Beer Lake and that would be much easier for him to get through this year because he had plans to see Laurie for a few days during the holiday season. One of those thoughts gave him a serious chubby.

CHAPTER TWENTY-EIGHT

The three men involved in The Oyster-Shucking Murders investigations were all seated in the private room reading the Forensic Report on the bodies found in the white Mercedes at Victoria Park and Danforth. The detectives had been at the scene and totally understood what Konkle was saying in the detailed report. However, Bill Speer had not been there first hand and it was all new to him.

"What the hell is he saying?" Speer asked. "It sounds like there was a gunfight in the car before the two guys in the front seat were actually killed."

"That's what it looks like," Carpenter answered with a bit of a smirk on his face. "The passenger in the front seat pulled a gun on the guy in the backseat and there was some kind of an altercation. It appears that the guy in the backseat won!"

"He definitely won the gunfight, but not before getting shot. The fact that the blood stains in the backseat are on the left rear door and window suggests that the killer got shot in the left arm. He leaned on the door and window while he killed the driver with the oyster-shucking knife," Everdell added.

Speer went on, "It really isn't his bag to kill his victims with other people around. Don't you find it all a bit strange?"

"Yeah. He's been more careful in the past," Carpenter said.

"Let's think about it." Everdell went on, "If he was after Ruffus Allan because he was a drug trafficker, maybe the other guy just happened to be in the wrong place at the wrong time and something bad went down."

"The killer usually finds some way to get his victims alone. Maybe the guy hadn't planned on killing anyone at that moment in time," Speer added.

"Ruffus Allan had to be his target," Carpenter said. "Something must have happened in the car that caused the killer to act sooner than he had planned."

"That would account for the fact that he had to kill someone else with a gun and not in his usual way," Speer went on.

"For some reason," Everdell added, "the killer was in the car with those two drug traffickers. He was more than likely looking for an opportunity to kill Ruffus, but something must have happened?"

"My guess is that the killer has always been ready to deal with things if they didn't go according to plan. He probably always had a gun with him, and in the past, he had been lucky enough not to need one," Carpenter commented.

"Look at the blood reports," Everdell went on, "the victims in the front seat are O Rh Positive and the blood on the back window and door is AB Rh Negative. It's very rare and it has to belong to the shooter."

"Is there any information on the bullet that was fired from the backseat?" Speer asked.

"The shell casing from the handgun that was fired by the guy in the backseat wasn't found. It must have been picked up by the killer," Everdell said.

"Konkle said there wasn't much left of the bullet in the front seat and Forensics couldn't tell what it was, but they think it's a thirty-eight," Carpenter went on.

"Other than that information, it appears from the report that there isn't much more evidence from the car or the surrounding area that we can go on," Speer said.

"That's right." Everdell answered, "We've got the oyster-shucking knife that appears to be the same as the others, the RH Negative blood on the back door and the disintegrated slug that *might* be a thirty-eight. All of the hospitals and doctors have to report any gun-shot wounds they treat but we haven't heard a thing yet."

"If the guy shot the passenger and then killed the driver with the knife, after he got shot, he sure the hell wasn't hurt very badly," Carpenter suggested.

"What did you learn at the house where the two victims lived?" Speer asked.

"It was a beautiful home in an exclusive neighbourhood and appeared to be owned by Ruffus Allan. Some of the members of his posse seemed to be sharing the house with him," Everdell said.

"There was a substantial amount of money in the master bedroom, which was decorated for sex orgies, and a very small amount of cocaine, but we didn't really search the place because we didn't have a Search Warrant," Carpenter continued.

"There were four or five trophies in the pool room of the house from a place called Willie's Billiards. It's located at Victoria Park and Eglinton," Everdell added.

"We're going to start there and see if we can find some people who knew the victims. Maybe we can put some kind of a timetable together about what the men were doing and who they were with the night they died," Carpenter said.

Everdell continued. "The guys from Forensics are going through the house as we speak, under the authority of the Search Warrant that you got for them. They may find something in the house to add to the whole puzzle."

"You two had better get out there and find out how those three guys got together. The two Jamaicans frequented Willie's Billiards so someone must know them," Speer said as he got ready to leave the small room, but stopped because the phone rang.

"Detective Graham Everdell, can I help you?"

As soon as he heard the voice, a chill went through his body. He knew it was the killer. He had spoken to him before. He frantically waved his free hand at Carpenter and Speer to try to get a trace on the line and they rushed to the outer office. Unfortunately, the conversation didn't last long enough. By the time Everdell hung up, Carpenter and Speer were standing over him. He passed on the contents of the conversation.

"The two Jamaicans were going to rob him and kill him! That's why that whole thing went down the way it did in the Mercedes. He hadn't planned on killing the two guys at that time."

"They sure as hell picked the wrong guy to rob," Carpenter commented.

"Do you want to hear the good news?" Everdell asked.

"What the hell kind of good news would the killer have for us?" Speer asked.

"He said that he's only got one more drug trafficker on his hit list. It sounds like he has plans for just one more murder."

"Christ! There are lots of them in city, I wonder who the lucky guy is?" Speer commented with a half smile.

Everdell was feeling tired and spoke directly to Speer, "Billy, can you get someone to see where the call came from just in case it was a pay phone. Also if it is, get one of the other guys to take someone from Forensics to wherever the hell it originated to try to get some prints. I'm sure there won't be any because this guy seems to be way too cool. Jack and I really have more important things to do this afternoon."

"Sure, no problem," Speer answered, "it's done."

* * *

It was one o'clock by the time Everdell and Carpenter got to Willie's Billiards and as soon as they walked into the huge room, they sat down on stools at the bar. About fifteen tables had customers playing pool and two other guys were sitting at the bar having a beer. The bartender approached the detectives.

"What can I get you guys?"

"We'd just like a little information," Carpenter said as he showed his badge. "You obviously heard that Ruffus Allan and Arthur Jacobi were murdered the other night. Did they spend any time here at the pool hall the night they were killed?"

"Too bad, they were really good customers. Yeah, they almost lived here."

"What time did they arrive and leave that day?" Everdell asked.

"There was always half a dozen of them who would arrive mid-afternoon and often stay through until eight or nine o'clock at night. The day they were killed was no exception," the bartender said as he pointed. "That pool table back there in the corner, by the windows, is where they hang out."

"We all know that Ruffus Allan and his posse trafficked drugs all over Scarborough. Did he or his associates deal drugs out of here?" Everdell asked.

"No way! If they ever did, they would have been banned."

"Do you know most of Allan's buddies?" Carpenter asked.

"Yeah, I know them, they still come in. They should be here any-time now."

"Why don't we have lunch and wait and talk to them," Everdell suggested. "Are your burgers any good?"

"They're the best in town. I'd recommend the banquet burger because it comes loaded with cheese and bacon and our fries are super!"

"Sounds good to me and I'll have a diet Coke," Everdell replied.

"The same for me," Carpenter added.

The bartender turned away for a few moments to put the food orders into the kitchen and came back to talk to the policemen. He liked to chat.

"Ruffus and his posse were in here all afternoon and evening the day that he and Artie were killed. They played pool back there until close to nine o'clock."

"Was it just a usual day for them? Do they just play pool with their own group or did they meet some other people that day?" Carpenter asked.

"It was just a normal day. Ruffus fancied himself a pool shark so he often challenged other guys to games of pool for serious money," the bartender said. "Come to think of it, he did have a mark late Friday afternoon. Some guy had been playing a couple of tables over from Ruffus for a few hours and they eventually played a num-ber of games together. I remember that Ruffus came by here to go to the can and he made some comment that the guy had a real bank roll. I know the guy lost money to Ruffus because he paid for the table when they were done."

"Is the guy a regular here at the pool hall?" Everdell asked.

"No, but I think that he was in here a couple of days in a row."

"Do you remember what the guy looked like?" Everdell asked.

"Yeah, he had lunch right where you two are sitting. He was a white guy, about thirty-five or so, six feet tall and in really good shape. He had dark hair, with sideburns and a mustache and a bit of a goatee. He wore a Blue Jays cap."

Everdell and Carpenter glanced at each other as Carpenter continued, "Would you recognize him again if you saw him?"

"Sure, I'd recognize him. We talked a bit while he had his lunch and he seemed like a nice guy. Actually, here comes Ben through the door right now. He played pool with the guy for a couple of hours before he started to play with Ruffus. Ben, these two cops probably want to talk to you."

The policemen introduced themselves to Ben and suggested that they move to a table away from the bar so that they could speak in private. Ben complied.

"Do you want a beer or anything?" the bartender asked Ben before they left.

"Sure, I'll have a Coor's Light."

The cops picked up their diet Cokes and Ben grabbed his beer and they walked over and sat together at a small table to the right of the bar.

"We're investigating the deaths of Ruffus Allan and Arthur Jacobi which took place sometime late Friday night," Carpenter explained.

"We understand that you played pool in here for a couple of hours on Friday afternoon with a guy who ended up playing with Ruffus after you left. Did you know the two men who were killed?" Everdell asked.

"Yeah, I knew them to see them. I played pool with Gord and I think he said that he was from Oshawa or somewhere. I played with him one other time a couple of weeks ago and won some money and I won some more from him the other day too. You can't think that he had anything to do with the murders, can you? He's a really nice guy!"

"You just never know with people. We have to look at everything and everybody," Carpenter explained.

The detectives asked Ben for a full description of his friend Gord and it matched exactly what the bartender had said. They questioned Ben at length while they ate and took his personal data so he could be contacted again. As soon as they finished with him, they sent him on his way and continued to sit and talk about the latest information. They waited for Ruffus Allan's posse to arrive.

"The description matches the one we got from the witnesses at the hospital and at Sweethearts when Eddie Firestone got it. I can't believe the similarities. He's gotta be the same guy," Everdell said shaking his head.

"This is the closest we've got to him," Carpenter commented.

Just as they started to chat, five black guys came through the main door of the pool hall. As they walked toward the bar, Everdell got up quickly with his badge outstretched in his hand and spoke to them.

"I'm Detective Graham Everdell and I'm investigating the deaths of Ruffus Allan and Arthur Jacobi. My partner and I would like to have a few words with you guys."

"No bloody problem, mon, we do what we kin do to help fin' the bastards that do it," the brother who appeared to be leading the gang into the pool hall answered.

Carpenter stood up and said, "All of you guys come and sit down here with us. Grab some chairs from that other table."

The five Jamaicans joined the policemen at the small table. The cops thought that they were dressed like rappers, in baggy, bright colored clothes with toques. Everdell spoke to the one who appeared to have become the new leader since Ruffus Allan's untimely departure.

"First of all, what's your name?"

"I'm Leroy Thomas."

"Leroy, we understand that you guys spent all of Friday afternoon and the early evening in here shooting pool with Ruffus and Arthur?"

"Not all of us," Leroy answered pointing to a couple of his friends, "these two guys weren't round 'ere Friday, jus' the rest of us."

"We've been told that Ruffus played pool for two or three hours with some white guy who was here most of Friday afternoon and evening. Is that true?" Carpenter asked.

"Yeah, we was just hangin' round, like we always do, at our table over 'dere in the corner and two white boys was shootin' pool a couple o' tables away. They was passin' money back and fort. Ruffus noticed the one guy had a really big bankroll that he kept peelin' them bills off when he lost the games, so Ruffus decided that he wanted ta git it from 'im."

"What do you mean, get it from him?" Everdell asked.

"I mean beat 'im at pool for it, mon! Ruffus was a pretty good pool player if he wasn't all fucked-up. So when the one white boy left, Ruffus ask this guy Gord if he want ta play fer some real money 'an he took up the challenge. O'er the next couple o' hours Ruffus beat him good. He was up 'bout five or six hundred dollar when we left 'em here."

"We all decided ta go down ta the Danforth ta a club that we go ta all the time and I think the white guy was gonna go with us. The three of us left first, in my own car, and we was gonna meet the rest o' dem 'dere later. Dey never show up."

"So the white guy, who everyone calls Gord, went with Ruffus and Artie in their car?"

"I tink dat wen' down, mon. We wen' straight down ta da club on da Danforth and never saw dem agin' after we left 'ere."

The detectives took the personal information from the Jamaicans and took notes as they spoke. The description of the white man who had played pool with Ruffus Allan matched what the others had said. All the witnesses who were interviewed at the pool hall gave the same information. At about nine o'clock on Friday evening, Allan and Jacobi had left the building with the white man they all remembered and described.

"Let's go back to headquarters and put all of this information together and report to Speer," Everdell suggested.

"OK, let's do it," Carpenter agreed. "This is the first time that we've had any serious evidence to work with and I'm getting pumped again."

CHAPTER TWENTY-NINE

I t snowed four or five times before Christmas and Beer Lake looked like a winter wonderland. Paul hung around and relaxed in his favorite chair by the fire and read or watched television. He did his daily work out and lifted weights to stay in shape. Every afternoon, he went for a long hike in the bush and enjoyed the scenery. As Christmas Day approached, he felt a bit down as he remembered the old days and the holiday seasons with Liz and Ricky. He still missed them terribly, but realized that his life had changed substantially since Ricky had gone. He had done things, that years ago, he wouldn't have even contemplated doing and he was feeling better for doing them. There were eight drug dealers and traffickers off the streets of the city and not poisoning teenagers any longer. Paul knew that others would take their place, but he still felt that he had accomplished something.

During those days, Paul thought about his lost family often, but he also thought about Laurie in New York City and was looking forward to spending some more time with her. He really did miss having a woman in his life, someone to touch, to hold. He knew that he hadn't fallen totally in love with Laurie, but he really liked her a lot and they had fun together. She had sounded glad to hear from him. He was counting the days until he could head for *The Big Apple*.

Christmas and the few days that followed turned out to be quite sad and lonely for Paul as time moved very slowly at Beer Lake. On Friday, he packed for the trip to New York and made sure that he took enough clothing to last through to the second of January. He remembered that Laurie had wanted him to bring some dressy clothes so he threw in a couple of sports jackets and slacks. As he got his things together, he opened the passport that he had been using in the name of Gordon William Thoburn and looked at it for a long time. He decided that he had been using that name far too long and it was time for a change. Laurie knew him as Jack Randall so that's who he would be while he was around her, but he would travel under his other alias, Clive Edward Lyons.

Paul drove into the long-term parking lot at Casino Niagara, in Niagara Falls, at close to five-thirty that afternoon. He parked his old Ford and carried his bags to the main foyer of the casino where he called the Airport Express shuttle that he had used on his last trip. He arrived at the Buffalo Niagara International Airport around eight and called Laurie on his disposable cell phone. He wasn't sure if she would be back in New York after spending Christmas with her folks in Boston because she wasn't expecting him until the next day. If she wasn't home or was busy, he would stay in Buffalo for the night and fly out on his original schedule in the morning. She answered the phone on the second ring.

"It's your Canadian buddy calling. Merry Christmas! I hope you had a nice time with your family."

"I did, Jack. Merry Christmas. I wasn't expecting to hear from you until the morning."

"The weather report said that a terrible snowstorm is coming to the Toronto area, so I drove to Buffalo today and I'm either going to get a hotel room here for the night and come to New York in the morning like I had planned or I'm gonna jump on a Jet Blue and be there in a couple of hours. It's up to you."

"This is great! I want you here in an hour, not two!" Laurie said sounding excited. "I'm really looking forward to seeing you again."

"I'll grab the next flight outta here and I'll cab it from Kennedy. I've got your address memorized, 568 E. 8th St., in the east part of Greenwich Village, so I'll be there as soon as I can!"

"That's great! I'll have a bottle of my favorite red wine open and breathing."

* * *

Paul was glad that he had made the call because Laurie really did sound excited to hear from him. The next flight to J.F.K. was in just thirty minutes and he was on it. The plane got to the airport in no time and his luggage cleared quickly. The traffic was slow because of snow flurries, but it kept moving across Highway 495, through Queens, and into Manhattan. As Paul passed through Union Square, he knew that he was heading toward the East Village and the Brownstone that Laurie called home. The closer he got to her place the more anxious he was to see her. Paul gave the cabby a twenty dollar tip since it was Christmas. He was happier than he had been in a long time.

As soon as the door opened, Laurie, dressed in dark slacks and a pretty, off-white blouse, almost jumped into Paul's arms and kissed him. She was glad to see him and he was happy to be there. As she stepped back, and Paul had a chance to look at her, she was much more attractive than he had remembered. The unbelieveable body was the same though. He realized, right at that moment, that he had really missed her.

"Jack, this is really a nice Christmas present. I'm glad you were able to get here tonight."

"I almost didn't call just in case you had a date or something. I didn't want to interfere with any plans that you might have had this evening. You never know, it is the Christmas season and I'm sure that I'm not the only guy who wants to be with you during the holiday season."

"I told you before that I'm not dating anyone. I wasn't when we met in Florida, and I'm not now. I must admit, ever since you called and we made these plans, I've been really wishing that you would get here!"

"Well, I'm here now!"

"Just leave your bags by the stairs and come with me. I'll pour you a glass of the red wine that's been waiting for you."

Paul followed her into the well-decorated living room with a gas fireplace burning. There was a new bottle of red wine sitting on the coffee table with two glasses and as they sat down on the leather sofa, Laurie poured.

"I hope that you like this wine, it's a California Merlot called Charles Shaw. I drink it a lot, but it's very hard to find. I've really been enjoying it."

"Don't worry about me and what I drink. I've never met a bottle of red that I didn't like."

"I'll tell you an interesting story about it after you've tasted it."

"Here's to a fabulous few days for two people who seem to have missed each other and to a great New Year's Eve!" Paul said with a caring smile.

"I'll drink to that," Laurie said as she looked into his eyes in a way that he could tell that she was happy too.

They clinked their glasses together and Laurie spoke, "Do you like the wine?"

"It tastes great. It's very smooth."

"I have to tell you the wine story. Charles Shaw won a number of awards for this wine and I think it's only made once a year and put on the market. It sells for only two dollars and everyone calls it *Two Buck Chuck*!"

"I can't believe it's only two dollars a bottle. It tastes great!"

They leaned toward each other and kissed, slowly, intimately and for a long time. When their lips finally parted, they both took another sip of *Two Buck Chuck*.

"I really had a nice Christmas with my family in Boston and after I got there, I had a serious case of the guilts. I was really sorry that I hadn't thought to invite you to come with me. I'm sure that Christmas is not a great time for you back home and you would have been more than welcomed at my parents' place."

"It was nice of you to even think about me. My Christmas was fine. The thing that really made it wonderful was I knew that I was coming to see you."

"Well, I felt badly. Our family has a very relaxed Christmas; we just eat and drink. I must have gained about five pounds over the holidays that I'm gonna have to get rid of soon."

"You have nothing to worry about, you look great!" Paul said as he looked her up and down and kissed her again.

She kissed him back. They felt good together. They kissed a number of times through the first glass of wine and as Paul was about to pour the second glass, Laurie stopped him and came up with a great idea.

"I don't know about you, but I haven't had a hug since you and I were in Florida almost a month ago. I think that we should take the wine upstairs and get more comfortable because it's starting to get late anyway."

"That suits me fine. I haven't had a cuddle since then either."

"Grab your luggage and I'll bring the wine and turn out the lights down here."

Paul followed Laurie up to the master bedroom on the second floor. As he opened his suitcase on a chair in the corner and hung up his things that were in the suit-bag, she got a clean bath towel out of the closet and put it in the bathroom. He took his shaving kit in, put it on the sink and then joined her in the bedroom.

"I love your home. Did you do all of the decorating yourself?"

"I did most of it myself, but I did have some input from a friend of mine who is an interior designer. I came up with most of the ideas and colors."

"It looks great and so do you," Paul said as he pulled her toward him and as they finished kissing, he asked, "Do you want me to pour the wine?"

"No, I want you to kiss me some more. I was going to have a shower after you called, but decided to wait because I have a lot of trouble washing my back."

"I just happen to be a back-scrubbing expert, so let's do it before we both get carried away and don't make it to the shower."

They kissed as they undressed each other. Laurie went into the bathroom and started the shower and stepped into the warm water. Paul followed. There were two bars of soap so each one had something to rub all over the other. The almost healed scar on his arm was explained as a home accident. They kissed and washed and washed and kissed until they were squeaky clean and it became quite obvious that they were both ready for something more. Paul reached out of the shower for a condom from his shaving kit and tore it open. As the warm water poured down on them, Laurie took it out of his hand and knelt down to put it on for him, but she didn't put it on immediately. Paul thought that he was in heaven. As soon as it was in place, Laurie stood up and kissed him deeply. As he lifted her up and the warm water flooded over them, she put both of her feet on the sides of the tub and raised herself up as if to help. At the right moment, she lowered herself back down, up and down, up and down in the warm water and steam.

A little while later, they sat with their backs against the headboard with glasses of wine in their hands and caught up on what they had been doing during the past month. Laurie had done the Christmas party circuit with clients. She had also spent lots of time shopping for family presents. Paul had to make up things because he couldn't tell her the truth. He had done nothing that he could actually talk about. They drank their wine and laughed. As soon as the wine was gone they settled in under the covers and made love again. This time, it was two lonely people involved in plain, old, dirty sex, in every position that they could imagine, for a long, long time. They really enjoyed each other. By the time they were ready to go to sleep, they had to remake the bed.

* * *

Sunday turned out to be a cold and crisp, sunny day. Bright sunlight shone in through a large window and woke Paul and Laurie at about ten o'clock. They decided that it was too nice a day to waste in bed, so they got up and got moving. Laurie put on the coffee while Paul shaved and then they showered together, much more calmly than the night before. While they were drying each other and playing around, Paul got aroused, so Laurie sat down on the lid of the toilet and pulled him close to her and took almost all of him into her mouth. She did it well and liked what she was doing. As it happened, Paul's head started to spin as he tried to remember the last time that he had received a blowjob. He couldn't remember, but he knew that it had been far too long ago. By eleven, they were seated in the kitchen drinking coffee.

"I'm really glad that you decided to come to New York last night. I really enjoy being with you. You feel soooo good!"

"I enjoy you too. This was a lot more fun than spending the night in Buffalo."

"Let's go for breakfast to one of my favorite restaurants in Greenwich Village and then, if it's not too cold, we can take a walk in Central Park."

"That sounds great! How do you get around this town? Do we have to call a cab or can we catch one outside on the street?"

"I'll call the company I always use. They only take about ten minutes," Laurie answered as she picked up the phone on the counter. "The restaurant I love is called the Durham Café and they serve a fantastic Spanish omelette and great bacon and eggs."

They went outside to wait for the cab and to a beautiful, cold day, full of fresh air. The temperature was hovering around freezing, but it seemed warmer because of the sunshine. The cab went onto Park Avenue and headed north into the village. Paul had never been in that part of the city and found it quite fascinating. Everything was neat, the buildings, the stores and the restaurants. Breakfast turned out to be lots of fun and the food was the best. Laurie introduced him to the owners of the Durham Café, Steve and Debbie Green, who were clients of hers. They took a cab to Central Park right after they ate and walked for about an hour. They stopped for Cappuccinos around three o'clock and shortly after that, took a cab back to Laurie's brownstone.

"I'm kind of tired after that long walk in the park," Laurie said with a smile, "do you feel like an afternoon nap?"

"I sure do. As long as I don't have to go to sleep."

"You don't and by the way, after that treat this morning, I think you owe me!"

"It's very strange you should say that because that was exactly what I was thinking," Paul answered with a laugh.

They walked upstairs together and got ready for a cuddle. They dropped their clothes, freshened up in the bathroom and got into bed. They enjoyed each other and seemed to be a perfect fit. They did end up having a nap and decided to stay in bed for the rest of the night. They watched the eight o'clock movie. The two of them talked and laughed and had a lot of fun. The evening was wonderful and they made love quietly and gently before they both had a good night's sleep. Their feelings for each other were growing stronger without them even realizing it was happening.

Sunday evening was the cocktail party at Frank and Jan Smeenk's lovely condo that overlooked the city. Paul had a good time and hit it off with Laurie's boss. The next couple of days were spent just hanging out together and having a few laughs. On Monday night, Paul took Laurie to one of his favorite restaurants, The Palm, and they both had great steak dinners with lots of red wine, of course. On Tuesday, New Year's Eve, Paul took Laurie to one of his old hang-outs, the Bull and the Bear at the Waldorf Astoria. Oscar, the Cuban bartender, who had been there since the beginning of time, poured the best drinks in town. They got there around nine and eventually made it to Times Square by eleven-thirty in lots of time to bring in the New Year with the thousands of people in the streets. On New Year's day, Paul got up to shave and as he was in the shower, Laurie joined him. They ended up staying in bed all day. It was to be their last one together for awhile and it was fantastic.

* * *

As Paul sat in the cab on his way to JFK on Thursday morning, Laurie was all he could think about. He could still smell her special aroma. He could still taste her. He missed her already. It had been a wonderful five days and quite to his surprise, he was beginning to fall for the gal from New York. She was successful, attractive, had a body to die for and had been lots of fun, not only in the sack, but out of it too. They seemed very compatible and enjoyed being together. He had the feeling that she really liked him too. The only thing that he wondered about was when he might be able to see her again. He still had something to do. He had to delete that one last name from his list.

Since Paul had met Laurie, he had been thinking about the drug dealers and traffickers and although they all deserved to pay for what they had done to so many families, he was getting tired of the killing. He couldn't keep committing murders forever. However, he wasn't so tired that he wasn't going to finish off the Russian, but he knew that he couldn't just keep killing people without eventually getting caught. He would make a mistake one day. Paul decided that as soon as the Russian got what was coming to him, he would cease and desist and try to decide what to do with the rest of his life. Subconsciously, his feelings for Laurie had something to do with his new line of thinking. He had lots of money that was safely placed in offshore bank accounts. He was dead to the world, so if he was to start a life in some other country, he would use the third and final identity that he had for himself. The one that Laurie knew him as, Jack Melville Randall. The one that had absolutely no ties to his law firm.

As soon as he got back to Canada and Beer Lake, Gordon William Thoburn, was definitely retired because that identity had been used long enough. He had used the name, Clive Edward Lyons, another deceased client of his that was tied to his law firm, to fly to New York. He would use that alias one more time, to take care of Vladmir Rousinsky, and then that identity would be retired. He would become his old friend, Jack Melville Randall, a man who now had a future and he would travel to South America, Europe or the Pacific Rim and start a new life. As he considered his options, Laurie Crawford's face kept flashing through his mind.

CHAPTER THIRTY

Everdell and Carpenter used their overtime from The Oyster-Shucking Murders to take two full weeks off during the Christmas holidays. Their wives and families had been delighted to have them home for a change. Prior to leaving for the holidays, they made sure that the lists of airline passengers from the carriers out of Toronto and Buffalo who flew to Lauderdale during the week before Morelli was murdered, the ballistic reports on the bullets found in Ruffus Allan's Mercedes and the blood report on the smudges that were found on the backseat door, would be on their desk by the time they returned to work.

In the new year, the detectives planned to revisit all aspects of the first murder in the chain of mission killings, the murder of Steven Shackleton. Someone was on a *mission* to rid the streets of Toronto of all of the drug dealers and traffickers who were involved in the deaths of the students so long ago. Shackleton's murder was so different from the other seven that it continually haunted the detectives as they probed their files.

"Happy New Year! Now that you two have rested for a couple of weeks, I want you to get right into The Oyster-Shucking Murders and I don't want you to let up until you get this guy," Bill Speer said as he came through the door of the small room. "I'm under some real pressure here from the Chief and the Mayor."

"Happy New Year to you too!" Everdell said. "It's really nice to be missed."

"Bill, we have the reports on the Morelli and Allan murders. We've heard from absolutely everyone," Carpenter said. "We have every piece of evidence that is available."

"Great! Now get the hell through it all and nail that guy!" Speer snapped as he left the two detectives alone in their cubby-hole.

"He's in a great fuckin' mood to start the new year," Everdell commented.

"He'll settle down. Now where do you think we should start."

"Jack, look at the length of the passenger lists. I don't think there's any point in us looking through them. Let's give them to Judy, in Admin, and she can put them into the computer by airport and give us a list of the passengers who live in the metro area. As far as Buffalo, maybe she can just list the Canadians who were flying that week."

"That's a great idea. It'll save us a lot of screwing around."

"I'll run them up to her. She's probably swamped, but I'm sure that she'll take care of it for us," Everdell said as he got up and left the room.

Carpenter put the Shackleton murder file in front of him and started to go through it. He had read it so many times, he knew it off by heart. As he read, he glanced at the notes on the blackboard and recalled that there were three victims from Medford, two dead and one permanently in the hospital.

"Why was that murder so different from the rest?" Carpenter said to his partner as he came back into the room.

"The obvious answer is that the killer had a relationship with one of the victims who attended Medford. That has to be the case, unless the killer is some crazy vigilante and I don't think so. Let's assume that he is a relative or friend of one of the kids."

"Let's take that approach and look at the families again. We've already talked to the relatives, on two occasions, without coming up with anything."

"Andrew McKenzie is probably in the hospital for the rest of his life with brain damage. That would certainly piss me off if he was my kid!" Everdell commented.

"June McKenzie is a widow with three other kids who all seem to share in the responsibility to visit Andrew almost daily. Andrew's brother is too young to be a suspect and there were no other close relatives. The only person who would be mad enough to take revenge out on drug dealers would likely be a father. Remember your comment about what if it had happened to one of your boys? You said that you even have a gun! As I recall, Andrew's father passed away some years back."

"Jack, I could easily spin out if something like that happened to one of my kids. Now, what about Kenneth Wilson? His parents, Charles and Betty, seem to be getting on with their lives and all of their friends confirmed that they seemed fine."

"Charles, the accountant, isn't a very big guy. I don't think that he could have handled Shackleton and Firestone; they were both tough bastards."

"There was also no indication that the Wilsons had any relatives who fit the profile. We talked to everyone."

"That leaves Richard Taylor, the kid who's mother had died of cancer two or three years ago and who's father committed suicide a year or so after the boy died of the drug overdose," Carpenter went on as he shuffled papers from the file.

"We spoke to the wife's sister, what was her name? Ah, Farwell or something, and she confirmed that she is the only living relative of that whole family. Didn't we decide that she didn't have the resources to fund a killer-for-hire?"

"Yeah, she seems to be getting on with her life too."

"Jack, we keep talking about what we, as fathers, would do if those terrible things happened to one of our kids. The fathers of the Medford victims that we haven't had an opportunity to talk to are Mr. McKenzie, who has been dead for like ten years, and Richard's father, who has been dead for about four months."

"The Farwell woman and the dead father are the only people connected to Ricky Taylor and Medford. We have her statement but nothing about the father. I think we should send for a copy of the police report on the suicide just to paper our file."

"We've done everthing else, so why not," Everdell agreed.

Two days later, the Ontario Provincial Police report had been obtained from the General Headquarters in Orillia and while the two detectives were drinking their second coffee of the morning, they both had a copy in front of them.

"Jesus Christ! Do you see what I see in this report?" Everdell asked. "Take a close look!"

"Yeah. Paul Taylor's body has never been found! All the evidence points to a suicide, but the damn body has never surfaced in Lake Simcoe!" Carpenter answered.

"He rented a fishing boat at the Pefferlaw Marina and went out in late afternoon and never came back. They found the boat washed up on the shore, about five miles from the marina, with the life-jacket that he had been wearing, a fishing rod that looked unused, an almost empty bottle of vodka and framed pictures of his dead wife and dead son."

"I can't believe it, the body hasn't been found! Why didn't someone tell us?"

"The report says that Taylor left a four or five year old Saab at the marina with some sort of suicide note in it, but they didn't even send us a copy of the note," Everdell commented. "I wonder what happened to the car?"

"I'll call the OPP right now and get them to fax us a copy. It'll be interesting to see exactly what it says."

* * *

The copy of the suicide note from the OPP didn't arrive until late Friday afternoon when Everdell and Carpenter were out working on one of their other cases so they didn't get it until the following Monday. Everdell took a look at it as soon as he settled in with his first coffee of the day. As he read it carefully, something suddenly caught his attention and he passed it to his partner.

"Jack, look at the suicide note they found in Taylor's Saab. Do you see anything that seems unusual?"

"Nothing out of the ordinary. He just left instructions to dispose of his car," Carpenter answered. "Just a minute, you're right! He directed that the money go to the Hospital For Sick Children!" Carpenter commented as he stared at Everdell.

"Let's not get excited. It might be just a coincidence, but that's where the killer dropped off Stevie Shackleton's fifty grand after he was murdered."

"It's time to have another chat with the lawyer from the law firm who we spoke to a few weeks ago. He and Taylor were buddies."

"Maybe we can get a picture of Paul Taylor from him and if he doesn't have one, we'll pay another visit to the sister-in-law," Everdell suggested.

* * *

Rod Farn was more than happy to make time to see Everdell and Carpenter as their investigations continued. He was surprised when another appointment was made by the detectives because he had already told them everything he knew about his friend. The next afternoon at three o'clock, the policemen were led into Farn's spacious office by his legal assistant. Farn rose to greet them.

"Please sit down and make yourselves comfortable. Would you like a coffee or some kind of a cold drink?" Farn asked almost immediately.

"Not for me, thanks," Carpenter said and his partner nodded in agreement.

"What can I do for you today?"

"As I mentioned on the telephone," Everdell confirmed, "we're still investigating the murders of what now appears to be eight drug dealers from the Toronto area and we've run into another dead end. All we're doing now is back-tracking and going over everything again to be sure that we haven't missed something."

"The evidence we've accumulated surrounding the murders has gone nowhere," Carpenter added so Farn wouldn't know what direction their questions were taking.

"I'll try to give you whatever information I can, but I'm sure that I told you everything I know the last time we talked."

"What we'd like you to do is think back to the months before Paul Taylor killed himself," Everdell said. "Perhaps you could describe his mental state and any strange quirks or comments that you may have noticed or heard."

"We had better start with the time period before he left the firm," Carpenter added.

"Well, he was never really the same after his wife passed away. He was totally devastated by her loss and had a hard time getting back on track. I talked to him a number of times to see if there was anything that I could do or the firm could do to help, but there was never anything he wanted. He continued to work hard and I knew that he was having some problems dealing with his son, Ricky. The youngster was a terrible mess after his mother died. We had two people with total emotional breakdowns trying to help each other and nothing worked. Paul never did really improve and when Ricky died, that was just the icing on the cake."

"Did his behaviour change very much after his son died?" Everdell asked.

"He had been working hard prior to that, but I think he thought that he was helping things by staying away from his son. As I said, he was working hard, but from a business point of view, he was just spinning his wheels. He was working, but he was in another world. Nothing was being accomplished. He was a total mess after his wife died and his relationship with his son deteriorated. When Ricky died, Paul was a disaster."

"How did you handle him at that point?" Carpenter asked.

"I finally talked him into taking some time off. He left the firm on a medical leave, so money was never an issue. Sometime later, he contacted me and told me that he had decided not to return to the firm and he wanted to be paid out for his interest."

"Then what?" Everdell asked.

"The firm arranged to pay him and Paul just disappeared for five or six months. I never heard from him again until the week he committed suicide. Out of the blue, he called me and wanted to take me out for dinner."

"How was your evening out with him?" Carpenter asked.

"The first shock that I had was the way that Paul looked. He must have worked out regularly during all those months because he was extremely fit, almost muscular, and he looked years younger. He looked fabulous, but the conversation was kind of weird. He indicated that he had sold all his assets and had donated all of the money to charity. It all sounded very strange. It was in the tone of his voice. As he left the restaurant, he made a comment that I really didn't need to worry about him because everything was going to be all right or something like that. I didn't know what the hell it all meant until I read about his suicide. I think that he took me out for dinner just to say goodbye."

"Why didn't you tell us Paul Taylor's body was never found?" Carpenter asked.

"It never crossed my mind. I assumed that you, as policemen, would know all of the particulars of his death," Farn answered.

"There's only one more thing we need before we let you get back to work. Do you happen to have any photographs of Paul Taylor that might have been taken while he was still a partner?" Everdell asked. "As near to the time of his death as possible."

"Sure we do. Our social committee takes pictures at all firm events. Why do you want a picture of him? Do you guys really think that he might still be alive?"

"The thought recently crossed our minds, but his body will likely come to the surface of Lake Simcoe during the spring thaw," Carpenter commented.

"There's no way that Paul could be involved in those murders. He just wasn't that kind of a guy. That couldn't be!"

"I'm a father and have two sons and I'd hate to think what I might be capable of if something terrible like that happened to one of them," Everdell said.

"Christ! This is all hard to believe. I'll call the co-ordinator who handles all of the firm's social events and ask her to find two or three pictures of Paul and deliver them to you in the reception area right away."

"We want to thank you for all your help," Carpenter said as the policemen shook hands with Farn.

"Now you've got me upset. I don't know whether to hope that Paul drowned in Lake Simcoe or hope that he's still alive!"

"We'll let you know if we turn up anything important," Everdell said as he and his partner left the office. "Thanks again."

The detectives didn't have to wait long in the firm's reception area before a woman arrived with a brown envelope. She handed it to Carpenter and indicated that they were the three most recent pictures of Paul Taylor that the firm had in their files. Carpenter pulled the pictures out and he and his partner looked at them.

"He's a nice looking man. What a shame that his life turned out to be such a disaster," Carpenter commented.

CHAPTER THIRTY-ONE

The plane trip from J.F.K. to Buffalo was right on time and the Airport Express shuttle was waiting for Paul to deplane. The weather was clear and the short trip back to Niagara Falls and the casino was over in no time. By the time he got his car out of the parking lot and pulled onto the Queen Elizabeth Way, eastbound toward Toronto, he figured that he would be back at Beer Lake by early afternoon.

As Paul drove leisurely along the expressway, thoughts of Laurie kept flashing through his mind. He had enjoyed spending part of the Christmas season with her. In Florida, when they had first met, he liked her, but had been more interested in getting into her pants. He had been finally ready to spend some time with a woman, any woman, and at that moment, it just happened to be her. Their few days together in The Sunshine State had been sexually charged and he had enjoyed every moment. When he left Florida, he wasn't sure if he would ever see her again. As Christmas approached, he found himself thinking about her more and more often and wondered if the urge to go to New York had been just coming from his penis. In retrospect, when he first saw her at her home, he realized that it wasn't just the sex. He had actually missed her. The few days over the New Year had been wonderful and he would have liked to have stayed longer. He was starting to care for her.

As Paul's Taurus cruised up and over the Burlington Skyway, which soared above the entrance to Hamilton Harbour, his thoughts of Laurie were wiped from his mind. He looked west at the downtown area and thoughts of Vladmir Rousinsky flooded into his head. He knew that the scumbag was spending the holiday season with his associates at his strip club and fancy restaurant. Paul also knew that he was getting tired of killing people, but he had to take care of one more drug trafficker before he retired.

He thought about the eight men he had murdered and felt no remorse because he believed that they had all deserved to die. As Paul mentally went through his list of victims and how he had killed them, he thought that he was getting progressively more careless and it was time to smarten up. There was no need to take risks. He would hate to get caught just as he was about to kill the last drug trafficker on his list. With Laurie's aroma still with him, he thought of stopping the revenge killings, but Rousinsky was the last one. He needed to hand out the same justice to him that he had to the others.

* * *

Back at Beer Lake, Paul sat in his leather chair with a glass of scotch and water in his hand in front of the fire. He was glad to be home, but he kept thinking about Laurie and the wonderful few days that he had in New York. He knew that he wanted to see her again, but he had to finish his mission before he could make any personal plans to do that.

As he stared into the flames, he recalled that Vladmir Rousinsky and all his cronies had talked about going on a vacation to Colorado early in the new year, but they hadn't mentioned a specific date. He decided that he had to visit Hamilton because if he waited too long, he might miss their ski trip. Paul had skied Vail a number of times and knew his way around. He knew that it would be a great place to get to know the Russian. Besides, after the last killings of Ruffus Allan and Artie Jacobi, he thought that it was time for him to stop pressing his luck in Toronto. He knew that Detectives Everdell and Carpenter had been assigned The Oyster-Shucking Murders and since Rousinsky would be his last, he didn't want to give them anymore clues just in case they got lucky.

Paul went to bed after the eleven o'clock news because he was heading back to Hamilton for a couple of days in the morning. It would be Friday and he knew that the Russian would be out and about entertaining himself at week's end. He figured that he would not have to be in Hamilton until mid-afternoon.

He got up early the next morning, had a decent breakfast, and did a few things around the house. Then he took care of something extremely important. He collected all of his Gordon William Thoburn documents and hid them in a small metal box below a loose board in the bedroom floor where he kept his Jack Melville Randall papers. At the same time, he made sure that he had all of the papers for his new identity, Clive Edward Lyons, in his wallet, where they were supposed to be. The overnight bag and the hang-up bag had enough clothes and personal effects for two nights, even three if necessary. He didn't pack any tools for this trip because he had decided that he was going to do his last job in Colorado.

* * *

The old Ford Taurus left Beer Lake around noon. Paul would be in Hamilton before three o'clock which would give him lots of time to find a hotel and get organized for his visit. He could still get to Lovely Natasha's for the busy Friday afternoon performances. He had a feeling that Rousinsky and his Russian friends would be at the strip joint later that day to start the weekend off in style.

There were light snow flurries during the trip south to Toronto and west to *The Steel City*, so the traffic was slower than Paul had expected. It was about twenty past three when he parked in the parking garage of a Best Western in the downtown area. By the time he checked-in and changed his clothes for the evening, it was four o'clock. He put on a sports shirt and slacks with a winter wind-breaker so he would look fairly casual for the strip joint. He also had a sports jacket and trench coat that he could change into later just in case he ended up dining at The Russia House.

Paul took a cab to Lovely Natasha's which was packed with guys who had just got off work. The tall, attractive, foreign looking women danced one after the other and the crowd of men cheered them on. Between the music played by a disc jockey and the cheering from the men, the place was very noisy. Paul joined two other guys, at a table for four, and sat down and ordered a Canadian from one of the number of waitresses wandering throughout the establishment. From where he was seated, he was close enough to the bar that he could hear the bartender and other employees talking between songs. He could also see the dark glass of the VIP lounge, but couldn't tell if anyone was inside. He would have to wait and see if any of the waitresses delivered drinks there.

Paul had been there for two hours and none of the waitresses had gone near the VIP room, so he assumed that the owners and their entourage were not around. There were about ten guys standing at one end of the bar watching the show, so Paul left his table and joined that group at around six-thirty, just to see if he could pick something up from the chatter of the employees around the bar. He hoped to be able to learn the whereabouts of Vladmir Rousinsky and his friends. As soon as he got to the bar, Paul ordered another beer and blended in with the group watching the girls as they danced across the stage and up and down the runway. Paul joined in with the odd comment about the dancers right along with the other guys.

He stood at the bar for over an hour before he heard anything that made any sense to him. The bartender was talking to an attractive Shooter Girl who was wearing about six bottles of liqueurs and Tequila in a leather holster type belt that also held hundreds of small plastic shooter glasses. She was extremely well put together, with enough cleavage to turn most eyes from the stage. Her job was to wander around the room selling shooters to the screaming men and she was always very busy. Paul listened as she and the bartender talked while there was a lull in the music.

"You must be having a good night, Loren. This is the biggest crowd that we've had on a Friday afternoon for a long time," the bartender commented.

"Yeah, it's great for a change. I need the money after Christmas," the gal answered. *"Have you heard from Ivan tonight? I'm supposed to be off at nine for the weekend and he said that he was gonna take me out for dinner tonight. I don't know why the hell he doesn't call and let me know what's going on."*

"Ivan called about ten minutes ago and told me that he and Vlad are doing some business in Toronto and they likely won't be back here until around closing."

"Did he mention me or leave a message?"

"Sorry, Loren, he didn't say a word about you."

"What an asshole! I sent my kid to my mother's place for a couple of nights and he doesn't even have the decency to call me and tell me what the hell's going on. I finally got a weekend off without my kid and I'm goin' out to have some fun. Fuck him!" The shooter gal said as she headed back into the crowd.

Paul found out that Ivan and Vlad were in Toronto and they wouldn't be back until late that night. He was relieved to hear that they were around and not away. He thought that there was no point in him hanging around Lovely Natasha's for the whole evening if the Russian wasn't going to be back till closing time. He decided that he would have to come back the next day to see what he could find out. The bartender had said that they would be back in town so they would likely be around the next day. As he finished his beer, Loren, the Shooter Girl, came back toward the bar and the bartender spoke to her.

"If your dinner plans are screwed up, you may as well work tonight. We could use you around here because it's so damn busy."

"There's no fuckin' way that I'm workin'! I just called my girlfriend and when I'm done here at nine, we're goin' down to the Gown and Gavel to get pissed and have some real fun," Loren answered. *"I'm not wasting my weekend off with no kid."*

As she went back into the crowd, Paul finished his Canadian and headed toward the door. A couple of cabs were waiting outside the entrance so he hopped into one and asked to be taken downtown. He got out of the cab a block from his hotel and walked the rest of the way. He was back in his room by eight-fifteen and made plans for the rest of the evening. He thought about the Gown and Gavel because it wasn't that far away. He also thought about Loren, the attractive Shooter Girl, who was pissed off at her boyfriend. He thought, *Maybe I should go out and have some fun too!* He soon decided that he would go out for a few laughs, but he hadn't eaten since morning. If he was going to drink, he needed to eat, so he ordered a cheeseburger and fries from room service.

As he ate and flipped channels on the television, he thought about the Shooter Girl. She was cute and had a body to die for. If she really wanted to party that night, he would try to accommodate her. Besides, he might gain some important information about the Russians that could help him set up his final target. He began to really hope that he would be able to meet Loren and get close to her. Before he left his room, he grabbed three condoms just in case. Since he had met Laurie in Florida and renewed his interest in the opposite sex, he always made sure that he carried protection.

* * *

At about nine thirty, Paul walked the few blocks from his hotel to the Gown and Gavel. It was one of those English pubs styled like all the others that someone tried to move from the British Isles to North America. There was English ambiance combined with North American flavor. There was a long bar to the right and a number of seating areas to the left with a small stage and dance floor in a far corner. As Paul moved to a vacant spot at the bar, he looked around for Loren. She was nowhere to be seen.

As his pint of Keith's arrived, Paul watched as a gentleman with a British accent stepped up to the microphone on the small stage and started to strum a banjo and sing. He was the entertainment. He was pretty loose and easy going and sang all of those songs that drunks like to sing along to and clap their hands. During the fourth song, Loren and another girl came into the pub and walked along the bar to where Paul was standing.

Loren wore the same outfit she had on at the strip club, with her cleavage in full view. As she stood there, all the guys in the room couldn't help but stare. Her girlfriend took off her jacket and she was in a matching blue jean outfit that also looked sexy. Loren looked right at Paul and smiled, just to be friendly. She hadn't even noticed him at Lovely Natasha's because he had been in the middle of a crowd of guys at the bar. He took advantage of the opportunity and spoke to her.

"You two look like you're ready to have some fun tonight!"

"We're definitely ready for something. We both worked our asses off all day," Loren answered with a smile.

"Well, if you worked all day long, you probably need a beer," Paul said. "Can I buy you and your friend a pint?"

"You sure can," Loren answered. "I'm Loren and this is my girl-friend, Roxanne."

"Nice to meet you, I'm Clive, but all my friends call me Eddie."

"What the hell's that supposed to mean?" Loren asked with a laugh. "Do you use two names?"

"Clive's my first name but I don't like it, so I use my middle name, Edward."

"No problem, Clive," Loren laughed. "I hope you don't mind if I call you by that name. I really don't like the name Eddie very much. It reminds me of an old boyfriend who was a total asshole, but it doesn't matter, because he's dead anyway."

As Loren made that comment, Paul swallowed a mouthful of air with his next swig of beer and started to choke as he thought about Eddie Firestone and the fact that Vladmir Rousinsky had been his main supplier. Eddie had likely been to the Hamilton strip club in the past and they could have dated. Paul thought that the connection was a long shot.

As Paul and the girls got to know each other, he danced with one, then the other, however, he spent most of his time with Loren. Throughout the evening they knocked back a few shooters along with other drinks, and by twelve-thirty, they were both feeling no pain. During a slow dance later in the evening, Loren became quite cuddly and suggested to Clive that they leave the bar and go to her place. They said goodbye to Roxanne.

Loren lived in the downtown area of Hamilton, not far from the English pub, on the fourteenth floor of a fifteen story apartment building that had a concierge at the front entrance. As she pushed the button for her floor in the elevator, she stepped over close to Paul and kissed him. She felt good as he rubbed his hands up and down her sides inside her coat. As soon as they got into the apartment, she poured a couple of shooters of Baileys and excused herself and went to the washroom. As Paul sipped his drink, he wandered around the living room and checked things out. On a shelf, by the window, he found a few framed pictures, one of which was a group of employees from the strip club and one was of Loren and Ivan, Vladmir's buddy. Paul found it all quite interesting.

Loren came out of the bathroom dressed only in her housecoat. She went directly to the kitchen for her drink and then joined Paul in the other room.

"Let's finish these shooters and go into the bedroom. It's not often my kid stays over at my mother's for the night," she said as she leaned close to Paul and kissed him.

"That's a great idea," Paul said, as he clinked glasses with her. "Here's to your kid having a great time at Grandma's place."

In the bedroom, Loren moved close to Paul and they kissed. Between the first and second kiss, she let her housecoat fall to the floor and started to undo the buttons on Paul's shirt, then his belt and pants. He couldn't believe her body as he cupped her firm breasts and kissed her. She knew how to kiss and it wasn't long before she could tell that Paul was ready to play. She slowly kneeled down as she lowered his pants and Paul thought that he had died and gone to heaven. She knew what she wanted and she was extremely good at it. Later, they were seated in the bed, leaning on pillows and sipping Bailey shooters.

"That was as good as it gets," Paul commented. "You actually have a better body than most of the dancers at Lovely Natasha's. Have you ever stripped?"

"No, I'm not into that scene. Besides, I usually make more money than they do just being the Shooter Girl. If I dress right and let my tits hang out, I make great tips. I've had lots of one thousand dollar nights."

"That's quite amazing! I noticed a few pictures in the living room earlier. Is that a picture of you and your old boyfriend beside the group picture?"

"No, he's the guy I still date, but he treats me like shit. He's one of the partners in the club where I work. He just makes plans to see me whenever he feels like it, so I've decided that I'm not just sitting around and waiting for him anymore."

"Good for you. You mentioned that my name reminds you of an old boyfriend who's now dead. What the hell happened to him?"

"He was a guy from Toronto who knew one of the partners at the club. He was a street dealer who got himself into trouble and ended up murdered about four months ago. They found him in the bathroom of a strip joint in the west end of the city."

"I guess that business can be pretty dangerous," Paul answered somewhat shocked.

"He really got off on strippers. A jealous boyfriend probably whacked him."

"The club where you work seems busy. With a name like Lovely Natasha's, it must be owned by Russians?"

"Yeah, it is. The three partners are Russian and they also own a fancy restaurant."

"You must have lots of fun if you're dating one of the owners," Paul commented hoping to get her to talk about the Russians. "You probably get to go out for dinner a lot and go on all kinds of trips and things with the guy. Has he ever taken you to Russia?"

"I go for dinner to the restaurant often, it's called The Russia House. The food is fabulous. Tomorrow night, he's supposed to take me to a club in Toronto for dinner and dancing, just the two of us. As far as the asshole taking me anywhere very exciting, that never happens. A few of them are going skiing to Vail, Colorado the week before Super Bowl and they're staying through the weekend to watch the game. If the jerk took me with him, he wouldn't be able to chase that American pussy!"

"It sounds like he doesn't pay enough attention to you," Paul said kissing her.

"He doesn't, so why don't you pay some more attention to me?"

It wasn't long before Loren was laying between his legs doing that thing that men love so much. After awhile, she slid one of the condoms into place. She was taking her time and fooling around, but Paul didn't mind. He was enjoying himself. It was one of those lubricated rubbers that almost shone in the darkness. She was so adept, it was obvious that she had put them on before. Then she crawled on top of him and dangled those gorgeous breasts above his face. They were absolutely fantastic. It wasn't long before she slipped him inside her and was pounding away. He was having a good time. He had really missed the sex.

Paul and Loren eventually fell asleep and slept through until eight in the morning. They woke up about the same time and started to cuddle. It wasn't long before Paul used the last condom that he had brought with him. The morning sex was more sedated than the night before and as they finished, and Paul rolled off her onto his own side of the bed, the telephone on the bedside table rang and startled them.

Loren put her finger to her lips to ask Paul to be quiet as she took the call. It sounded like her boyfriend was checking in to see what she was doing. As soon as she hung up the phone, she turned and spoke to Paul.

"I'm afraid that you have to leave now. Ivan is going to pick me up and take me for breakfast and he'll be here in about an hour."

"Just use me and throw me out," Paul laughed.

"The way my pussy feels, I think you used me a lot more than I used you. I sure hope he doesn't want to have sex," she said as she kissed him. "I'm sorry. I really had a nice time, but you do have to get the hell outta here."

"Don't worry, I'll be dressed and gone in a few minutes. I'll shower later."

It wasn't long before Paul was walking down the street in front of Loren's building looking for a cab. As he walked, he thought to himself with a grin on his face, *The things that I have to do to get information!*

* * *

As Paul showered, he thought about Eddie Firestone and how small the world had become. His thoughts soon turned to the information that he had learned from Loren. The Russian's ski trip to Vail was planned for the week before Super Bowl Sunday so they would be leaving in two weeks. Paul thought that the timing was perfect. The next conundrum was to decide what to do for the rest of the weekend. He wondered, *Do I trust the information I got from Loren or should I try to have it confirmed while I'm here in Hamilton?*

Loren had said that she wasn't working that weekend and was going to Toronto for the evening with Ivan. If Paul hung around the strip club and even ended up going to The Russia House for dinner, he wouldn't bump into her. He decided to stay over another night and spend some time at the club and see if Rousinsky and his friends were around. *Who knows?* he thought, *Maybe they will all be going out for dinner on a Saturday night.* He might be able to confirm that the ski trip was definitely on for Super Bowl week. He had no other plans and the worst thing that could happen was that he would enjoy another great meal at the upscale restaurant.

Paul got a paper and went to a restaurant across the street from his hotel for breakfast. He spent the rest of the day just lounging around his room and watching television. He fell asleep because the activities from the night before had caught up with him. He had an enjoyable afternoon doing nothing.

* * *

By five o'clock, Lovely Natasha's was full of guys who were half in the bag. The crowd had attractive girls doing lap dances all over the room and the men continually cheered the strippers on the stage as they performed. Paul sat at a table with a couple of other guys near the bar and had a full view of the VIP lounge. There was no activity at all around it. Just as Paul was thinking about leaving, in walked Ivan and Loren. She was all dolled up for a night on the town and looked very attractive in a slutty sort of way. *She's one horny looking lady*, Paul thought as they walked past him and directly to the bar. It appeared that Ivan gave the manager some last minute instructions about the evening and confirmed that he and his date were on their way to the city. He told the manager that they might be back by closing. Paul didn't think that Loren had seen him, but as she left, walking a few feet behind her date, she looked directly at him and winked with a smile.

* * *

Paul arrived at The Russia House by cab at eight o'clock and as he took off his coat at the coat-check, he looked down the hall toward the far end of the dimly lit eating area. The large, empty table in the back corner, where the Russians had sat during his last visit, had a *Reserved* sign in the middle of it. *Maybe Vladmir Rousinsky and his friends will show up after all*, Paul thought. If they didn't, he would have a nice dinner anyway and go back to the strip joint for a beer on the way back to his hotel.

The maitre d' asked Paul where he would like to sit and he chose the same place as his last visit. He was almost above the reserved table and hidden from view, but he would still be able to hear most of their conversations if they showed up.

Paul ordered a large martini, to be followed by a bottle of Chateauneuf-du-Pape, to be opened and left on his table to breathe. He remembered that he had King Crab legs the last time he was there, so he ordered a Caesar salad and the surf and turf; a ten ounce filet and a large lobster tail. He started on the appetizer tray of pickles and cottage cheese and the large bowl of rolls. He was hungry.

Just as Paul placed his order, eight people were led to the reserved table in the corner, five men and three women. Paul bent down slightly, to look through the slats on his balcony, to see if he recognized anyone in the crowd. The first person who caught his eye was a beautiful, dark-haired, European looking woman. Vladmir Rousinsky was sliding her chair in for her. He had lucked out. The Russian had come to the restaurant for dinner and Paul hoped to confirm the story about the plans for Colorado.

Paul's dinner arrived fairly quickly and he really enjoyed it. The lobster tail had been cooked to perfection and the steak was excellent. He took his time eating and kept his ears glued to the conversations at the table below. He finished his dinner without hearing anything interesting and the waiter was just putting a cappuccino and a double Grand Marnier in front of him when the Russian caught his attention.

"It looks like the only guys who are going skiing in Vail for the Super Bowl this year are me and Ivan. Those other two assholes cancelled," Rousinsky said.

"If just the two of you are going, why don't you and Ivan take me and Loren with you for the week?" the pretty girl beside him asked.

"I told you before, no women! It's Super Bowl Week and it's for guys only. Ivan and I ski a lot better than the other two anyway, so we'll have a great holiday."

"All you guys do when you're away is chase girls! You probably don't even take your skis with you!" the gal replied.

"That's bullshit, we ski all day, every day, and usually end up at the Red Lion at the bottom of the mountain for a few drinks before we go out for dinner. After dinner, the whole village goes to bed because everyone is tired from skiing all day."

Paul listened until he finished his coffee and drink and knew that he had heard all that he needed to hear. The Vail trip was on and had been confirmed by Rousinsky, so Paul could now start to make whatever plans he needed to make so he could join them.

* * *

Paul slept like a log that night and left downtown Hamilton the next morning. He skipped breakfast and picked up a coffee and muffin at a Starbucks. The Sunday traffic wasn't heavy so the trip home was fairly easy. He was back at Beer Lake by noon feeling that his trip had been quite successful, in more ways than one. After so many years of abstinence, Paul had enjoyed the encounter with Loren and had a hard time not thinking about her wicked body. He felt a little bit guilty about having slept with her just to get information, but soon decided, with a smile, that he had to do whatever he had to do.

As his thoughts turned to Laurie, pangs of guilt went right through his body. Deep down, he felt that he had cheated on her and didn't feel comfortable about it. Paul was starting to care for Laurie much more than he realized. He wished that she lived closer.

CHAPTER THIRTY-TWO

The detectives spent most of the following week sorting through the new evidence gathered since the murders of Ruffus Allan and Arthur Jacobi. They finally had all the reports they were waiting for; blood, ballistics, fingerprints and computer comparisons of the lists of airline travelers from Toronto and Buffalo to Florida. They went through everything, one piece at a time, with more excitement and determination than they had been able to muster for weeks. Paul Taylor was now their prime suspect.

"There was more evidence at the scene of the last two murders than all of the others combined," Everdell commented.

"You're right. It seems that the killer didn't plan these killings as well as he had planned the first six that were done with no fuss and no muss," Carpenter answered.

"The killer said that the traffickers were going to kill him so he had to react."

"Look at the ballistics report. The bullet in the backseat came from the passenger's Colt .45 semi-automatic and it was in pretty good shape. They even got some blood off of it. The same blood type that was on the back door and window."

"The killer's slug, in the front, was so smashed it couldn't be processed," Everdell went on. "The best guess is that it's a .38."

"The report on finger prints shows that there are a number of prints in the car, both in the front and back. If Ruffus Allan was the ring leader of the Jamaican gang, he would likely have had guys in and out of his car all the time. They'll just have to be processed to see if any of them are out of place," Carpenter said.

"My guess is that our guy didn't leave prints anywhere."

"If he had to reacte to a situation unexpectedly, he might have inadvertently left us some evidence."

"The lab report indicates that the blood on the bullet and on the backseat door and window is AB Rh Negative and the two guys in the front seat are both O Rh Positive," Everdell went on. "It seems to me, if my memory serves me right, that the most common blood type is O Rh Positive and AB Rh Negative is very rare. The AB Rh Negative has to belong to the killer. I wonder what Taylor's blood type is?"

"The law firm may have access to that information. How did Judy make out with the airline lists of passengers?"

"Here's the breakdown. There were eighty Canadians who flew out of Buffalo to Fort Lauderdale during the week before Morelli's murder and, I almost hate to tell you, three thousand and eighty-two from the Toronto area on the flights out of Pearson."

"Damn! I guess that means we have to contact each and every one of them and try and find out if there's any connection to the victims," Carpenter whined. "It's gonna be a lot of hard work."

"I've got another idea! I almost forgot about the list of reservations that I got from the restaurant where Morelli had his last supper, I think it was called Yesterdays," Everdell said a bit excited. "Why don't I have Judy put those names in the computer with the names that are on the airline lists and see what happens."

"That's a hell of an idea, but we couldn't be that lucky could we?"

"You just never know where our next lead will come from."

"Rod Farn should be able to tell us where the partners have their medicals for the various insurance coverages," Carpenter suggested. "I'll call him and get that information. They might even have some records on file right there."

"While you do that, I'll take this restaurant reservation list to Judy," Everdell said. "Then we can take the pictures of Paul Taylor and show them to the nurses at the Hospital For Sick Children and the witnesses out at Sweethearts and Willie's Billiards. Maybe we'll have some luck. I'll be right back."

Carpenter got lucky with his call to Farn and his assistant put him right through to the busy lawyer. After a short discussion, he hung up with a big smile on his face.

"What are you so happy about?" Everdell asked as he returned.

"Farn checked with his administration office and they have what we need. He won't give us a copy of Taylor's last medical, but he will fax us his blood type."

"Perfect!" Everdell said. "Let's hit Sick Kids first and then go out to Etobicoke and watch some dancing girls. We'll catch the pool hall later or in the morning."

* * *

The detectives parked outside of the main doors and entered the foyer of the hospital. They immediately recognized the woman on duty in the lobby coffee shop as the one who had noticed the man who had dropped off the money weeks before. The policemen pulled her aside and explained that they wanted her to look at a photo line-up of twelve individuals because one of them might be the guy who dropped off the money last September. She took a few minutes and carefully studied the pictures of the men one at a time. None of the men shown to her looked familiar. She apologized to the detectives and went back to work.

Joan Markey was on duty too and was ready for her coffee break when the detectives arrived at her window off the main lobby. She told them she drank her coffee black and suggested they meet in the basement cafeteria in about five minutes.

"Do you think you have a lead on the man who dropped the money off that night?" Joan Markey asked as she sat down in front of a steaming cup of coffee and some pictures of men spread out nearby.

"We haven't had a lot of luck and seem to be chasing long-shots all the time," Everdell explained. "If you would take a look at these twelve pictures and try to remember back to that night, one of the men might look familiar. Take your time and look carefully. You were closer to him than any of the other witnesses."

"They're a nice looking group," Joan said with a smile. "It was a long time ago."

"Take your time," Carpenter said. "We're in no hurry."

After about a minute, Joan picked up the picture of Paul Taylor and tilted it back and forth in the dull light of the cafeteria. Everdell and Carpenter held their breath. She seemed to study it for awhile but then put it back down.

"I'm really sorry. None of these men look familiar."

"You're sure?" a disappointed Everdell asked. "You picked up a couple of them."

"I'm positive, I don't recognize any of them," Joan answered. "It's just that the lighting in here is not very good."

"Well, thanks for your help," Carpenter said as they got up to leave. "We still have a full day's work ahead of us so we'd better get back on the job."

As the two men got into their car, Everdell spoke, "I hope we have better luck with the witnesses at Sweethearts, but even if we don't, the interviews will be more fun."

* * *

The detectives took the Gardiner Expressway west to Etobicoke and reached their destination around three-thirty. As the unmarked police car pulled into the parking lot at Sweethearts, they talked to each other.

"The first two we interviewed, Honey and Candy, told us that they didn't see anything because they had been watching the dancer with the big boobs. Didn't someone say that they both liked girls anyway?" Everdell asked.

"I'm pretty sure Firestone's old girlfriend, Danielle, told us that," Carpenter answered, "and there was the waitress who served the guy who may have gone to the can just before Eddie. Her name was Lori-Ann Murphy."

"If they're working today, we should let them see the pictures just in case."

"The bartender, Eddie's old girlfriend, said she saw him follow someone else into the washroom. It was so dark for the special show she couldn't describe the guy. He had been sitting between Eddie and the pisser and no one else went in there after Eddie did."

"Think about it. If someone wanted to get Eddie alone in the can, he could've just sat nearby and waited for his chance. If he saw Eddie head for the washroom, there's no reason why he couldn't get there first if he was sitting in the right place," Everdell said. "That way, he wouldn't look suspicious because he didn't actually follow him there."

"Right," Carpenter answered. "Then there was Jack Spratt, the guy who could eat no fat, who actually noticed the killer. He said that he had long dark hair, a bushy mustache and sideburns."

"Do you think there's much chance of him picking the guy out of these pictures? Taylor has short hair, no mustache and is in a suit."

"Hell, who knows? There's a parking spot near the main door!"

The interior of the strip bar was the same as the policemen remembered. It was half-full of guys who were cheering the girl on the stage. It took a few minutes for their eyes to adjust to the darkness of the large room, but they recognized the bartender.

"Dani," Everdell said, "do you remember us from the time we spent around here when Eddie Firestone was murdered?"

"Sure. I've still got your card on my dresser at home. What can I do for you?"

"Can you take a short break to look at some pictures for us and maybe answer a few more questions?" Carpenter asked.

"Sure, we can go into the office. I've got a key," she said as she walked around the bar and headed toward the main entrance.

As soon as the lights were turned on, Everdell scattered the twelve pictures across the top of the desk and spoke to her.

"Were any of these men in Sweethearts that day or any other day that you know of?"

"Remember, you told us that some guy went into the washroom just ahead of Eddie that afternoon," Carpenter said. "Do any of these guys look like that man?"

"No one looks familiar. None of these guys are customers here."

"Are Candy and Honey still working here?" Everdell went on.

"Honey is still around, but Candy is long gone. I think that Honey is about to start work so she should be here."

"What about Lori-Ann Murphy, does she still work here?" Everdell asked.

"She sure does and she's working today, so she'll be able to take a look at the pictures too."

"There's one other thing you can help us with before you go back to work. We interviewed one of your customers named Jack Spratt and we'd like to talk to him again. Do you see him very often?" Carpenter asked.

"He drops in a couple of times a week and has a beer or two. I gotta tell ya', you guys got lucky today because I just saw him come in when I was coming to the office. Do you want me to send him in to see you?"

"Yeah, if you don't mind. Also see if you can find Honey and Lori-Ann and ask them to stick their heads in here and talk to us too," Carpenter said. "Sure, but when you finish, lock the door and return the keys to me at the bar."

Dani left them there alone talking to each other about the lack of evidence that was turning up from the use of the pictures. All of a sudden, Jack Spratt walked in.

"Mr. Spratt, thanks for coming back to talk to us," Everdell said and shook his hand. "We want you to look at a few pictures to see if you recognize the guy who was in the washroom area with Eddie Firestone when he got killed."

"It was pretty dark, but I remember that the guy had long hair, sideburns and a mustache. I don't see the guy in any one of these pictures."

"If you're sure, then that's all we need you for today," Carpenter responded.

"Do you think one of these guys did the murder?"

"There's nothing definite yet. Thanks for your help."

Just as the detectives were saying goodbye to Jack Spratt, Honey walked in, showing bare breasts from under a see-through top, just to embarrass them.

"I told you guys everything I knew the last time you were here."

"We just need you to take a look at some pictures for us," Everdell said.

"No, problem," she said, as she bent over the pictures that were on the desk.

Everdell and Carpenter glanced at each other and then back at her large breasts. She was fairly well built, but had quite a few miles on her.

"Do any of these guys look familiar?" Carpenter asked.

"I've never seen any of these guys. None of them have ever been here before."

Everdell and Carpenter also showed the pictures to Lori-Ann Murphy, but she didn't recognize anyone. However, she thought that she might be able to pick the guy who she had served out of a line-up, if the police ever happen to make an arrest.

The detectives returned the key to Dani and left.

* * *

Everdell and Carpenter went north to Highway 401 and then east. They were extremely disappointed because they believed that someone would at least finger Paul Taylor as a *possible* suspect. No one had even made a partial identification. They parked below Willie's Billiard Hall and walked up to the second floor emporium. The Jamaican posse was at their usual pool table and there appeared to be a new leader to whom the gang members were expected to pay homage. The detectives remembered Leroy Thomas from their first interview with the brothers.

"Leroy," Everdell said, "we're Detectives Everdell and Carpenter and we'd like to have a few words with all of you about the death of Ruffus Allan. I'm sure you remember that we spoke shortly after he was killed."

"Yah, mon, what kin we all do for ya'?"

"We'd like you all to take a look at these pictures and see if you recognize any of the men as being customers of this pool hall and maybe even playing pool with Ruffus Allan on the day that he was murdered," Carpenter explained.

"Christ, mon, these guys too clean and neat to hang roun' a place like dis," Leroy commented. "I never seen any o' dem before."

The rest of the posse agreed with their new leader so there was absolutely no help from the Jamaicans. They got the same response from the bartender.

"Remember Ben, the guy who played pool with the suspect on at least two occasions? He just lives a couple of blocks from here, so we should drop by and see him while we're in the east end," Everdell suggested.

"Good idea, let's do it," Carpenter agreed.

Five minutes later they knocked on Ben's front door. They were in luck. He answered it. After the policemen explained to him what they needed, he invited them into his living room. As soon as the pictures were spread out on his coffee table, he leaned over them and took his time to study them.

"These men don't look like they hang around pool halls, but there's something familiar about this guy," Ben was almost thinking out loud as he picked up the picture of Paul Taylor. "I can't really be certain, but if this guy had a mustache, sideburns and longer hair, he might look a bit like that Gord guy who I shot pool with on those two occasions."

Everdell took the picture from him and pulled his pen out of his pocket. He wasn't much of an artist, but one didn't need to be to draw a mustache, sideburns and long hair.

"Does this look anymore like the guy now?"

"Christ! It really does look like the Gord guy I played pool with, but I wouldn't want to swear on a stack of bibles."

"Take another good look at it, because this is really important," Carpenter said.

"I'm looking," Ben said as he leaned over under the light on the end table, "but like I said, with those changes he looks like the guy

I met but I don't think that I can be one hundred percent sure from this picture."

"If we put this guy in a line-up, could you pick him out?"

"I'm sure that I could if I saw him in person," Ben answered.

"Well, you've certainly been helpful and we want to thank you for your time," Everdell said as he and his partner stood up to leave.

* * *

As Everdell and Carpenter drove back downtown in the rush hour traffic, they wondered if what Ben had told them meant anything because he had waffled a bit with the identification. Carpenter was the first to speak.

"He wasn't a hundred percent, but he did pick Taylor out of the twelve pictures. There must be a resemblance to the guy he met in the pool hall. That's the best evidence we have to date. Who knows? The way all the small things are building up, we may have something important very soon."

"I've got a gut feeling that we're onto something and I wouldn't be the least bit surprised if some new evidence turns up shortly."

CHAPTER THIRTY-THREE

During the couple of weeks leading up to the Vail trip, Paul spent a lot of time thinking about his son's death, the other kids who had died and the families that had been torn apart by the poisonous drugs on that terrible weekend. Deep inside, he could feel his crusade of revenge coming to an end. No matter how deserving the drug traffickers and dealers were, he had just about had enough of the killing. In the beginning, it was easy because he had been operating on adrenaline, but as time went on, the killing started to get to him. When he killed Shackleton, he was mad enough that he thought that he could kill those bastards forever. Time had changed all that. Since he had met Laurie, there was a glimmer of hope that life might be worth living after all.

As Paul got his ski gear together and laid it out in his living room, he thought about the good times that he, Liz and Ricky had skiing in years long past. The last time he had skied in Vail, they were with him. They had wonderful times together. He still felt a special sadness when he thought about them, but the tears didn't flow as readily as they used to. It wasn't that he didn't miss them, he was just getting used to reality. They were gone and nothing could bring them back.

A couple of days before Paul was to leave for Vail, he drove to Peterborough and went to four sporting goods stores to look for a new ski jacket that would go with his black ski pants. He was looking for something very special and couldn't find the one that he wanted anywhere. He decided to drive to the shop at Devil's Elbow near Bethany, twenty minutes south of the town, to see if they had what he was looking for, but again, he was disappointed. All of a sudden, it struck him. The Old Fire Hall in Unionville, just north of the city, would have exactly what he needed. The large store had hundreds of ski outfits. It was just about an hour's drive south from the Elbow.

The trip turned out to be worthwhile because he found the exact jacket that he was looking for and bought it. His new jacket was reversible, one side was black and the other red. He thought that it might come in handy in Vail. The only other thing he needed was an oyster-shucking knife which he would buy after he got there.

Paul had always enjoyed skiing and was looking forward to spending some time in ski-country. He had been a good intermediate skier and would tackle any of the runs on the mountain. He hoped that he hadn't lost his touch. The Taurus was loaded with all of his ski equipment and enough clothes for the trip when he pulled out of Beer Lake on the Friday morning, ten days before Super Bowl Sunday.

He decided to fly out of his favorite airport in Buffalo once again and he got there in his usual fashion through Niagara Falls. He took a direct SouthWest flight to Denver, the mile high city, and with the time change, landed at Denver International at one o'clock. Rather than rent a car, he grabbed one of the shuttle buses for the three hour trip to Vail and squeezed into the large van with six other skiers. The drive from the airport in the east end of the city, through the downtown area and onto Highway 70 was a bit slow, but the traffic improved as the shuttle headed west into the mountains. A number of shuttles travel back and forth between the ski areas and the airport on a regular basis, twenty-four hours a day. It was the best way to travel because the highways climb another seven thousand feet up into the mountains and the roads can be hazardous during snowstorms. Vail was just over eight thousand feet above sea level and situated right in the center of the White River National Forest.

Paul was dropped off at the bus station at just after four o'clock that afternoon and carried his things about six blocks up Bridge and turned left on East Gore Creek Drive. The Matterhorn Inn, a small hotel on the main street, was set among a number of busy restaurants and popular night spots. He wasn't sure if they would have a room available, but it didn't matter, because there were a dozen small inns nearby. As it turned out, Paul got a room with a loft and after he checked-in, under his new name, C. Edward Lyons, he threw his things on the couch and went outside to look around. He decided to wander around the village to get his bearings and see what had changed in the years since he had been there.

The walk around town was enjoyable but it was right at the time when all of the skiers were coming off the mountains and pouring down the streets into the dozens of bars. The night life started at four in the afternoon and never let up. As Paul got back to his hotel, he noticed that Pepi's Restaurant & Bar, across the street, was filled with people so he decided to drop by for a beer. As he pushed the door open, he could hear the singer, in a cowboy hat, who was sitting in the far corner of the large room. The guy was backed up by an electric orchestra and he played a guitar and harmonica at the same time. There were eight people squeezed onto a small dance floor right in front of him, still in their ski outfits, dancing up a storm. Paul slipped his way through the crowd and went to the bar to the left and ordered a glass of Stella.

Paul got caught up in a conversation with a couple from New Jersey who were standing next to him at the bar. Unfortunately, his new friends, Howie and Lynn, had been skiing for a week, in fabulous conditions, but were leaving the next day. Before Paul knew it, he had sucked back six pints and was starting to feel the booze because he had missed dinner. He ended up grabbing a bite to eat in the small restaurant on the main level of his hotel and then went to his room. The loft-style room had a kitchen, eating area and living room on the main level with a large bedroom upstairs overlooking the lower floor. To make the place more comfortable, Paul decided that he would shop for food and booze some time the next afternoon, after a day of skiing. He flipped on the television and lay on the chesterfield. It had been a long day. He fell asleep immediately and woke up as the eleven o'clock news was ending and went upstairs to bed.

* * *

The morning skiing was unbelievable. Paul skied alone and could always get on the lifts quickly by lining up in the singles lines, which were always much faster than the other line-ups. Besides, he kept meeting new and interesting people from all over North America and Europe. It didn't take him long to get back into the groove. Paul stopped at Two Elk Lodge on top of the mountain for lunch and then hit the trails again. About three o'clock, he stopped at Centerville or Mid-Vail, halfway up the mountain, for a couple of beers and then went to the top one last time. He did the ski-out from the highest peak, all the way down Riva Ridge, and arrived back in the village at about four, just as the snow started to come down. He had some errands to do.

Paul took the public transit to Beaver Creek, about fifteen minutes away, to do some shopping. He wanted to get out of Vail Village to find the object he really needed, an oyster-shucking knife. He got lucky. The light snow became a blizzard and gave him the opportunity to purchase the knife without his face being seen. As he got off the bus at the local station, he spotted a large hardware store in a plaza. He immediately pulled the balaclava out of the inside of his toque and it covered most of his face. By the time he got to the store, his coat, toque and balaclava were covered in snow. He left it on as he went inside. Paul immediately found what he was looking for and merely pulled one glove off a hand as he paid for it. The clerk could only see his eyes. He immediately went back to the bus stop and returned to Vail. He did the rest of his shopping at a grocery store and liquor store in the village near his hotel. At that point, he was ready for the week. All he had left to do was find his Russian friends who should arrive at any time.

After shopping, Paul walked up East Gore Creek Drive and turned left on Bridge Street. He went directly to the Red Lion which was full of people. He squeezed his way into the bar and looked around. If his friends from Hamilton were in Vail, they would be at the hottest spot in the village for the après skiing. He hung around until about eight, but there was no sign of the men he was looking for, so he went back to his hotel. He poured himself a scotch and lay back on the bed and watched television with full intentions of going out on the town later in the evening. He fell asleep about eight-thirty and didn't wake up until close to ten. His next decision was whether to go out for some fun or go to bed.

Paul loved Vail, but would have rather been there with someone special. He started to think about Laurie in New York City and even with the time change, he decided that it wasn't too late to call her. The phone rang about four times and was just about to flip onto the answering machine, when she picked it up.

"Hello," Laurie said.

"Hi, it's your buddy from Canada. I hope that I'm not calling you too late."

"No, not at all. I've been watching Letterman and Leno. I'm glad that you called. I was in the bathroom brushing my teeth and getting ready for bed. That's why it took me a minute to get to the phone," Laurie explained, as she noticed the area code on the number that was calling on her telephone window. "Where are you calling from?"

"I had to go to Denver on business, so I took a few extra days to ski in Vail. The conditions are so good I'm thinking about staying over for the Super Bowl."

"How lucky can you be? There's nothing but wet snow here in New York."

"I may have all my business completed by mid-week. Is there any chance that you could fly out here on Wednesday or Thursday and maybe stay until say Monday?"

"I probably could. It's a whole new year for holidays."

"We can ski for a few days and watch the Super Bowl somewhere on Sunday."

"That sounds great. I'll see if there are any problems at work.

When will you know if your business will be concluded or not?"

"I should know for sure in a couple of days, but what the hell, if things are all right at work, why don't you plan on coming out here on Wednesday or Thursday anyway. If I have to leave you alone for awhile, it won't be that big a deal."

"You met my boss, Frank Smeenk, before. He's always telling me to get out and have some fun. I'm sure I'll get the time off. Give me a call Tuesday and I'll confirm everything."

"I can't wait to see you."

"Me too. I miss you."

* * *

Paul was on the Riva Bohn Express quad-lift bright and early the next morning on his way to the top of the mountain. He was really enjoying himself for a change. The snow conditions were perfect and there wasn't a cloud in the sky. The bright sun kept the temperature just above freezing and there was absolutely no wind. He couldn't have asked for a better day. Paul skied hard and covered most of the mountainous runs in the area. He skied all the way from Vail Village to Lionshead and back and cruised most of the runs in between. At three-thirty, he found himself down in the village and caught the last ride on the Vista Bahn Express before it closed. At Mid-Vail, he took the last lift of the day to the highest peak. The ski-out, back to the village, would take about fifteen or twenty minutes depending on how fast he skied. The day had been spectacular.

Paul was tired, a good kind of tired, by the time he stuck his skis in the deep snow and hung his poles on top of them out in front of the Red Lion. He had taken the last run of the day so the bar was already packed with tired skiers sucking back the booze. As Paul squeezed his way into the large, crowded room, he noticed that the entertainment had started. A good-looking college kid was playing an electronic piano, with some background instrumentals, and singing those familiar songs that people enjoy. Paul made his way across the room to a tall table that allowed a dozen people to stand around it. He found a spot among five guys and six girls. They were all about to toast the wonderful ski conditions with tequila shooters as Paul joined them, so they handed him one too.

The music and drinking continued and Paul met the whole gang at his table. David Tausendfreund from St. Catherines, Ontario, introduced Jay Robinson, from Oakville, Doug Flett, from Toronto, Gene Bearinger, from Phoenix and Dave Stoddart, from Las Vegas. The girls from Houston, Diana, Gwen, Lee, Catherine, Gerri and Tracey were a lot of fun. Over the next three hours, there were seven more rounds of tequila shooters and Paul was included in various toasts that were just excuses to suck back the burning booze. He bought a couple of rounds in appreciation for being made welcome. The gals from Texas had no trouble keeping up with the guys. Paul was really getting into the party mode when some newcomers caught his attention.

Vladmir and Ivan had just walked in through the main entrance and were looking around to find a place to have a few drinks. They were in their street clothes, rather than ski outfits, so Paul assumed that they had just arrived in the village and hadn't skied that day. They had likely gone to where they were staying, got rid of their belongings, and headed directly to the Red Lion to get right into the evening's entertainment. As Paul kept an eye on them, they made their way through the crowded room and over to one of the stand-up tables two down from where Paul and his group were partying.

About an hour later, the two Russians left the Red Lion. Paul thanked his new friends for the company and told them that he would look for them later that evening. He was sure that he would be out and about. After he got outside and picked up his skis and poles, he followed the Russians down Bridge Street that was crowded with partiers and shoppers. They turned left at East Gore Creek Drive and walked toward a darker area of the village. Five minutes later, they turned right at a circular road called Willow Place that looped toward the creek and back to the main road. About halfway around the circle, the men entered a small building on the banks of the fast flowing Gore Creek. It had eight condos on the first two floors and one large one on the top floor. As the two men walked toward the building, Paul continued along the main road as if he was going to walk right on by, but he stopped as they went inside. Five of the seven apartments were in darkness, so he waited and watched. About a minute after the men disappeared, the lights in the huge penthouse came on. Once Paul found out where the Russians were staying, he headed back to his own hotel.

It wasn't long before he had showered and shaved and was wandering down East Gore Creek Drive on his way to Blu's for dinner. He had a real buzz on and knew that he had to eat. He hadn't eaten very much all day because the skiing had been so good and he was starving. He ended up ordering a huge steak, baked potato and Caesar salad and by the time he finished dinner, he was pooped, so he headed back to his hotel room to get a good night's sleep. He was very tired from the day's activities and was looking forward to skiing the next day. He hoped that the Russians skied well, because he wouldn't be far behind them until he got his job done. He also hoped that he would run into his new friends again too.

* * *

By eight-thirty the next morning, another beautiful day, Paul was waiting at the bottom of the main ski lifts that leave the village for different parts of the mountains starting a nine o'clock. Everyone staying in Vail Village starts off from there each morning and the Russians would be no exception. Paul had only skied in his black ski jacket and black pants and that was the color that was showing that morning. As he sat on a bench, with his skis in front of him, he sipped on a Starbuck's coffee and ate an apple fritter. It was the Russians' first day, so he assumed that they would be there for the first lift. As Paul waited, his friends from the Red Lion walked by.

"Good morning, Ed. We're all going to ski to Lionshead and do some runs over there today. Why don't you come with us?" Gene asked.

"Thanks, Gene, but I'm just waiting for some other friends to show up. I'll come over that way a little later and see if I can find you guys," Paul answered.

"We'll probably have lunch at that restaurant at the bottom of the main lift right in Lionshead. See you later," David from St. Catherines added.

As Paul took his last sip of coffee, he saw the Russians in the line-up for the Vista Bahn Express. He slipped his skis on and got into the line several skiers behind them.

At Centerville, the Russians took the Mountaintop Express to the peak and Paul was in the quad-lift two back from them. As soon as they got to the top, they poled over the back of the mountain to the more challenging runs, in the Northwoods area, and Paul followed. He just melted into the crowd of hundreds of skiers and made sure that he didn't get too close to them. They skied well and basically skied the runs that Paul would have if he had been on his own. He skied with them until mid-day and got in a lot of good runs. By then, Paul knew their ski outfits and would be able to pick them out of the crowds from time to time either on the slopes or the lifts. The two Russians stopped at Mid-Vail for lunch and Paul decided that he had spent enough time with them. He would catch up to them at the après ski party in the village at the end of the day.

He took the Wildwood Express toward Lionshead and as he skied, run after run, on the way to Eagle's Nest just above that village, he tried to come up with a plan to deal with the drug trafficker. He could kill him at night in the village, but then he would have to deal with his friend, Ivan. On the other hand, Paul could continue to ski with them and at some point in time, Ivan might leave Vladmir alone on the mountain. He might have an opportunity to meet him on a secluded part of one of the runs. The next day, Paul would carry his tools with him. He would be ready just in case an opportunity presented itself.

Paul caught up with his new friends at Lionshead and skied with them through the afternoon and they all ended up at the Red Lion. Paul was with his group at one end of the room and the Russians were seated at the far end near the singer. Paul and his buddies got carried away and really got into the sauce. Between the Long Island Iced Teas and the shots of tequila, they were all drunk as skunks by eight o'clock. The girls from Houston wanted to go dancing at the club in the basement of Pepi's, right near Paul's hotel, so that's where they went. Paul had way too much to drink to think about Vladmir and Ivan, so he wrote them off for the rest of the day. After having lots of fun with the gang, he got back to his room at midnight feeling no pain. He had enough sense to set the alarm for eight in the morning so he wouldn't miss the first lift.

* * *

Paul jumped out of bed the next morning, got dressed and was ready in no time. He looked out the window and was shocked to see over a foot of snow in the village and it was still coming down in a blizzard. He could hardly see across the street. He knew there would be twice as much fresh snow up in the mountains, but the visibility would be terrible if the snow continued. It would be tough and tiring to ski in the fresh powder. He had to catch up to the Russians at the base of the mountain because the snowstorm that was going through the area might give him the opportunity to introduce himself to Vlad. The black side of Paul's jacket showed again and by the time he put on his toque, tinted goggles and pulled down the balaclava, it was virtually impossible to see his face. He put the oyster-shucking knife in his right zippered pocket.

As Paul waited at the base of the mountain near the express quads, the heavy flakes of snow continued to hamper visibility. He nearly missed seeing the Russians in the line for the Riva Bahn Express. They were well ahead of him before he noticed their outfits, so he had no choice but to race for the singles line. Paul was almost shocked when he and another single, a gal just ahead of him, were waved onto the same quad-seat as the two Russians. Paul sat in the outside seat and didn't say much because he didn't want to be noticed. The Russians ignored him anyway and spoke to the pretty girl beside him.

There was a total blizzard at the top of the mountain and the visibility was only a hundred yards or so. Paul followed the two men down the mountain as they looked for runs where the snow wasn't too deep or blowing so much. The skiing was tiring because of all the fresh snow that had to be pushed around. It was work as they skied the ski-out with the idea that they would be able to see better lower down on the mountain. The three men finally got back to the base at the village. Paul followed them into the line for the Vista Bahn Express back to Mid-Vail and rode up a couple of quads behind them. They all took the Mountaintop Express to the peak and the snow was still coming down in a swirling blanket. There were few people that high on the mountain in the storm. Paul was close enough to hear the men speak to each other.

"Vlad, let's ski down to Mid-Vail and take a break for awhile. I feel like a couple of beers."

"All right. I'm going to take the black run, Lox, that runs along side Whistling Pig, the one you like. I'll see you at the bottom where we usually leave our skis."

Ivan led off the summit and Vlad followed with Paul right behind them. About a half a mile across the mountain top, Ivan went straight through and Vlad made a quick left turn onto Lox, a steep black run, that had mounds of snow and no tracks from other skiers. It ran parallel to the Whistling Pig run that Ivan was going to go down and the skiers on the two runs could actually see each other, through the breaks in the patches of evergreen trees, if the falling and swirling snow let up long enough for any visibility. As Vlad made his turn onto Lox, Paul knew that this would be his best opportunity and even the weather seemed to be cooperating. He unzipped his right pocket as he turned and followed the Russian.

Paul caught up to Vlad as he made a turn and they crisscrossed on the trail through the knee-deep snow very close to each other. Halfway down the run, Vlad made a quick stop for a rest on top of a crest and Paul purposely made a wrong turn and collided with him with enough force to knock him over. Vlad landed on his stomach, face first in the snow, and Paul landed right on top of him and held him down in the snow as he pulled the small knife out of his jacket pocket.

"What the hell are you doing you stupid bastard? Don't you know how to fuckin' ski? Get the hell off me!" the Russian yelled.

Paul ripped Vlad's toque and goggles off him with his left hand as he put his arm around his neck and under his chin. Just as he got a grip on the Russian, he stuck the small knife into the back of his neck just far enough to get his attention.

"Jesus Christ! That hurts like hell! Get off me?"

"There's a knife right in the back of your neck and if you move again, it's gonna hurt a helluva lot more."

"What the hell do you want?"

"Your name is Vladmir Rousinsky from Hamilton?"

"Yeah, so who the fuck wants to know?"

"You distribute drugs to Eddie Firestone?"

"No I don't. That asshole's dead!"

"Do you remember that bad shipment of Ecstasy that killed all those kids in Toronto close to two years ago?"

"Yeah. That shit came outta California."

"My fourteen year old son died, and so did a lot of other kids, from that shit you put on the streets! By the way, I know Eddie is dead. I'm the guy who killed him. I also have some bad news for you . . . you're dead too," Paul said.

Paul jammed the small knife into the back of the Russian's neck as hard as he could and twisted it strongly. Even over the sound of the wind and snow, he heard the crunch as the bones separated and he felt the Russian go limp. As Paul got up slowly and straightened his skis and snapped his boots into place, he could see Ivan through the evergreen trees over on Whistling Pig, about a hundred feet away from him. As Paul got reorganized and ready to continue on down the hill, he heard Ivan yell to him.

"Did you two guys run into each other? Is he all right?"

"No, he's hurt pretty bad. You'd better get over here fast!"

"Where the hell are you going?" Ivan yelled as he started walking his skis in the direction of his friend who was lying face down and almost covered in the deep, loose powder.

Paul yelled back, "I'm going skiing, it's gonna be a great day!"

"You fuckin' asshole!"

Paul barely heard Ivan's last remark as he turned toward the bottom of the hill and set out for Centerville. He could barely see the shapes of the buildings through the snow. As soon as he got there, he left his poles and skis stuck in a snow bank outside the huge chalet and went inside and directly to the men's room. He found an empty cubicle. When he came back out, he was wearing a red ski jacket, a red ear-warmer and goggles. His black toque and the attached balaclava was rolled up and in a jacket pocket. As he left the washroom, he looked at himself in the mirrors along the wall and felt very comfortable because he didn't even resemble the guy who had collided with the Russian.

The snow was deep and the visibility was so poor that Paul decided it was time to go back to the village. His job was done but his adrenaline was flowing. He decided to take the Mountaintop Express to the summit one last time and take the ski-out all the way to the bottom. He went off the peak and onto Lox once again and briefly stopped halfway down the hill to see why a small crowd had gathered. He stopped about three or four feet from Ivan who was kneeling over his friend.

"What's going on?" Paul asked a bystander.

"Someone has been stabbed and they think he's dead!"

"That's terrible!" Paul answered as he left and continued skiing down the hill with a few others who had also seen enough.

The skiing in the blizzard had not been great but Paul had completed his mission. It was early when he returned to the village, so he headed back to his hotel. He was quite relaxed because he knew in his heart that the Russian was his last victim. He decided to rest for the afternoon and show up at the Red Lion to meet his new buddies and the gals from Houston around four o'clock to do some celebrating. Paul did get to the pub in time for the party, but Ivan, the other Russian, didn't show up for cocktails at the end of the day. Paul really hadn't expected to see him that evening.

* * *

Paul skied all day Wednesday in unbelievable conditions. Laurie's shuttle bus from Denver International Airport arrived at seven o'clock and Paul met her and helped her carry her things to his hotel. As soon as they got to his room, their clothes went in all directions and they made love up in the loft. They had to make up for lost time.

By nine, they were walking hand-in-hand up East Gore Creek and stopped in front of one of Paul's favorite restaurants, Sweet Basil, to look at the menu posted in the window. He had eaten there a couple of times on past trips and had enjoyed the ambiance. They had a long, drawn out, romantic dinner and drank a couple of bottles of his favorite Bordeaux, St-Emilion. The food was exquisite. The restaurant was abuzz with news that a murder had taken place up on the mountain the day before. A Russian from Canada had been stabbed to death.

"A murder on the mountain! Things like that don't happen in Vail," Paul said.

"That's terrible news for a ski resort! Everyone here on vacation will be really nervous," Laurie commented.

"I doubt that there's anything to worry about. If the guy was a Russian, he was probably one of those gangsters or drug traffickers who we're always reading about in the newspapers. Those guys are always fighting."

"It's still scary to think that there's a killer roaming the ski area."

"I wouldn't worry about it. The murder was probably a planned hit and the guy who did it is likely long gone," Paul said to make her feel better.

"Jack, I'm sure you're right, but didn't a Canadian get killed in Ft. Lauderdale when we were there? You're not a hit-man in your spare time are you?" Laurie laughed.

"I make way too much money doing what I do to need a part-time job."

The two lovers had a wonderful dinner and shortly after eleven, found themselves walking back toward Paul's hotel. After eating and drinking so much, they felt like a walk, so they turned right at Bridge Street. They walked to the end of the road near the Red Lion and then back down to East Gore Creek and made a right toward the inn.

"You seem tired after your trip from New York. Do you want to have a drink somewhere or do you want to go back and crash for the night?"

"If you feel like a drink, I'll have one, but I don't want to stay out too late."

"Let's drop in to Pepi's across from our hotel for a nightcap. Then we'll get to bed so we can hit the slopes bright and early in the morning."

* * *

Paul and Laurie had five wonderful days. They spent everyday on the mountain and skied most of the open runs. Laurie kept up with Paul without any trouble. The snow storm passed through the area and the sun came out again. It did snow several inches each night, but the days were beautiful and sunny. They hit the runs early every morning and usually stopped for lunch around one o'clock at one of the many different restaurants in the resort. One day they ate in the cafeteria at Two Elk Lodge, the next, in the more posh restaurant at Centerville, and on another day, they skied all the way over to Lionshead for pasta at Fredo's Italian. They had a great time together. On the Sunday, they skied most of the day and ended up at a huge Super Bowl party at the Sundance Saloon, the village's only true western bar, with Gene, Doug, Jay, the two Daves and the girls from Houston. That night, they made love for a long time. They hardly slept at all.

At ten o'clock on Monday morning, they took the shuttle back to Denver airport and spent an hour and a half together before their separate flights left for Buffalo and New York. They sat together in a quiet airport bar as they waited to say goodbye.

"I had a wonderful time," Laurie said. "I don't want to go back to New York."

"I'm gonna miss you too, but we'll make arrangements to see each other soon. I've got a large, very lucrative real estate deal pending back in Toronto and it's scheduled to close in the next week or so," Paul lied. "If it does, I've been thinking about taking an extended vacation to Europe and doing some traveling for six months or a year. Is there any way that you would be interested in taking a leave of absence from work and coming with me? You won't have to worry about money."

"You really want me to come with you for six months or a year?"

"Yeah, I do. I find myself always thinking about you and missing you when you're not around," he smiled.

"I miss you too when I don't see you, but do you think that we could stand being with each other for such an extended period of time?" Laurie laughed.

"When you're not around, I miss you. I think we should spend some time together and see what happens. Who knows? We might really like each other."

"I think that we just might," Laurie smiled, "so if you decide to go away for an extended holiday, I would love to go with you. You'd better be careful, if we spend much more time with each other, we're liable to fall in love!"

"That wouldn't surprise me at all!"

Laurie's flight to New York City left first and he accompanied her to the gate. They kissed each other goodbye and Paul watched her disappear into the crowd. As soon as she got out of sight, he missed her. He hadn't had feelings like that for a woman for a long time.

CHAPTER THIRTY-FOUR

O n Friday morning, Everdell and Carpenter were seated at their table drinking their first coffee of the day when the door opened. It was Bill Speer and he had a piece of paper in his hand.

"Good morning! Are you guys waiting for a fax from a Rod Farn at Gemmill, Farn? It just came in and I thought that I'd deliver it to you and see what's going on with The Oyster-Shucking Murders investigation."

"Good morning," Everdell said as he took the paper from Speer and looked at it quickly. "We're looking for a blood-type on the father of one of the kids from Medford. He supposedly committed suicide a year or so after his son died. We're just turning some stones over to see what's under them."

"We've got a qualified identification of a Paul Taylor from one of the witnesses at the pool hall where Ruffus Allan and his gang hung out. The killer shot pool with both the witness and Ruffus on the evening of the murders," Carpenter commented.

"Taylor has been on our minds a lot. He committed suicide in Lake Simcoe back in September and we just learned that his body was never found," Everdell added.

"Bill, all of this goes back to that very first murder of Steven Shackleton that was so different from the others. There seemed to be some personal touches," Carpenter added.

"You'll never guess what it says," Everdell commented. "Paul Taylor's blood type is, or was, AB Rh Negative and that's the same type that was on the rear door of Ruffus Allan's Mercedes and on the bullet that we got out of the back seat."

"That's interesting," Speer commented, "but lots of people are AB Rh Negative."

"Believe it or not," Carpenter said, "only one percent has that blood type."

Carpenter was in the process of convincing his boss that he was right when Judy from Administration burst into the room.

"You guys really owe me big time! I've got a match for you! One of the names on a Jet Blue flight out of Buffalo matches a name on the reservation list that you gave me from that restaurant in Fort Lauderdale."

"I can't believe it! Maybe we finally got the break that we've been looking for," Carpenter said quite excited.

"What the hell is the guy's name?" Everdell asked his partner with anticipation.

"*Gordon W. Thoburn!* He took a Jet Blue flight to Florida three days before Morelli was killed and a *Gord Thoburn* also ate at that restaurant, Yesterdays, the night of the murder!" Judy excitedly said as she handed him the list.

"You're a doll," Everdell said. "We owe you an expensive lunch."

"I get to pick the restaurant too," Judy said as she left the room.

"The witnesses at Willie's Billiards said that the name of the man who spent the last night with Ruffus and Artie was named *Gord!*" Everdell said in disbelief.

"It looks like this Paul Taylor is off the hook," Carpenter answered.

"I can't believe it, after beating ourselves up all of these months, things are finally coming together," Everdell commented.

"You guys sound like you're starting to get somewhere. You have a blood type from the Allan murder and the name of a man from Toronto who was in Florida when Morelli was murdered," Speer said as he left. "Find out how it all fits together!"

Carpenter reached for the Toronto phone book and Everdell sat and studied the flight information that Judy had given them.

"There are ten Thoburns in the phone book and not one of

them is listed as a Gordon but there is one G.W. We couldn't get lucky?" Carpenter asked. "There are also two other names using a single G only or a G as a second initial."

"Let's split them up," Everdell suggested. "We'll each call half of them."

"I'm gonna call this G.W. right now!" Carpenter said as he picked up his phone.

As the phone connected to the number he dialed, a busy signal beeped. He called one of the other two and got an answering machine, but didn't bother to leave a message. He tried the third and got no answer. He would try them again during the evening. Carpenter then redialed the *G.W.* number. It was still busy.

Everdell got through to two of the numbers he called and asked for a Gordon Thoburn. Both parties who answered indicated that he must have the wrong number because no Gordons lived there. When he called the third number, he got an answering machine. He would call again later that evening.

Carpenter tried his original number again and the ringing tone buzzed in his ear.

"Is this the Thoburn residence?"

"Yes, who's calling please?"

"I'm Detective Jack Carpenter calling from the Toronto Police Department and I am looking for Gordon W. Thoburn."

"I'm Evelyn. Thoburn. What is this call all about? My husband Gordon passed away almost two years ago."

"I'm very sorry for your loss and I'm sorry to have to bother you, Mrs. Thoburn, but during the investigation of one of our cases, the name Gordon W. Thoburn came up. It may very well be someone other than your husband, but we have to enquire into these things. Could my partner and I meet with you, at your convenience, and get a few questions answered just to straighten this matter out?"

"Certainly, I'm home all day today if that's good for you."

"The telephone book says that you're on Dalewood. Are you still there?"

"Yes, I am. Do you know where my street is located?"

"I know exactly where you live. We'll drop by about eleven-thirty if that's OK."

It was just after eleven o'clock when Everdell and Carpenter finished doing the rest of the things that they had to do at headquarters that morning. They were both looking forward to visiting with Gordon W. Thoburn's widow.

* * *

The Thoburn residence was a classy, older home right in the central part of the city just north of Eglinton and west of Yonge in an area called North Toronto. It was an eighty year old, two story house that had been totally refurbished. The two detectives climbed the front steps to the large porch that went right across the front of the house and rang the door bell. Mrs. Thoburn turned out to be an attractive woman who appeared to be in her late thirties. She was quite receptive and invited them into her home.

"I'm Detective Jack Carpenter and this is my partner, Detective Graham Everdell," Carpenter said as he showed her his badge.

"I'm Evelyn Thoburn. What's this all about?" She asked as they sat down in the living room that was just to the left of the inner hallway.

"During one of our current investigations, the name of a Gordon W. Thoburn came up on an airline roster on a flight to Florida and we're just trying to sort through the various Thoburns with the same name so we can cross them off our list," Carpenter explained. "If you could answer a few questions it will help us clear things up."

"I have no problem trying to help if I can, but as I mentioned on the telephone, my husband has been gone for almost two years."

"We just need some general information such as his full name, including all of his middle names, the date that he passed away, the cause of his death, his age when he passed away, what he did for a living. That sort of thing," Everdell went on.

"His full name was Gordon William Thoburn and he passed away two years ago this April. He was sick for eight months before he died of stomach cancer at thirty-six."

"It sounds like that must have been awfully terrible for you," Carpenter said.

"Yes, it was awful. When Gordie finally passed on, it was almost a blessing."

"What did your husband do for a living?" Everdell asked.

"He was a Chartered Accountant who had his own practice. Most of his clients were here in the city but he did have some that lived out of town."

"Do you have any children?" Everdell asked.

"Yes, twin girls and they're both in first year at Western."

"It would be helpful if you could give us the name of the doctor who took care of your husband when he was ill," Carpenter asked.

"My husband was treated by Dr. Paul Dowdall down at Princess Margaret Hospital."

"Do you happen to know his blood type?" Carpenter asked.

"He was A Positive."

Everdell and Carpenter looked at each other and both appeared to be very disappointed. Their thoughts immediately went back to Paul Taylor.

"After your husband passed away, did you require any legal services to help you with estate matters or anything like that?" Everdell asked.

"Yes, we've used the same law firm for years. My husband went to undergrad with a lawyer at Gemmill, Farn, one of the larger law firms downtown."

"What's your lawyer's name?" Everdell asked, almost knowing the answer.

"Paul Taylor. He handled Gordie's estate for me," Mrs. Thoburn explained and went on. "However, he had some terrible family tragedies of his own and ended up committing suicide about six months ago."

"We do recall that unfortunate situation," Carpenter answered.

"Why do you ask? Is the law firm involved with the case you're working on?"

"No, the law firm has nothing to do with what we're working on," Carpenter said.

"That's all the information that we need for now so we'll carry on and bother some other people named Thoburn," Everdell said as the two men got up to leave.

"We're very sorry for your loss and also for having to bring all of these things up once again when I'm sure you're trying to put them behind you," Carpenter said.

"Thanks so much for your help," Everdell said as the door shut behind them.

As the two detectives walked toward their car in the street, Everdell was the first to speak, "What the hell do you think of that information."

"Maybe Paul Taylor isn't off the hook after all," Carpenter commented.

* * *

Everdell and Carpenter arrived back at headquarters just before one o'clock in the afternoon. They knew exactly what their next step had to be so they buzzed Bill Speer.

"What the hell do you guys want now?" Speer asked as he came through the door. "Everytime I get in the middle of something, you seem to bother me."

"After spending time with Mrs. Thoburn, we really need a Search Warrant. Paul Taylor, the lawyer whose son died of the drug over-dose at Medford, and who may have drowned himself early last fall in Lake Simcoe, was the lawyer on the estate of Gordon William Thoburn," Everdell explained. "We have to take a look at the estate file at Gemmill, Farn and can't without a warrant."

"No problem, I'll get it for you."

"We had better call that Dr. Dowdall at Princess Margaret and see if he'll confirm Thoburn's blood type," Everdell went on. "Mrs. Thoburn may have to call him for us."

"Have you got the information I need for the Warrant?"

"It's all right here," Everdell said handing Speer a completed sheet of paper.

"I'll have the Warrant for you in the morning. I'll try to have it broadly worded just in case there are other files that you have to examine later on," Speer said as he left the room. "It looks like you guys are finally onto something."

"I'll phone Rod Farn and make an appointment to see him tomorrow afternoon. I'll ask him to have the Thoburn Estate file available," Carpenter commented.

"If this guy went to all the trouble to fake his death and he had access to the identification documents of men his age who had passed away, there's no telling how many aliases he might have set up," Everdell surmised.

As the two detectives ate their lunch, they did whatever paper work had to be done to update their files and made the necessary phone calls.

"We can see Farn at two tomorrow," Carpenter confirmed.

About half an hour after Bill Speer had gone back to his own office, he burst through the door with a piece of paper in his hand.

"You two aren't gonna fuckin' believe this!" he said as he handed Everdell a copy of a report he had just received. "I just got this faxed to me from Hamilton."

"Christ, Jack! He's done it again! Vladmir Rousinsky, a Russian who lived in Hamilton, has been murdered while on holidays in Vail, Colorado. Rousinsky is a known drug trafficker who the local police have been trying to prosecute for a number of years. He was found halfway down a ski hill with an oyster-shucking knife sticking out of the back of his neck."

"The last time the killer called and talked to you here at the station, he said that there was only one more victim left on his list," Carpenter remembered. "Do you really think this is the end of The Oyster-Shucking Murders?"

"Hell, it could be the end. Why would he say it, if he didn't mean it?"

"It doesn't matter if it's the last one or not," Speer said as he reached for the door. "Follow up on the Vail killing and keep me advised."

"I don't think that either one of us should have to travel to Colorado on this one," Everdell suggested. "We can probably get everything we need by phone, fax and courier. We can also get a list of passengers from the airlines that fly into Denver from Toronto and Buffalo. We'll concentrate on the week before Rousinsky's death. We may just get lucky and find Gordon W. Thoburn on one of the rosters."

"We'll make a few calls this afternoon to Vail and Hamilton to see what they can send us and we'll make arrangements to slip over to Hamilton in the morning. We can be back for our two o'clock appointment with Farn," Carpenter suggested.

"I'll have your Warrant for you before you head for Hamilton," Speer said as he left the room. "Keep up the good work!"

* * *

Everdell spoke to the Colorado State Troopers in Vail and explained what had been going on in Toronto and Florida. They were very cooperative. They faxed everything they had on Rousinsky's murder to Hamilton and Toronto. The detectives had about thirty faxed pages to go through before the afternoon was over.

"Jack, it looks like the State Troopers sent us copies of everything they have."

"Were there any witnesses or is it the same old story?"

"It looks like there was one witness, another Russian who was vacationing with Rousinsky and it says here that he actually spoke to the killer."

"Does that mean that he actually got a look at him?"

"I don't think so. The report says that the murder took place up on the mountain, halfway down a ski run, in the middle of a blizzard and the visibility was very poor. The witness saw the killer and the victim lying in the snow and thought that they had just run into each other and had fallen down. It sounds like he watched from about a hundred feet away as his buddy was being killed. The witness and the killer had words."

"What the hell did they talk about?"

"The witness asked the killer if his friend was hurt and the guy said that he was hurt pretty badly and then took off skiing."

"Did the other Russian get a good look at the guy?"

"The killer had a black toque on his head, a balaclava and goggles on his face and a black ski outfit and he was covered in snow. That's all the witness saw and by the time he got to his friend, the killer had disappeared down the hill in the blizzard."

* * *

The next morning, the two detectives met at headquarters and picked up their Search Warrant for the Thoburn Estate file. They also asked Mrs. Thoburn to contact the doctor who had treated her husband to have him confirm the blood type for them. The trip to Hamilton only took them about an hour and they pulled into the Hamilton police station at around nine-thirty.

Their discussions and the additional information that they were given didn't provide them with anything new other than some background information about Vladmir Rousinsky. He was definitely a local drug trafficker who the police had been trying to put out of business for a long time. As the metro detectives left the station, a Hamilton police detective asked them to thank the killer for his help in getting Rousinsky off their streets if they happen to arrest him anytime soon. Other witnesses close to The Oyster-Shucking Murders had expressed similar sentiments; now that attitude was coming from a policeman. They all believed that the killer was doing society a favor by disposing of all the garbage that the police couldn't get their hands on because of the reams of red tape.

At noon, the detectives stopped by Sweethearts on the way back into the city. They wanted to speak to the manager of the bar and talk to Danielle, the bartender who had dated Eddie, if she happened to be around. The cops got lucky because Dani was in her usual place behind the bar and the manager was expected at anytime.

"Dani, I'm sure you remember Detective Carpenter and myself, Detective Everdell. How have you been doing since we saw you last?"

"Great! I must've got over Eddie because I'm engaged now."

"Congratulations! We just want to ask you a quick question," Everdell said. "Do you recognize the guy in this picture?"

"Yeah, he's been in here before to meet Eddie when he was alive. It seems to me that he was a foreign guy, Russian maybe, from Hamilton or somewhere west of here."

"You're sure that you saw him with Eddie?" Carpenter asked.

"Positive, he was here quite a few times."

"Thanks for your help," Everdell said. "Is the manager in his office?"

"No, but he should be here soon."

"We can see him the next time we're out this way or maybe you could just give him my card and have him call me at headquarters. Thanks for your help," Carpenter said as the two detectives headed for the front door.

They were just getting into their car when the manager pulled into a reserved spot near the door. They walked back over to where he had parked and he spoke to them.

"Did you ever find out who killed Eddie Firestone?"

"No, we haven't yet, but we're still working on it," Carpenter answered.

"Take a look at this picture. Have you seen this guy before?" Everdell asked.

"Sure, he used to come here to see Eddie. I saw him here a number of times before Eddie was killed. Do you think he's the guy who did it?"

"No, he didn't do it. He was killed last week in Vail, Colorado. Do you know why he met with Eddie?" Everdell asked.

"Not really, but I got the impression that he was his supplier or something."

"Did you ever know the guy's name?"

"No, but he spoke with some kind of an accent. I never had anything to do with those guys, the liquor license ya' know!"

"Thanks for your help," Carpenter said as he and his partner headed to their car.

* * *

On the way back into the city, they stopped at Pazzia, a great little Italian restaurant, on the Queensway at Islington, for lunch. Frank, one of the owners, treated them like long lost cousins and by the time they headed downtown to their two o'clock appointment with Rod Farn, they were stuffed. They arrived on time and Farn had pulled the old estate estate file on Gordon W. Thoburn out of storage and had it on his desk.

"I'm really sorry, but I can't let you look through the Thoburn Estate file because it's privileged information. However, I will answer any questions that you might have if I feel comfortable doing so," Farn advised.

"I think the easiest way to handle this is to let us sit in your boardroom and look through the file on our own. If we need copies of anything, maybe your assistant could help us," Everdell said smiling as he handed him the Search Warrant.

"Well, I think that you might be right," Farn answered as he quickly read the contents of the court document. "The last time we spoke, you gave me the impression that you thought Paul may still be alive. Do you still think that is a possibility?"

"We still seem to be backed up against a wall in this investigation so we're looking at everything that might make sense, but we have no real evidence or definite leads of any kind to date," Carpenter answered.

"Laura, please come in here and show the detectives to a boardroom with this estate file and if they are all occupied, find them an empty office. Gentlemen, if you need copies of anything, Laura will accommodate you and if you need to ask me any further questions about the file, I'll be glad to be of assistance."

"Thanks for your cooperation," Carpenter said as they left his office.

Farn's legal assistant led them to a boardroom, got them both a coffee and gave them her phone extension number so they could call if and when they needed her. The detectives spent about an hour going through the file and came up with very little information they wanted to copy, but they did find something interesting. A list of the documents that had been provided to the lawyer by the widow so the estate could be processed. They called Laura and she ran them the copies that they wanted.

"We have a couple of questions for Mr. Farn, but if you can answer them for us, we won't have to bother him," Everdell said.

"I'll try to help, but I'll get him for you if you need him."

"You copied this list of file contents for us and it included things like passport, birth certificate and driver's license, but none of those things are in the file," Everdell commented. "Where would such things normally go when an estate is being processed? Are they kept in the file or given back to the relatives?"

"They are usually just left in the file unless the relatives want them back as keepsakes. Does the reporting letter to Mrs. Thoburn say anything about them?"

"No, it doesn't mention them. The file contents list says that they were received, but they just aren't in the file," Everdell went on.

"I really don't know. Perhaps Mrs. Thoburn would know where they are."

"We just have one more question and we'll let you go back to work," Carpenter said. "When a person applies for a new passport or a renewal, what is the procedure and what has to be sent in with the application?"

"The application is completed and signed by the applicant. It requires some personal information and a couple of references. The signature is validated or guaranteed by a lawyer, or one of the other qualified parties described in the applications. The old passport is usually sent in with it only if it hasn't expired or been lost, along with a birth certificate and two qualifying pictures. One of the pictures is signed by the applicant and is validated by the guarantor as well, on the back side."

"And that guarantor just signs the application and the pictures and provides basically a birth certificate that doesn't have a picture?" Carpenter asked.

"That's right, that's all there is to it. The only check that appears to be done by the department involved is to contact the party who guaranteed the signature by telephone. Mr. Farn often gets calls, but I've never had one being named as a Reference."

* * *

As Everdell and Carpenter fought their way through the traffic to headquarters, they considered the information they had gathered that day. It all appeared to lead to Paul Taylor and the fact the he might still be alive. He could be responsible for all of The Oyster-Shucking Murders.

"There is the connection between Firestone and Rousinsky. The Russian was Eddie's supplier and now he's dead too," Carpenter commented.

"Vito Morelli and Ruffus Allan were also distributors and they probably supplied Shackleton, Chung, Rastone and Jones."

"Graham, that estate file is interesting too. The items that are missing from the file are things that can be used for a new identity and a new passport with the right picture in it. What a great system we have to obtain passports!"

"We're going to need a list of the other estate files that Paul Taylor worked on for the time period after his wife died and up until he committed suicide. I wonder how many other identities he has set up if he's really our guy."

"Do you think that Farn will give us the list of Taylor's estate clients based on the Search Warrant that we already served him with?"

"Probably," Everdell answered, "because we won't need to look in any more of the files, at least for the time being. All we want is a list of the names of his estate clients so we can see if any of them turn up on any of our passenger lists."

CHAPTER THIRTY-FIVE

P aul's return flight to Buffalo and his trips to Niagara Falls and on to Beer Lake went well. He was dead tired from the week of skiing and the four days and five nights that he had spent with Laurie. The on-hill and off-hill activities had been demanding. He went to bed as soon as he got home and slept for twelve hours. As he cooked himself a small strip loin and a couple of eggs for lunch the next day, he thought about his friend from New York. The two of them seemed to get along extremely well, both in and out of the sack, and he was starting to miss having her around. She was a lot of fun and he was beginning to really care for her.

The fact that Paul had met Laurie and had developed some kind of a relationship with her definitely had an effect on him. All of a sudden he had a future. The darkness where he had spent so many years seemed much brighter. He was glad that his mission was finally over. He had held the persons, who were responsible for destroying the lives of so many young people, accountable. He had absolutely no remorse for the nine men he had killed. None of their communities would miss them. Revenge was his.

* * *

After lunch, he poured himself a scotch and water and sat in front of the fire and thought about the last few years of his life. A life that had once been absolutely perfect but had gone haywire. He had been happily married to the girl of his dreams and she had passed away at a very early age. He might have been able to cope with that tragedy, but to lose his only child so soon after he had lost his wife was too much for him to handle. As he sat by the fire, he realized that for him to do the terrible things that he had done over the past few months, he must have suffered some kind of a nervous breakdown. The pressure must have been so great that he had spun-out of control and done all of those terrible things while he wasn't thinking straight. Everything that he did had been totally out of character for him, even the staged suicide, let alone murdering all of those drug dealers and traffickers. *Oh, well! Now that I'm better, I'll get on with my life!* he thought with a smile as he sat there and sipped his scotch. Being in love gave the world a totally different complexion.

Gordon W. Thoburn and Clive Edward Lyons had committed those crimes and the need for revenge had been flushed from his being. Paul was ready to try to get back to normal. He had met a new woman who had helped get him through the feelings of hatred and hopelessness. She made him realize that life was worth living after all. The fact that he had killed himself, to begin his mission for revenge, complicated things to the point that he knew that he had to leave the country as soon as possible or he would have no life at all. The police would eventually put it all together and determine that he was the likely suspect because his body was never going to be found. There was no way that Lake Simcoe was going to give up a body that wasn't there. He may have made some mistakes along the way that the detectives would eventually find. Paul knew that there was always the possibility that he might be caught at some time in the future. The best thing for him to do was to leave Canada immediately.

Before he left Denver, he had talked to Laurie about taking a sabbatical from work and the two of them going on an extended vacation to Europe or somewhere else. At that time, he hadn't been sure how serious he was. Now that he was thinking more clearly, he thought that it was a great idea. The longer he stayed in the country, the more of a chance someone might figure out what had happened and tie him to the killings. He decided to call Laurie and find out if she had even considered his proposal. He picked up his cell and made the call to New York City.

"Good afternoon. You're speaking to Ms. Crawford's assistant, Nancy, can I help you?"

"Hi, it's Jack Randall calling. Is Laurie available?"

"Oh, just a minute, she's away from her desk but she'll be right back," Nancy said, more excited than Laurie would have been had she answered the phone herself.

Nancy knew that her boss was down the hall chatting in someone else's office so she quickly found her. Laurie noticed her agitated state and wondered what was going on.

"Ms. Crawford. I need to speak to you privately, right now!"

As Laurie got up from her chair and moved out into the hall, she asked, "Nancy, what are you so excited about?"

"You have a call waiting for you at your desk. It's your friend from New Year's Eve and Vail!"

"Will you settle down for heaven's sake and get the hell out of the way so I can get to my phone!"

Laurie got back to her desk very quickly and picked up the phone. "Hello."

"Hi, I was just sitting up here in the north country thinking about you and thought that I'd give you a call."

"This is a pleasant surprise! Does it mean that you miss me a little?"

"Actually, I miss you a lot, but that's not why I'm calling. I just got word that the deal I'm working on is definitely going to close and I was wondering if you had given anymore thought about the extended holiday I had mentioned?"

"I really didn't know how serious you were. Are you?"

"Yeah, I am. I think that you and I should go away together."

"What are you talking about? A few weeks or a few months?"

"I'm thinking that we should plan for at least a year or so and who knows, if it turns out that we actually like each other, maybe a little longer."

"If you're serious, we just hired a guy from San Francisco and he and his wife are looking for a place to rent in Manhattan and I think that they would take mine furnished."

"I'm dead serious. I think that I can be outta here in the next week or so, but you don't have to leave New York that quickly if you have to get things organized. I can let you know where I'll be and you can catch up to me when you're ready."

"Leave it with me and I'll see what I can do. I have to deal with the company and my house," Laurie answered. "Are you sure that this is what you want?"

"Laurie, when I spend time with you and then go home, I really miss you a lot. I honestly think I'm in love with you," Paul said. "Is that a problem?"

"No, it's not a problem! I think I love you too and I would like to spend a lot more time with you. All the better if it's on vacation."

"See what you can work out down there and I'll talk to you in a few days. By that time I'll have a timetable."

"It all sounds so wonderful, but I want to hear it again. Do you really think that you love me?"

"Laurie, I do love you and I really do miss you. I'll call you in a couple of days."

Paul was shocked. He had said it. He had told her that he loved her and he had really meant it. After he spoke to her, he wished that she was with him at that moment. He did miss having her around. Thoughts of Liz went through his mind, but he knew that she would understand. Paul was ready to try and get his life, or what there was left of it, back together and he hoped that Laurie would be part of it.

* * *

Paul had a lot of sleep the night before so he wasn't tired. He made himself a nice dinner, another steak and a garden salad, and watched the nine o'clock movie. The old movie couldn't have come on at a better time because Paul, in his own mind, had been trying to justify the past few months and had wondered if he had made a terrible mistake. The movie stared Charles Bronson and was called

Death Wish. It really hit home. The cops almost thanked Bronson's character for cleaning up the streets. Paul had a feeling that he wouldn't be so lucky if he was caught. As the movie ended, Paul flipped the channel for the CTV News and sat back with his third scotch and water of the evening.

Lloyd Robertson went right to the national news that included a top story from Toronto: "There has been another killing in what the Toronto police and media are calling The Oyster-Shucking Murders. The police have reported that the most recent murder has taken place in Vail, Colorado. The victim was Vladmir Rousinsky, a local Hamilton businessman, known to have ties to the drug community. The police have confirmed that Rousinsky's death is the ninth in a string of killings that started last fall. All of the victims have been drug dealers or drug traffickers. The police have ruled out a turf war among competing drug gangs and are investigating leads that may point to a vigilante. The police say the suspect may have suffered a terrible loss because of drugs on the streets of Toronto and is exacting his revenge on dealers and traffickers. The police further advise that they have new evidence that they are considering that may lead them to the person responsible for The Oyster-Shucking Murders. They have promised to elaborate on that new evidence in the near future."

Paul listened carefully to the broadcast and knew that it had been much more informative than usual in that the police actually mentioned a vigilante who might have suffered a terrible loss. The police had gone out of their way to provide the media with the additional information and he got the feeling that maybe they were actually onto something this time. It was the perfect time for him to leave the country.

* * *

During the next few days, Paul thought seriously about what he had to do to make the necessary arrangements to disappear. There were only three or four things and all of those things were relatively simple. Beer Lake had been purchased in one of his fictitious names from an elderly local man who held the first mortgage. Paul had put down as little as possible because he wasn't quite sure of his future plans. He made all of the monthly payments regularly, in cash and on time, because the original owner lived close by. If he stopped, the guy would just take the place back and resell it without much difficulty. Paul would lose his minimal down payment and that would be the end of it. He would just walk away from the cottage. All he had to do was drop in and see the old fellow and pay him four months mortgage payments in advance. He would tell him that he was heading south for the rest of the winter and would be back later in the spring. That way, the arrears wouldn't even become an issue to the old guy until early summer. By the time the property was put up for sale, the Oyster-Shucking Murders would have been long forgotten.

There were only a few personal things in the house by the time Paul had faked his suicide. He had discarded everything except for some family pictures. Now he would get rid of anything that might tie him or the cottage to Gordon William Thoburn or Clive Edward Lyons. The place could be cleaned out very quickly and everything that he didn't take with him could be burned or disposed of in some way.

The old Taurus wasn't worth much and it had served its purpose. Rather than just leave it sitting at Beer Lake, Paul could sell it to one of the auto wreckers in the area before he left. He would receive very little money for it, but at least it would be gone.

As he made his plans, he looked at the wooden box of oyster-shucking knives that sat in the corner of the room. There were still thirty or forty of them left in the box and they had outlived their usefulness. He wondered, *Should they be left in the Beer Lake cottage with all of the other strange stuff or should they be destroyed or disposed of once and for all?* He wondered if it even mattered one way or the other. He thought that if he left the knives in the cottage at Beer Lake and the authorities found them, it wouldn't matter, because by that time, they would have figured out who he was anyway. Then he thought, *Why should I take the chance?* He picked up the box and carried it a couple of hundred yards out onto the frozen lake and dumped the contents into the snow. They would sink to the bottom as the ice melted in the spring.

He would become Jack Melville Randall for the rest of time, at least the rest of his time. The new identity that he had saved for last had absolutely no ties to clients at his law firm, so it would be safe. The other two, Thoburn and Lyons, could at some point be traced to Gemmill, Farn's clients and his real identity. If that ever happened, he would be linked to the murders. Paul knew that the police weren't dummies and that they had been working on The Oyster-Shucking Murders for a number of months. It could only be a matter of time. He hoped that would never happen, but there was always the possibility.

Paul knew that his days as a vigilante were over. He was going to pick up the pieces of his life that he had left, if it was at all possible, and he was going to include Laurie in those plans. He planned to fly from Toronto to Europe, probably Amsterdam, because it was the hub of the continent. From there, he could head in any direction. He could access any of the European countries.

By the end of the week, Paul was ready to leave Beer Lake forever. He thought back in time and wished that when he, Liz and Ricky had been looking for a cottage that they had found the place, because he would have loved to have shared it with his family. That was then. He had put that part of his life behind him and was looking forward to a new life with Laurie, the stockbroker from New York City; if it wasn't too late.

* * *

By the weekend, Paul had done everything that he had to do and he was ready to leave Canada. He called Laurie on his cell to see if she had been able to arrange for a sabbatical from her job and see if the new employee in her firm had rented her furnished home for the next year. It was Saturday and she had been waiting for him to call.

"After our discussion earlier in the week, I thought that you would have called me before now. What have you been doing?"

"I've been extremely busy, but I wanted you to think about what I had asked you to do, so you would be sure that you wanted to go a little crazy with me for awhile. I didn't want to interfere with your own decision making process, just in case you had some reservations about me."

"The only reservations that I've had are that you haven't called me back two or three more times to tell me that you love me! That would have made me feel a lot better while I was trying to make arrangements to leave New York. What's with you? Since we met, you've only told me how you really feel once!"

"Laurie, I'm sorry. I really have a lot of things on my mind, important things, things that you wouldn't understand even if I explained them to you. Lately, I've been in a total fog. You know where I'm coming from since my wife and child died. It has been hard for me, but I honestly want you to know that *I love you! I love you! I love you!*"

"I just wanted to hear it again. I know that business is on your mind too. I spoke to Frank and I can have a year's leave of absence starting at the end of February. I have a lot of things to clean up before I can actually disappear and hand all my clients over to the new guy from San Francisco."

"The end of the month is fine. The deal that I was working on is closed and it was very lucrative so, as I mentioned, we won't have any money worries. I have completely organized everything here so I'm ready to leave right now. I'm heading for Europe next week to do a little business, so by month's end when you are ready to join me, I'll have a game plan as to where we'll meet and what we'll do."

"The other good news is that the guy from the west coast, who happens to like my house, has a deal with the company to pay his rent for a year."

"That sounds great!"

"Frank said that the company will deposit the rent right into my bank account every month and, it's unbelievable, the new guy will pay me a percentage of what he earns from my clients each month while I'm away."

"You sound like you're better organized than I am."

"I can confirm this whole thing tomorrow with my tenant and my company, if you are serious and really want me to be with you for the next year!"

"I really do. You never know, a year may turn into a lifetime!"

"You say the nicest things!"

"As soon as I know when I'm leaving Toronto, I'll give you a call. It'll be in the next few days. I might even call you before that just to tell you that I love you a couple of more times."

"You can call and tell me that anytime. Call me everyday if you want to."

"By the way, do you have a valid passport? You'll need one!"

"I renewed mine a few months ago so that's not a problem."

* * *

Late Sunday afternoon, Paul drove to Peterborough, about forty-five miles to the southeast, and checked into the Days Inn right downtown. His room was quite nice with a sitting area, wet-bar and fireplace. After Paul settled in for the night, he wandered up the main street to find a place to have dinner and came across a restaurant that looked very popular judging by the crowd that was there for Sunday dinner. Paul went into the Kitchen Table and had a drink at the bar, until he was led to a table at the rear of the restaurant, next to a fireplace. The Caesar salad, followed by the prime rib, was excellent and he washed it all down with a bottle of Chateau de Pizay, a great Beaujolais. After dinner, he watched a movie in his room and went to sleep right after the eleven o'clock news. The next day was going to be busy and he needed to get a good night's sleep.

Paul took advantage of the complimentary orange juice, coffee and toast, in the breakfast nook off the main lobby and relaxed while he read the morning Toronto Star. Shortly after nine o'clock, he walked back up the main street toward the restaurant where he had dinner the night before and went into the travel agents' office that was nearby. Jack M. Randall wanted a one-way ticket on the next flight to Amsterdam. KLM Royal Dutch Airlines had a non-stop flight leaving for the Netherlands at ten o'clock the next morning, Tuesday, and there were a number of seats available. The flight was booked and paid for in cash. When that was finalized, Paul went back to his hotel room to put his ticket into his suitcase and then arranged to do some last minute things.

As soon as Paul got back to the lobby, he paid for another night and made arrangements with the clerk to contact the Peterborough Airline Shuttle Service that went from Peterborough to Pearson International Airport, two or three times a day. The shuttle was booked and scheduled to pick him up at the hotel at five o'clock the following morning. That would get him to the airport by seven which would give him lots of time to be processed for the international flight.

Paul drove up Water Street, turned left on Parkhill and then drove all the way through town and out to the Highway 7 bypass. It wasn't long before he saw the sign, *AAA Auto Wreckers Limited*. Paul got three hundred bucks for the old Taurus. It had always run well for him even though it had over two hundred thousand miles on it. He called a cab to pick him up and take him back into town.

The rest of the day was spent relaxing. At noon, Paul walked a couple of blocks to the Montreal House, one of the older pubs in town, for a few draught beers and a burger. He met a couple of local characters, Doug Atchison and Mercury Moyle, and spent the afternoon trying to match them drink for drink. He was able to keep up to the guys but was totally pissed by the time he got back to his room at about six o'clock. He turned on the television and fell asleep almost immediately. He woke up as the eleven o'clock news was being introduced.

Beverly Thomson was as pretty as ever as the Global News broadcast began. She went directly into the Toronto local news: "The Metropolitan Toronto Police Department has provided an up-date on the investigation into The Oyster-Shucking Murders. Chief of Detectives, Bill Speer, has said that the detectives in charge are concentrating on one specific suspect and have been meeting with witnesses to the various murders in the hopes of having the suspect identified. The detectives have uncovered a number of inconsistencies in the evidence from the nine murders of the known drug dealers, two of which took place outside of Canada. As Detectives Everdell and Carpenter sort through the previous evidence and the new evidence that has come to light, they are hopeful that a witness will step forward and be able to identify a photo of the suspect. More information will be released by the department as it becomes available."

Paul wasn't quite sure what the news broadcast meant, but he had a gut feeling that it was the right time for him to retire and get out of the country. The only thing that crossed his mind about the suspect, that the news report had mentioned, was that the detectives may have been able to tie together a number of loose ends. Obviously, his body had never been found after his suicide. The killer did have some connection to the deaths at Medford and he had been seen at The Hospital For Sick Children, Sweethearts and Willie's Billiard Hall. He also felt that he may have made some mistakes along the way. He wasn't sure if the police had been able to tie him to his deceased clients at Gemmill, Farn, but there was always that possibility.

As Paul thought about the contents of the newscast, he wondered more and more if he was actually the suspect that the police had told the media about. He should really try to find out as he would have to be extremely careful in Europe if his identity was known to the Toronto police. He would be glad when the KLM flight to Amsterdam touched down on the continent and he disappeared.

CHAPTER THIRTY-SIX

The detectives called Rod Farn as soon as they got back to headquarters, but he had already left for the day. He didn't return the call until late the next morning. Everdell explained to him that they needed a list of the names of all of the decedents in the estates that Paul Taylor had acted on, during the years following the death of his wife until he left the firm. He made it clear that they needed the compiled list quickly.

"I don't know if I can just provide you with all of that information without some authority to do so," Farn said showing reluctance to provide deceased clients' names.

"Have you got the Search Warrant that I gave you yesterday?"

"Yeah, it's right here in my hand."

"I think that it's very broadly worded so you should feel comfortable giving us what we need," Everdell explained. "We only need the client names or we can get a Search Warrant that allows us to pick up the files and bring them here to the station."

"You're right. I think I can give you that information as long as you don't have to get into the files. I'll make immediate arrangements for a list of the names to be made for you and it will be faxed to the number you gave me the other day."

"If we have to look in a file or two in the future and you don't feel that the Warrant you have is sufficient, we'll get another one that will be more specific."

"We'll deal with that when and if the time comes."

"How soon do you think the list will be available?"

"I'll get my legal assistant to deal with it right away so she should have the information available later today."

"That's great. Thanks for your help."

"Would you let me know what you turn up on Paul Taylor? If he is in fact alive, his actions might have compromised the firm in some way and we may have to take some immediate steps to minimize the damage."

"We'll be sure to keep you advised. You've been very helpful to us," Everdell assured him as he hung up. "Jack, the list of estate names should be here today. Why don't you call the airlines again and get a list of passengers who flew out of Toronto and Buffallo to Denver during the week before Rousinsky was murdered? Call the Buffalo airlines first because that's where the killer flew from on his way to Florida."

"I'll do it right now."

The detectives made all the calls they had to make by noon and when they were done, Everdell slipped across the street and brought back some coffee and sandwiches. As soon as he returned, they shut themselves in their room and discussed the case.

"Let's plug Paul Richard Taylor into the equation as if he's not really dead and see what we come up with," Everdell said as he rubbed off part of the blackboard.

"OK, the murder of Steven Shackleton was totally different from the rest of them because he was killed downtown and the body was moved to Medford. Just that fact alone should have convinced us that the killer was connected to Ricky Taylor's school. Shackleton was the street dealer who sold drugs at that high school."

"The other evidence that we can't forget is that Stevie was stabbed twice. Once in the back of the neck like the rest of them and for some reason he was stabbed a second time in the middle of his forehead," Everdell recalled. "Either strong hatred or something that Shackleton said caused the killer to pull the knife out of the dead man's neck and implant it in his forehead. Maybe the kind of hatred someone might have for the drug dealer who supplied the drugs to Medford on the weekend his son died."

"Graham, that makes a whole lot of sense."

"Those facts clearly tie Paul Taylor to the first murder and as far as we can tell, Shackleton's supplier was Morelli. So it ties Taylor to him too. There were no witnesses to Stevie's murder except for the women at the hospital. They described a white man with long, dark hair, sideburns and a goatee. The size and shape of the guy they saw fits Taylor. Farn confirmed that he was in extremely good condition."

"The next murder we investigated was Edward Firestone who got it the same way at Sweethearts in the west end. The only witness there who actually noticed him, Jack Spratt, gave the same description of the guy as the women at the hospital. We know that Firestone worked Trudeau Collegiate, where another kid died. We also know that his supplier was Vladmir Rousinsky," Carpenter went on.

"Those facts tie Firestone and Rousinsky together, but not to Taylor."

"The next body we found, a few days later, was Liang Chung and it appeared that he died the same day as Firestone. Ruffus Allan had Scarborough tied up tight."

"Cedarview Secondary School in the east end was on Chung's beat and another kid died there. There is really no tie-in to Taylor," Everdell said as he wrote on the blackboard.

"The next dealer to get killed was Clarence Jones, in Downsview, where he hung around Pinehurst Secondary two or three days a week. Two students died there. We can tie Morelli to Jones in the north west end of the city."

"That still doesn't bring Paul Taylor into the picture."

"Shortly after that, the body of Darvel Rastone showed up out in the Beach. He seems to have hung around The Bluffs Collegiate where one kid died and another ended up with brain damage. We can tie Rastone to Ruffus Allan as his supplier, but there's nothing to link Taylor to that murder either."

"Jack, at that point in time, five street dealers had been killed and they all sold drugs at high schools where teenagers had died on the same weekend as Ricky Taylor. Next on the hit parade was Vito

Morelli, in Florida, and that was where the killer started making mistakes."

"Someone using the name Gordon W. Thoburn flies to Fort Lauderdale and has dinner at the same restaurant where Morelli eats in on the night he is murdered. We can definitely tie Paul Taylor to Thoburn, not only because they were university friends, but because of the lawyer-client relationship and the fact that Taylor acted for the estate. He had all of the documentation in the Thoburn estate file to build himself a new identity if he wanted to do that."

"Sometime after that, Ruffus Allan and a buddy got to know the killer at the pool hall in Scarborough. They try to rob the guy and he kills both of them. Ruffus probably had no idea that his new friend was setting up an opportunity to kill him anyway. In the process, the killer gets shot and the blood type, AB Rh Negative, in the backseat of Allan's car matches Taylor's blood type exactly."

"The descriptions that we got from the witnesses in the pool hall were similar to all the other witnesses' accounts, if you change a beard or mustache or haircut," Carpenter said. "The guy was white, mid to late thirties and in extremely good physical condition."

"As far as the Vladmir Rousinsky murder in Vail, there's really nothing to go on because the witness didn't see the guy's face in the snowstorm. We might get lucky and find that Gordon W. Thoburn was on a flight out of Buffalo or Toronto to Denver."

"The more you and I go through this stuff, the more I'm convinced that Paul Taylor didn't drown in Lake Simcoe and he is the vigilante who is avenging the deaths of his son and all of those other kids. Some adults also died from the bad drugs, but the killer has only concentrated on dealers who pushed drugs around high schools."

"There are too many things that keep leading us back to Taylor," Everdell agreed.

"There isn't much more we can do until we get the list of Taylor's estate clients from Farn. We're still waiting for the lists of passengers from the airlines too. Why don't we pack it in for the weekend while we're in a waiting mode? I'm sure that we'll have everything we need first thing Monday morning."

* * *

Everdell and Carpenter walked into Homicide headquarters at their usual time on Monday morning and met in the front office. They exchanged a few pleasantries about the weekend and went right into their room.

"Here's the list of Taylor's estate clients that Gemmill, Farn faxed over to us. It looks like it arrived late Saturday afternoon," Everdell commented.

"I'll wait until just after nine to make a few calls to see where the airlines' lists are that we requested. They should've been here by now."

Carpenter followed up on the evidence that they were waiting for from the airlines and Everdell made a few calls in relation to one of their other cases. There wasn't much more to do until they got the lists from the airlines. Everdell called Judy in the office and asked her to keep her afternoon free because they would soon have some evidence that they would need her to sift through as quickly as possible. She would have to input the names on the list from the law firm into the computer, with the names on the flights to Denver. It would take her a lot of time.

While they waited for the airline information, the detectives left their office for a long overdue interview of a witness for one of their other murder cases because The Oyster-Shucking Murders had taken most of their time. They got back to the office at about one-thirty and the lists from the airlines that flew out of Buffalo and Toronto to Denver were on the table. Everdell took them upstairs to Judy to have them processed.

Everdell spoke to Judy as he handed her the papers, "There are a lot of names on these lists. Do you think you can run them for comparisons this afternoon?"

"You gotta be kidding, there are hundreds of names here," Judy commented.

"It's gonna take more than the afternoon just to put the information into the computer, but once that's done, the comparisons are easy. From the look of it, I'm afraid that I'm gonna have to work some overtime tonight. I promise that I'll have it all on your desk first thing in the morning. By the way, forget about the lunch, it'll have to be dinner!"

"No problem. You're a sweetheart."

Everdell went back to his room and explained to his partner that it would be morning before they would get the comparisons back so they decided to go back to the murder case they had worked on earlier. The rest of the day passed in the usual fashion and just before the two men went home to their families at about five-thirty, Everdell stuck his head into Judy's department to see how she was making out.

"I'll have all the information loaded in a couple of hours and I'll make sure that a full report will be waiting for you when you get in tomorrow morning."

* * *

The next morning, Tuesday, Everdell arrived at headquarters before his partner. After he grabbed a coffee from the Starbucks across the street, he went directly to the room. The reports from Judy were there, in a neat pile, and the top page had notations in yellow marker. As he was trying to compare the notations on the paperwork and determine what Judy was trying to tell him, Carpenter came in and sat down.

"Good morning, Graham. It looks like Judy got all the computer work done last night. Any good news?"

"Yeah, Jack, she did and I was just looking at it. It looks like there's a match."

"Did our Gordon W. Thoburn show up again?"

"No, he didn't but a C. Edward Lyons flew out of Buffalo to Vail on the Friday before Rousinsky was killed and returned to Buffalo ten days later, on the Monday."

"Does that name match one of the names on the list that we got from Gemmill, Farn?"

"It certainly does and our friend Paul Taylor was the lawyer who acted for the estate of Clive Edward Lyons who passed away about two years ago."

"Graham, I think that pretty well seals it! Paul Richard Taylor is alive and well and didn't drown in Lake Simcoe last September. It would appear that the loss of his wife from cancer and the death of his only child, Ricky, from a drug overdose, put him over the edge."

"I'm almost disappointed that it's him. Most of the people that we've spoken to, including other policemen, want us to thank him for cleaning up the streets but our system says that we have to hunt him down and arrest him. The problem is that no sooner than one of those dealers is killed or arrested, another one takes his place."

"Graham, I better call Rod Farn at the law firm and tell him what we've found out from the information that we've collected to date. I'll tell him that we need to take a look at the Lyons Estate file and that we'd like to do it under the authority of the Search Warrant that we already served him with to save time."

"Yeah, we have to see it. Farn was concerned about us going through his clients' files, but it'll be the only one, so under the circumstances, he'll probably cooperate."

"It may be too early to get Farn. In the meantime, I guess we should get Speer in here and tell him that we've found The Oyster-Shucking Killer."

"Let's do that right now because we'll have to decide how to proceed in terms of the media and pictures of Taylor," Everdell answered. "We're gonna need the public's help to find him because as far as anyone who knew him is concerned, he's dead and has completely disappeared off the face of the earth."

"The problem is that he doesn't look like his pictures anymore."

"Jack, I'll go and get Billy. Why don't you try Farn?"

It was nine-fifteen when Bill Speer sat down with the detectives. As he arrived, Carpenter was just hanging up from speaking with Rod Farn.

Carpenter was first to speak. "I just talked to Farn at the law firm and everything's fine. We can go through the Lyons file later this morning. He remembered something strange that Taylor had said to him during their last dinner meeting. Taylor made a comment about turning to the *other edge of justice*. Farn didn't know what he meant at that time, but he now realizes that the *other edge of justice* is *revenge*."

"Why couldn't he have remembered that when we started our investigation?" Everdell commented.

"I want to compliment you guys. It looks like you finally have some solid evidence pointing to this lawyer, Paul Richard Taylor, as the vigilante," Speer said.

"I noticed that you called him a vigilante and not a killer," Everdell commented."

"You're right," Speer answered. "He has actually cleaned a lot of garbage off the streets of Toronto for us, but he really is and should be referred to as a killer."

"I think that we now have enough evidence to say, unequivocally, that Taylor is our man. It started back with the murder of Stevie Shackleton and the facts that he had been stabbed twice and his body was moved to Medford where Taylor's son went to school. Then the phone call to me suggesting they weren't just random killings. The victims all sold drugs at high schools where students died the same weekend that Taylor's son died. The name of one of Taylor's dead clients, Gordon William Thoburn, came up in Florida at the restaurant where Morelli had his last supper and on the flights to and from Buffalo. The name of another one of Taylor's clients, Clive Edward Lyons, came up on the flights from Buffalo to and from Denver during the week that Rousinsky was killed in Vail. The blood found in the backseat of Ruffus Allan's car, on the bullet and on the back door and window, is a match for Taylor's not so common blood type, AB Rh Negative. I don't think that there's any doubt that his suicide was staged and that he is our vigilante."

"Where the hell do we go from here?" Carpenter asked. "As far as anyone who ever knew Paul Richard Taylor is concerned, he has disappeared. He's dead to the world. Even his sister-in-law believes he committed suicide."

"We'll have to use the pictures of him that were provided by the law firm and develop an approach for the media to help us find this guy," Speer suggested. "We'll have to splash his picture on all of the news broadcasts and in all of the newspapers and see if we can find someone who recognizes him."

"Even if someone does recognize him, with the attitude of the public around these murders, they may not step forward and help us anyway," Carpenter suggested.

"We'll slip over to the law firm and take a look in the Clive Edward Lyons estate file and see what's there," Everdell said, "but I'm sure we'll find the same thing as in the Thoburn file. The passport, birth certificate and driver's license will be missing."

"As soon as you finish doing that, get back here and draft a news release for the media including a good picture of our killer and let me take a look at it. If I don't get back from my meeting this afternoon, leave it on my desk and we'll finalize it tomorrow. We had better get that information out to the public as soon as possible because this investigation has been going on way too long," Speer said as he got up to leave.

CHAPTER THIRTY-SEVEN

Paul woke up before the alarm went off and had a leisurely shower and shave. He trimmed his mustache so that it looked neat and put on his sunglasses that lightened and darkened depending on the brightness of the day. He was waiting in the lobby of the hotel at five o'clock in the morning for the Airport Shuttle and it arrived right on time. The driver had already picked up two other couples from Peterborough, who were on their way to Mexico for a week in the sun. As soon as Paul and his luggage were in the vehicle, the van headed out Lansdowne toward Highway 115 and eventually Highway 401 on its way to Pearson International Airport. It was dark but it wasn't long before the passengers could tell that it was going to be a beautiful day. There was little traffic until the van got close to the city, but even then, it was moving well. He got to the airport before seven o'clock.

Terminal Three was very busy that morning and there were long line-ups at most of the airline counters including KLM. It took Paul over an hour to get his luggage checked and his boarding pass, but even then he had lots of time to relax. He decided to stay in the main part of the airport and not go through security to the gate where his KLM flight to Amsterdam would be boarding. He got a copy of the Globe and Mail and found a restaurant. He read the paper during breakfast, however, his mind kept wandering.

Paul kept thinking about the detectives who had been working on the murders for the past five months. He had an awful urge to contact them to confirm that there would be no more killings and to try to find out if the new evidence they had involved him. By the time he left the restaurant at close to nine-thirty, he had decided to make one last call and he wanted to make it as close to his departure time as possible. He would make the call from the main part of the airport. He knew that the police would quickly find the location of the pay phone where the call originated, so he couldn't make it from the other side of security near his KLM gate. He felt lucky that it was so busy that morning with thousands of people coming and going to and from hundreds of different destinations.

Paul knew that he didn't have to call Detective Everdell. He had already told him that there was only going to be one more killing. The detectives probably already knew that Vladmir Rousinsky was the last one. He needed to call the detective. He thought that if he did, he could get some sort of clarification of Beverly Thomson's newscast, from the night before, about a suspect in the murders. If he was the suspect, Interpol would be automatically alerted. It was essential for him to know before he arrived at his destination in Europe. He also needed the police to know that the murders over the past months were not just the acts of some crazy person. Paul wanted them to know that there was a reason why each of those men had died. He wanted the police to know that he was not just on a killing spree.

Paul picked a bank of telephones in the middle of the airport, near one of the main entrances to the huge complex, to make his call. There were people everywhere. There were long line-ups at the counters of the many different airlines that had flights leaving Canada. As soon as he made the call to Detective Everdell, he hung up the phone and immediately headed toward the security search area that he had to pass through for the departure gate for his KLM flight to Amsterdam. As he walked, he realized that there was no need for him to have held the receiver with a handkerchief because Everdell had confirmed that they had figured out that he was the killer and that his suicide had been faked. He had left some evidence in Florida when he had killed Morelli and they had been able to put it together with some airline records and came up with him.

Paul was quite amazed that they had been able to find out who he was because he thought that he had been extremely careful and had left very little evidence for them to consider. The detectives deserved a lot of credit from the department. As soon as they got to Gemmill, Farn and came up with two of his aliases, they must have figured out his name. He thought to himself, *Thank God that I knew enough to set up an identity that had nothing to do with the law firm!*

* * *

It took Paul about twenty minutes to get through the very busy security area and as he walked down the long hallway toward the gate for his ten o'clock KLM flight to Amsterdam, he noticed there was still a huge crowd of passengers waiting in the gate area to be boarded. It appeared that his flight was not going to leave on time. He started to get concerned about how long the delay might be because he guessed that the police already knew where his call had originated and were likely closing in on the airport at that moment. There were so many people milling about, he was unable to find a seat, so he stood by the windows that overlooked the tarmac. As he settled in and tried to relax, the flight attendants started to load the passengers by calling for those who needed assistance and those with young children. By the time the numbers for the seats at the back of the plane where Paul was seated were called, it was close to ten-thirty. The flight attendant who ripped the boarding passes was so busy, she barely looked up as Paul passed through. He walked down the boarding ramp to the Airbus and settled into his window seat at the rear of the plane. He anxiously waited for it to depart.

Paul was more than relieved when the loading door was finally closed and the plane was slowly towed backwards out onto the tarmac. He felt progressively more comfortable as the engines screamed and the plane began to move forward under its own power. Paul kept looking out of the small window that was beside him and into the waiting area where he had been standing minutes ago. He happened to notice a uniformed policeman rush into the gate area with another man in a suit right behind him. Moments later, the man in the suit leaned against the window sill and stared at the taxiing plane. Suddenly, he turned and disappeared. Paul wondered if it was Everdell or Carpenter and if they were showing his picture to various airline employees in one last ditch effort to locate him before he left the country.

If the police knew who he was, they would have pictures of him, but they would be very out-dated pictures. He didn't look a bit like the Paul Richard Taylor of old who used to work at Gemmill, Farn, LLP. He honestly believed that it would be very unlikely that anyone would tie him, as Jack Randall, to any picture of Paul Taylor that the police might have in their possession at the airport. He sat back in his seat, crossed his fingers and tried to relax as the Captain announced that there were two other planes ahead of them on the runway and that they would be taking off within five minutes.

As the Airbus lifted into the air, Paul looked out of his small window once more. He stared out over Toronto which had been his home for a long time. He wondered if he would ever see it again. There was nothing left for him there, so it didn't really matter. As he thought about the future, he wondered what Pandora had in store for him.

CHAPTER THIRTY-EIGHT

Just as Bill Speer left the room and Everdell and Carpenter were getting ready to go downtown to meet with Rod Farn at the law firm to look at the Clive Edward Lyons estate file, the telephone rang. Carpenter, who was closest, picked it up. A moment later, he handed it to his partner.

"It's a call for you, Graham."

"Detective Graham Everdell, what can I do for you?"

"I just called to tell you that it's all over. There will be no more killings. All of the drug dealers and their suppliers who were responsible for that bad shipment of Ecstasy and for the deaths of all of the high school students across the city are now dead. They have paid for the terrible grief that they inflicted on so many Toronto families."

Carpenter immediately noticed the shocked look on his partner's face and stopped what he was doing to listen intently. He had seen that look before.

Everdell immediately recognized the voice and tried to pull himself together as he spoke, "We have finally figured out who you are! We know that it was the loss of your son, Ricky, from an overdose of those bad drugs that caused all of these killings. We know who you are, so the best thing that you can do now is turn yourself in so you can get some help!"

"I don't need any help, thanks. I had a job to do and now it's done. I just want you to know that it's all over. There will be no more killings."

"Give yourself up and we'll do everything we can to help you."

"I just want you and the public to know that all the drug dealers and traffickers were killed because they deserved to die. They ruined the lives of countless people in our city."

"We know why you targeted the men you killed. We know that Ricky died from an overdose from that bad shipment of Ecstasy that hit the streets so long ago."

"Then you know why all of those killers had to die."

"We also know that you are Paul Richard Taylor and that you have been using the aliases, Gordon William Thoburn and Clive Edward Lyons! It's just a matter of time before we catch up with you. Give up! We'll do everything we can to help you!"

"I'm sure you know that I can't do that right now."

"Your name isn't Thoburn or Lyons, it's Paul Richard Taylor. Let us help you!"

There was a short lull on the line as Paul got over the shock of what Detective Everdell had just told him. They had found out everything there was to know about him and he had absolutely no idea how they had done it. As he listened to the last comment that Detective Everdell made, he only had one thought.

"How did you find out? What did I do wrong?"

"Killers always make mistakes. We matched your Thoburn alias from the flight out of Buffalo to Yesterday's reservation list in Fort Lauderdale. Then we found the Thoburn widow and traced the estate work to you at Gemmill, Farn."

"You guys are good!"

"We're smart enough to know that what you went through caused you to go on this killing rampage. There is a lot of sympathy for you both in the public and in this department. We also know that if you give yourself up right now, we can help you!"

"Detective Everdell, Paul Richard Taylor is dead. He died a terrible death, a long, long time ago," Paul answered as he quietly hung up the telephone.

As the buzzing sound hummed in Everdell's ear, he almost yelled at Carpenter, "It was Taylor! He called to tell us that there will be no more killings! It's over! He said that all of the drug dealers and suppliers responsible for the deaths of the students have now been killed. Christ! We have to find out if that call was made from a pay phone quickly!"

"I'll get Speer while you call Bell Canada," Carpenter blurted out.

Everdell hung up and quickly called the special Bell Canada operator who was available for situations like this and provided his codes and the information that she required for clearance. He told her that it was an emergency and that he needed the search done immediately. He prayed that she would call back quickly. While they waited for information on the pay phone that Taylor had used, the minutes that passed by felt like hours. Carpenter and Speer quickly returned to the small room and waited with Everdell for the call from the Bell operator. It took ten minutes.

"The call that you received came from a pay phone at Pearson International Airport, Terminal Three. The serial number on the phone is PI 652-857."

"Thanks for your help," Everdell said as he hung up and turned to the others. "He called from the fuckin' airport, Terminal Three! All of the flights from that terminal are international!"

"You two get the hell out there as fast as you can and take those pictures of Taylor with you," Speer said excitedly. "I'll call the detachment of the Royal Canadian Mounted Police who are stationed at the airport and have them find the pay telephone that Taylor used. Maybe, once you provide them with pictures, they can help. Take Ward and Johnson with you. They can help you cover some territory out there."

* * *

The detectives' unmarked car, with the red light flashing on the dash, slid to a stop at one of the main doors of Terminal Three where a couple of uniformed RCMP Officers waved them down. The four detectives rushed inside, right behind the two officers who led them to a bank of pay telephones where two other Mounties were waiting.

"This is the phone with the Serial Number PI 652-857," the officer called out, "but there was no one suspicious around it when we got here."

"The son-of-bitch is flying outta the country as we speak, to Europe or South America or somewhere," Everdell commented and turned to the other detectives. "We don't have time to check passenger lists for Taylor's two aliases at all of the outgoing airlines so why don't we each take a Mountie and a picture of Taylor and head for the departure gates. All we can do is check the crowds and see if any of the flight attendants who are loading passengers remember seeing him. "

"We have to try. Who the hell knows? We might just get lucky," Carpenter answered and spoke to one of the Mounties who was there. "You come with me and take a look at this picture. This guy's name is Paul Richard Taylor and he is The Oyster-Shucking Killer."

The four detectives, each with a uniformed Mountie from the special airport contingent, were allowed through the various security areas of the huge complex without delay. There were twenty gates in each one, with crowds of people waiting for departures at most of them. Everdell and his RCMP officer rushed down the hall toward the gate where a KLM Airbus had just backed away from the loading area. The Mountie talked to the airline employees in the various passenger loading zones and Everdell scanned as many passengers as he possibly could as he looked for his suspect's face in the crowds. He quickly walked through the people and looked at every man he could see. It was not the best way to find Taylor, but under the circumstances, that was the best he could do. As he got through the crowds of passengers, Everdell stopped and talked to the flight attendants at a number of gates that were vacant, where the planes had obviously already left. Taylor's KLM gate was one of the last ones where he stopped.

"I'm Detective Graham Everdell. How long ago did the plane leave this gate?"

"Just a few minutes ago," the attractive gal answered, "that's it there, the KLM that is just leaving the loading area."

"Do you happen to remember if the man in this picture was among your passengers?"

The flight attendants looked at the picture and shook their heads as one gal answered, "I don't recall seeing anyone who even looked a bit like him."

"Where is this flight headed?"

"Amsterdam."

Everdell, totally frustrated, took a brief moment and leaned against the window sill and stared at the plane as it moved slowly toward the runway. He abruptly left the area and went through the same process at four or five more gates and got nowhere. The detective knew deep down that they had missed him. The only thing left for them to do was to get copies of the passenger manifests for all of the airlines that were flying out of the country that morning and give them to Judy in Administration back at headquarters to do her thing with the computer. It would be a terrible, time-consuming job and Judy would not be happy.

* * *

On the way back into the city, Everdell was the first to speak, "You know what really bothers me a whole lot?"

"No, what?" Carpenter asked as he looked at his partner.

"Taylor has been very careful and left little evidence for us to go on at all the murder scenes. He's a lawyer, so he's a pretty smart guy. I wonder if he didn't just drive out to the airport this morning and make that call to headquarters, then get right back into his car and go to wherever he now lives right here in Ontario. He may have just wanted us to think that he left the country!"

"That wouldn't surprise me in the least."

"The only good thing that happened today was that Taylor confirmed that it is the end of The Oyster-Shucking Murders."

CHAPTER THIRTY-NINE

Jack Randall had a very relaxed KLM flight across the Atlantic and landed at Schiphol International Airport in Amsterdam around midnight. He had been unable to sleep on the plane because his discussion with Detective Everdell kept spinning around in his mind. He couldn't believe that it was something as simple as a Buffalo airline ticket tied to a dinner reservation in Fort Lauderdale that had clued them in. He tried to keep himself busy on the plane by eating, watching movies and reading, but he could not stop thinking about how good those Toronto cops had been. As soon as Jack arrived at Schiphol and cleared customs and immigration with his new identity, he took the Hilton Shuttle Bus to the hotel and booked a room for the night.

Jack had a good night's sleep and ordered breakfast from room service as soon as he woke up. He trimmed his mustache, shaved and was out of the shower before the food arrived. He took a moment to call Eurostar, one of the continental railway systems, to find out the easiest way for him to travel south to Spain. A flight would leave a paper trail. Even though he had a new identity, the train would be safer. He was taking no more chances. He was still shocked and impressed at the same time with the work that Everdell and Carpenter had done in Toronto because he had been so careful. They had broken the case wide open. Now that he had made it out of Canada, he was going to be extremely careful because Interpol would be looking for him too.

Jack took the Amsterdam subway system directly from the airport area to the downtown train station. As soon as he arrived, he bought a ticket on the Eurostar, non-stop to Paris, and checked his luggage. His train wasn't scheduled to leave until four-fifteen in the afternoon so he had almost five hours to spend in the city center.

Not far from the station, Jack came across a pub and dropped in to have a beer; after all, he was on vacation. The pub was unbelievable by Canadian standards. Along the left wall was a standard, long bar, with stools that served all kinds of beer and alcoholic beverages. On the other wall, there was a small bar that advertised a dozen different kinds of marijuana and hashish imported from all over the world. As Jack drank his beer, he looked around the room at the dozen or so customers. At least four or five patrons were smoking joints and reading or chatting, rather than drinking. The drinkers and tokers mixed together well. He was impressed with the casual and relaxed way that the Dutch people lived and as he sat there, he struck up a conversation with an older gentleman who was seated near him at the bar.

"Do all of the bars in Amsterdam sell booze and pot?"

"They sure do, mate. You can drink or toke up anywhere you want to in this city and everyone is happy, really happy!"

"I'm Jack Randall. I just arrived here on holidays from Canada and I've got some time to kill before my train leaves for Paris."

"Len Swaby. Nice to meet you," he said and extended his hand. "It's a great city. You should take a look around the downtown area while you're here."

"Len, you sound British. Are you visiting Amsterdam?"

"I've lived here for about ten years. I'm originally from London and came here on a two week holiday. I loved the country so much I retired here. What I love about it is that you can almost feel the freedom in the air."

"Does the legalized pot cause any problems here? Back home, most of the crime is drug related."

"Hell no! All that petty crime that you have in your country around soft drugs doesn't exist here. The government sets a reasonable price for the pot and collects lots of taxes on it too."

"I have a few more hours to put in. Is there anything that you suggest I should see while I'm here?"

"Blimy! You gotta go over to The Red Light District. It's just three or four blocks behind the railway station and it's well worth seeing. Legalized prostitution is one of the main tourist attractions in the city. All the women are government inspected for diseases on a regular basis. It all means more tax revenue for the government and all of the crime around that industry doesn't exist here either."

"Len, I want to thank you for all the tourist information and I'm gonna go and see what The Red Light District is all about right now. Nice meeting you."

"Nice to meet you too , Jack, 'ave a good holiday."

It wasn't long before Jack found himself walking through The Red Light District of downtown Amsterdam. It was pretty neat and trendy. There were dozens of sex shops that sold every piece of paraphernalia made for sex, kinky or otherwise. The number of people in the streets proved what old Len Swaby had said; that part of the city was quite obviously a major tourist attraction. The hookers were licensed, government inspected and paid their taxes. There were women of all colors, shapes, sizes and nationalities stationed in small, one room units. Each room had a window that opened onto the street out of which they propositioned men as they walked by. Jack listened as one attractive gal propositioned a couple.

An absolutely stunning blonde, Scandinavian gal, about twenty-five years old, who looked like Marilyn Monroe's twin sister, caught Jack's attention as he went by her window. She called to him. He had to stop and say hello because it was likely the only time that he would ever be in Amsterdam without the girl he loved. He allowed himself to be drawn under her spell and they chatted about what was for sale. It sounded and looked exciting. He had always been true to Liz because he loved her. He knew that this was likely his last time to be a little foolish, but he couldn't even think about it. At that moment, Jack knew in his heart that he was truly in love with Laurie.

* * *

In Paris, Jack connected with a trans-continental train on the Talgo Trans Pyrenees System that traveled south through France and into the Pyrenees Mountains at the Spanish border. The train ride was very enjoyable and the scenery through the wine country of southern France was breathtaking. It only got better as the train climbed into the mountains on the French-Spanish border and continued south to Barcelona, the capital of what the locals call Catalonia, on the Mediterranean Sea.

Jack got off the train in that beautiful, ancient city, and since he was in no hurry to go anywhere, he decided to spend some time there and relax before he headed south toward the Costa del Sol. The Barcelona area of Spain, in the northeast part of the Iberian Peninsula, was separated from France by the Pyrenees Mountains. The architecturally-magnificent train station of the old city of one and a half million people was right in the downtown core and city center in what appeared to be one of the city's main squares. Pl. de Catalunya was just north of the old part of town. The large square was at the intersection of two major thoroughfares, La Rambla and Rda. St. Pere.

Jack found a small pension nearby that had rooms available and booked in for a few days. He decided to take it easy and unwind after all of the stress and excitement of the past few months. He acted like a tourist and wandered around the old city looking at all of the sights. Not far from his hotel, he came across an interesting old church with four tall spires pointing toward the heavens that looked very old but was still under construction. As he wandered through La Sagrada Familia, he learned that the name meant *The Holy Family* and that construction had started back in eighteen eighty-four and it wasn't expected to be completed until well into the twenty-second century. Jack enjoyed the history of the city so much that he stayed for almost a week before he decided to rent a car and head further south. His plan was to head south to Malaga and find a place to stay for a month or two.

* * *

As Jack left Barcelona, he bid the city adieu, but knew that he would bring Laurie back for a visit in the not too distant future. He rented a small Citroen convertible that could be dropped off in Malaga, on the Costa del Sol, and headed south on Highway A 16. Just north of the city of Valencia, the original highway became Highway A-7 and continued to curl south, well inland, as it followed the natural curvature of the Mediterranean coastline. As Jack drove south, he decided to get off the main road and follow the coast highway to see some real scenery. His map showed Highway CV 690 heading south, so he turned off at Alicante and soon found a beautiful road along the shores of the sea. The scenery was breathtaking as he wound along two and three hundred foot cliffs high above the rolling surf of the light blue Mediterranean. It wasn't long before he found Highway A-7 again and traveled west toward his destination, Malaga.

Jack found a small hotel on the main street of Malaga, in the center of the business district, right near the sea. He had intended to turn the car into the rental agency, but decided to keep it for a few more days so he could reacquaint himself with the area and get his bearings. His plan was for Laurie to fly into Malaga International Airport to meet him. They would then travel further south and find a condo or apartment for a month or so and take it easy until they decided what they wanted to do.

Early the next day, Jack drove to Torremolinos, the first main vacation area twelve kilometers south of the city. He fell in love with the town. It was absolutely beautiful. It had major hotels, waterfront complexes and the town center was filled with shops, restaurants and outside patios. It was busier and had more things to do than in those quiet fishing villages further south. The main street had a wide boulevard decorated with green shrubbery and colorful flowers. He felt that it was an ideal place for them to spend some time, so he went apartment hunting. Jack found a large, two bedroom condo on the top of a five story building, with an open kitchen, dining room and living room that had a huge, outdoor patio. The floors were done in an earth-tone tile and it was also fully furnished in that unique Spanish style. It overlooked the Mediterranean Sea and most of the quaint seaside resort town. He knew that Laurie would love the place, so he rented it until the end of March with the possibility of staying for another month or two if they decided not to travel.

Jack returned the Citroen to the car rental office in Malaga, packed all of his belongings and checked out of his hotel. He took a cab back to Torremolinos and his new home, at least for the time being. He went shopping for food, booze, toiletries and all the other necessities that would be needed for their holiday. He wanted to have the place ready for Laurie when she arrived at the end of the month so they could just relax and really get to know each other.

* * *

On March the third, at two in the afternoon, Jack stood out in front of the arrivals area at Malaga International Airport and waited for the woman he loved. He had missed Laurie more than he thought he would and realized that he did truly love this fun gal from New York. As he stood and leaned against the rail near the luggage belt, she came through the door in the midst of a couple of dozen other travelers and she glanced around, looking for him. She didn't see him at first, but he saw her. She looked beautiful and fresh with no evidence that she had been on a plane for six hours.

Laurie's eyes soon found his and her walk sped up as she headed directly for him. She leaned over the rail and kissed him, a long, tender kiss, and hugged him tight. He could tell that she had missed him too. They kissed again, and again, and held each other and talked quietly while they waited for her luggage. It wasn't long before they heard the conveyor belt begin to move and bags started to come out of the opening in the back wall toward the travelers.

"It's so wonderful that you're here. I've really missed you. How was your trip?"

"The flight was fine and I missed you too. It's so good to see you and so great to be in Spain!"

"The bags are coming. You'll have to carry your own out here past the fence because they won't let me in there to help you."

"No problem. I'll be right back."

It wasn't long before they were kissing each other in the back of a cab on their way to Torremolinos and their new home; their first home together. They were both ecstatic. As they kissed, hugged and talked, they couldn't keep their hands off of each other. Any doubts that they each had about the relatively new twist in their relationship, disappeared immediately upon seeing one and other. They knew that it was right for them to be together. They knew that they were truly in love.

As Jack put the luggage in the master bedroom, Laurie walked through the spacious kitchen and living room and out onto the huge patio that overlooked most of the town and the sea. She took a few moments and leaned on the railing to take in the view. It was the most beautiful that she had ever seen.

As she turned and walked back to where Jack was standing in the living room, she had a broad, happy smile on her face. They embraced and Jack spoke first.

"How do you like our new home?"

"It's unbelievable, absolutely gorgeous, but more important, you look great. Look at the suntan!"

"You look fabulous too. I've really missed you," Jack said as they kissed.

"I've missed you too, it's been way too long," she said as she started to undo his shirt buttons and they headed for the bedroom. Jack and Laurie made love for a couple of hours and afterwards, stayed in bed. They talked about how happy they were to be together and hoped it would be for a long time. They eventually went out on the town and walked along the beautiful boulevard of the main street, Calle Hoya. Jack eventually led her down Calle San Miquel, one of the side streets, to Quitapenas, one of Jack's favorite drinking spots. It was filled with patrons for the cocktail hour. As he and Laurie approached the outside patio, a couple who Jack had met during the past couple of weeks beckoned them to their table.

Jack had met the fellow Canadians shortly after he had arrived and they had partied together a few times.

"This is Laurie, my sweetheart from New York who I was telling you about. Laurie, these are my new friends, Joe and Trizzi."

"It's really nice to meet you. This guy hasn't quit talking about you since we met him," Joe commented.

"It's nice to know that he missed me," Laurie smiled.

"Joe and Trizzi are Canadians and they're on an extended sailing trip around the Mediterranean," Jack explained.

"Sounds wonderful," Laurie answered and went on. "Trizzi, maybe you can show me around the shopping district here in the village tomorrow."

"I'd love to do that because I can never get Joe to go shopping with me."

"I know what you mean. It's not something men do."

Jack and Laurie were celebrating that evening and insisted that Joe and Trizzi join them for a wonderful dinner on a terraced restaurant overlooking the sea. The sound of the rolling waves was very soothing and they all had a lovely evening. The two couples really enjoyed each others company. Jack and Joe seemed to have some kind of special connection from their first meeting. They were all to become great friends.

Back at their own place, Jack and Laurie shared a bottle of Cristal and sat on their patio looking at the millions of stars in the clear night sky. They eventually went to bed and made love again. They talked about their love for each other and how happy they were to be together. The lust of their initial encounters had somehow changed. Their love had grown slowly and was sincere and from their hearts. They made love again and Jack cuddled up to Laurie's back as she fell into a deep sleep and was soon lost to the world.

* * *

Paul couldn't sleep at all. He was fully relaxed and comfortable but wasn't tired. The events of the past few years flowed through his mind, one after the other, as he lay awake for a long time. He thought about all those things that had truly affected him over the years. He often thought about Liz and Ricky and he knew that they would be happy for him.

He looked at the woman lying beside him and had a wonderful feeling about her. She felt good. She felt comfortable. He was content that they had fallen in love with each other slowly, not overnight, and he was looking forward to spending the rest of his life with her. *The rest of my life. I wonder where the hell that will take me!* he thought.

Paul thought of Liz's terrible disease and her suffering. Her image kept going through his mind. He still missed her. He still loved her. He missed his son so much it hurt. The thought of Ricky's tragic death still haunted him. He wondered if things would have been different if he and Ricky had been able to cope with losing Liz.

He thought about the men he had killed, the drug dealers and the drug traffickers, and felt absolutely no remorse. He was glad they were off the streets of Toronto. He knew they had families too, but he didn't let those thoughts in.

Paul thought about Detectives Everdell and Carpenter with admiration and knew that they must be the best that the Toronto Police Department had to offer. He wondered if they would ever be able to close their files on The Oyster-Shucking Murders.

Paul Richard Taylor thought about that day last fall when he had opened Pandora's Box. He wondered if he would ever be able to close it completely.

IF YOU ENJOYED THIS NOVEL BY

FLETCHER DOUGLAS

PLEASE TAKE A LOOK AT

"RIDE A CROOKED ROAD"

Frustrated by a waning law career and the disappearance of Trizzi, the love-of-his-life, Joe McConnell escapes from life's dilemmas, with five other Weekend Warriors, on a motorcycle trip through northeastern United States from Toronto to Alexandria Bay, Boston, Cape Cod, New York, Philadelphia and Atlantic City. One of the bikers secretly steals millions of dollars from a drug plane that crashes in the mountains of Vermont and the gang inadvertently becomes mired in Colombians, cocaine, money and murder. After an associate of the bikers is murdered, Joe risks his life to make a deal with the drug traffickers that could save the lives of his friends. As fate intervenes, money and death draws Joe's world and the dangerous world of his lost love together once again and he has to cross the line for the woman he loves.

THANKS FOR YOUR SUPPORT